THE
SHADOW
SORCERESS

BOOK FOUR OF *THE SPELLSONG CYCLE*

·····································

L. E. MODESITT, JR.

TOR®
fantasy

A TOM DOHERTY ASSOCIATES BOOK
NEW YORK

For Susan, Kacy, and Ava

This is a work of fiction. All the characters and events portrayed in this book are either products of the author's imagination or are used fictitiously.

THE SHADOW SORCERESS

Copyright © 2001 by L. E. Modesitt, Jr.

All rights reserved, including the right to reproduce this book, or portions thereof, in any form.

Edited by David G. Hartwell

A Tor Book
Published by Tom Doherty Associates, LLC.
175 Fifth Avenue
New York, NY 10010

www.tor.com

Tor® is a registered trademark of Tom Doherty Associates, LLC.

ISBN: 0-765-34013-5
Library of Congress Catalog Card Number: 2001027048

First edition: June 2001
First mass market edition: May 2002

Printed in the United States of America

0 9 8 7 6 5 4 3 2 1

CHARACTERS

Anna *Former Regent of Defalk; Sorceress and Lady of Loiseau (Mencha)*

Secca *Lady of Flossbend (Synope) and sorceress; sorceress heir to Loiseau.*

Robero *Lord of Defalk, and Lord of Elheld, Falcor, and Synfal (Cheor)*

Alyssa *Consort of Robero*

Dythya *Counselor of Finance*

Jirsit *Arms-commander of Defalk*

LORDS OF DEFALK: THE THIRTY-THREE:

Birke *Lord of Abenfel; consort is Reylana; mother is Fylena*

Cataryzna *Lady of Sudwei; consort is Skent; heir is Skansor*

Chelshay *Lady of Wendel; consort is Nerylt, son of Clethner*

Clethner *Lord of Nordland; son and heir is Lythner*

Dinfan *Lady of Suhl; consort is Wasle, brother of Birke*

Dostal *Lord of Aroch; consort is Ruetha*

Ebraak *Lord of Nordfels*

Falar *Warder of Uslyn, heir to Fussen; also consort to Herene, Lady of Pamr*

Fustar *Lord of Issl; son and sole heir is Kylar*

Gylaron *Lord of Lerona; consort is Reylan; heir is Gylan; father of Reylana*

Herene *Lady of Pamr; consort is Falar; heir is Kysar*

Kinor *Lord of Westfort [Denguic] and Lord of the Western Marches*

Mietchel *Lord of Morra, brother of Lady Wendella of Stromwer*

Selber *Lord of Silberfels; heir is Helbar; sister is Belvera*

Tiersen *Lord of Dubaria; consort is Lysara; eldest son and heir is Lystar*

Uslyn *Lord heir of Fussen; father was Ustal, mother Yelean*

Ytrude *Lady of Mossbach, sister of Tiersen; consort is Cens*

Wendella *Lady of Stromwer, heir is Condell*

Zybar *Lord of Arien*

SORCERERS AND SORCERESSES:

Anandra *Sorceress assistant to Clayre*

Clayre *Sorceress of Defalk*

Jolyn *Assistant Sorceress of Defalk*

FOSTERLINGS, APPRENTICES, AND PAGES:

Jeagyn *Fosterling/sorceress apprentice at Loiseau*

Kerisel *Fosterling/sorceress apprentice at Loiseau*

Richina *Apprentice sorceress to Secca; daughter of Dinfan*

DEFALKAN ARMSMEN:

Elfens *Chief Archer, Loiseau*

Drysel *Captain, Loiseau*

Quebar *Captain, Loiseau*

Rickel *Lord's Guard-Captain, Falcor*

Wilten *Overcaptain, Loiseau*

DEFALKAN PLAYERS:

Bretnay *Violino, Loiseau*
Delvor *Chief of second players, Loiseau*
Duralt *Falk-horn, Loiseau*
Palian *Chief Player, Loiseau*
Rowal *Woodwind, Loiseau*
Yuarl *Chief Player, Falcor*

OTHERS OUTSIDE DEFALK:

Alya *Matriarch of Ranuak; consort is Aetlen*
Alcaren *Cousin to the Matriarch*
Ashtaar *Leader, Council of Wei, Nordwei*
Ayselin *Holder of Netzla, Neserea*
Belmar *Holder of Worlan, Neserea*
Clehar *Lord High Counselor of Dumar; without consort*
Hadrenn *Lord High Counselor of Ebra; Lord of Synek, Ebra; consort is Belvera; heir is Haddev; younger son is Verad.*
Hanfor *Lord High Counselor of Neserea; consort is Aerlya; eldest daughter and heiress is Annayal*
Kestrin *Liedfuhr of Mansuur; brother of Aerlya*
Maitre of Sturinn *Leader of Sturinn; master of the Sea-Priests*
Motolla *Holder of Itzel, Neserea; heir is Chyalar*
Mynntar *Lord of Dolov, Ebra*
Stepan *Arms-master of Synek*
Svenmar *Holder of Nesalia, Neserea*
Veria *Second Counselor, Freewomen of Elahwa*

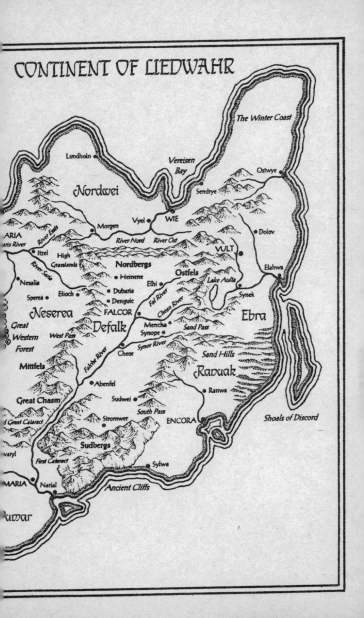

CONTINENT OF LIEDWAHR

The Winter Coast

Lundholn

Nordwei

Vereisen
Bay

Ostwye

Sendrye

ARIA
Vyel   WIE
...ris River   Morgen

River Eass

River Nord   River Ost

Itzel

Dolov

High
Grasslands

River Sarta

Nordbergs   VULT

Heinene

Elahwa

Ostfels

Nesalia

Elhi

Lake Aulta

Eloich   Dubaria

Sperea

Denguic

FALCOR

Chean River

Fal River

Synek

Neserea

Defalk

Ebra

Mencha

Sand Pass

Great
Western

West Pass

Synope

Synor River

Falche River

Cheor

Sand Hills

Forest

Mittfels

Ravuak

Great Chasm

Abenfel

Ranwa

Sudwei

Great Cataract

Stromwer   South Pass   ENCORA

Shoals of Discord

Sudbergs

...varyl

First Cataract

Sylwa

MARIA   Narial

Ancient Cliffs

...uwar

1

Two sorceresses stood beside the scrying pool in the domed outbuilding that lay to the south of the main keep of Loiseau. The taller woman had fine white-blonde hair, hair that could have belonged to the young woman of nineteen that her appearance conveyed. Her thin and finely drawn face was without blemish, without lines, and her piercing blue eyes were clear. Only the fineness of Anna's features attested to her true age. Her figure was nearly as slender, and far more girlish than that of the smaller redhead who stood next to her.

Anna eased into a straight-backed chair behind the small writing table, then looked at the redhead. "Secca . . . our good Lord Robero has requested that you visit him at El-held, preferably within the next two weeks."

"Doubtless he has yet another heir or lord for me to meet, Lady Anna." Secca's mouth offered a sardonic smile as she perched on the tiled edge of the scrying pool. Part of her smile was because Anna had never been able to say "Robero" without a twist to her lips. Then Secca had difficulty herself. When Secca had been growing up in Falcor under Anna's tutelege, Robero had been "Jimbob." Only when he'd become Lord of Defalk had he decided "Jimbob" was too undignified and changed his name to Robero. "After all these years, he would still have me consorted."

"You aren't *that* old." Anna added, "He doesn't understand you, but he does care for you."

"That may be, for he understands women not at all. He understands but strength and power, and that is why he respects you, lady."

Anna sighed gently. "I wish it were otherwise. Certainly we tried."

Secca nodded sympathetically. While Anna almost never used Lord Jecks' name, Anna often said "we" when referring to what the two had accomplished for Defalk in the less than half score of years when Anna had been regent and sole ruler of Defalk. The former regent spoke seldom of Lord Jecks, but Secca had seen the lamps of Anna's rooms still lit late into many nights over the ten years since his death. While Anna and Jecks had been friends and certainly lovers, consorting had been out of the question. *That* Secca had understood from the beginning, when Anna had effectively adopted her after the deaths of Secca's parents, for Jecks had been a powerful lord in his own right, and the grandsire of Lord Robero, during the time when Anna had been Sorceress-Regent for the underage Robero.

"Despite his inclinations, Robero has learned much," Anna continued, "and I am thankful for Alyssa."

"So am I," replied Secca.

"You know I never would have consorted you to him."

"Alyssa made it that much easier."

The two sorceresses laughed. Then Anna cleared her throat.

"You have something else I am to do?" asked Secca.

"Kylar . . ." Anna said.

Secca winced. "The one who suffocated his consort and claimed she died of consumption?" Anna nodded.

"You wish me to go to Issl as well?"

"I think you should go there first." The older sorceress smiled. "You will be paying my respects to Lord Fustar. He will be most happy to see your young and smiling face." The smile vanished. "The pool shows that Kylar does not understand what has happened in Defalk, and that he will abuse any woman he can. He now seeks yet another consort." Anna looked at Secca. "You understand how you must deal with Kylar, and with Lord Fustar? Nothing must happen to Kylar while you are at Issl."

"I understand, lady. Nothing will occur." Secca inclined her head. "I could take the players, and we could stop and add a dek to the road between Mencha and the River Chean on the south end, and then add another dek or so on our return journey from Elheld."

Anna shook her head. "You dislike Robero, and yet you would work to finish paving the road he demands."

"Why not? He is likely to be lord for many years to come, and it will speed our travel from Loiseau to Elheld." She laughed. "At times, I would that there were other ways to build his roads."

"In Defalk, there are no other ways." Anna shook her head. "Robero doesn't have enough men or engineers—or the golds to pay for them—and he cannot call on the Lords for anything other than their liedgeld and their levies in battle."

"So we must build roads and bridges."

"It's not all drudgery without rewards, Secca," Anna pointed out. "People know we build roads and bridges, and it helps associate sorcery with good things. Given how this land has regarded sorceresses in the past, that's not all bad."

"I know." Secca grinned suddenly. "I could also use sorcery to repair a wall or bridge or something for Lord Fustar . . . as a gesture from Loiseau."

The older sorceress smiled. "That might help."

"It is hard to see shadows in the light of a favor."

"Sometimes," Anna replied. "Sometimes. Other times, light makes the shadows more obvious. This time, I think you're right."

"When should I leave? Tomorrow?"

"If you wish to spend time on the highway and several days being a charming guest at Issl."

Secca nodded, then tilted her head. "Lady Anna?"

"Yes? You have that serious tone."

"I would that you would wait until I return before you send your next scroll to your daughter in the Mist Worlds."

Anna nodded politely.

"At least I could play for you and lessen the effort."

"We will see," replied the Sorceress and Lady of Mencha. "I'm not ancient yet."

"Lady . . ." Secca tried not to plead, but to convey her concern.

"Secca . . ." Anna laughed. "Don't turn me into a doddering old lady."

"No one could do that." The younger sorceress smiled at Anna's tone, smiled in spite of her worries, for she had seen the deepening darkness behind her foster-mother's eyes, and sensed the ever-increasing strain that even the lightest of Clearsong spells placed on Anna, for all that Anna looked little different from what she had more than a score of years earlier when first she had arrived in Defalk from the Mist Worlds.

2

In the midmorning light of early fall, before harvest, a half-score of players stood on the low rise to the west of the dusty road. The majority held violinos or violas, but there were also two woodwinds and a falk-horn in the group. Another half-score of players bearing lutars of various sizes stood behind the first group.

Secca, wearing a pale blue tunic, walked toward Palian, the gray-haired and gray-eyed woman who held a violino, and who stood before the first group of players. "Chief player?"

"Yes, Lady Secca," replied Palian. "We have almost finished tuning."

"Good." Secca nodded, accepting as always the necessary formality of Palian's address. "We will be using the second building spell." That too was a formality, since Secca and Lady Anna had always used the second building spell for road-building, although it had been years since Anna had done heavy building sorcery.

Secca glanced out at the dusty road that stretched northward toward the River Chean from Mencha. Behind her, nearly thirty deks of sorcery-laid stone paving extended back to Mencha. The gap between where she stood and the paved section stretching south from the river bridge was less than ten deks, and she hoped that she would be able to complete that section within the next few years, but that depended on what other tasks Lady Anna and Lord Robero laid upon her. She looked toward the lank-haired Delvor, catching his eye.

"Second players are ready, lady."

Secca studied the image on the portable easel, an image with which she was all too familiar, and began to bring up both the image of the road, and the spellsong itself, into her mind. "The second building spell, chief player."

"The second building spell, on my mark," declared Palian. "Mark!"

As the notes from the players and their instruments rose into the morning, the first two bars merely to stabilize the players, Secca waited, and then began the spell proper with the first note of the third measure.

> ". . . replicate the earth and stones.
> Place them in their proper zones . . .
> Set all firm, and set all square,
> weld them to their pattern there . . ."

Even before the notes of the players and Secca's voice died away, an intense bluish glow settled over the dusty track, initially so bright that neither Secca nor the players could have looked at it, had they wanted to, but all had seen the brightness over the years with each new section of road built.

Secca held herself erect against the faint dizziness that always came with heavy sorcery such as road-building, then walked to her mount, a gray mare, and took out her water bottle for a long swallow, before eating several biscuits from her provisions bag. After eating, she turned and looked at the newly created section of paved road.

Like the sections created before over the years, the roadway itself was exactly eight yards across, and raised almost a third of a yard above the surrounding ground. On each side was a stone rain gutter, and every hundred yards, there was a side drain. The stone roadbed had a slight crown, enough that the infrequent rains of eastern Defalk would run off into the lower rain gutters. Beneath were layers of stone and gravel going almost a yard deep.

"How do you feel, sorceress?" asked Palian.

"Fine." Secca smiled. "How are the players?"

"We can do another spell, perhaps two."

"We'll move up to the end of what we've finished here and do another section," Secca said. "Then we'll ride north and see how we feel when we reach where the paved section coming from the north begins. I'd like to finish this road before . . ." She shrugged, not certain what comparison might even be useful. "I'd like to see it finished."

"We can add another dek or so on our return from Issl and Elheld, can we not?" asked Palian.

"I would think so," Secca replied. "I'd like to be able to tell Lady Anna that we can have the entire road paved within a few more years." Generally, a road spell was good for about five hundred yards—half a dek.

"You will." Palian smiled.

"I hope so." Secca nodded.

"Players, prepare to mount and ride!" ordered the chief player.

Secca folded the small easel, and turned back toward her own mount.

3

The harvest-time sun was hot and beat down upon the two riders, and upon the column of players and lancers in the green of Loiseau who followed them along the dusty lane that led between two hills, hills covered with hardwoods whose leaves had begun to turn yellow, gold, and deep red. Beside Secca rode Kylar, the stocky and blond heir of Lord Fustar. Kylar, a good ten years older than Secca, wore a nondescript tan tunic and an indifferent smile.

"Why do you remain an assistant to Lady Anna?" His tone was casual.

"I do owe her my life, and my lands." Secca did not look at Kylar but at the narrow and winding road that paralleled the ancient wooden aqueduct leading farther back into the low hills.

"Your lands?"

Secca smiled, although she felt more like drawing her sabre and spitting the condescending heir to Issl. "I am already Lady of Flossbend."

"You are that Lady Secca?" He frowned as if he had not made the connection.

"I am that Lady Secca. I have been for many years. Since I was nine."

"And yet you serve . . . ?"

"I'm also sorceress heir to Loiseau."

"Oh . . . you are an ambitious woman."

"No. I'm still learning," Secca pointed out. She saw no need to say that she was ambitious, at least in the sense that she wished to rule her own lands rather than surrender them to a consort, and that she had no intention of becoming a brood mare for some brainless lord.

"You are well past the age—"

"When most women have long since consorted and produced heirs?" interrupted Secca gently. "That is true. Some women see that as their calling. Others see arms, or sorcery."

"Arms? There are few indeed in Defalk."

"But not in Elahwa or in Ranuak or in Nordwei," Secca replied. "And there are some lords now in Defalk who have women as armsmen."

"Because they cannot find men who will serve them, no doubt," rejoined Kylar. "We have no such difficulties here."

"I am most certain you do not." Secca gestured at the low line of earth and rock visible through the passlike opening between two low hills. "Is that the dam your sire mentioned?"

"It is."

Secca rode along the narrow lane, so close to the maples and oaks that she could almost reach out and touch them, before the lane turned uphill to the east and narrowed even more. Secca found herself riding single file, with Kylar behind her. As she neared the hilltop, she could see an expanse that had once been cleared, but now held low bushes, including blackberries that had long since been picked.

Guiding the mare around the browning and thorny berry bushes, Secca made her way to an area that had been grazed relatively clear, just above a dried mud flat. She reined up and studied the earth-and-rock dam, noting the streaks of dampness on both rock and earth. Then her eyes went to the wooden planks that comprised the beginning of the crude aqueduct.

"My sire would have you repair the dam and the aqueduct to the keep," said Kylar, reining up beside her.

"I would have to be here longer than I can be for such," Secca replied politely. "The dam appears to be failing. That I can replace, and perhaps the bridgework to the beginning of the aqueduct."

"I had understood that you were among the more powerful of sorceresses . . ." Another shade of condescension crept into Kylar's voice.

Secca looked evenly at the far taller man. "It would take scores of men more than a season to rip down and replace that dam. I will do so in less than a glass. I cannot do more, for I must leave within a few days, at the command of Lord Robero, and I must arrive at Elheld able to do whatever sorcery he may require."

Kylar looked from the failing dam to Secca and then back to the packed rock and earth. "I suppose any small aid you could provide would be helpful."

"I will certainly endeavor to be helpful." Secca dismounted and handed the gray's reins to Kylar. "If you would."

Kylar took the reins with another condescending smile.

Secca turned and walked downhill to where the players had begun to form up on the slope to the east of the ancient structure, above the blue waters held in place by the dam. The sound of tuning began to issue from the strings, the falk-horn, and the woodwinds, and the lutars of the second players.

Palian turned toward Secca. "Lady Secca."

"I've made some word changes to the second building spell, but the melody will be the same," Secca told the chief player. "This will take as much as a long section of road. It could take more."

"We will be ready shortly." Palian smiled.

"Thank you." Secca stood beside the chief player and waited, not wanting to go back anywhere near Kylar for the moment.

Shortly, the sounds of tuning faded, and Palian turned to Secca. "We stand ready."

"At your mark, then," Secca said.

"The second building spell, at my mark," Palian said, her voice firm. "Mark!"

Secca waited for the opening bars, then launched into the spellsong itself.

". . . replicate with measured stones.
Place them in their proper zones . . .
Set all firm, and set all square,
weld them to their pattern there . . .

. . . lock each block in solid place
ɔ no water goes beyond its proper space . . ."

Even before the spell was complete, gouts of steam flared upward, white against the blue-green of the clear sky. Rowal and several other players stutter-stepped backward, while the far older Delvor and Palian merely exchanged knowing glances.

As her last notes faded into the afternoon, a wave of faintness and dizziness swept over Secca, and she knew she had pushed harder than she should have. For several moments, she stood facing the narrow gorge, watching as the clean lines of sorcery-dressed and -formed stone replaced the irregular rock and earthen berm that had been the older dam. A graceful arched chute now carried water—water that steamed as it streamed down the hot stone and flowed into the old wooden aqueduct. She also observed that the water level had dropped several feet—doubtless as a result of the stone taken from beneath the reservoir by the spellsong.

Secca gave a small smile of success before turning and walking back toward the gray mare, where she lifted the water bottle from its saddle holder and took a long swallow. Then she reached for the provisions bag and extracted a biscuit.

"Doesn't seem all that hard," offered Kylar from where he had remained mounted, watching the entire spellsong.

"It's not," Secca said politely. "Not after a score of years of training and practice. Just like blade handling doesn't look very hard when the person using it is an expert."

"You just sang."

Secca took another swallow of water, debating whether to answer. Finally, she looked up again at the stocky blond heir. "Each one of those stones in that dam weighs between five and ten stone. It takes work to move them, even with sorcery. The players might be able to do that twice today. They wouldn't be able to play another spell for several days."

"What about you?" A glint glittered in Kylar's blood-shot eyes.

"I've trained longer. I could sing several more spells, even without the players." Secca smiled politely. "Enough to kill a few armsmen, but not enough to destroy a large force."

She turned and walked back down to where the players were casing their instruments.

"Will that be all, Lady Secca?" asked Palian.

"It's more than either Lord Fustar or his heir deserve, but manners require the effort."

A faint smile crossed Palian's lips. "It was always that way, even from the beginning, when Lady Anna first came to Liedwahr."

"I recall, young as I was." Secca could remember most of those days, and she had no desire to relive them—not at all. "I suppose we should have everyone mount up. We'll need to ride back to the keep."

The chief player nodded, then turned. "Prepare to mount."

Secca walked back to the gray, taking the reins from Kylar. "Thank you." She offered a pleasant smile, then mounted.

Once the players appeared ready, Palian lifted a hand.

Secca turned her mount. "If you would not mind, Kylar, we can return to the keep." She let the stocky man lead the way down the narrow trail, then forced herself to draw abreast of his mount as they passed through the gap in the hills.

"You have many hardwoods here." Secca gestured

toward the red-leafed maples. "Do you have crafters for the wood?"

"No." Kylar shook his head. "My sire allows the mastercrafters from Falcor to cut a wagonload of the oldest timber every few years."

"For golds, I imagine."

"Why else?" The stocky heir laughed.

"What do your tenants grow?"

"Corn, mostly. We have a mill, and there is no other for deks."

"So you collect more golds from that?"

"Not so many as we might, for my sire lets the tenants keep a fourth part for themselves. He is far too generous, and they know it not." Kylar frowned as his eyes strayed to the south, beyond the ancient brownish walls of Issl, still more than a dek away.

"What else feeds your prosperity?"

"Our wool. Few have flocks and fleeces of such quality as do we . . ."

Secca nodded, listening as Kylar waxed on.

Before long, the road had widened and neared the beginning of the causeway leading to the gates of the keep. Kylar reined up, and Secca followed his example, as did the players and the company of lancers from Loiseau that followed the column.

"Sorceress, if you will pardon me . . ." Kylar offered a diffident half-bow from the saddle. "I needs must attend to another matter before the evening meal."

"I look forward to seeing you then," lied Secca with a smile. "I know you will deal with what must be dealt with great skill."

"One would hope so." With a broad smile, Kylar turned his mount and began to ride westward toward the hamlet that held the cots of many of Fustar's tenants.

Secca continued riding toward the causeway.

Palian edged her mount up beside Secca's mare. "You do not care for him."

"Is it obvious to all?"

Palian laughed. "No. I have known you from the time when you would turn red at trying to utter a falsehood. Few others would see the signs, I would wager."

"What do you think of the honorable Kylar?"

"Less, if possible, than do you," replied Palian dryly. "He reminds me too much of lords like Dannel and your uncle."

Secca nodded. Both had tried to have her killed as a child. "We need to prepare for dinner. You and Delvor will be above the salt at table."

"I hope the food is good," Palian said.

"It will be better than travel fare, and more honest than the conversation that accompanies it," Secca replied.

Both women smiled as they neared the open gates of Issl.

4

Secca sat to the left of Lord Fustar, a man ancient, thin-faced and beak-nosed, with thin wispy white hair. The lord's green eyes were intent as he turned to the sorceress. "I know I have said this before, but it is indeed a pleasure to have you in Issl." There was a twinkle in his eyes as he added, "You have not said why you offered your skills to rebuild an old lord's dam or why you present these old eyes such a feast."

Secca inclined her head slightly before replying. "Lady Anna would have liked to have been here to offer her best wishes, but she could not. She also felt it was best that I come to know all the lands in the north and east. I have never been to Issl before."

"Ah, yes . . . the Sorceress-Protector. I have but met her

a bare handful of times, and always she looks the same. She will doubtless see us all go and still preside over the defenses of the east." Fustar laughed, but the laugh turned into a wheezing cough. He reached for the goblet and took a small swallow of the wine. "Dissonant time when wine's best used to kill a cough." He shook his head as he set the goblet down.

"She was granted the appearance of youth after she crossed from the Mist Worlds," Secca said, "but not immortality."

"She seems to have such."

"She says she will die as do we all."

"That . . . that will be interesting," cackled Fustar. His eye flicked toward the figure striding through the door. "Here comes our wayward heir. Much longer and he would have been eating scraps."

"I beg your pardon, ser, for coming to table late." Now wearing a shimmering purple silk tunic, Kylar approached the table and offered an indifferent bow, then turned his eyes upon Secca. "A pleasure to see you again, Lady Secca." was overly hearty, the cheerfulness forced.

Upon closer inspection, Secca could see that his thick hair was as much silver as blonde, and that fine lines radiated from the slightly bloodshot eyes. "You look well in purple, Kylar," she replied politely.

Kylar settled into the empty seat across from Secca. "I had a matter to attend to, except someone had already taken care of it." His eyes flicked lazily toward his father, but did not actually meet the gaze of the older man.

"Ah, yes . . . the peasant's woman, wasn't it?" asked Fustar mildly.

"She seems to have vanished, along with the peasant. I cannot imagine what happened." Kylar filled his goblet from the pitcher on the table, then inclined his head to Secca. "Would you like more, lady?"

"Not for a bit," Secca demurred. "Until we eat."

"I cannot understand why a peasant would leave his cot

. . . or how anyone could suffer such to happen." Kylar looked at neither Secca nor his father, using his knife to spear two slabs of meat from the platter tendered by the serving woman, then his fingers to seize and break off a large chunk of the rye bread in the basket to his left.

Secca also took two hefty slabs of the mutton, knowing she needed at least that much food after the day's sorcery, and hoping she could force it all down.

"Peasants do leave, you know. That happens when they obtain coins and a chance at something they see as better." Fustar sipped from the pewter goblet.

"Or when they fear they have done wrong," suggested the son. "I had thought, ser, that the peasants deserved a lesson. They should not have been hunting the pheasants. Those are reserved for us."

"Kylar, do you think that they like a good fowl any less than do we?"

"But . . . they are peasants."

"Yes . . . they are. They eat; they drink; and they piss just like we do." Fustar offered a dry and cackling laugh.

"They are little better than trained animals."

"They must be somewhat better." Fustar smiled politely. "Else you would not be so wroth at one leaving the lands. Or was it his consort you wished to discipline?"

"That he would have understood."

"I am certain he understands now. He did not remain here to receive such punishment."

"How . . . ?" Kylar shakes his head in disgust. "How . . ."

"It might be better just to let the matter lie, Kylar." Fustar's voice was again mild, deceptively so, with but the slightest accent upon the words "let the matter lie."

Kylar offered another indifferent nod. "As you wish, ser." His eyes glittered for but a moment before he turned to Secca. "How are you finding Issl, lady?"

"Your sire has been most instructive and kind," Secca replied.

"He has always enjoyed instructing others," Kylar said,

continuing after the slightest of pauses, "Have you seen the mews?"

"No, I have not."

"The falcons are Kylar's pride," observed Fustar. "Along with his daughters."

"You have several daughters?" asked Secca.

"Seven," admitted the stocky heir. "As you doubtless have heard, my dear Tressa did not long survive the last."

Secca had heard that, and more, considering that Tressa was his second consort, and that Kylar had approached several other lords of the Thirty-three for the hands of their daughters. "I was most sorry to hear that."

"As were we all," said Fustar. "But enough of sadness." He raised his goblet. "To the lady and sorceress who graces Issl."

After a moment, Secca raised her goblet. "And to those who have so graciously hosted us all and made us most welcome."

Fustar smiled broadly, Kylar politely, before both drank.

Secca trusted neither smile, nor her own, but she drank, if far less than they, before quickly cutting a chunk of the mutton and beginning to eat.

She had finished both slabs, had taken a third, and was halfway through that and her second large chunk of bread, when Kylar spoke.

"You are not large, lady . . ." He gestured toward her platter. "Yet . . ."

"I think I mentioned that sorcery takes much energy," Secca replied. "You will never see a fat sorcerer or sorceress."

"Would you like another slice?" Kylar smiled slyly.

"Yes, please." Secca smiled demurely, and quickly ate the fourth large slab of the mutton, which was not nearly so strong in taste as she had feared.

"She'll eat you under the table." Fustar laughed once more, grinning at Kylar. "Never underestimate a sorceress. Those who do have paid most dearly."

Secca was beginning to understand the old lord. While

Fustar certainly believed in the older standards of masculine rule, he was sharp enough to understand that times had changed, and wise enough to alter his course and actions just enough to avoid having Anna or Robero act against him.

"I defer to your judgment, as I do in all matters such as these." Kylar refilled his goblet and glanced at Secca.

"Half please," she said politely, before turning to Fustar. "Your family has been at Issl long, has it not?"

"Aye, lady. We date to the Corians, if not before. The first of the line . . . he was said to be able to plow twice what any of his peasants did in a morning. That was why people once asked whether they measured by an Issl morgen or a Corian morgen."

Secca nodded. Although a morgen had long since been set at a square of land a hundred yards on a side, it had once meant the area plowed in a morning.

"Why . . . in the upper tower," continued Fustar, "there is an inscription still in the original Corian . . ."

Secca sipped, smiled, and asked a question every time the old lord paused, or added a few words, and then asked something that demanded a long answer.

In time, Kylar pushed back his chair. "If you would . . ."

Fustar stifled a yawn. "We all should." He smiled at Secca. "You have been most charming and gracious, and you may tell the Lady Anna that either of you are welcome here at my table at any time."

"I enjoyed greatly hearing about Issl and your family," replied Secca, not entirely untruthfully.

Followed by Achar, one of the younger lancers from Loiseau who was acting as her guard, Secca made her way, led by Fustar, to the third level of the keep, and the corner guest room. Once inside, with Achar outside, she stretched, then took a deep breath, and ran through one soft vocalise, then a second, before taking her lutar from its case and softly checking its tuning.

From her saddlebag, she extracted a single small bottle,

opening the stopper and setting the bottle on the window ledge.

Then she stood in the shadows, just back of the casement, behind the open window that faced the casement—and the windows of Kylar's chamber—watching.

When she was certain Kylar was in his room, from the play of shadow and light, she lifted the lutar and began to sing.

> *"Infuse in droplets, slow and strong,*
> *through this coming week along . . ."*

As the last couplet died away, she swallowed and stepped back, shivering. Methodically, she recased the lutar, then lifted the bottle and poured the contents down the outside of the stone wall below the window, so that the liquid left a thin and almost colorless line on the ancient stone. After the bottle was empty, she restoppered it and replaced it in her saddlebag.

The spell would put a drain on her for several days, but she would be well away from Fustar before Kylar felt the effects. At least, that was what Lady Anna had said.

The physical drain was the easy part. The knowledge of what she had done would weigh on her—as Secca knew it weighed on Anna, for all that the older sorceress had done over the years. When Anna had first introduced Secca to the shadow side of sorcery, Secca had asked one question: Why?

"Because it is better that one sorceress bear the burden of deciding wrong than for scores or scores of scores to die for the vanity of justification." That was what Anna had said to Secca, and what Secca might well have to say to Richina in years to come.

Kylar had abused peasants, and worse, according to the glass, and he was the sole heir to Issl. It would be so much easier to let time show Kylar to all Defalk for what he was, to wait until scores more died, another consort or two, until either all the peasants fled or a revolt occurred. People were always people, Secca reflected. Always reacting, always thinking that to act before a disaster was cold-blooded. Yet it was always perfectly acceptable to react to a large cruelty with battles and war, or even assassination—*after* scores or scores of scores had died.

For all the arguments, there was still the other question: Who was she—or Anna—to make such decisions?

Part of that answer was simple. There was no one else who could decide on the fate of just one man. Lords were supreme on their own lands—unless the Lord of Defalk or another lord wanted to go to war. So, acting openly created even more suffering for far more than a lord or heir. Yet . . . a life was a life.

Secca shook her head. If she and Anna were wrong, and a revolt did not occur, then one man already proven at least cruel, if not far worse, would have died before his time. If they were right, years of suffering and scores of deaths were prevented.

Still . . . all the reasoning didn't make it much easier. A life was a life. But Kylar's peasants hadn't deserved beatings and abuse; his former consorts hadn't deserved to be suffocated in their pillows when they were already ill.

Secca had to keep in mind that Kylar—and the others—had already demonstrated their cruelty. She had to keep that well in mind. She had to.

Secca walked to the door of the guest chamber, checking the iron bolt.

She turned back to the high guest bed, laying out her short sabre on the table beside her bed. While she doubted Kylar would be foolish enough to try to enter her chamber, even if there were a secret entrance, she wanted to be prepared. For a moment, she *almost* hoped he would.

Then she shook her head. Far better to remove him

from the shadows. Acting in the open always created more anger and resentment, and led to the need for ever greater force. That had become most clear over the years she had been at Loiseau . . . and before.

5

ENCORA, RANUAK

The woman in pale blue stands and walks to the window of her study, gazing out into the darkness, a darkness that bears the faint hint of salt air and the ripeness of harvest time.

Her consort, also sandy-haired, if with less silver-gray in his thick, short thatch of hair, also stands and turns. He eases up behind her and slips his arms around her waist. "You are worried, are you not?"

She nods.

"Why?"

"There is a time of great change coming. I can sense it. Much will change, and the Harmonies themselves will suffer dissonance and disharmony." Her lips form a crooked smile. "And I, as Matriarch, can say not a word yet, except to you."

"Do you know where these changes will strike?"

"All Erde will change."

"But you cannot tell anyone else?"

She laughs. "A Matriarch *knows*, but how she knows, that cannot be explained, and what she senses cannot be explained or revealed too soon because the Matriarch is either disbelieved or blamed for being the cause of the trouble."

"How bad is this trouble?"

"I fear it could be as bad as the Spell-Fire Wars. It could be worse."

"How soon?"

"Soon." The Matriarch shrugs. "We will know when it begins."

The two look silently into the darkness for a time.

6

Secca had no more stepped in through the arched doorway of the main hall at Elheld when she was greeted by a young woman—one of the fosterling pages from Falcor, she thought.

"Lady Secca . . . ? Lord Robero will await you in the private study, a half-glass before dinner is served."

"Oh . . . thank you."

"I am to escort you to your guest chamber." The rangy blonde page bowed a second time. Secca wondered if the fosterling were a daughter of Ytrude, but decided against asking as she followed her guide up the wide polished wooden steps to the second level. The guest chamber was modest, but not cramped, with a single double-width high bed, an armoire, a working desk and chair, and tables on both sides of the bed. Adjoining the guest chamber was a bath chamber, clearly added later, and probably converted from half of another adjoining chamber, from the way the paneling on the inside walls did not match.

Secca enjoyed the bath, even if she did get a slight headache from using her lutar and a spellsong to reheat the water in the long tub which swallowed her. She managed to lie back on the bed and doze for almost a glass before rising and donning the single blue gown she had carried with her from Loiseau. Then she took a deep breath and ventured forth into the ancient and dimly lit hall, making her way back down toward the private study.

"Lord Robero, Lady Secca," announced the guard at the

door to the study, opening the door almost immediately, and then closing it behind Secca.

The study was as it always had been, its dark wood paneling warm and welcoming in the illumination cast by nearly a score of polished bronze lamps, some in wall sconces, others on the desk and side tables.

Robero stood and offered a boyish grin, an expression somehow at odds with his thickening midsection and the thinning mahogany hair above his bushy eyebrows. The grin also reminded Secca that, changed name or not, the Lord of Defalk was in some ways still a "Jimbob."

"Secca, it is good to see you."

"It's good to be here," she replied, bowing, as much to his office as to him.

The Lord of Defalk gestured to the armchair set at an angle to the one in which he had been seated, then sat down as Secca did. "How was your journey?"

"Long enough," she replied with a smile. "Mencha is not close to anything."

"That's why you will be glad when you finish the road." He grinned.

"We did add another dek or so along the way, but the journey is still long."

"You visited Lord Fustar, did you not?" asked Robero.

"You know I did. Lady Anna has suggested that I visit many of the lords of the east and north. She requested that I convey her greetings and best wishes to Lord Fustar." Secca smiled and added, "While we were there, I rebuilt the dam that gathers and supplies the water to his keep. It would have failed within seasons."

"I am certain he was pleased."

"Not particularly," Secca admitted. "He and Kylar wanted me to replace three deks of wooden aqueduct as well. With stone."

"Fustar has never been the kind to appreciate generosity. I am surprised that Lady Anna wished to gift him so." Robero's smile turned chill. "I understand that less than a week after your departure, his son and sole heir sickened and died. Before he could consort again."

"He did?" asked Secca.

"He did, and I have my doubts as to your surprise."

"Rulers must have doubts," Secca said quietly. "From what I saw, I would have been less astounded had he been murdered by someone on his sire's lands."

Robero shook his head. "Just because . . ."

"Because what?" Secca asked politely.

"Lord Fustar cannot live that much longer, can he?" Robero's eyes narrowed.

"I would not know. Using sorcery to seek such is Darksong. I do believe Kylar left a number of daughters," Secca said. "One of them might well be suited to inherit."

Robero sighed. "Are you going to continue the shadow legacy?"

"The shadow legacy?"

"You know very well what I mean, Secca. I may not see everything, but I see enough. Disloyal lords break their necks when a bridge collapses or a mount stumbles. Heirs who are arrogant and stupid die when no one is around."

Secca laughed gently. "If such have happened, well . . . they are far better than what once occurred. I recall vividly armsmen running toward me with blades and screaming for my head."

"Lady Anna cannot live forever."

"No. But her mind is most clear."

"She is not that strong, is she?"

"Do you want to spend your armsmen reining in unruly lords? Or returning to a time when the Lord of Falcor could count on but a handful of the Thirty-three? Do you really think her death will allow you to go back to the days of Donjim?"

This time, Robero was the one to laugh. "With three sorceresses and a handful of apprentices trained by Anna filling Defalk?"

Secca smiled and waited.

"What will you do now?" he finally asked.

"Return to Loiseau. I had thought that I would spend a day or so adding to the paved section of the road between Mencha and the River Chean. Within another year or so, the paving will run all the way from Loiseau to Elheld."

"After almost thirty years."

"You have better roads and bridges than any land in Liedwahr," Secca said lightly. "And the one from Nordfels to Denguic serves as much for defense as trade."

"I believe I do . . . and the cost has been high."

"I think I'd like you better if you weren't always feeling sorry for yourself." Secca kept her tone light.

"I think it would be better for you if you did not accept all that Lady Anna says as truth."

"It might be better for you, you mean." Secca shook her head. For Robero, it had always been Anna. He had never accepted fully the debt he owed her, first for restoring his kingdom, and second, for forcing him to accept women as equals. Or maybe it had been as simple as his inability to accept that Anna was stronger and had been a better ruler in the years she had been regent, until she had handed the land back to him.

"Let us not argue," he offered, flashing his boyish grin again. "We must do as each of us sees best. You have always supported what you thought best for Defalk, as has Lady Anna."

"We have always supported you, if not precisely as you have wished." Secca smiled. "I will not argue more . . . tonight."

"That is all I can hope for." The Lord of Defalk chuckled. "I have taken the liberty of inviting a guest. He is waiting for us."

"I cannot say that I am surprised."

"He is someone I wanted you to meet. It has always seemed odd that you have not."

Secca did not conceal a frown.

"You certainly have heard of Lythner. You have met his sire, Lord Clethner, I believe." Robero stood. "And he is my neighbor."

Secca also rose. "But not your closest." She offered an impish grin.

"It is but dinner." He turned and headed toward the study door.

The man who waited for them outside the dining hall was not especially tall, nor was he short, but a good head and a half taller than Secca and clean-shaven. His dark black hair was cut short. Brilliant blue eyes dominated a face that somehow was both masculine and square-jawed, yet slightly elfin. With his smile, the hallway seemed to warm. "Lady Secca, my sire has said much of you." He bowed deferentially, but not excessively. "I can now see why he has done so."

"Lord Clethner has always been honorable and straightforward. I see that you take after him," replied Secca, returning the bow.

"Since Lythner lives not that far from Elheld, and since you had never met nor been introduced, I thought you should." Robero smiled, before turning to the slightly taller and younger man. "I appreciate your delaying your departure for an additional day."

"For the pleasure and honor of meeting Lady Secca, and dining with her, it is well worth the delay." Lythner spoke in a way that the compliment was delivered as a fact, and not flattery.

Secca managed not to flush. "It is indeed a pleasure to meet you."

Robero turned to Lythner. "We should eat before whatever is fixed becomes too cold."

There were but the three of them at the end of the long table—and that was the smallest grouping for a meal Secca had had with Robero in more than a score of years.

She could not help but smile at the half fowl presented on her platter, covered with a pear glaze, and accompanied with sweet-fried late apples and crisp lace potatoes.

"I thought you might like something like this after Fustar's table," Robero said. "He has very good mutton, and more very good mutton, and even more very good mutton."

"I did eat a great deal of mutton," Secca admitted.

A warm twinkle appeared in Lythner's eyes.

"It is solid fare for sorcery," Secca continued, "but this fowl is most welcome."

"Alyssa did not come with you?" Lythner asked Robero.

"She will be joining me tomorrow," replied Robero. "She was visiting her sister."

"In Wendel?"

His mouth full, Robero nodded.

"Lady Chelshay has done wonders with Wendel . . ."

"No doubt due to the advice of your brother," suggested Robero.

The faintest trace of a frown crossed Lythner's forehead, then vanished. "Nerylt is a dear fellow . . . and he does well with arms, far better than I . . ."

Secca repressed a smile, knowing that Nerylt was a well-meaning bumbler whose principal virtues were his love of his children, an understanding that his consort was far his better, and his willingness to follow her directions. Secca was glad to see that Lythner had few illusions about his younger sibling.

"He is a good fellow," Robero agreed, "and a fair instructor in arms, I've heard."

"He loves the practice yard, though there is little need of that skill at present in Defalk."

"It may not always be so." Robero lifted a goblet and took a sip of the amber wine.

"Oh?" asked Lythner.

"There is some young fellow in Neserea, scion of one of the old families. Rumors are that he's trying to suggest he's the true heir of the Prophet of Music."

"Rabyn didn't have heirs," Secca pointed out. "Not that he didn't try with every woman he could find." She resisted smiling as the server slipped another half fowl onto her platter.

"This one traces his lineage back to Behlem's brother

or cousin." Robero broke off another chunk of bread. "Lady Jolyn reported that the Sturinnese have sent another fleet to the Ostisles."

"They have held the isles for a generation." Lythner paused. "You think they may attack somewhere in Liedwahr?"

"Anything is possible, but when the Maitre starts amassing fleets, one should watch closely."

Secca continued to eat, but nodded. Sturinn had been quiet for years, and that had scarcely been the pattern of the Sea-Priests throughout the history of the sea-warriors.

"We are most fortunate that they cannot land on the coast and harbors we do not have," Lythner said with a smile.

"This is a good vintage. I appreciate your sending it to us." Robero held up his goblet. "How are the vineyards coming?"

"The root rot is a problem . . . but we've begun to graft the white grapes to wild root stock, and it looks like . . ."

Secca continued to eat, to smile, and to ask an occasional question, but she had to work even to keep her eyes open.

". . . too much water . . . as much of a problem as too little . . . going to try for ice-wine in the higher fields this fall . . ."

Secca jerked, realizing she had almost fallen asleep at the table. She could not help but yawn. She managed to stifle the first, but not the second.

"Am I boring you?" Lythner disarmed the question with his warm smile.

"No. Quite the contrary. I have been trying not to show how tired I am. I rode here from Issl, where I had used sorcery to repair a water dam. Before that, the players and I were extending the finished sections of the road between the River Chean and Mencha."

"Some day, it may even be completed," suggested Robero.

"Shortly," promised Secca, trying to hold back another yawn and keep her eyes open.

Robero shook his head. "Ever were you among the first to bed and the first to rise." He stood and glanced at Lythner. "I will see Lady Secca to her chamber, if you do not mind. I appreciate your courtesy, and trust you will convey my best to your sire."

"That I will. That I will." Lythner stood and bowed, first to Secca, then to Robero, before the two turned and departed.

"He did not see me at my best," said Secca once they were outside.

"It was an introduction, not a matchmaking," Robero said dryly. "He might as well know that you do not chatter into the night. Then—as I learned early—you never did offer idle chatter."

"I had thought he was consorted, and even has some children." Secca raised her eyebrows.

"He was consorted. His consort died last summer of a consumptive flux, and even Lady Jolyn was unable to save her." Robero's voice was even.

Secca started up the steps to the second level. "So . . . you thought . . ."

"You, Lady Sorceress, would not cross the corridor to meet someone suited to you," Robero pointed out. "He may be suited to you or the reverse, but it could not hurt to have you meet. I did not intend more than that at this point." He continued walking along the corridor.

"I suppose Jolyn recommended him?"

"Hardly. What recommended him to me was that he was not interested in her." Robero laughed.

So did Secca, if more gently. "You still would like to see me consorted."

Robero shook his head. "Secca . . . we have known each other since we were scarce more than children. I am not the Lord of Defalk you would want, but I do wish you well. I do not think you are so happy as you insist you are."

Secca opened her mouth, then shut it. After a moment, she said, "Thank you."

"I do admit I thought of Lythner because he already has two sons and a daughter. Were you attracted to him, you would not . . ."

Secca nodded. "The choice would truly be mine and free. Thank you for that. After I return to Mencha, I will consider all you have said."

"That is all I ask." Robero continued walking until they reached the door to the guest chamber, where Achar still stood guard.

Secca turned. "Thank you."

"Good dreams, Secca."

Secca offered a tired smile before she slipped into the guest chamber, holding off yawning until she was alone. Lythner had a warm smile . . . and seemed like a good man—but did she really wish to settle for just a good man?

Abruptly, she stiffened. Why did she want to settle for any man? Anna certainly had not settled for just any man, and Jecks had had to meet Anna's terms, not anyone else's. Why did Robero—or most of the lords and even the ladies of the Thirty-three—think that a woman wasn't happy without a man?

She shook her head, suddenly awake again, and wondering if she would soon sleep.

7

Still brushing the dust off her riding jacket, Secca hurried across the paving stones of the north courtyard and up the front steps into the arched front entry hall of Loiseau, cool and dim, and lit but by a single pair of wall lamps. Her boots echoed in the high-ceilinged hall as she made her way toward the second archway and the main staircase beyond. The spaciousness of Loiseau always amazed her when she returned.

"Lady Secca!"

At the sound of the voice, Secca stopped and turned.

The white-haired but energetic and round-faced Florenda hastened through the side archway from the formal dining hall to join the sorceress at the base of the staircase. "I thought that had to be you, riding in so late," puffed the household head as she stopped and bowed.

"Is everything all right? How is Lady Anna?"

"She be fine, lady. She ate well, down in the salon with Richina and young Kerisel and Jeagyn. She, Lady Anna, was . . . she was telling Lizyrel that she'd better be careful with that young fellow of hers, because he took after his father."

"That sounds like her." Secca took a slow breath, relaxing slightly. She'd felt tense for the entire day's ride, and she'd been worrying the whole time about the extra day she'd taken on the journey back to add another dek and a half to the road from Mencha to the Chean. Yet, if she didn't squeeze it in, she'd never finish it, because it wasn't something that she wanted to ride two days in order to put in a day's work and then ride two back. Nor did Secca wish to spend a week or so camping on the road to finish it, especially when neither Anna nor Robero liked the idea of the players being out of touch that long for roadwork, even though Robero also complained about the length of time it had taken to build the road system.

"She was fussing about something, but didn't say what. She's been doing that for years, and she will be after I'm long gone. You know the way she does."

Secca did. "I'll go on up and see how she is. Is everything else all right?"

"Nothing that Halde 'n me couldn't handle."

The sorceress smiled. There was very little the two couldn't handle between them. Still, she hurried up the wide stone stairs to the second level, her boots echoing on the stone steps and the stone floor of the upper corridor leading back to the main suite that was Anna's.

After a hurried knock, Secca bowed as she entered Anna's quarters. "Lady . . ."

Anna sat behind the small desk in the alcove in her quarters, appearing, as always, young and beautiful, blonde hair in perfect position, blue eyes firm and focused, and wearing her trademark green vest over a white silk tunic-shirt. "You seem to be no worse for the wear, or from the ride, Secca." Anna smiled good-humoredly.

"I did take an extra day on the way back to add to the road."

"You shouldn't have much left before it's done."

"Six deks or so, I would judge." Secca perched on the chest at the foot of the bed.

"Robero sent me a message." Anna's smile turned sardonic. "About the unfortunate illness afflicting Kylar."

"He did not become ill until I was gone several days from Issl. Robero informed me when I reached Elheld."

"Heavens . . . I'm not unhappy with you, Secca." Anna shook her head. "Robero still doesn't have a grain of sense in that balding skull. Anyone could have read that scroll and figured out what he meant. What good would writing something like that do? Alyssa's not around for a week, and he's already in trouble. Robero has known for years, as well as we have, that Issl would have been a mess, worse than the revolt in Pamr, within seasons if Kylar had inherited the holding. But Robero still had to warn me, as if he didn't need the protection we provide." The Sorceress-Protector snorted.

"You used the pool to find that out?"

"A little scrying won't hurt me. I'm not trying to see Elizabetta." The touch of a frown remained on the unlined forehead as she continued, "I'd like you to try to call up her image tomorrow . . . when you're rested."

"I can do that." Secca managed to keep her voice level. Anna had never asked Secca to use the glass to bring up an image of the older sorceress's daughter. "Are you all right?"

"I'm fine. You're the one who's always telling me to be careful." Anna paused, if but briefly, before asking, "How is our Lord of Defalk?" Her tone verged on the sarcastic, as it often did when she mentioned Robero.

"He was most cheerful. He set up a dinner for just three of us—me, him, and Lythner. Lythner's—"

"Lord Clethner's eldest. I know. Robero wrote about that, too. The smartest thing Clethner ever did was to consort Nerylt with Chelshay. Robero's trying to do the same for Lythner."

"Lythner seems quite nice."

Anna laughed. "I've always hated that word. Nice. It's like cute. Baby ducks are cute. Simpering idiots are nice."

Secca couldn't help but laugh at Anna's phrases.

"Robero was sort of cute as a boy," Anna went on. "He never grew out of it, not all the way," mused Anna. "You're going to have to watch out for him."

"Me? You'll be around—"

"For a few years, I hope, but not forever. Clayre's a good woman, but she's an old-style sorceress, and Jolyn . . ." Anna shrugged. "We know about her."

"What are you worried about?" Secca shifted her weight on the footchest. She was sore from all the riding.

"I didn't sleep that well last night. I had this dream that the Harmonies were shifting. They weren't the Harmonies, exactly, either. I'm not sure it was a dream." The ageless blue eyes focused on Secca. "You have to learn to trust how you feel."

"I know. You've told me that . . ."

"Something's going to happen, and you'll be the one who'll have to deal with it. I can give you advice."

Again, Secca wanted to frown. Anna had never talked that way about Secca being the one to deal with problems, especially major ones. That had been true even when Anna had sent Secca out to sing shadow sorcery or do the mining spells to get the iron and gold that sustained Loiseau. Anna had just told Secca what to do, as if each occasion had been an exception or a learning experience.

"Do you know what it is?" asked Secca.

The older sorceress shook her head. "With the Harmonies, you don't."

"Robero?"

"No. It could be the Maitre of Sturinn. Jolyn sent a message about his sending more fleets to the Ostisles. Or it could be something in Ebra. Hadrenn's always been a weak reed. Or Dumar. Dumar's always bothered me, ever since Alvar died anyway."

"Have you heard from Hanfor recently?"

"His younger daughter's happy with young Eryhal, but he still doesn't have a consort for Annayal, and she's the heir. He should have consorted Annayal to Eryhal, not Aerfor." Anna paused, adding soberly, "It's hard to find a good match. If Robero's boy Robal were even five years older . . . but he's not. Maybe Verad, that younger son of Hadrenn."

Secca waited, then asked, "Is there anything you need from me tonight?"

Anna smiled, warmly. "Not a thing. I'm glad you're back safely. I do still worry, even at your age."

"At more than a score and a half?"

"You never get over it, Secca." Anna rose and stepped from behind the desk. "Go on. You're tired. I can see it in your eyes. They're almost pink. I won't be up that much longer myself."

Secca eased herself up from the chest, then stepped forward and hugged Anna. Then, with a smile, Secca turned and slipped from the room, somehow both relieved to see Anna in such good spirits, and slightly troubled by what the older sorceress had said.

Trouble with the Harmonies?

8

Secca reined up the chestnut outside the domed sorcery building to the south of the main keep of Loiseau. Vyren—the head ostler—had insisted Secca take the chestnut and give the gray mare she preferred a rest, even if the ride down to the outbuilding was little more than half a dek. As she dismounted, Secca glanced at the saddled raider mount tied outside the domed sorcery building, then at the pair of guards who had straightened at her arrival.

"Lady Anna must have been up early," she said. Usually Anna was anything but someone who rose early.

"She said she couldn't sleep, Lady Secca, and might as well do something useful," said Mureyn, the older of the two guards in the green of Loiseau.

That did sound just like Anna, reflected Secca with a brief smile. "Richina should be here shortly, and the players later."

"Yes, lady."

Secca slipped into the building, closing the door behind her and walking down the corridor toward the room that held the scrying pool—and the area where she and Anna usually worked. The building was silent except for the muted echo of Secca's boots. Secca paused. Never had it been so still, or so it seemed.

She opened the door to the scrying room, and the pool.

"Anna!"

The blonde and slender form of the older sorceress lay slumped across the working desk. A quill lay on the stone floor beside the desk. Secca ran the few steps to the desk and bent, touching Anna's forehead—still warm. Anna was breathing, but so lightly that Secca had trouble discerning that.

She eased Anna out of the chair and laid her gently on her back on the floor.

Anna's eyes opened. "No . . . Darksong . . . once . . . enough." Then her eyes flicked shut.

Secca knelt and listened, but Anna continued to breathe lightly. The younger sorceress straightened and ran back to the door, and then along the corridor and out to the front of the building, bursting out into the early morning light of the fall day.

"Get the carriage!" Secca snapped. "Lady Anna is most ill! Get Richina to help me!"

"Yes, lady!" Mureyn untied his mount and swung up into the saddle, urging the bay gelding back toward the keep.

Secca turned to the other guard—the young-faced one. Albar, she thought. "Let me know when the carriage comes. I'll be with her by the scrying pond. Send Richina to me as soon as she gets here."

Even before Albar could respond, Secca had turned and rushed back to be with Anna.

The Sorceress-Protector was yet breathing when Secca returned, perhaps more strongly. As Secca bent over Anna again, she listened to her mentor's heartbeat, but could hear nothing irregular, although the beating seemed faint. Nor could she find any sign of any wound, or bruise, or any injury.

"Lady Secca?" Albar stood in the door. "The carriage is here, and I can see Richina riding down from the keep."

Without even a thought, Secca bent and lifted Anna into her arms—the older sorceress's form was so light—and carried her down the corridor.

Mureyn stepped forward as she neared the outer door and helped Secca through the door, and then to ease Anna into the waiting carriage—the blue-lacquered carriage created more than a generation earlier by Lord Brill, seldom used, and still in close-to-pristine condition.

"We didn't know, lady . . . we didn't know." Mureyn's eyes were bright.

"You couldn't have known." Secca managed to choke out the words.

Richina reined up beside the carriage. The apprentice's sandy-blonde hair was disheveled, her eyes wide. "Lady Secca!"

"She's most ill. Ride back to the house. Have her bed ready. We'll need some help getting her up there."

"Yes, lady." Richina turned her mount.

Secca slid into the carriage, and Mureyn closed the door behind her.

As the carriage began to move, Secca's eyes burned, and her nose itched from the faintly musty smell of the old velvet upholstery. She bent over Anna again, but the sorceress was still breathing, lightly but regularly.

Secca could not help but wonder what had happened. There had been no sign of sorcery. Anna's lutar had been nowhere in sight, and the strong room with the notebooks had still been sealed. Anna wouldn't have tried even mild scrying without a lutar.

Secca glanced at Anna again, through the burning of unshed tears, willing the carriage to move more quickly, hoping that Anna had merely fainted, and that rest was all she needed.

But, thinking about all that Anna had said the night before, Secca's eyes burned as the carriage rolled up the paved road toward the main buildings of the hold.

9

Although it was after harvest and the sun hung just over the western walls of Loiseau, ready to set, the Sorceress-Protector's room was warm, not just from the sun, but from the heated air coming through the louvers underneath the windows.

The breathing of the young-appearing sorceress on the high bed was shallow, becoming intermittent at times before returning to an irregular pattern. Anna had scarcely moved since she had been laid in the bed by Secca, and her hair remained fine, blonde, almost like spun gold, and still almost perfectly in place. Her eyes were closed, but had they been open, their piercing blue would have dominated the chamber. Her face was thin and drawn, and her figure was so slender, almost tiny, that it looked more like that of a young girl before maturity than that of a sorceress who had dominated Defalk for more than a score of years.

Secca sat in a blue-lacquered and delicate-appearing chair at the side of the bed. She held the dying woman's hand in her own, swallowing as the older sorceress's breathing lapsed into silence for a moment before resuming once more.

"So . . . tired . . . promise   me . . . no   Darksong . . . no spells," Anna had whispered less than a half a glass before. "Defalk . . . everyone . . . they need you . . . more than me."

Nodding agreement had been hard for Secca, but she had, and now she waited, her guts tied into knots, her eyes burning, wondering why she had offered that promise.

". . . won't be long . . ." The smile on the drawn face of the sorceress had been more a rictus than a true expression. "Elizabetta . . . got . . . my last letter . . . told her . . . be the last . . . didn't tell you . . . tried to . . . last night . . ."

Every time Anna had sent a missive across the void to the Mist Worlds, it shortened her life. That had been the one thing about which Secca and Anna had always disagreed, but Anna had been adamant, her only concessions having been limiting the frequency of such spell-transmissions and letting Secca sing the spells to retrieve Elizabetta's missives.

The effort of merely retrieving those missives had prostrated Secca, leaving her exhausted for one to two days, even despite her comparative youth, and the effect reminded her how short she fell of the sheer power that Anna had been able to bring to her sorcery. Yet Anna had insisted that using Clearsong to cross the Mist Worlds was easier for her than for those born in Liedwahr, and that the trio—Secca, Clayre, and Jolyn—were as powerful as Anna had been.

At the slightest whisper of a knock on the door, Secca turned in the chair.

Richina slipped just inside the door. The sandy-haired young woman, although but a few years more than a girl, stood nearly a head taller than Secca. Richina's face was blotchy, and her green eyes were reddened.

Touching her finger to her lips, Secca nodded for Richina to join her, waiting until the apprentice sorceress stood next to the chair.

Richina bent and whispered. "There's so little left. I can sense it. Can I do anything . . . please?"

Secca shook her head, murmuring back. "She's forbidden it, and it won't change anything. I don't even think Darksong would work."

"It's unfair," replied Richina in a whisper.

"Life is unfair, child," said the dying woman, her voice momentarily strong, her eyes opening for a moment and fixing on the pair beside her bed, before they slowly closed. "Don't . . . ask . . . for fairness . . . create it."

"Her mind is all there," murmured the apprentice, "but the Harmonies are leaving."

Secca nodded. "You can stay."

Her eyes burning, Secca looked at the dying sorceress again, squeezing Anna's hand ever so gently, trying to let Anna know that she was there. Sometimes the slim and smooth fingers offered the faintest pressure back, but most of the time Anna's hand was limp, cool, but not cold. Not yet.

Secca swallowed again, blinking back tears, sensing, knowing that there was nothing she could do—not that Anna would have accepted.

So light was Anna's breathing that Secca hadn't been

certain she would know when the pale blonde woman on the high bed stopped breathing.

She needn't have worried . . . because a long and low chord, perfect in harmony, filled the room, if but for a timeless instant. Even the sorcery-warmed air flowing from the window louvers halted for a moment.

Secca stood, bent forward, and offered a last kiss.

She found she wasn't crying. Perhaps the time for tears had been earlier, after she had found Anna collapsed beside the reflecting pool in the domed building that had been the elder sorceress's working space. Secca had brought Anna back to her chamber, fearing the worst, as it had happened.

There would be more tears later. That she also knew.

Richina was standing at the foot of the bed, sobbing silently.

Behind the sorceress and the apprentice, the door opened quietly.

The red-haired sorceress turned. So did Richina.

Two figures stood in the doorway—the graying saalmeister Halde and the white-haired household head Florenda.

"We heard . . . like a single note of farewell." Florenda's voice broke on the last word.

Halde nodded. He swallowed wordlessly.

Secca returned the nod. Richina also swallowed, blotting her eyes.

The four stood in silence, a long silence following a single harmonic chord that had announced a great loss to Erde, a loss so great that even those who had never heard the chords of Harmony had done so.

10

WEI, NORDWEI

The dark-haired seer enters the study and bows to the Council Leader. "Leader Ashtaar . . ."

"I know. I heard the Harmonies chime." Ashtaar brushes back a lock of fine silver hair. Her eyes are now as dark as once her hair was, and black circles ring those eyes, eyes set in a finely wrinkled skin, but her voice is clear and hard.

"The sorceress just breathed her last," announces the seer, her face contorted in confusion, "moments ago."

"You think the Harmonies would not mark her passing, Escadra?" Ashtaar blinks, as if something has irritated her eyes, and she blots them with a dark green cloth.

Escadra lowers her head, her pale gray eyes on the green and maroon carpet that covers the polished stones of the study floor. "I am sorry to have bothered you, Leader Ashtaar."

"I asked you to let me know, and you have." Ashtaar gestures to one of the polished wooden armchairs across the ebony desk from her. "Sit down."

The slightest frown creases Escadra's forehead, then vanishes as the chunky seer seats herself.

"You are what . . . a score less a year?" asks the older woman.

"Yes, your Mightiness."

"All your life you have heard of the Sorceress of Defalk, that forbidding presence from the Mist Worlds. Is that not so?"

Escadra nods.

"How she buried hundreds of scores of armsmen under lakes, entombed the Evult of Ebra with molten rock, killed every last man in a town that revolted? Or how she pulled down an entire city upon its innocent inhabitants to destroy the Lord of Dumar?"

"Yes, leader."

Ashtaar brushes away the honorific.

"Do you remember the story of Gretslen?"

A quizzical expression fleets across Escadra's eyes, quickly, but not quickly enough to escape the scrutiny of the older woman.

"You wonder why I ask that now?" Ashtaar's laugh is light, with a sense of brittleness. "Because it is appropriate. Gretslen never understood why things changed, or what power is. She thought power could be separated from its use. The great sorceress is dead, but those who would use power as she did are not. Yet too many in Liedwahr will believe that matters will return to what they were now that she is dead. We in Wei must not entertain that alluring temptation."

Ashtaar's eyebrows lift. "What does that have to do with the horrible stories about the sorceress? It is simple, if one thinks. What the sorceress did was to use power for ends she thought worthwhile. She has taught others both how to use power as she did, and, equally important, the ends she favored, and the reasons for those ends. There will be struggles, even here in Wei, because many will not believe the changes she wrought are enduring." An ironic smile crosses her lips. "Those who question those changes will fail, but they will make us all suffer, and for that reason alone, I would mourn her passing."

Escadra's mouth opens, then closes.

"You wonder why I question the legends, or why I am disturbed at the passing of one seen as the eternal enemy of Wei?" Ashtaar laughs. "Dear child, for more than a score of years, we have prospered from trade with Defalk, Neserea, and Ebra—and even farther across the oceans. We have built our ships and our fleets, and we have managed to secure safety for our traders against the Sea-Priests and their fleets. We could do this because our borders to the south were guarded by the sorceress. Never have we been safer." She laughs. "The Lady of the Shadows and her followers even grudgingly admit that, much as they fear and dislike sorcery."

"It was to the sorceress's interest as well," ventures the young seer.

"Indeed it was. But people are not merely interests. Did you know she had children? And was forcibly separated from them by the sorcery that hurled her into our world? Or that once, for nearly a half-score of years, she effectively ruled all of eastern Liedwahr? And then stepped aside? Did you know that before her, not a single one of the Thirty-three of Defalk had ever been a woman?" Ashtaar coughs, covering her mouth with the dark green cloth. After a moment, she sets the cloth beside the time-and-finger-polished black agate oval on the desk. "Leaders are people, Escadra. Their pasts influence their present—and ours. Never forget that."

Escadra nods.

Ashtaar's dark eyes burn into the seer. "Use your pool to scry Defalk in the days ahead. See what you can of how the people feel about her death. See how the younger sorceresses of Defalk feel, if you can. See how Liedfuhr Kestrin feels, and the young Matriarch of Ranuak. And if you can, the Ladies of the Shadows in Ranuak. Then we will talk again." After a moment of silence, the Council Leader of Wei adds, "You may go."

Once the door closes, Ashtaar looks toward the window, and the late twilight beyond.

11

In the midafternoon light, Secca glanced around the entry hall of Loiseau, looking at the pale blue stone of the walls, then up, to the brass chandelier, its candles dark, and then to the trapezoidal cupola that topped the foyer. Slowly, she let her eyes follow the blue-tinted stone blocks of the walls downward until her eyes rested on the polished black and white interlocking stone triangles of the floor, the regularity of the triangles emphasized by the inlaid strips of curlicued brass.

In the center of the soaring hall, directly under the cupola, was a rectangle of wooden planks—two yards deep and three wide. On three sides of the rectangle were stacks of copper and tin ingots, almost half a yard high.

The red-haired sorceress stepped back to the easel and studied the drawings there, noting the simple lines, but also the inner support struts. Even if Anna were not being paraded in state through Falcor, as the greatest sorceress ever in the history of Defalk, she deserved some measure of grandeur in the ceremony that would mark her farewell to Loiseau and the people of Mencha. For a moment, Secca's eyes burned. She blotted them with the back of her sleeve, took a slow breath, and then studied her drawing again. After a moment, she closed her eyes and attempted to visualize just how the funeral catafalque would look.

At the squeak of ill-lubricated wheels, Secca glanced up to see the two lancers wheeling in the handcart laden with another load—the last one—of copper ingots from the storeroom. Secca watched as Richina followed the example Secca had set earlier and motioned to the rectangle of wooden planks set directly under the center of the entry hall. "Put them on the planks, evenly spaced, like the others."

The lancers began to stack the ingots on the section of planking that had none.

Secca nodded to herself and went back to studying the schematic drawing, another innovation of Anna's. From what Secca had read and studied in the old books Anna had inherited from Lord Brill, the only images used to aid in sorcery had been simple line drawings. Soon after she had become regent, Anna had started using multiple drawings, some even of internal supports unseen when a device or structure was finally fabricated through Clearsong. But the more detailed schematics had come after Lord Jecks' death, and after Anna had turned Defalk over to Lord Robero and returned to Mencha.

"Lady Secca?" Richina stood, respectfully, a yard back from the easel and the drawings it held. "Will you need more of the copper?"

Secca studied the ingots stacked neatly on the plank rectangle, then the two lancers standing by the empty cart. "No, thank you, Richina. What we have should be enough." She smiled. "How are you coming on your spell to return the catafalque to ingots once . . ." The words trailed off.

"Ah . . . it's hard."

"You haven't started?" Secca raised her eyebrows.

Richina dropped her eyes. "It's hard to think . . . she's gone."

"You don't think I don't care?" asked Secca gently. "She was my mother from the time I was eight."

"Oh, no, lady. Never. It's just . . ." Richina looked down, but not before Secca could see the tears welling up.

Secca reached out and touched her hand. "I know. We still . . . she would want us to go on . . . and she deserves our best."

Richina lifted her eyes. "I will start once I am through here." This time Richina paused, as if she had more to say. "There is one thing."

Secca smiled. There was always "one thing" more with students and apprentices.

"Kerisel and Jeagyn would like to watch you do the spell," Richina ventured.

"They may, if they stand well back, and behind me. You may get them." Secca grinned momentarily. "That is, if they're not already hiding just inside the dining hall."

Richina flushed. "They had hoped . . ."

Secca shook her head ruefully. "Just tell them." Her eyes flicked to the lancers and the empty cart. "You had better dismiss the lancers. They're still waiting to know about whether you need them."

Richina's hand went to her mouth. "I'm sorry." She turned and walked quickly to the two men. "Lady Secca says that you may go and put the cart away. She has the copper she needs."

The shorter of the two rankers inclined his head momentarily. Both turned. The taller man took the handcart and turned it, wheeling it out the front entry doors before him. Without the ingots on it, the cart did not squeak.

Richina headed back past Secca, bowing her head as she hurried past, in the direction of the formal grand dining hall—seldom used in recent years.

Secca pulled on the gloves with the copper-tipped fingers, then picked up the grand lutar and began to check the tuning. Even before she had finished, she heard careful footsteps on the polished stone behind her. Looking over her shoulder, she took in the three figures, putting a finger to her lips before returning her full attention to the task before her.

Her eyes went to the drawing of the catafalque on which Anna's coffin would rest. She began to play, the spell melody first, one time through, without words, to smooth the way for the full spell. Then came melody and spell, welling out into the stillness of the entry hall.

> *"Build of bronze, with this song*
> *shining true, hard and strong . . ."*

The air above the planks was filled with a glowing haze that flashed a near-brilliant blue before subsiding into a blue-gold fog that surrounded the planks and ingots. With a second flash, of golden white and a single harmonic chord that was, as always, heard only by the sorceresses and the apprentices and students, and the more gifted players, the fog lifted to reveal a rectangular structure not quite a yard high, but three yards wide and

two deep. Each surface of the catafalque glistened as if
it were lit from within.

"Oh . . ." The involuntary murmur came from one of
the students. The slender Kerisel, Secca thought as she
slowly lowered the grand lutar.

"It's beautiful," Richina said quietly, stepping forward and bowing her head. "It's almost too beautiful—"

"It's for her only," Secca replied firmly. "Just once,
just hers."

Richina nodded slowly.

As she stripped off the insulating gloves and slipped
them into the pouch on the right side of her belt, beside
the dagger and opposite the short sabre on the left side,
Secca hoped the sandy-haired apprentice truly understood why Anna deserved the best Secca—or any of
them—could provide her.

12

Later . . . after Secca had completed what else needed to
be done, sent short scrolls to Clayre for Lord Robero,
and helped Florenda and Halde with what only she could
do for Anna, the red-haired sorceress stopped by the
smaller room on the lower level to see Richina.

As Secca knocked and stepped into Richina's room, the
sandy-haired young sorceress looked up from where she
sat in the single chair near the foot of the bed.

"Lady Secca . . ."

"I wanted to see how you were. You were troubled,
more than I realized . . ." Secca let the words die away.

"She still looked so young," blurted the young sorceress,
"but there was no Harmony left in her."

"That was the death Darksong of Lord Brill. It did not

change her years, only her shape. You know that," Secca said gently.

"Mother . . . she said that . . . the sorceress would never change. But . . . it's hard. Two days ago . . . she was so alive."

"Death is like that," Secca reminded her apprentice. "We must never forget that it is sudden and forever."

"I know. Lady Anna said that all the time." Richina frowned. "Sometimes, she was so stern, but I know she cared."

"She did. More than most people ever knew. She didn't let people see. You know . . . once, when I was much younger than you, nine, I think, she carried me to bed. That was when she was regent. She didn't have to, but she carried me there and tucked me in, and promised that I could stay with her." Secca swallowed. "She was the one who saw that your mother would be better at holding Suhl than her brothers would be."

"My uncle Keithen . . . he wanted Suhl."

"I know. He tried to kill your mother, and then poison her. She never asked Anna for help."

"Not until I came along." A faint smile crossed Richina's lips. "She cared not for sorcery in the hold."

Secca nodded. "Are you unhappy to be here?"

"No. I'm thankful. I know enough to know I'd be unhappy without the Harmonies. Jyrll . . . he loves the land and the people. He'll listen to me, if it comes to that, but he wouldn't do anything to hurt people, except to stop a greater hurt."

Secca wondered if Richina hadn't just summarized ruling—do no harm except to stop a greater evil. "You'll be all right." Secca rose.

"I know." Richina smiled wanly. "Thank you, lady."

After Secca closed Richina's door, she walked farther down the lower corridor—away from the entry hall—and stepped out the side door into the cool night air that had descended upon Loiseau and brought a chill into the courtyard. Above her, the liedburg loomed, seemingly lightless, for all the lamps and candles within.

Her feet carried her toward the gates. Above the near-silent hold, in a clear sky, the stars shone bright—and cold. Secca shivered, despite her green leather riding jacket, and her hand brushed the hilt of the sabre—another gift of sorts from Anna.

The white disk of the moon Clearsong shimmered near its zenith, and Secca was grateful that the red point of light that was Darksong had not yet risen. She stopped in the space between the open gates of Loiseau, looking to the east, not quite sure why. Neither the stars nor Clearsong offered any answer to her unvoiced questions. To her right, to the south, lay the domed work building, dark and empty.

In time, she turned and walked back up the stone steps and back into the soaring space of the entry hall. Neither guard looked at her as she passed, her steps slow as she neared the center of the spacious foyer and what awaited her there.

She looked up to the brass chandelier, its white candles still dark, for a moment before her eyes skipped over the blue-tinted stone blocks of the walls and dropped to the polished black and white interlocking triangular floor stones. Finally, the red-haired sorceress lifted her eyes to the shimmering bronze catafalque that held a simple and ancient oak casket, one that had once been meant for Lord Brill's sire, three generations back, polished so that it shimmered under the light from the candles of the single four-branched sconce set behind the catafalque.

There . . . against the green velvet of the open silvered coffin, lay the body of the woman who had transformed Defalk, the woman who had saved Secca time and again, who had taught her music and sorcery . . . and life.

Anna's face was drawn, but she looked almost as young as when Secca had first seen her more than twenty years before, and Secca wondered if, perhaps, her body would remain incorrupt forever, like a statue. Anna still looked young, her features too drawn, too fine, to be beautiful without the fierce spirit that had animated them. But she was dead, perhaps because she had demanded too much from herself, in life, in sorcery . . . and perhaps because she was tired.

Lord Jecks had died nearly a half-score of years before, his heart bursting as he had been instructing young armsmen at his own hold of Eldheld. Anna had been quieter, more withdrawn, since Jecks' death, leaving more and more of the day-to-day sorcery to the trio, only occasionally traveling to Falcor. After Lord Jecks' death, Anna seldom had seen or conferred with Lord Robero, and when she had, neither had been particularly happy, not from what Secca had overheard and seen, although Robero had always taken Anna's advice.

Secca shook her head.

She doubted that Robero would care that much personally about Anna's death, although he would regret deeply the loss of the power Anna had held and always used for the benefit of Defalk and its people.

Secca took a deep breath. Now she would have to deal more with Robero, as Anna had suggested—and with Jolyn and Clayre. She pushed that thought away. Those problems could wait.

How long she stood, looking at Anna's visage, missing the fierce blue eyes, forever closed in what seemed endless sleep, Secca neither knew nor cared. A deep void had opened within her, like a wound she doubted would ever close, always aching, even beneath any smile she might offer.

So motionless had she stood, wrapped in grief, that only the aching of legs locked too tightly finally broke through the concentration of her vigil.

Slowly, slowly, she stepped back and then slipped around the catafalque and walked slowly through the second archway and toward the grand staircase, her boots murmuring on the hard stone.

Behind her remained the guards, watching over the sorceress who had watched over them for all their lives.

13

In the bedchamber right at the top of the grand stair-case—the one Anna had first used when she had come to Loiseau, a chamber larger than the master chamber in Secca's own hold of Flossbend—the red-haired sorceress dressed slowly in the grayness before dawn. She donned dark green trousers and a lighter colored silky green shirt, but with a black vest and a black mourning scarf.

She looked at her image in the robing room mirror, a mirror fringed with moisture from the hot bath she had hoped would relieve the stiffness that had come with an uneasy sleep. Amber eyes ringed with dark circles and set above still-freckled and youthful-looking cheeks looked back at her. She frowned, if wryly. More than a score and a half of years behind her, and she still stood little taller than the youngest of apprentice sorceresses. After a moment, she turned, heading toward the door to face a day she dreaded.

She had to talk about Anna, and she wasn't quite sure she'd ever understood Anna. "But maybe I will . . . like the vocalises . . ." While Secca had appreciated Anna's insis-tence on all the women apprentice sorceresses and foster-lings learning skills with blades, perhaps because of the attack on Falcor when Secca had been a child, Secca had been well into her twenties before she had begun to un-derstand fully the value of the vocal exercises and endless technique—or the songs from the Mist Worlds that were scarcely spells at all, except perhaps love spells. And the thought of learning songs or spells in five or six languages, as Anna had . . . Secca wondered if anyone besides Clayre or Jolyn really understood, or even whether they truly did.

Today . . . all she could do was to express the feeling of

loss, and that would have to do, but, inside, she knew that was far from enough.

Would Secca ever understand—or would she be old and unable to explain to anyone else before she did?

For all the older sorceress's love and kindness to Secca, Anna had not shied from delivering tongue-lashings to Secca herself—or even to Robero, or to Lord Jecks, or to apprentices, like Richina. Yet Anna had gone out of her way for all of them, and for people she had scarcely even met, and she had tried her best to heal a land that had been wounded throughout most of its long and bloody history.

Perhaps Secca's father had said it best, decades past, when he had told Secca, before sending her to Anna in Falcor, "She is a good woman, but far from perfect. Accept her goodness, and do not expect perfection."

But then, in ruling Defalk or any land, could anyone be perfect? Secca's lips twisted into another wry expression as she opened the door into the upper corridor.

"Your thoughts are wandering," she murmured to herself. How could they not wander? In most ways, for almost all of Secca's life—or at least the last twenty-five years—Anna had been her mother, the one Secca looked to, talked to, and had wanted to please. And Anna was gone, gone far earlier than she had to have died. Because . . . ? Because she had spent too much of her life and energy to ensure Defalk was strong, too much energy teaching the sorceresses who were to succeed her?

It was strange, too, in a way, because the older three were all so different—Jolyn, blonde, almost what Anna had called a contralto; the brown-haired Clayre with her middle voice, in some ways the closest to Anna's, if without the power the older sorceress had always projected; and Secca, the redhead with the voice that had turned all too many glasses into crystal powdered almost like fine sand.

For another moment, Secca stood at the top of the grand staircase. Then, halfway down the wide stone steps, as she caught sight of the score of lancers in green—one com-

pany of the five that had comprised Anna's personal armsmen—Secca found her face stiffening into a mask of grave
composure.

Wilten, overcaptain of the Loiseau armsmen, met her at
the base of the stairs. He bowed. "They're lined up for
leagues, it seems, Lady Secca. Some have been waiting
outside the gates since a good two glasses before dawn."

Secca nodded. "Thank you. I suppose we should open
the doors and let them pay their last respects. Are your
men ready?"

"Yes, lady."

From the rear lower corridor, Richina appeared, as if
she had been waiting, as she doubtless had, slipping up to
follow Secca wordlessly. Like Secca, the younger sorceress wore green and black. Behind her were Kerisel and
Jeagyn, without vests, but with black scarves.

The red-haired sorceress walked toward the front entry
doors, her steps curving away from the open coffin and
the glistening bronze catafalque. Behind her followed the
three younger women.

At the entry hall doors, Secca looked out into the morning—a morning seemingly like many other fall mornings,
with scattered clouds and blue skies. She'd almost wished
for something dramatic, like a storm, or even heavy clouds.

Her eyes focused on the open gates of Loiseau. Beyond
them, the line of men and women, most of them older—
gray-haired, silver-haired, or bald—stretched along the
dusty stone road, back down the hill, winding almost back
to the yellow-and-red-leaved orchards, in the direction of
Mencha itself. Some of them had to have come from other
towns, because there were more in the long line than could
have ever lived in Mencha.

Secca turned to Wilten, who had also followed her. "Let
them in."

"Yes, Lady Secca."

Secca nodded at Richina. "Stay at my shoulder."

"Yes, lady."

Secca reached out and squeezed Richina's hand. "Thank you."

The sandy-haired young woman flushed, then lowered her eyes.

Secca's eyes went to the two students. "You two may stand just behind Richina."

Both inclined their heads silently.

The four walked back toward the coffin, turning before the catafalque and waiting. A half-score of Loiseau lancers eased up behind and beside her before the first of the mourners stepped into the entry hall.

As the men and women, but mostly women, filed past, Secca smiled politely and nodded—and listened.

"Can't believe . . . like as she's gone."

". . . looks like she's sleeping . . ."

". . . so thin, like a child . . ."

"The redheaded one there, say she was like her own daughter . . . sorceress, too."

". . . hope she's as strong and good . . ."

So did Secca.

". . . never be anyone like her again . . ."

Secca smiled briefly at those words, knowing all too well their understatement. All too many past lords of the Thirty-three and some of those still holding lands hoped fervently that there would never be another like Anna.

"Seems . . . a shame . . . all she did for him, and Lord Robero not even here . . ."

Secca kept her face emotionless. Anna had demanded that she not be paraded like a trophy in the event of her death, but laid to rest in the small mausoleum Anna and Secca had designed and created through sorcery on the hill overlooking the orchards.

A small wizened woman stopped after viewing the coffin. Her bright brown eyes fixed on Secca. "You carry on like her, sorceress, you'll be all right, and so will everything."

"Thank you," Secca murmured, not quite sure what else she could say.

In the end, Secca had to stand before the casket and the catafalque on which it rested . . . and speak.

"A score and a six years past, a tired woman appeared in a house in Mencha. She had been ripped from her own world. She had been separated from her own children. She was a sorceress who knew nothing of Defalk. She may have wept and raged. If she did, no one saw it. Instead, from the first moment, she did what she thought was right. For this, she was attacked. She suffered more wounds than most armsmen. For the first years she lived in Defalk, she was always attacked, if not by arrows and sorcery, then by words. Defalk was poor and starving and suffering from a terrible drought caused by sorcery. She destroyed the invaders and stopped the drought. Time after time, she almost died trying to put things right.

"Along the way, she helped people—a player here, a miller's consort there, an orphaned child. I know. I was one of those orphans. Along the way, she became powerful. But she still helped people. She restored Defalk and gave a stronger land back to Lord Robero.

"She was not perfect. I will not say she was, but I will say that never has Defalk or Liedwahr had a ruler so powerful who was also so good. She came from another world, but she made Loiseau and Mencha and Defalk her home." Secca paused. With each sentence, the words got harder, and her eyes blurred more.

"Because of her, we all have what we have. Because of her, we have seen nearly a score of years of peace and prosperity in a land that scarce knew weeks of peace before her." Secca swallowed again. She had more to say, but there was no way she could express it all.

"My father said it best. The sorceress was a good woman. She asked more of herself than of anyone, and she never stopped trying to do her best. Because she never spared herself, others did more than they thought they could, and Liedwahr is a far better place. . . . May we all remember that. Forever."

Secca just stood before the coffin, the rest of the words

she would have said choked within her, her eyes burning and unable to take in the hundred or so who had crowded into the foyer—or those who filled the courtyard outside, or even the holding's staff and the guards who flanked her. Finally, she just bowed her head, then, after another long moment, turned and walked back toward the staircase.

There, halfway up the steps, she stood, silently. Beside her stood Richina, equally silent. On the step below, one to each side, stood Kerisel and Jeagyn.

As the mourners shuffled out into the bright fall sunlight, the four sorceresses watched. Secca stared almost sightlessly toward the front of the entry hall, her throat thick, her stomach knotted so tightly she could scarcely breathe, her cheeks streaked with tears.

Outside, the high puffy clouds drifted westward—toward Falcor—in the light chill breeze.

14

MANSUUS, MANSUUR

Kestrin, Liedfuhr of Mansuur, paces back and forth in front of the desk in the upper-level private study. On his left arm is a mourning band of black and maroon, standing out against the sky-blue velvet of his tunic sleeve. After a time, he stops and laughs.

"And you used to tease your father for his pacing." Murmuring to himself, he walks to the window behind the desk and stands there, looking out from the hillside palace at the wide river Toksul, smooth and broad, leading westward to the port of Wharsus.

With a deep breath, he walks to the bellpull and tugs it firmly, but not violently. Then he walks back to the broad desk and picks up the scroll. He has barely reread the short report when the study door opens.

"Yes, sire?" The trim lancer overcaptain steps inside,

closes the outer door, and bows. His hair, mostly gray, with a few streaks of raven black, does not stir as he straightens.

"I read your latest report, Bassil." Kestrin smiles, then shakes his head. "How long have you been writing these reports? Two-score years?"

"A score and six, sire."

"Since just before the appearance of the sorceress."

"Just after, actually."

Kestrin pauses. "Does it not seem strange that she and father died within weeks of each other?"

"Given that they were the greatest rulers in Liedwahr," Bassil says slowly, "and given that we have a world ruled by unseen Harmonies, perhaps it was not so strange."

"Was she that great?"

Bassil pauses, almost imperceptibly. "Greater than that, sire."

"Greater than my father?"

"Not in Mansuur, sire."

Kestrin laughs. "Father warned me about you, Bassil. He said you would tell me the truth whether I liked it or not, and that the more questions I asked whose answers I didn't like, the more I'd understand."

Bassil smiles, not quite indulgently.

"How great was she?"

"Great enough that, had she more years and children, all Liedwahr would be united and at peace." Bassil shrugs. "That is but my poor opinion, sire."

"You don't think much of Lord Robero, do you?"

"He is capable enough that he understood to change his name and that he listens to his sorceresses and his consort, and they appear most capable. And there are more sorceresses in Defalk than in all of Liedwahr. They train others, as well."

"So . . . perhaps the long-departed Lord Ehara was right, that the men of Liedwahr will be ruled by women?"

"No, sire. There cannot be enough sorceresses to rule that way, and in all lands there are Ladies of the Shadows who oppose sorcery. Yet even with such opposition, there can be enough sorceresses that it will be dangerous for lords and holders to abuse women."

Kestrin nods. "We cannot change that, one way or the other. What of Lord High Counselor Hanfor?"

"He is a most capable man tasked with governing a land that despises ability in anything but intrigue and plotting. Without your sister, he would have had a much more difficult time."

"Father and I were glad that worked out. He seems to be a good man, and Aerlya is happy."

"Your sister was most fortunate." Bassil waits.

Kestrin lifts the short scroll. "I've read this several times. There is one question that remains unanswered. How did an entire company of lancers vanish? Where did they go?"

The older overcaptain shrugs. "Sire, I do not know. No one knows."

"You're telling me that a company of Mansuuran lancers stationed on port duty at Hafen just vanished? And my wretched seers cannot find them?"

"No, sire."

Kestrin smiles lazily. "What ships ported there?"

"Ah . . . the port records—"

"—are missing," concludes the Liedfuhr. "The lancers are on a ship, because that's the only place where a seer would have trouble finding them. Someone bought them— and their captain—and they want to make trouble. It has to be the Sea-Priests." He fingers his chin. "Where? Can't be Defalk . . . no ports. Could be Nordwei . . . or Neserea or Ebra. Probably not Dumar."

"Nordwei?"

"Just how would I explain to the bitch traders of Wei that I had no control over my own lancers after they raided or sacked some outlying port like Lundholn?"

"Dumar is the weakest land of all those bordering Mansuur," Bassil points out.

"True enough, although without the sorceress-protectors

of Defalk, Ebra would certainly be a ripe plum ready to
fall, but . . ." Kestrin frowns. "With the golds it took, they
could have bribed a company in Cealur, and it would have
taken longer for us to learn, and it would have been far
closer to Dumar. We will see. Too soon, I fear." After a
pause, Kestrin adds, "The sorceress is dead less than two
weeks, my father less than four, and the world is changing."

"Change it will, sire, for they were the two strongest
rulers in Liedwahr."

"Can I be that strong, Bassil?" Kestrin's eyes fix upon
the lancer overcaptain.

"If you work as your father did, sire. If you spend every
moment thinking of Mansuur, and not of yourself."

"And if I listen . . . carefully." Kestrin laughs, ruefully.

Bassil nods.

"See if anyone can discover more about the missing
lancers—before they appear in a dispatch I will not wish
to read."

"I can but try, sire."

"I know." As Bassil steps back, Kestrin turns and looks
out at the river below, and at the gray clouds that herald
winter sweeping in from the northwest. He does not move
as the study door closes behind the overcaptain.

15

As she stepped into the large workroom, Secca glanced
at the harp beside the reflecting pool, noting absently
that the mute bars had not been applied. "You're the one
who didn't apply them." She had been the last to use the
pool, since Richina did not yet use it without Secca's su-
pervision.

While it would have taken a powerful sorcerer or sorceress to overhear her in Anna's workroom—hers, now, Secca realized sadly—it was possible. She turned toward the harp, but before she could fasten the muting bars in place, the bell on the top of the harp rang—twice. Clayre, rather than Jolyn.

Secca picked up the lutar, turned to the reflecting pool, and strummed the receiving song.

"... *let me hear,*
in tones so clear ..."

The clear water silvered over, then the image of a dark-haired woman with hazel-green eyes appeared. "How are you doing?" asked the image, although the words vibrated from the harp strings rather than coming from the image in the pool.

"It's hard," Secca admitted. "I haven't been sleeping that well. There's been more to do than I'd thought, and it's hard to keep my mind on it."

"She was more like your mother."

"She is ... was ... my mother. You know that. I was always an inconvenience to Anientta."

"I understand that."

Secca nodded in acknowledgment. Clayre's mother had died at Clayre's birth, and Clayre had never seen eye to eye with her stepmother. "How is Birke?"

"Doing well. He always sends scrolls." Clayre laughed. "He'll feel guilty to the end of his days, and that will be good for him."

"At least he feels guilty."

"Have you heard anything from Wasle?" asked Clayre.

"Richina hasn't said anything; there haven't been any scrolls from Suhl."

"He never was much for writing." Clayre paused.

Secca waited.

"There's more bad news," Clayre said slowly. "From the west."

"On top of Konsstin's death?"

"This is worse. Konsstin had been ailing for years. Kestrin has been acting as Liedfuhr for the past year, even if most people didn't know it."

"What is it?" Secca couldn't say she was surprised. Anna had been such a force that people were bound to react upon learning of her death, especially combined with the death of the old Liedfuhr of Mansuur.

"Hanfor died. Some sort of bloody flux. Jolyn's convinced it was poison . . . assassins. I'd believe it. Robero *says* it's just an unfortunate occurrence. What he thinks . . . who knows?"

"Who?"

"The most likely suspect is someone named Belmar. No one knows much about him, except that he's a Neserean holder from an old family. He claims descent from the Prophet, and he's got an ancient castle overlooking a place on the Bitter Sea called Worlan. We can't catch him at it, but the Harmonies are disrupted around him, and he has more armsmen than his holding and lands could support for long. All the pools show is a good-looking young man with a charming smile. Until two years ago, no one had ever heard of him. He was making eyes at Annayal, but never enough for Hanfor to reject him outright. But he's sharp enough to have gotten the message."

"And sent one of his own?" asked Secca.

"I'm not sure. There are several others with reasons of their own. Another holder named Svenmar. Besides Belmar, he's the closest relative of the last prophet, a cousin of some sort. And then there's Chyalar, the son of the holder of Itzel."

"But this Belmar is special? I suppose he has black hair." Secca smiled. "And deep blue eyes."

"What else?" Clayre laughed. "But I wouldn't trust him anywhere near my chamber. Nor would Jolyn."

"They didn't wait long." Secca took a long breath. "There's more."

"Oh?" Secca could feel her stomach tightening.

"Lord Robero has a scroll from Lord High Counselor Clehar. He's asking for a consort—one who can protect Dumar. Lady Ryvyn died two seasons ago."

"You?" asked Secca. "Doesn't he know about sorceresses?"

"He has three sons and a daughter. His brothers have sons. He's requested a consortship that will not require . . ." Clayre snorted.

"He's just doing that to get Robero to reduce Dumar's liedgeld. Crying poverty, and claiming that he won't be as well protected now that Anna's gone."

"As if we haven't been . . ."

Secca raised a finger to her lips.

"I know. I still don't think the seers of Wei are that good."

"They probably aren't, but we still don't know that much about the Sea-Priests."

"You think they're involved?"

"They've been quiet for a long time," Secca pointed out. "Anna destroyed their forces everywhere in Liedwahr. But just before . . . you said they had massed fleets in the Ostisles. Do you think . . ."

"Who knows? They kept their secrets well."

"She stopped them . . . but only in Liedwahr. I know you do not like to leave Loiseau . . ." Clayre ventured, her voice humming as translated by the harp.

"You're telling me I should visit our Lord of Defalk."

"He does listen to you." Clayre paused. "He doesn't like it, but he does."

"He's never liked it, not since I told him he was a bully when he was fourteen."

"You did?"

Secca let the question pass. "I'm not comfortable . . . burying Anna, and then just leaving. But . . . too many things could happen if I don't."

"It has to be your decision." Clayre's words were slow and measured.

"I'll leave in the morning."

"Who will you bring?"

"A company of lancers, the players, and Richina."

"Is that wise?"

"She's seventeen and old enough to travel with me, and she needs to see Falcor again."

"And what it is?"

"What it is not," Secca added dryly. "I won't bring the junior fosterlings. Kerisel and Jeagyn are too likely to be awed by Falcor."

"And Richina won't be?"

"That one is wise beyond her years. Perhaps too wise."

"I'll let Robero know you're coming. That way, he won't be as likely to do something rash."

"We'll see." As she let the image in the pool fade, Secca wasn't sure she had Clayre's faith in her own influence over the Lord of Defalk, and much as she had appreciated Robero's concerns about her happiness, the business with Lythner still nagged at her.

Before she stepped over to the desk and the bookcases that surrounded it, with the notebooks Anna had written and dictated to Secca over the years—notes on music, spells, and what Anna had called relevant science—Secca did remember to replace the muting bars on the harp.

16

WORLAN, NESEREA

How much longer?" Belmar glances through the heavily glazed windows of the bluff-top castle toward the gray and cold waters of the small harbor below, then at the figure who sits languidly in the dark wooden armchair next to the side table. "The winds that bring winter strengthen with each day."

"Tomorrow or the next day, I would guess. No longer than the day after," answers the man in nondescript traveler's gray. "No master would delay in these waters longer than necessary." He gestures toward the Bitter Sea.

"Especially not a Sturinnese master, even if he is claiming to be Pelaran," replies the dark-haired holder. "You are sure the deed is done, master jerGlien?"

"The Lord High Counselor is already dead." The man in gray smiles. "And soon Neserea will need a skilled and strong leader to repulse the adventuresome Liedfuhr, who would annex Neserea under the guise of protecting his sister."

"What the father tried . . . would not the son?" Belmar laughed. "The scrolls are ready to dispatch as well—once we act in preserving Neserea." ·

"Are your players ready?" JerGlien's eyebrows lift as he straightens in the chair and takes a small sip from the goblet on the side table.

"They've been ready for a season. Each week, they add another spell. Soon we will have enough for any condition we might encounter in battle in Neserea."

"One must still have armsmen."

"We already have five score fully trained. The sorceress conquered Dumar with less than that."

"She could risk them all, for she could call upon the levies of Jecks and Birfels," counters the gray-clad man.

"And I cannot?" half-queries Belmar.

"No. You cannot. You must be seen as both strong and cautious. No one wishes a firebrand. The memories of the previous prophets are still too rancid."

"Those memories will work to my aid, especially in a Neserea with no real heir, and one where many of the more venerable holders would like the old customs back."

"I cannot say I understand the customs of Liedwahr. The eldest daughter of the Lord High Counselor has no consort, yet the second eldest—what might be her name—she is already consorted to that youngster in Dumar."

"You are right. Annayal has no consort. The problem is that there is no one suitable, or none the Lord High Counselor found suitable. Aerfor was consorted to Eryhal early in the fall, a love match, but that was permitted because no one would accept a younger daughter as Lady High Counselor of Neserea."

"Perhaps you should offer a suit to Annayal," suggests jerGlien. "She is pretty, if not ravishingly attractive, and you are a holder of note."

"I have made my appearances, and that was enough for the time." Belmar smiles. "I cannot act, not until others suggest such is appropriate. In the meantime, we need to proceed as we have planned."

Without replying, jerGlien takes another sip from the goblet.

17

The rear courtyard at Loiseau was still gray in the glass before dawn when Secca strapped her gear in place, making sure that the grand lutar was securely fastened behind the saddle, balanced by the traveling scrying glass. She glanced to the sky, frowning momentarily as she caught the tiny red disk of light that was Darksong, the moon of misused sorcery and evil. Then, pushing any thought of omens out of her mind, she took the reins of the gray mare from the head ostler. Unlike Anna, she did not ride one of the enormous raider beasts—and had no desire to do so. Her words to the ostler caught in her throat as she realized that she would never see Anna on a raider beast again. She swallowed, and said, "Thank you, Vyren."

"My pleasure, Lady Secca."

Secca checked her gear a last time before she swung up

into the saddle. Behind her, Richina had already mounted a larger chestnut gelding.

Palian, chief player of Anna's—now Secca's—players, eased her dapple toward the sorceress. "The first players are ready, Lady Secca." The gray eyes almost matched the swatches of gray hair amid the black.

"Thank you. Have you seen Delvor?"

"He and the second players are over by the side entrance to the stables," replied the graying chief player. Palian— who had taught Secca all her instruments—offered a wry smile.

"He's thought up another harmonic variation?" Secca repressed a sigh.

"A new fingering scheme, I believe."

Secca nodded, ignoring the barely concealed snort from Richina, and eased the gray mare toward the back of the courtyard. After passing the lancers, she slowed as she came by the special archers. "Is everyone ready, Elfens?"

"Yes, lady. Perhaps we can bring down some of those big pheasants in the flats."

"Only while in our lands," Secca reminded the chief archer. "Lady Herene's pheasants are for her archers."

Elfens grinned. "But, of course."

"You're a rogue, chief archer."

"One loyal to Loiseau and to you, lady."

Secca shook her head with a quick smile and eased toward the stable where Delvor stood on the paving stones beside his mount, a lutar in his hand. "If you finger like so—"

"Chief Player Delvor!" Secca called cheerily.

The lank-haired Delvor glanced up from where the lutarists had gathered around him. "Lady! We are ready. I was just showing the lutarists—"

Secca barely held in a grin. "I appreciate your diligence. Perhaps you can show them later. We do have a long ride before us."

"Ah . . . yes, lady." He bowed.

Secca turned her mount back in the direction of the front

courtyard, and the gates where the lancers of the purple company of Mencha were already mounted in formation.

The painfully thin captain with an equally thin black mustache eased his mount around to wait for the redheaded sorceress. When she reined up, he inclined his head. "The purple company is ready, lady,"

"How is Filcar, Quebar?"

"Well enough to ride, and use a blade." Quebar smiled. "He will not be so careless in drills again, lady."

"I would hope not."

"Vyren, he said it best. Some horses have to step into deep water before they would swim."

"And what is he saying that you said?" Secca laughed. Vyren and Quebar were cousins, and each was always attributing some odd saying to the other.

Quebar offered an overelaborate shrug. "Perhaps that the only danger a dull blade bears is to its wielder."

Or a dull mind. Secca hoped hers remained sharp, both on the journey and once she arrived in Falcor.

18

WORLAN, NESEREA

In the dull gray morning, a light wind whispers from the northwest, across the cold waters of Bitter Sea. The wind is strong enough to have carried the merchant vessel bearing no ensign to the long pier, but not powerful enough to hamper a speedy docking. The customs' enumerator waddles up the gangway, then vanishes into the master's cabin.

From the flat roof of the baker's, across the square from the warehouse, Belmar watches. Behind him, the four players wait, occasionally blowing on their fingers. The two violino players check the tuning on their instruments, while the woodwind player moistens his reed.

Shortly, maroon-clad troops march down the gangway and south to make their way shoreward along the pier.

"It won't be long now," cautions Belmar. "Stand ready."

The players take up their instruments. Belmar watches the far side of the square, and the narrow street beyond where the maroon-clad troops march quickly toward the warehouse.

Although the lancers have drawn their blades, they move toward the warehouse door quickly, as though they expect little opposition.

One of the pair of guards by the iron-gated door sees the oncoming lancers, turns, and sprints down the narrow street away from the oncoming company. The second just stares.

Belmar gestures toward the four players. "Now!"

With the notes of the players comes Belmar's bass voice.

"Turn each blade to cut its bearer..."

The Mansuuran captain barely has time to yell, "Treachery!" before his own sabre slashes through his neck.

"But, of course," murmurs the dark-haired sorcerer after he completes the spell.

Other blades perform improbable actions upon those who bore them, so swiftly that but few curses or cries echo across the square. The body of the single remaining warehouse guard also lies before the iron gate, his neck slashed by his own blade as well.

Belmar looks at the figures sprawled on the cobblestones before the warehouse doors, then at the gray-clad figure who has appeared from the shadows of the staircase from the side street below. "That should do. Now we should inform his Mightiness Lord High Counselor Hanfor. We know nothing of events in Neserea, of course. We are but loyal subjects, protecting our coast from Mansuuran depredations."

"Of course," echoes jerGlien quietly.

Belmar turns to the players, and the half-score guards behind them. "You may go back to the hold."

The head player nods. The players slip instruments into cases covered with oiled leather, then file down the narrow steps, followed by all but a pair of the guards in dark green tunics.

Once the roof is clear, except for Belmar's personal guards, the sorcerer steps to the edge of the roof and turns to jerGlien. "And the golds?"

"The ship's master keeps half, remember?"

"I remember, and you retain a third of the other half." JerGlien smiles modestly.

"It's not a bad investment. Sturinn gets back two-thirds of the cost of bribing the Mansuurans; we kill an entire company, which reduces the forces facing the Maitre, and everyone thinks that either Kestrin is bent on conquest or can't control his own land." Belmar smiles.

JerGlien provides a noncommittal shrug.

"I am sure that is the idea, or something close to it, if not more ingenious." Belmar's voice carries more than a trace of amusement. "However, you did promise."

"I did, and we do keep our promises. You will recall the small matter of scrolls."

"Ah . . . yes. Tomorrow, they will be dispatched. For the moment, I need to inspect the damage below. I look forward to seeing you then."

"Until tomorrow." The man in gray bows, then slips silently to the steps.

With a nod to his guards, Belmar follows the other down to the street, where they proceed in different directions.

19

The wind whistled out of the northeast, chilling Secca as she rode westward out of Sorprat toward Pamr, and toward the holding of Lady Herene that lay north of the town center of Pamr. Absently, as she refastened the top buttons of her riding jacket, the sorceress wondered if young Kysar would be there, or if he were in Fussen with his father, Falar, since Falar was about to turn the holding over formally to his ward and nephew Uslyn on the young lord's twentieth birthday.

The death of Uslyn's older brother, Vlastal, had resulted from another need for sorcery set in the shadows, but not nearly so visible as the incident of the broken bridge at Aroch. Thankfully, Lord Ustal had been so unpopular that no one had looked closely into the snapped crossbow catch, and the frayed cable that had shredded his throat— or the consumption that had claimed Vlastal and had run its course well before Ustal's death. Still, luck had aided Jolyn, luck and the fact that no one in Fussen had ever seen the sorceress.

Secca straightened in the saddle. The gray's hoofs clopped on the smooth stones of the road, the sound sharp despite the low moaning of the wind that seemed to foreshadow a long and cold winter. The cold haze above the horizon was thick enough to have swallowed the disk of the bright moon Clearsong, although it would be setting shortly in any case.

Beside Secca rode Richina, silent for the moment, wrapped in a blue leather jacket similar to Secca's green jacket. Before them rode Quebar and Savyn, one of the squad leaders of the purple company. At the head of the column was a single lancer bearing the blue banner with the two gold musical notes upon it that signified that Secca was a sorceress of Defalk—the banner that had been Anna's. Palian and Delvor followed Secca and Richina.

Secca's eyes dropped from the haze above the horizon to the broad road that stretched—straight as a quarrel—from Sorprat to Pamr. The stones were even and level, and showed no sign of wear, and the road itself was a constant eight yards wide—enough for the largest wagons to pass side by side. A faint smile crossed Secca's lips. The lowland section had been one of the last paved between Mencha and Falcor, and it had been the first major sorcery Anna had let Secca do. More than fifteen years later, her work looked almost new. Then, so did the roads done by Anna, Clayre, and Jolyn. They still hadn't finished the network laid out by Anna, but there were completed metaled roads running from Falcor to the borders of Defalk in all the cardinal directions, as well as a few others.

Before long, Secca would be working with Richina on road- and bridge-building, perhaps initially on the last section of the road between Mencha and the River Chean bridge. With only six deks or so to complete, perhaps she and Richina could finish it before summer. The northern section, from the north side of the River Chean to the Fal River and Elhi, had been one of the first roads paved through sorcery.

"Lady, how much longer?" asked Richina quietly.

"Two glasses, if we're not stopped in the town." She smiled. "Kysar may be in Fussen, you know, for the celebration?"

"He's not for me, even if mother has a soft spot for Lady Herene," Richina replied.

"She was your mother's first warder and tutor."

"They've remained friends, and I like Kysar well enough, but he's too charming."

Like his father, Secca thought, nodding, reflecting that Anna had been smart to keep Falar from ever controlling a holding directly.

"Irenia is the one I'd rather see. She's like Lady Herene," Richina added.

"I thought she was in Falcor."

"She left. Her last scroll said Counselor Dythya told her she was ready to work as an assistant saalmeister. She's hoping Lord Tiersen or Lord Kinor will let her train in their holds."

"Something's headed our way, lady," offered Quebar.

Secca squinted, trying to make out the object on the road ahead, an object that resolved itself into a large long-haul trader's wagon, one moving quickly eastward. Drawn by six rough-coated dray horses, the heavy trader's wagon rolled toward Secca's vanguard. Then, as though the driver saw the golden notes upon the blue banner, the wagon slowed immediately, and the driver edged it to the left.

"Sorceress." The bearded driver bowed his head. "Our respects." Beside him, the armed guard also inclined his head.

"Thank you," Secca responded cheerfully. "A good journey to you."

"Thank you."

Even the pair of guards on the rear seat nodded as they passed, and Secca returned the gesture.

The legend painted on the side of the long wagon was simple, gold letters set within a green rectangular frame: "Teryn & Son, Factors in Spirits, Falcor."

Secca nodded, as behind her the wagon again picked up speed, its iron-bound wheels rumbling on the hard stone, on its way toward Mencha, the Sand Pass, and then into Ebra. While the road was stone-paved only for roughly thirty deks into Ebra, the route farther eastward was well-traveled enough that it had been packed into a hard surface—except in the early spring or after heavy rains.

The sorceress shifted her weight in the saddle again, a saddle that was getting harder with each dek she rode.

....

20

In the late afternoon, under a still-cloudless sky, Secca reined up the gray mare in the liedburg courtyard in Falcor. She was scarcely surprised that Lord Robero had not come down to greet her and her party upon her arrival. The silver-haired Dythya, who had been Counselor of Finance ever since Secca could remember, stood on the mounting block by the main west entrance.

"Greetings, Lady Secca." Dythya's smile was as friendly as ever.

"It's good to see you again." The courtyard was warmer than the open road or the streets of Falcor had been, and Secca unfastened the green leather riding jacket.

"Lord Robero is engaged, but he will be free shortly and would hope you would stop by the audience chamber." Dythya smiled again, professionally, rather than personally.

Understanding, Secca grinned. "I will indeed."

"I will convey that." Dythya's smile broadened.

Secca urged the mare toward the stables. Just ahead, the dark-haired Clayre stood by the second west entrance to the main section of the liedburg, smiling and raising an arm to greet Secca as the younger sorceress rode toward the stables.

By the time Secca had unloaded her gear, then waited for Richina to do the same, Clayre had crossed the damp paving stones to meet them. "You still look the same."

"So do you," Secca replied to the taller sorceress.

"You look older," Clayre added, with a grin to Richina.

The apprentice bowed slightly, clearly unsure of how to respond to Clayre's pleasantry.

"The older fosterling boys, especially those from the

north, will drool, but don't mind them," Clayre added. "They're still not used to . . . Falcor."

Richina nodded, trying to keep from frowning, as the three walked from the stables to the side door and then up the stairs to the second floor corridor that held the major chambers of the liedburg. Behind them followed Quebar and two lancers.

Clayre led the way to the chamber that had been Anna's, in the middle of the eastern side of the liedburg, where she opened the door. "Lord Robero suggested that it be for the Sorceress of Loiseau." Her voice carried a tone of both concern and apology.

"He wasted little time, did he not?"

The dark-haired older sorceress offered a nervous smile.

As Quebar cleared his throat, Secca turned to the lancer captain.

Quebar nodded at the pair of lancers. "Dyvan and Easlon will be your guards."

"I'm sorry. You have other things to do." Secca inclined her head to Quebar. "I'll be fine. Thank you."

Quebar bowed, before turning and heading toward the stairs.

"We need to talk. I will be back in a moment." Clayre nodded to Richina. "Your quarters are in the south tower, with the other fosterlings."

Secca watched for a moment as Clayre led the sandy-haired apprentice down the corridor, then looked at the older and shorter lancer. "Dyvan, I'll be unpacking until Lady Clayre returns."

"Yes, lady."

Secca smiled, then turned and closed the door. She carried the saddlebags to the footchest, where she deposited them, before setting the lutar case on the bed, then unfastening the sabre scabbard and laying blade and sheath on the footchest as well.

The chamber looked little different from what it had before harvest—or a score of years before—with the high bed, the small desk, the narrow window, and the attached bath chamber.

Clayre had her permanent quarters farther north along the corridor, in the larger chambers that had once belonged to Lady Essan, who had died almost a score of years before. Robero, of course, had combined the three southeast corner chambers into a suite for himself and Alyssa.

Secca had hung her riding jacket in the small armoire, washed up, after heating the cold water in the basin with the elemental spell, and was brushing her hair when there was a knock on the heavy door.

"Come in."

Clayre stepped inside. "I am sorry. About the chamber. But the liedburg grows ever more crowded."

"You aren't the one who made the choice." Secca shrugged. "I know I can't grieve forever, but . . ." She paused. "If I don't take the chamber, I'll be seen as petty and foolish."

"He was going to give it to Jolyn. We both protested."

"Thank you."

There was another silence. "We do need to talk." Clayre inclined her head toward the chamber beyond the door and across the hall—the one that held the reflecting pool created by Anna's sorcery.

"It's still shielded?" asked Secca.

"Yes. Whatever she did affected the stones themselves." Clayre opened the heavy oak door and motioned.

Marveling and wondering how much of what Anna had done would last well beyond her death, Secca followed Clayre out and across the corridor. Dyvan followed Secca, while Easlon remained at the door to Secca's chamber. Clayre opened the door to the scrying chamber, and both sorceresses stepped inside. Behind them Dyvan gulped even before Clayre shut the oak door. Secca smiled. Lancers were not used to sorceresses vanishing from view in plain sight.

"I added a spell to keep words from leaving the chamber."

"Ears everywhere?" asked Secca.

"More than I'd like. Anna hated it. I think that was one reason she left Falcor."

"One of many." Secca's voice was dry. "What's wrong?"

"You know me too well." Clayre laughed, mirthlessly. "Not only is Hanfor dead, but there's been an attack by Mansuuran armsmen on a coastal town in Neserea. The local lord killed all the attackers, but he's sent bodies and tunics and a few other proofs from Worlan to Esaria."

"And scrolls here?" asked Secca.

"I assume they're on the way."

"This is your friend Belmar?"

"Not my friend," Clayre protested. "He never was. Good-looking through a glass, but never more than that, especially not now."

"It seems rather convenient."

"All too convenient, but Lord Robero won't be willing to say that it's suspicious. There's no proof. If he says too much, then he's viewed as wanting to take over Neserea, and Hanfor's suspicious death is laid at his feet—or ours."

"Then, you haven't told Robero? Or Jolyn?"

Clayre shook her head. "I just found out last night, and I wanted to talk to you to see if you knew anything. Jolyn's at Elheld. Robero has her rebuilding the stables. There's no harp there."

"What did she tell him this time?" asked Secca with a laugh. "That the stables were collapsing?"

"Something like that. Except there was the hint that he'd be compared unfavorably to his grandsire."

"She'll do anything to get out of Falcor."

"Almost anything," Clayre amended. "Except she won't take a consort. She claims that she feels more like an aunt or a mother to anyone her age."

"With as many lovers as she's had—all of them a decade older—she should know."

"Jealous?" asked Clayre.

"No," replied the younger sorceress simply. Somehow

. . . in some fashion, Secca had always thought there would be someone, but there never had been. Robero had been far too self-centered, wanting someone to adore him, or at least pretend that, while Secca herself had been looking for someone like her father—or Lord Jecks. And after seeing the closeness between Anna and Jecks, Secca had never wanted to settle for a consorting of convenience, especially not if it meant losing her powers—or some of them—to have children to provide an heir . . . for what?

"She's also going to work on the road from Elheld north to Wendel?"

"I did suggest that," Clayre said with a laugh. "The way things are going, we may need more than one way northward . . . or in any direction."

"There's no new trouble in Ebra," Secca said.

"No, but Hadrenn's always been a rotten timber."

"Not rotten, just weak," Secca corrected.

"They both give way under weight."

"With Anna . . . gone . . . you think Mynntar will try something?"

"You've followed him more than we have," Clayre said. "What do you think?"

"Mynntar won't do anything directly against Defalk, but he could attack Hadrenn. Even so, he won't act unless he can finish whatever it is before we could deal with him."

"But with trouble in Neserea . . . ?"

"He'll bear watching," Secca admitted. "We'd best tell Robero about the Mansuuran attack on Neserea. Tell him we just found out now, and that it could be a ploy by anyone, not necessarily by Kestrin."

"Kestrin couldn't be that stupid."

"No. But what if someone wanted to show he didn't control his land?" asked Secca. "That he is weak or ineffectual? Then what?"

Clayre winced. "I don't like that at all."

Neither did Secca. "We might as well tell Robero now. I should present myself to his lordship."

"You still don't care for him, do you?"

"Robero has always been too impressed with Robero, and I worry that without Anna . . ." Secca let the words trail off.

"That we'll have to go through the same trials she did?"

"Haven't you thought about it? She was a mighty sorceress from the Mist Worlds. How could we know or have the powers she did?"

"They'll learn," Clayre prophesied.

"We'd best go."

Clayre nodded, and the two stepped from the reflecting pool chamber.

Dyvan's eyes widened as they appeared from what seemed to be an empty chamber, but he did not swallow or gulp as he turned to follow Secca down the steps to the main level and the audience chamber.

Two guards and a page Secca didn't recognize waited outside the closed doors.

"Lady Secca and Lady Clayre to see Lord Robero," Secca said quietly.

The two guards inclined their heads slightly, and the shorter one turned and edged the door open. "The lady sorceresses, Lord Robero."

After a moment, in which Robero must have gestured, for Secca heard nothing, the guard opened the door. Dyvan remained in the corridor with the other two guards. The blocky man in the gilded chair did not rise as Secca and Clayre entered the audience chamber.

Secca bowed, if just enough to convey respect for the position Robero held.

Behind and to the left of Lord Robero's chair was a smaller chair, occupied by a petite blonde woman, even more slender and shorter than Secca. Before her consort could speak, Alyssa rose and stepped forward with a warm smile. "Secca . . . it's so good to see you." She glanced at Clayre. "And you, too, if but since yesterday."

Rising belatedly, Robero offered the all-too-familiar boyish grin, then brushed back wisps of his thinning mahogany hair. "It is good to see you again." He added quickly. "Both of you."

"It is always good to see you and Alyssa, even when the occasion is sad." Secca was grateful to Alyssa, who served Robero as much as loved him, and who, somehow, quietly, managed to keep him from taking himself as seriously as he would have liked to do.

"How . . . ?" asked Alyssa. "She seemed strong last summer."

"She was working on something. She hadn't even tried to cast a spell. I found her collapsed by the reflecting pool. Usually, when that happened, she would rest and recover. This time . . . she didn't."

"We will miss her." Robero, surprisingly, sounded as though he would, as he reseated himself, leaving Secca and Clayre—and Alyssa—standing.

Secca had to believe that the Lord of Defalk had actually considered all of what Anna had meant to him and Defalk.

"Do you think . . . Hanfor's death . . . ? He was a good and a strong man," Robero said slowly.

"It could be," Secca said smoothly. "Clayre and I have just discovered that lancers clad in the uniforms of Mansuuran lancers attacked a town in Neserea."

"What town? Were they truly Mansuuran lancers?" Robero leaned forward in the gilded chair.

"Worlan," replied Clayre. "Apparently, the local lord slaughtered them all."

Robero shook his head. "That was most convenient for someone. Who was the local lord?"

"A young holder named Belmar. He had sought the hand of Annayal."

"He would prove he is worthy. Most convenient." The balding lord snorted.

"A costly way to prove such worth," offered Alyssa quietly.

Secca held in a faint smile as Robero turned in his chair and raised his eyebrows.

"As you yourself said last week, dearest," Alyssa continued almost apologetically, "the cost of maintaining a single company of lancers is dear. This Belmar must have had even more force at his command to destroy an entire company of Mansuuran armsmen. To maintain such, especially in an out-of-the-way holding, that could not be without cost, could it?"

"Sorcery, more likely." Robero looked to Clayre. "Could he have used spellsongs?"

"He has players, lord. Whether they are good and whether he can use them so . . . we have not seen."

"Why not?" Robero waved away his own question. "I know. Unless you spend all your time following but a single lord or holder, one cannot be certain. But is it likely?"

"More likely than his being able to maintain enough armsmen to destroy an entire company to the last man," conceded Clayre.

Secca thought either was highly unlikely of itself, but merely nodded agreement.

"We will have to think upon this. We will talk more tomorrow of it . . . when you are rested, Secca. And perhaps when you will have been able to learn more, Clayre." Robero smiled and nodded. "I thank you for your diligence in keeping us well-informed."

"We look forward to seeing you at supper," added Alyssa. "You can tell us more about how things are in Mencha and elsewhere in the east."

Secca bowed, not deeply.

"Until then, ladies." Robero continued to smile as the two left the audience chamber.

21

ENCORA, RANUAK

The golden light of late fall angling through the win-dowpanes is warm-colored but weak. At the desk sits a woman in a pale blue tunic and trousers. She studies the topmost scroll of the pile before her.

Thrap. At the knock on the door, she rises from behind the desk, setting the scroll down. "Come in."

A second woman enters the study. She has shimmering, short-cut, white hair and is stocky, but not heavy. Her sea-blue tunic and trousers are simple, yet of silk, and the sole piece of jewelry on her person is a collar pin that has been passed from generation to generation. The fine gold wires of the pin represent two sheaves of grain, crossed. Her lined face offers a pleasant smile as she bows. "Matriarch, you requested my presence. I trust you do not mind that I waited until the Exchange closed. I await your wisdom."

Alya laughs, gently. "You have far more experience than I, Dyleroy. That is why I have summoned you."

"Like your mother, Matriarch, you are modest."

"I trust I understand my limitations as well as she did." The comparatively young matriarch, whose blonde hair is but partly silver, smiles self-deprecatingly and gestures to the chairs opposite the simple desk. "You as Mistress of the Exchange know trade far better than I, and you hear what others fear to let me know."

"Can you blame them?" asks the Exchange Mistress with an amused smile as she seats herself.

"I do . . . privately, but even if I did so publicly, would it change matters?" Alya sits and eases the scrolls to one side of the desk.

"Not if you would remain strong," concedes Dyleroy.

"What did you wish to discuss? Certainly not your cousin Alcaren."

Alya lips curl into a wry expression. "Need I? Your daughter handled him well enough."

"For now. But you cannot keep him from sorcery . . . can you?"

"I have trained him, because the alternative is worse. After all, my father was a sorcerer, though few knew it."

"Your father was a modest and most remarkable man. All Ranuak is poorer for his absence. Alcaren needs must go far even to behold his memory. If I might ask, what will you do?"

"If I can, find him a proper consort, who will check his impulsiveness because he would protect her."

"And how will you manage that?"

"It does not seem possible, does it?" The Matriarch laughs. "As my mother once said, we must trust the Harmonies. Trust and watch." She pauses. "That was not why I requested your presence."

"I had thought not." Dyleroy smiles.

"We have lost another ship. The pattern is the same."

"Near a hazard, such as the Shoals of Discord? In darkness?" asks the Exchange Mistress. "Often on the routes to the Free State of Elahwa?"

"That makes near-on a half-score. Those are the ones I know of." Alya raises her eyebrows. "I would suspect that other traders would not disclose such losses."

"Your suspicions are well-founded."

"With the recent death of the sorceress, this bears the hidden hand of the new Maitre of Sturinn."

"The well-hidden hand."

"The young Liedfuhr has followed his sire's policy of keeping Mansuur strong and well-armed. The Council of Wei has built a fleet as well-equipped as that of Sturinn . . . and we are the weakest of those who must rely in part on trade and the bounty of the sea. Yet I cannot command that fleets be built," points out the Matriarch.

"Nor can I, Matriarch."

"It would seem there is little I can do," offers Alya, "save suggest that our traders sail in pairs when out of sight of land." Her lips twist. "Most will be loath to do such."

"You can but suggest, as will I."

"Young Mynntar has supposedly invested in vessels. He has near-on a half-score—they resemble those of the Sturinnese. Hadrenn has none."

"You doubt the possibility of coincidence?" Dyleroy laughs softly. "Or that they are truly his?"

"Let us say that those of Dolov—and its lords—have never been known for their love of the sea, but well-known for their opportunism."

"You believe that those vessels are captained and crewed by those of the Sea-Priests?"

"I would be most surprised were it otherwise," the Matriarch replies.

"Has your sister relayed any of this to you?" The Exchange Mistress bows her head. "It is not my business . . ."

"Veria has. That fuels my concerns."

"And mine also." Dyleroy moistens her lips, ever so slightly.

"There is yet another matter," Alya says slowly. "The Ladies of the Shadows."

"I have heard nothing." Dyleroy frowns.

"You know their goal?"

"Do not most? To prevent the use of sorcery by any means anywhere in Liedwahr." Dyleroy chuckles. "Given the horrors of the Spell-Fire Wars, a most worthy goal, if somewhat impractical in these times."

"They are especially adamant that no man should know sorcery."

"Have they threatened Alcaren?" asks Dyleroy.

"Not directly, but I have received a note expressing their concerns." Alya shakes her head. "I fear that we will have little choice in the years ahead." She smiles faintly. "You can do little with the Ladies of the Shadows save listen, but I would be pleased if you would do that."

"I will do what I can, as I can."

"Thank you. I would ask no more." Alya rises, gracefully.

"Not at present, at least, Matriarch." Dyleroy inclines her head as she stands. "I hope you do not have to request more."

"That would be best." Alya nods, and steps toward the study door. "I did want to share my concerns with the Exchange. I would not wish that the honored traders feel I was less than concerned about their losses." She pauses, her hand on the door lever. "Especially when a time of change lies before us all."

"The Exchange recognizes your concerns, Matriarch, and we will do what we can."

The two women exchange knowing smiles before they part.

22

Clayre looked across the corner of the table in the small dining hall. On her platter were only a few crumbs of the crusty bread. She took her second apple from the basket and began to slice it. Richina broke off another chunk of bread, then carefully cut a wedge of cheese. Secca sipped the heavy ale that neither Richina nor Clayre liked.

"Do you know any more . . . now?" asked Clayre.

"About what?" replied the petite sorceress. "Why would I know more now?"

"I never quite understood all that Anna did out there," Clayre mused. "Or all that you're doing. Even through the pool images, I can sense you're often exhausted, on the edge of dissonance."

"I'm just trying to carry on her work. That's all." Secca

took another chunk of bread, although she would have to force herself to eat it.

"I won't press. Still . . ."

After another mouthful and a swallow of ale, Secca answered. "You know about the boiling of water, and how, if the peasants and tradespeople do so, then there is less flux. And how cleaning wounds and the tears of childbirth with distilled winterwine and boiled water . . ."

"Of course."

"Where does one get the iron to make the kettles in Mencha?" asked Secca. "For there must be separate kettles in which to boil the water. How does one make sure that the water that goes into those kettles is clean enough that the boiling works? How does one make sure that the rainwater does not wash animal offings into the rivers and streams—or the wells?"

The slightest frown crossed Richina's brow, but the apprentice said nothing, for which Secca was most grateful.

"You do not use sorcery to make kettles. Please don't tell me that you do," said Clayre dryly.

"I use sorcery to take the iron from the Ostfels and copper and tin from the Silberfels. You know that. Would you care to try it often?" asked Secca.

"How often?"

"Enough," replied Secca.

"At least every three weeks," suggested Richina.

Clayre nodded. "I am just as glad our Lord of Defalk does not know that."

"You do not wish to become a source of metals?"

"Keeping the roads and rivers and bridges, and extending them, is not only tiring enough, but tiresome as well," Clayre countered. "Besides, there aren't any metals close to Falcor."

"And unlike Jolyn, you don't mind being in the center of things," Secca pointed out.

"After spending almost half my life in Abenfel? An ancient ruin in the middle of nowhere?"

Richina's eyes had been flicking back and forth between the two older sorceresses.

"Don't mind us, Richina," said Secca. "We always argue about this. Clayre wants me to believe her childhood was more lonely than mine."

"Not more lonely. Less valued."

"Perhaps. Anna rescued me when I was eight; you were near twice that." Secca took another mouthful of bread, then a last swallow of the ale—it was easier to get down than bread and helped keep her from wasting away under the demands of the sorcery, demands that were bound to increase.

"We should go," Clayre said, rising. "Our good Lord Robero's message did say before the beginning of his afternoon audiences." She glanced at Richina.

"She should get used to Falcor and Lord Robero," Secca replied as she stood, noting absently the faint sardonic tone in Clayre's use of the phrase "our good Lord Robero."

"You're right about that. Anandra still has trouble, and she's lived here all her life."

"There are other reasons for that."

"True." Clayre strode briskly out of the hall, not waiting to see if Secca and Richina followed.

The three walked northward along the lower main corridor until they came to the main audience hall, once the large dining hall, but which Robero had had rebuilt after Anna had turned Defalk over to him.

Already, outside the audience chamber doors waited a handful of tradesmen, including a fuller, a boatman, a miller, from the flour and dust ground into a tunic so deeply that neither fullering nor brushing was likely to remove either.

The five men all bowed. "Sorceresses . . ."

Secca returned the bows immediately, followed by Richina and Clayre.

"Lord Robero is expecting you," said Dythya, emerging from the audience chamber.

As the three stepped into the chamber, before the doors

shut, Secca could hear a few words behind them.

". . . when the shadow sorceresses come from Mencha . . ."

". . . always trouble . . ."

". . . best you go first, Benan . . ."

". . . be a while, I'd wager . . ."

"My sorceresses—and a new one, too," boomed out Robero's voice. The Lord of Defalk wore a purple satin jacket over a pale gold tunic. The purple of his trousers did not quite match that of the jacket. Unlike the day previous, Alyssa was not present, and he was alone on the dais. From the large gilt chair, he glanced at the young sandy-haired apprentice. "You must be Richina. You're Lady Dinfan's second, aren't you?"

Richina bowed again before replying. "Yes, ser."

"Good woman, your mother. Strong lady, too. How do you like sorcery?"

"I have learned much, ser."

"Good. Defalk needs its sorceresses." Robero turned his eyes on the two older sorceresses, first Clayre, then Secca, momentarily, before speaking again, his eyes not seemingly looking at any of the three. "Yesterday, we discussed the happenings in Neserea. I have been considering the matter." Robero looked sharply at Clayre. "Have you discovered anything else since yesterday?"

"No, lord."

"And you, Lady Secca?"

"Nothing that sheds any new light on matters."

"I would think not. Whoever plotted this will wait, knowing you all will be using your reflecting pools." Nodding to himself, he continued, "I think that Lady Clayre should pay a visit to offer our condolences and support to Lady Aerlya and her daughter the heiress of Neserea."

"You wish that I travel to Esaria?" asked Clayre.

"Someone must represent me, and you are the Sorceress of Defalk, as well as the sister of a noted member of the Thirty-three."

Secca repressed a smile. Robero avoided using Birke's name whenever possible.

"What of Anandra?" questioned Clayre.

"I would suggest that she remain here in Falcor. While road-building is ever more necessary, Jolyn perhaps should return to Falcor so that a full sorceress remains in residence in the liedburg," concluded Robero. "Your Anandra can assist Jolyn, can she not?"

"Anandra is a most capable young sorceress. I will also send Jolyn a message," said Clayre. "She might have to wait a day or so, since it would be foolish, if she is already working on a part of the road, not to finish that section."

"As you see fit." Robero turned to Secca, not quite meeting the redhead's eyes. "I think that you, Lady Secca, might be well advised to act as my representative to Lord High Counselor Hadrenn."

"If you think that necessary, I would be most pleased to do so," Secca agreed politely.

"Good." Robero smiled. "Lady Clayre . . . Richina . . . if you would excuse us, I need a word with Lady Secca."

"Of course." Clayre bowed.

Richina bowed almost as quickly, and the two turned.

Robero waited until the heavy doors closed again. "Have you thought more about Lythner?"

"He was most charming, and, no, I have not, not that much. With Lady Anna's death . . . and all these matters . . ." Secca shook her head.

"I would that you give the matter some thought."

"In a short time, I will. Anna was more my mother than Anientta was. If you hear from Lythner, you may point that out."

"With your permission, I will." Robero smiled, half-wryly. "There is one other matter to consider." The balding lord fingered his chin before going on. "Now that you hold Mencha, Secca, have you thought about an heir for Floss-bend?" asked Robero.

Secca blocked the question she wanted to offer in return—asking if Robero had thought about naming another

heir for his holding at Synfal—the hold Anna had taken
by sorcery and bestowed upon him. Instead, she frowned.
"I cannot say I have given it much thought, not so closely
upon Anna's death. After all, none of us had expected her
to die . . . and not so suddenly."

"There is that," mused the Lord of Defalk. He smiled
the false smile Secca had grown up learning to see through.
"Perhaps you should."

"I will give it that thought . . . although . . . I've also
been thinking that, unlike Anna, I may not wish to practice
sorcery until it spells my end. In that case, Mencha might
better go to Clayre or Jolyn . . . or perhaps young Anandra
in a half-score of years or so."

The smile remained upon Robero's face as he nodded.
"I can see that might be for the best, but, in time, you
would still need heirs for both holdings. There is no great
hurry, for you are young as sorceresses go. Yet I would
not wish to decide where your lands would go . . . against
your wishes."

"You are most thoughtful, Robero. As always." Secca
smiled pleasantly. "I will consider the matter as I return to
Mencha." She paused. "You have not said what you wish
me to convey to Hadrenn."

"I leave the words to you. The message must be that
times may become difficult, but that he must support Defalk."

"And not someone like Mynntar?"

"Exactly."

"I will convey your message." Secca bowed her head,
very slightly.

"There is one last matter." Robero cleared his throat.

Secca waited.

"Liedgeld. If matters continue as they have, and usurp-
ers raise forces in Ebra or Neserea, we may need to raise
more armsmen and lancers, and that will require raising
the liedgeld." Robero smiled apologetically.

Secca nodded. She understood the troubles that would
cause. She also understood the message behind the infor-

mation. If the sorceresses of Defalk did not support Robero in one way, they would certainly have to support him more directly against those traditional lords still holding lands in Defalk.

"We will have some appropriate gifts for you to convey to Hadrenn. By tomorrow, or the next day, so that you could leave on the day following." Robero stood. "I know it is a troubling time for you, for Anna was close to you, but we cannot squander what she gave us by failing to act."

Secca understood that, she suspected, far better than Robero, as she bowed before departing the audience chamber.

23

As the two sorceresses stood beside the reflecting pool in the liedburg of Falcor, Clayre's voice filled the chamber.

"Show us now, and as you can,
the acts of Belmar, lord and man . . ."

The waters of the pool rippled, then silvered before presenting an image. The dark-haired young lord stood in a chamber, apparently an audience hall that had been emptied, with six players behind him. Secca squinted to make out the room. Then her eyes focused on the pair of players to the left side of the group.

"That's a dancing hall . . . or it was," Clayre said. "Just like the one that once was in Abenfel."

"Two of those players are using small thunder-drums," Secca said. "I can't tell how, but that would allow him to mix Clearsong and Darksong."

After a moment, Clayre released the image and turned to the younger sorceress. "It's a good thing I'm taking the players from Falcor."

"You keep checking on him. You don't want him sneaking up on you. You know what trouble Anna had with drums and Darksong. And he comes from a heritage where drums and dancing run in the blood. That is not good."

"I will be *very* careful. He is a sorcerer."

"He's probably very sneaky because he's not that strong. If he were strong enough to wrest gold or silver from the earth, we would probably know it from disruptions in the Harmonies."

Clayre raised her eyebrows.

Without answering, Secca thought for several moments, then lifted her own lutar.

"Show us now, whether near or far,
who pays and stands behind this Belmar . . ."

The water shivered, then silvered over, then presented two separate circular images that barely touched. The first was a thin figure in gray who stood at the railing of a ship. The second showed a man with a blonde beard seated at a writing table in a lamp-lit and paneled library of some sort.

"He could be any holder anywhere that we don't know," offered Clayre.

"He's probably Neserean," Secca suggested. "Only Kinor and Robero have libraries like that in Defalk."

"That looks like a Sturinnese vessel." Clayre pointed at the ship and the figure on the deck. "You don't even look surprised."

"Who else besides Sturinn?" asked Secca. "The Council of Wei likes the stability a strong Defalk provides. They wouldn't cause trouble in Neserea. Belmar can't possibly pay for armsmen and all those players. We know the Sturinnese have always wanted a foothold in Liedwahr. Why would they change now?" She cleared her throat and sang the release spell.

"Let this scene of scrying, silver filled with light,
vanish like the darkness when the sun is bright . . ."

"What about the Ladies of the Shadows?" asked Clayre as the image in the pool died away. "They don't like sorcery."

"No, but there don't seem to be many in Defalk."

"That we know of," Clayre pointed out.

"That's because Brill was the only sorcerer in the whole land for a generation, and because the Corians banned sorcery from the beginning—and they won."

Clayre shook her head. "Why did you think about the second spell?"

"If Belmar happened to be that strong a sorcerer, he wouldn't need backing from anyone. He isn't." Secca shrugged. "I thought I'd seek his backer, just to see if he had one."

"Because you can sense disruptions in the Harmonies as far away as Worlan?"

"Sometimes I can. Can't you?"

"You know I can't. I don't know why you're merely the Sorceress of Mencha."

Secca laughed gently. "You couldn't stand the quiet of Loiseau. Anna knew that." Just as she had known that leaving Secca in the same liedburg as Robero would have created too much friction.

"You and Robero don't do well together, either," Clayre acknowledged. "Redheads seldom do, and Robero's more stubborn even than Birke and Lysara put together."

Secca didn't comment.

"I heard he introduced you to Lythner."

"How did you find that out?"

"I have my ways." Clayre grinned.

"Lythner didn't seem *that* interested. He was most polite."

"How could he be otherwise? He's very handsome, and all say he was most kind and loving to Cynelya."

"You, too?"

Clayre shrugged.

Secca wondered. Did all of Defalk think she was miserable? Or somehow needed a man? Almost any man? "What do you plan to do with Belmar?"

"Whatever I must, I suppose." Clayre lifted her shoulders, then let them drop in a gesture that was not exactly a shrug.

"He'll be waiting for you."

"He would not try a sneak attack on a mere sorceress, do you think? He is, after all, a Neserean holder and a direct descendant of the Prophets of Music, the most rightful heirs to Neserea," said Clayre mockingly.

"How do you know he's in the line of descent?" questioned Secca, an amused tone in her voice.

"Besides his claim? I don't, except that I understood all holders in Neserea claimed to be descendants of the Prophets." Clayre grinned. "In some ways, I worry about the man in the study more. When I get to Esaria, I'll call up that image for Aerlya and Annayal and see if they recognize him. Someone has to know who he is."

"You'd best be careful getting there."

"I will be. I'm insisting on two companies of Robero's best lancers. He must be worried. He didn't even quibble." Clayre looked at the blank waters of the reflecting pool, then at Secca. "It must be nice to have your own lancers."

"It's still hard to believe they're mine. Paying them amounts to most of the rent coins. Five companies do not come cheaply." Secca hating hedging the answer, but Anna always had, and seldom had following Anna's example hurt Secca.

"That must be why she kept Loiseau so small," offered Clayre.

"It's one reason." Secca gave Clayre a wry smile. "Also, it makes it less attractive for those with large entourages to come and visit."

"Birke has observed that, but he's the lord of Abenfel, and that comes with having the largest liedburg in Liedwahr. Every time Robero visits, Reylana begs servitors from her father."

"Do you know how Gylaron is doing?"

"He's getting weaker. Gylan takes his father's guidance, but he really runs Lerona on a daily basis. Reylana has been traveling back and forth since summer. She usually takes one of the children on each trip."

"I always liked her," Secca said.

"Birke was very fortunate, but, then, father let him wait for a suitable consort. It irked Fylena greatly."

"She never had to worry. Your father was very traditional." Secca understood that. As Clayre's father's second consort, Fylena had pushed to make sure that both Clayre and Lysara had been consorted quickly and in a fashion that would not threaten her sons' inheritance of Abenfel. Fylena still worried about the unconsorted Clayre and the power she held in Falcor as the Lord's Sorceress.

"Anna wasn't." Clayre began to replace her lutar in the case.

Both sorceresses laughed.

Secca knew they had more scrying ahead, but trying it immediately would offer nothing new and tire them both. She lowered her own lutar into its case.

24

Although the noonday sun beamed through a cloudless sky, its weak light was not enough to offset the chill wind that blew out of the east and into Secca's face as she rode past the dekstone on the east side of the road town of Zechis. Hoping it would not be too dark before they reached Pamr, Secca glanced up as Richina cleared her throat.

"Is Lythner as handsome as they say?" asked the younger sorceress.

Secca shook her head, wondering what Clayre had planted in Richina's thoughts. Or had it been Alyssa?

"He is not?"

"No. He is very handsome, and very charming. Some say that he is intelligent, loving, and kind—and no, I am not considering consorting to him. That is a decision that must wait until after our trip to Synek."

"Our trip? I can come?"

"You had best come. You trust too much in the words of others, even mine." Secca laughed.

"I could not help but overhear your words with the Lady Clayre before you went to see Lord Robero." Richina eased her mount closer to Secca's.

"I am most grateful for your discretion." Secca paused, then asked, "What do you think of Falcor?"

"I would rather live in Loiseau or even Suhl." Richina frowned.

"Why?"

"I could not say, save I feel all watch in Falcor, and none would care should any slip upon a stone step or tumble from a parapet."

"It's not that bad," Secca said with a slight laugh. "You

must recall that those in Falcor must balance the wishes and the needs of all of the Thirty-three, and never can a ruler satisfy all. Many who walk the corridors there, while not wishing ill directly upon others, may not be all that displeased at misfortunes falling on others."

"And the Lady Clayre contends with such daily."

Secca nodded. "So does Jolyn. That is why she is willing to undertake road-building and arduous sorcery anywhere away from the liedstadt."

"You did not tell Lady Clayre, yet she is also a sorceress," Richina pressed.

"Nor did Anna, and, as you will come to see, nor should any sorceress who holds Loiseau."

"There is that much difference in how a sorceress in Falcor and one in Loiseau views Defalk?"

"No. There is much difference in how each would use the knowledge of Loiseau. You will see, I promise you."

Another long silence followed, a stillness broken only by the low moan of the fall wind. Secca adjusted her jacket again.

"Lady, why did she stay so much in the shadows?" asked Richina abruptly. "The Lady Anna, I mean."

Secca leaned forward slightly in the saddle and raised her voice. "If you would allow us a few moments in the van and some space, Quebar . . . ?"

"Yes, lady." With a knowing smile, Quebar reined his mount to the left edge of the dusty stone road, and Savyn eased his mount to the right.

The red-haired sorceress waited until a good ten yards had opened between her mount and Quebar's before she gestured, and then turned her face to Richina. "Why did she stay in the shadows, you mean, when she could have ruled far better than Robero?"

Richina nodded.

"One must not only rule, but prepare for those who will follow you. Anna had no children here in Liedwahr, nor could she summon them from the Mist Worlds without risking their death, and she could have no more children here. Robero was the heir. Could she have done aught otherwise?"

"But why . . . did she not . . . ?" Richina broke off, gesturing almost helplessly.

Ignoring the implied direct question, Secca pondered for a moment before answering. "She kept Defalk and most of eastern Liedwahr safe, and she found a lord she could love, and a holding she appreciated. Would that all of us were so fortunate."

"Lady, please do not avoid my question."

Secca fumbled with the topmost button on her jacket. "When she was first regent . . . how did she rule?"

"She ruled well."

Secca shook her head, shifting her weight in the saddle. She feared the afternoon would be long. "How?"

"By sorcery. She destroyed the Black Monks, and killed the evil Prophet of Music, and cast down the rebellious Lord of Dumar, and—"

"With each action, she created the need for more action, did she not? Until she had to use her sorcery to replace almost half the Thirty-three and destroy armsmen across all of Liedwahr?"

Richina's brows furrowed in puzzlement. "We have had no wars and little fighting since."

"Do you think that all the men and women in Defalk suddenly changed, that they would so quickly stop their plotting and fighting?"

"But they did," Richina protested.

"The fighting stopped. Lady Anna saw to that, but long before Robero became Lord of Death. Do you remember the story of the broken bridge?"

"When the bridge over the Mittfal collapsed, and flung Lord Klestayr and his eldest into the river?" Richina nodded. "That was how young Dostal became Lord of Aroch."

"And what happened? Or did not happen?"

"His armsmen cast down their arms and did not proceed against Lord Kinor."

"Would Lord Kinor have lost?" Secca pressed.

"He had more armsmen, and armsmen better trained. He should not have had difficulty."

"But he would have lost armsmen, would he not?"

Richina nodded.

"Now . . . had I been there, or Clayre, or Anna, and called forth the flame arrows, could Kinor have lost?"

"Of course not."

"How many of the armsmen of Aroch would have died? And then, when he became Lord of Aroch, how would Dostal have raised levies?"

"Seldom have the levies been raised."

"True enough. But the armsmen are there to command the levies. Often they were not, not when Anna came to Defalk. Far too many died in skirmishes between lords. If Defalk is to remain strong, lords must not fight against each other."

"The bridge collapse wasn't an accident?" Richina said slowly.

"There is more than one way to use sorcery, child." Secca paused. "Folk forget that because of the first years of the Regency." She laughed without mirth. "That is all for the best. Anna had no choices when first she came to Defalk. She had power, and little knowledge of the people and the land, and no time to learn either. Nor were women or sorceresses respected. For many years, all that those in Liedwahr respected was the power that they could see. Many rebellious lords had heard of the destruction of others, yet would not believe until it befell them. It took many years before Anna could be assured that she could leave Falcor, and all believed that she would again raise the fire arrows or the floods, or cause the land to sink under those who would not support Lord Robero."

"That is why you fear the days ahead?"

Secca nodded. "All of us are considered pale shadows of Lady Anna."

"You? With all you have done?"

"Me, most of all, for I have indeed stood in the shadows." *And I fear the glare of an unforgiving sun, and what may need to be done.*

25

NARIAL, DUMAR

Darksong stands high in the clear night sky, and Clear-song has set more than two glasses earlier. Several trading vessels are moored in the deeper part of the harbor, but two tall-masted schooners are tied up at the deep-water piers on the western side, just south of the main part of the city of Narial. The night is still, with not even a whisper of wind.

The only sounds in the harbor are the gentle lapping of night-dark water against the piers and the hulls of the vessels, and the occasional reports of the Harbor Watch, words vanishing into the night, unheard except for those standing duty on the vessels in port.

Beyond the harbor, beyond the horizon, well out of earshot from the fleet of warships there rises the sound of thunder-drums. The skies darken, near instantly, clouding over the bright points of the stars and of Darksong, and there is a rumbling from deep beneath the sea.

A swell of water rises to the north of the warships, a hillock perhaps three yards high that disappears into the darkness as it races northward. The hillock swells with each furl it moves toward the shore, yet, before it, with a sucking, hissing sound, the sea recedes out of the harbor, seemingly before the rising water can reach the land.

The half-dozen vessels drop onto the harbor mud, their masts tilting at various angles. Yells and curses in a handful of languages fill the night air, but only for a handful of moments before a darkness looms out of the south, a darkness that rises swiftly into a wall of water more than thirty yards high. The wall of black water races northward across the exposed mud and sand, far faster than the swiftest of horses, engulfing the beached vessels, then the piers, before crashing nearly a dek inland.

Among the structures flattened are the barracks of both the Harbor Watch and the coastal guards.

When the waters recede, the only structure left intact within a dek of the harbor is the single stone bridge across the Falche, a structure dating back nearly three decades.

26

With the dull anguished chord that seemed to echo through the night, Secca sat bolt upright in the bed of the guest chamber at Pamr. Her eyes were gummy, and every muscle in her body protested, but the anguished chord seemed to reverberate on and on, intensifying the aches and the muscle strains caused by the riding she had done, riding whose extent was more than she had been used to doing recently.

Her first thought was that she was suffering a nightmare, but she could smell the scent of the perfumed oil she had rubbed into those muscles, and in the dimness of the room she could see the lutar case on the table, and her belt wallet beside it. And her muscles hurt.

Slowly, she slid from under the heavy covers, her feet touching first the woven rug beside the bed, and then the cold smooth stone of the floor beyond. Her right hand grasped the dagger on the table by the bed, slipping it from its sheath.

She cocked her head to one side, listening, but the hold at Pamr was silent, the stone cold and reassuringly solid beneath her feet.

One-handed, she used the striker to light the bedside lamp. As the glow grew, she looked around the room. Nothing looked different.

But what had been that awful anguished chord?

She glanced around the room again.

Something had disturbed the Harmonies mightily, but where?

Secca took a deep breath. There was little she could do. The ride to Pamr had been long, so long it had been well past sunset, into the second glass of the night, when she had slowly dismounted in the courtyard, and well into the fourth glass before she had pulled the covers in this strange guest chamber over her.

Even trying to search out the cause of that disruption would not be wise, not until she had more rest, and more food. In any case, there was little enough that she could do. Perhaps when she returned to Loiseau . . .

Still, she checked every corner of her chamber, and the latch bolt to the room, before she returned to her bed and blew out the lamp.

And . . . tired as she was, she found sleep was a long time returning.

27

Standing just back from the archway to the large practice room of the domed building that lay almost half a dek to the south of the walls of Loiseau, Secca listened as the second players worked through the spellsong.

Their copper-tipped finger guards struck the metal strings of the lutars with a precision that it had taken Anna—and Secca—years to develop. Then the three sizes of lutars had also taken years of effort to design and make. Finding a way to draw the wire strings had been the hardest, since spellsinging didn't work nearly so well in replicating tempered or highly forged objects, such as master blades or wire.

Although Delvor and the second players had accompanied Secca to Falcor, neither Secca nor Anna had employed the second players beyond the lands of Mencha, except for road- and bridge building. Mainly, they had been used in wresting metals from the hills west of the Ostfels, but always on the lands held by Loiseau. So far they had not been needed elsewhere and for other uses, although Anna had insisted that the time for their use would come.

Delvor nodded in time to the simple harmony, the hard, almost drumlike rhythms of the lutars shaking the windows in their casements. The lead player's lank brown hair flopped across his forehead. While his hair was far thinner than in years previous, it was still as long and brown and unkempt.

Secca smiled. Delvor was a far better lutarist and lutar leader than he had ever been a violino player. She slipped away, down the corridor to the smaller workroom where Richina was drilling Jeagyn and Kerisel in the simpler vocalises. For a time she stood in the door and listened. At the end of the first exercise, Richina glanced toward Secca.

"Your mouths aren't open wide enough," Secca said. "For a spellsong to carry, you must use all that you have with as little effort as possible. If your mouths are closed, you have to work harder, and the spell will not carry so far. In a battle, that could mean you would die under the arrows of archers loosing shafts from beyond your voice. In working the mines, that could mean more spells . . . or less iron."

"Yes, lady," chorused the three.

Secca smiled and nodded. "You will learn." Then she continued into the spell-shielded room that held the scrying pool. She closed the chamber door behind her. Her eyes slipped past the pool to the iron door of the safe room. Behind the door were the bookcase filled with notebooks and the rows of overlarge sealed jars on the shelves of the second bookcase, each containing a different substance, finely ground. There was also a second smaller strong

room within the safe room that contained strongboxes
filled with gold bars, coins, and a few other items.

Secca's eyes dropped to the desk she and Anna had
shared in recent years, when Anna had asked Secca to
write down yet more of the scraps of knowledge Anna had
remembered from the Mist Worlds. Secca shook her head,
recalling the reason for all the notebooks, remembering the
two times when she and Anna had tried to retrieve what
Anna had called textbooks. Both times, the volumes had
arrived as flaming masses, accompanied with ugly dissonant chords, and both times, Anna and Secca had been
prostrated.

Dissonant chords—with that thought, Secca lifted the
lutar case and opened it. She needed to find out exactly
who had been manipulating the Harmonies two nights before. She should have checked earlier, but she had hesitated to push herself. She'd seen too often what that had
done to Anna.

Still . . . both the power and the ugliness alarmed her,
and she couldn't imagine that it had been Clayre's or Jolyn's doing. After tuning the lutar, she concentrated on the
reflecting pool and the scrying spell.

"Show me now and in great detail
the source of that night's deadly wail . . ."

As the image filled the silvered waters of the pool,
Secca swallowed in spite of herself.

The harbor, for it had been a harbor, lay devastated—
and she was seeing it after two days. The heavy timbers
of the piers had been snapped as if they had been basket
withies ground under enormous wagon wheels and then
scattered carelessly. Ship timbers of various lengths and
colors floated on the muddy water, as did other objects,
including white specks that might have been bodies.
The buildings around the harbor had been reduced to
heaps of stone and bricks or snarled and twisted piles
of wood. In the distance, she could see a single solid

stone bridge—untouched except for the rubble heaped under and around it.

The bridge looked familiar, and she smiled wanly. The harbor had to be that of Narial.

She released the spell, singing a second version.

"Show Narial and in great detail
the results of last night's deadly wail . . ."

The scene was almost identical, except the silvered waters showed more of the shoreline, with a greater number of piles of shattered structures.

The third spell was to find who created the damage. That revealed a fleet of nearly two score ships—warships of Sturinnese design, sailing in formation, northward, from what Secca could tell from the lighting. With no land in sight, there was little way for her to determine just where that fleet was headed, except that it meant ill for some land.

"An invasion fleet . . ." She shook her head. Clayre was somewhere enroute to Neserea. Jolyn was traveling back to Falcor, if she hadn't deliberately mislaid or "misunderstood" the messages sent to her.

What about Hadrenn and Ebra? And the troublesome Mynntar? First, Mynntar.

The next image in the pool was that of a tall and broad-shouldered and clean-shaven blonde man, wearing a burgundy tunic, riding at the head of a very long column, a smile on his face.

Somehow, Mynntar's smile seemed even more dishonest than when Secca had studied him earlier. Was that because of the open honesty of Lythner's smile? Secca shook her head. Lythner might be honest and warm, but those qualities were not enough, and she hoped she would not find herself settling for such.

It took her several more attempts to scry enough of the column to determine that the lancers were riding westward along a river, and that at least five companies were clad in the white tunics of Sturinn. Almost as disturbing were the dozen wagons following the lancers.

After releasing the last scrying image, she poured the orderspelled water prepared by Richina into the goblet and took several long swallows. There was no way to reach Clayre, but she owed Robero a message with the news. It might arrive scorched on his conference table, but arrive it would.

She sat at the desk and began to write on the heavy parchment. When she was finished, she scanned the lines.

Most noble Lord of Defalk . . .
    . . . the harbor of Narial lies in ruins, destroyed by a giant wave raised through Darksong . . . Darksong undertaken by Sea-Priests . . . A fleet of near-on two score vessels sails northward toward Liedwahr . . .
    . . . Mynntar leads a large force of armsmen toward Synek . . . Inasmuch as you have already requested my travel to see Lord Hadrenn . . . as Protector of the East, I will do as I can to support Lord Hadrenn . . . ensure that Dolov remains a holding loyal to you . . .

She reread the scroll, then rolled it and sealed it. Then she placed it in the copper traveling tube, the tube lined with the fuzzy mineral Anna had called asbestos.

With a long deep breath, she picked up the lutar.

After dispatching the scroll, she found her entire body shivering. But then, that was expected. Parchment had once been living and even sending it was a form of Darksong, although it was encased in metal. A minor form, but Darksong, nonetheless—although many forms of sorcery bordered Darksong, and the line between Clearsong and Darksong was far less distinct than even most sorcerers or sorceresses would admit.

Secca sank onto the hard surface of the wooden desk

chair. *You haven't done that much scrying in seasons.* Not in so short a time, at least, and the message scroll hadn't helped. Then, everything associated with sorcery had its costs—as Anna had so often emphasized.

She sat for a time before the small desk, drinking water from the pitcher and slowly eating the hard biscuits that Anna had always insisted be kept in the tin by the reflecting pool.

Finally, she rose and walked down the corridor, stopping at the door of the first players' practice room, empty except for the chief player.

Palian turned. "What's wrong?"

"Everything. The Sea-Priests have raised a giant wave that has destroyed Narial, all except for the bridge Anna built. They have an invasion fleet somewhere south of Liedwahr, and Mynntar has raised armsmen and is riding toward Synek. There's plotting and a possible uprising being planned in Neserea, and the old Liedfuhr of Mansuur died less than half a season ago, and there are probably plots against Kestrin as well."

"And Wei?"

"The Council won't make trouble for Defalk, but I can't see them helping much either."

"Do you still plan to go to Synek?"

"More than ever. We'll take all the players and all but one company of lancers. We can do something about Mynntar. I don't know that I can do anything about a Sturinnese fleet."

"Where will they strike? The Sturinnese?"

Secca spread her hands. "Dumar is not so strong as it should be, and with Narial destroyed, Dumar would be easiest at first. But the Sturinnese have disliked the Matriarchs of Ranuak for generations, and they could also attack the Free City of Elahwa to support Mynntar."

"Ranuak or Dumar," Palian suggested. "They gain little from Elahwa."

"We will see."

"I will refresh the players with the battle spells when they return."

"Thank you." Secca offered a smile to the graying chief player before she turned.

Outside, in the blustery gray afternoon, she mounted the gray and rode back toward the open gates of Loiseau, followed as always by four lancers in green. Silently, she rode upon the stones of the side lane to the main road leading to the gates, then through the gates and the north courtyard to the stables. There, she dismounted.

"You'd be looking grim, lady," offered Vyren as he took the gray mare's reins after Secca dismounted. "I'd be wagering it not be the weather."

"You'd be right." Realizing the grimness of her tone, she added quickly, "I'm sorry, Vyren. I hadn't planned on all that has happened. It will be a hard winter, and a harder spring." She forced a smile. "We'll do what we can."

Vyren nodded sagely. "One doesn't lose a great lady often."

"No. Her loss is greater than any realized." That was certainly turning out to be true.

From the stables, Secca walked through the open iron gate into the rear bailey—the one she and Anna had added with sorcery ten years earlier—and toward the large structure set before the westernmost wall.

The dull impact of a hammer against hot metal filled the chill air of late fall as Secca stepped into the smithy. She stood well back from the forge, watching as Belan turned hot iron on the anvil and, with deft hammer blows, fullered the circular shape into a thinner and broader form.

Only when he had taken the tongs and replaced the cooling iron in the furnace did she speak. "How goes it, master smith?"

Turning to the sorceress, Belan blotted his brow with

the back of his forearm. "Would that I were a sorcerer, Lady Secca. Would that I were . . ."

"Sorcery does not work well for what you do. The Lady Anna tried, and so have I." She shrugged. "It takes hard work to forge what will change Defalk."

"I'd be knowing that. The parts, they be straight enough, but the seals . . . fitting them so that the steam does not burst forth . . ."

The smith gestured to the model of the engine upon the rear work shelf—the one that lay in pieces. "Even from it came steam."

"I know. We did tell you that you would be paid well—because the work would be hard."

"That you did, Lady Secca. That you did." Belan laughed. "I have had to learn casting, and casting iron such as this . . ." He shrugged. After a moment he added. "We will need more iron soon."

Secca nodded. "We'll go to the Sand Pass mine on the way to Synek. You can bring back what we take from the hills. You may have to use some of it for the special arrows and some for blades."

"Folk are talking about fighting. Not in a score of years . . ."

"There will be fighting," Secca admitted. "We will try to keep it from becoming war."

"You sorceresses will?"

She nodded.

Belan looked toward the iron in the forge, then back at the redhead, questioningly.

"Liedwahr will still need engines such as those, perhaps more than we thought."

"Be seasons yet, lady."

"I know." Secca smiled gently.

When Belan turned to the forge once more, Secca slipped from the smithy.

As she walked back toward her room to ponder all that was happening, thoughts swirled through her head. She needed to review the spells to use against thunder-drums and Darksong, and all sorts of other spells Anna had developed, spells unused in years. She couldn't count on there not being a Sea-Priest with the Sturinnese lancers.

She also needed to think about how far she dared to go. Anna had been regent when she had fought in Ebra, and Secca was far from a regent. Protector of the East, which allowed her to support and defend Hadrenn, but then what?

Would she have any choices? Would she recognize them?

28

Wearing the heavy leather trousers, the padded leather tunic, and carrying the cumbersome practice helmet, Secca walked under a leaden gray sky toward the small walled courtyard beyond the lancers' barracks. From the worn brown leather belt at her left side hung the battered scabbard that held her unedged practice sabre.

As she neared the archway to the practice yard, she could hear the sound of metal on metal, the scuffing of boots on the stone pavement, panting, more than a few grunts, and an occasional mutter.

"Lady's coming, Easlon said . . ."

". . . get one of the new ones to spar with her . . ."

". . . don't want any bruises, Gorkon?"

". . . can't win. Hard to touch her . . . strikes hard . . . and if you do hit her . . . then what?"

"She laughs . . . tries harder . . . better 'n a lot of lords."

Secca smiled and stepped through the archway. Almost a score of armsmen were practicing, half that number paired off and sparring with each other. Two were stood under the overhanging eaves in front of the armorer's shop, watching the ancient Albero while he used the pedal grind-stone, sharpening one of their sabres.

Everything stopped, and the lancers turned toward Secca. Secca didn't see any of the officers, but she often didn't if she came later in the day, since most had consorts.

"Lady?" asked Westl, one of the senior squad leaders, who had clearly been instructing a younger lancer.

"I need to sharpen my very rusty skills with a blade, Westl. We are leaving tomorrow." Secca smiled. "I'm sure there is someone here who won't mind." She looked across the lancers who had been sparring, then nodded toward the dark-haired Gorkon, who reminded her vaguely of Lyth-ner. "Gorkon? Would you spar with me?"

Gorkon bowed slightly. "As you wish, lady."

Secca could sense the suppressed laughter. She was al-ways amazed at how often people were surprised when she said something based on what she had overheard, thinking that she had somehow used sorcery instead of her ears.

She smiled pleasantly. "I realize I offer a smaller target than you seek." She shrugged expressively. "But since everyone is larger than I . . ."

That drew a few smiles, even from Gorkon.

She pulled on the practice helmet—her one concession to sorcerous practicality, since a blow to her throat or face would have consequences that she couldn't really afford, especially with the tasks before her. Then she stepped for-ward into the nearest empty practice circle and drew the sabre, setting her feet. The blade felt heavier than usual in her hand. Was it tiredness? That was something she also couldn't afford.

"Go on," Secca suggested to the lancer.

Gorkon's first move was little more than a halfhearted feint, as if he really didn't wish to strike at her.

Secca slammed the edge of her shorter sabre against his, then forced his blade down, and thwacked the bigger man across his right shoulder with the flat of the sabre, letting her blade return to a guard position. She tried to remember to keep her weight balanced.

His next moves were neither feints nor weak, and Secca had to fall back, parrying the furious slashes, waiting . . . until Gorkon overextended himself. Her blade slammed down on the back of his practice gauntlet, and he lurched backward, barely holding on to his blade.

As Secca stepped forward, her boot skidded on the sandy surface of the stone. Instead of trying to catch her balance, which would have gotten her spitted in a real fight, she ducked into a roll, and came up to the side with the sabre ready.

Gorkon's mouth was still open when she slammed the side of his arm with the flat of the sabre once more. His blade clanked on the stones.

"You're too kind, Gorkon. What would you do if you had to fight a woman trained by the Matriarch, or the Traders of Wei?"

The lancer rubbed his arm before bending to retrieve the blade. "I be remembering that, lady."

A few more murmurs whispered from the watching lancers.

". . . like a cat . . ."

". . . wildcat . . . red hair and all . . ."

She ignored the words and gestured with the sabre. "Would you like a turn, Rukor?"

"Begging your pardon, lady . . . but I fear you be far better than me."

"I doubt that, but you won't improve sparring with someone worse."

For all his protestations, Rukor was good with the blade, and his weapon was a good span and a half longer than Secca's sabre.

Still . . . she managed to avoid all but a few blows, but those would be bruises by evening, as would be the shoulder she'd hit on the stone rolling when she had slipped. She bruised all too easily, but there wasn't anything she could do about that.

By the time she was tired, and felt she had had the exercise she needed, despite the coolness of the day, and the chill wind out of the northeast, her hair was plastered flat with sweat, and her undertunic was dripping.

After pulling off the practice helmet and sheathing the sabre, she inclined her head to Rukor, and then Gorkon. "Thank you both. I needed the practice and the exercise."

"Our pleasure, lady," offered Rukor, then Gorkon, a moment later.

Secca listened to the faint murmurs as she turned and began to walk toward the archway, and back to the main building of the keep—for a bath before she dealt with the other problems she had to clear up before leaving Loiseau.

". . . know any other sorceresses—or ladies—spar with their lancers?"

". . . why she do it?"

". . . a fool, Nyrtal . . . She goes into battle . . . only do so much sorcery, you know . . . needs to be able to defend herself . . . All the lords do . . . why not her?"

". . . seems . . . strange . . ."

It didn't seem strange to Secca. She could still remember Lysara and Ytrude using blades to defend her when Hoede and Lord Dannel's armsmen had attacked Falcor. If Anna hadn't had them trained with blades, Secca would have died. On that night, Secca had made up her mind that she would master both blade and sorcery. While she would never be a true master blade, she wouldn't be an easy target, either. And neither would Richina or the other apprentices, for Anna hadn't stinted on their training, and Secca intended to carry on that example as well.

29

MANSUUS, MANSUUR

The Liedfuhr stands at the closed window, looking out into the gray afternoon where ice pellets bounce off the railings of the balcony beyond. The chill of the day seeps through the windows. At the knock on the study door, he turns.

"Yes?"

The graying Bassil steps through the door and bows. "You had summoned me, ser?"

"Has Overcaptain Tein arrived in Mansuus yet?"

"What do you plan, sire?" Bassil's eyebrows lifted. "If I might inquire."

"I don't know if the man is guilty, or innocent and incompetent, but he should have had some idea of what the problems were in Hafen."

"Oh?" Bassil's voice is neutral.

"We lost a company of armsmen. Someone paid off the captain, or promised to, and probably the men as well. Then they were murdered through sorcery in Neserea, and all of Liedwahr is thinking I'm either making a power play or so ineffectual that I can't control my own armsmen. It reeks of the Sea-Priests, but there's not a single bit of proof, and there won't be, as we both know."

"You do not think that the overcaptain can provide such?"

"I doubt it. The stupidest overcaptain wouldn't remain in Mansuur if he were a party to something like this. And if he'd found out, he would have fled or let me know. So I doubt he knows anything. But he should. If the overcaptain doesn't know his officers well enough to anticipate that, it can only mean two things. Either the promised payoff was extraordinarily high or the morale of the men was very low."

"A high payoff to the captain doesn't make his superior officer incompetent or guilty, sire."

"Oh?" asks Kestrin. "Would you ever have been able to afford that summer cottage in Cealur without the golds from your consort's parents' bond? Or would you have bought that matched pair of grays if you'd lost that wager to Commander Grymm? Or would your consort have silk outfits if her sister weren't consorted to a cloth factor?"

Bassil smiles. "You have a point, like your sire. A superior should know the officers under him."

"I think you had best have Commander Latollr report to me."

Clearing his throat gently, Bassil says quietly. "I already took that liberty, sire. He is waiting in the anteroom."

Kestrin laughs, a booming, self-deprecating sound. "And if I hadn't thought of it, you would have set it up so that I thought I had."

"One does learn after a few years, sire."

"What else have I missed, then?" Kestrin studies the older overcaptain. "I'm young enough to have missed something."

Bassil tilts his head. "I may be aging . . . but on this, I think not."

"There's something else, then."

"Yes, sire. Your seers report that the Sturinnese are attacking Dumar. They have used sorcery with the ocean to destroy most of Narial."

"When?"

"Several days ago."

"And they did not find out until now?" Kestrin's voice rises.

"You have but two that are well, sire, and they have been seeking the causes and those involved with the missing lancers."

Kestrin nods slowly. "We have much to discuss—after we deal with the commander." He motions to the door. "Have him come in."

30

In the dim gray predawn light of the late fall morning, Secca looked at the notebooks on the one bookshelf, then at the rows of the oversized jars with the substances she and Anna had gathered over the years. Her eyes dropped to the single saddlebag that held small stoppered jars of ingredients taken from certain of the jars. Then she closed the iron door to the safe room and its iron-lined interior walls, and slid the bar into place.

Picking up the lutar and accompanying herself, she began the spell.

"Within this iron, keep safe and under seal . . ."

As the words died away, Secca stepped back at the momentary flash of heat. She studied the bar welded to the door and the iron frame. The notebooks and all her notes were behind the iron. While the door and storeroom were not proof against metalsmiths with hammers and chisels, even those would take time to break into the room. The spelled iron would stop any sorcerer or sorceress less powerful than she was. For the moment, that was all she could do. She never left Loiseau without sealing the safe room and had no intention of ever doing otherwise, especially with two curious and only partly trained apprentices remaining at Loiseau.

She disliked leaving Kerisel and Jeagyn, but liked even less taking the two with her or sending them to Falcor. So she had handed each a small stack of books, asked them to read and write notes on each, and given them the notations for several simple spells.

After checking the spell-weld a last time, she replaced the lutar in its case and lifted the saddlebag onto her shoulder. She closed the chamber door behind her as she walked out to the waiting gray mare for the ride back across the hill to the lancers and wagons that were assembling in the north courtyard of Loiseau.

Her guards followed her silently as she rode through the gray of the glass before dawn.

31

The breeze that had barely ruffled hair at the Sand Pass fort had turned into a chill and steady blast at the backs of Secca and the lancers—and the wagons for the iron and their drivers—as the column rode back westward to the road that would lead to the red rock escarpments from which Secca would pull the iron Belan needed. While Secca could have tried the sorcery late the day before, after worrying about the effect on tired men and mounts she had decided against it and had the force ride directly to the fort for the night. That meant that, while they would be better on the day's ride after her sorcery, she would not be. Nor would the players.

The side road to the red rock escarpments turned south from the main paved highway between Ebra and Mencha just two deks east of the old Sand Pass fort. The side road, while half the width of the main thoroughfare, was stone-paved as well. Anna had insisted that she didn't want heavy-laden wagons mired in the mud. But then, Secca thought, Anna had been insistent on road-building throughout Defalk—road- and bridge-building—and Secca had done more than her share of both. Would she ever see a stone bridge in Defalk without thinking about Anna?

In the orangish light of the moments just past dawn, Secca turned the gray onto the narrower way to the mine, following Wilten and Dymen, a young standard bearer she barely knew except that he had come from Synope to serve in her lancers. Beside Secca rode Richina, wearing a new blue leather jacket Secca had given her two nights before at Loiseau. The apprentice's lutar was strapped behind her saddle and on top of her saddlebags, just as Secca's was.

The south road angled up the slope at a steady grade, running almost two deks before leveling out on the sorcery-flattened hilltop before the jagged red hills that signified the western edge of the Ostfels, the natural border between Defalk and Ebra.

Secca glanced back, taking in the players, and, behind them, Elfens and his half-score archers, and even farther back, the four companies of green-clad lancers, and well behind them, the wagons that would carry the iron back to Loiseau.

After Secca reached the artificial plateau and had ridden to the eastern end, a hundred yards short of the gaping pit filled with black water, the red-haired sorceress reined up the gray mare and brushed back the hair from her forehead, readjusting the green headband that was supposed to keep it out of her face. She turned in the saddle to check on the riders behind her—and the wagons still moving up the long incline—then glanced at Richina. "If you would please let me know when the wagons are here?"

"Yes, lady."

Secca dismounted, handing the gray's reins to Richina, and turned to study the skies to the north, relieved that they were clear. Then she began to run through the warm-up vocalises.

Behind her, the players had all dismounted and were beginning to tune their instruments.

Secca had finished three vocalises, and the tuning and warm-up melodies were fading away, when Richina spoke.

"Everyone is here."

Secca glanced at Wilten. "Are your men ready?"

"Yes, Lady Secca. They have their mounts reined in, and have been warned."

Secca glanced next at Palian, and the first players, then at Delvor.

"We stand ready," replied Palian.

Delvor nodded his readiness.

"Begin," Secca ordered.

"The mining spell . . . on my mark," Palian called. "Mark!"

The first three bars were all violino, before the woodwinds and falk-horn joined. Then came the massed chords of the lutars of the second players.

Secca concentrated first on matching her voice and words to the accompaniment of the two groups of players and then on visualizing the iron being pulled from the red rocks of the escarpments and being formed into the ingots that Belan—and Defalk—needed.

"Form, form, form the iron strong,
into ingots made pure by song,
verily, verily, verily . . ."

As usual, well before the end of the spell a low rumbling rolled out of the skies that had filled with a gauzy haze, a haze quickly thickening into interlinked thunderclouds. Spider lightning came next, bright enough that Secca had to force herself to concentrate even harder on finishing the spell.

With a single harmonic chord of the kind that only sorceresses or certain players heard, the ground shivered, then rolled ever so slightly. Secca shifted her weight and waited. A blast of hot air raked across her and the players, followed by one almost equally chill.

Another, longer, peal of thunder rumbled over Secca and the players.

Ignoring the burning in her eyes, she slowly looked at the ground between her and the gaping pit before and below the red cliffs, a pit now larger than it had been a glass earlier. The dark ingots of iron, each one weighing nearly two stones, lay in rows on the red-sand soil between the sorceress and the pit.

"Lady . . ." Richina extended a water bottle.

Flashes—daystars—flickered before Secca, as she took the water and began to sip slowly from the bottle.

"You need to eat," urged the apprentice.

Secca took a small mouthful of the bread that would get crustier with each day of travel, then a bite of the white cheese, then more bread, and another swallow from the water bottle.

Murmurs drifted from some of the ranked lancers.

". . . they all like that?"

". . . small . . . big voice . . ."

". . . early storm . . . all we need, going through the Sand Pass . . ."

Fine droplets of rain cascaded around Secca and then across the lancers, players, and the wagons that Belan had brought to carry the iron back to Loiseau. Almost as quickly as it had come, the rain stopped, and the sky began to clear under the chill wind out of the north.

Secca's eyes drifted northward, to the road, and to the Sand Pass fort, barely visible against the red stone cliffs. Only a squad of lancers from Loiseau maintained the fort, and they were rotated every two weeks. These days the fort served more as waystation for traders and travelers, who were grateful for the stark accommodations and the small copper per head charge.

"You need more, lady," Richina reminded Secca.

Dutifully, Secca took another mouthful of bread and cheese, aware that the dayflashes were beginning to fade.

She studied the sky, especially to the northeast, from where the worst storms came, but there were but a few scattered clouds, if moving swiftly westward. While it was not winter yet, not for a few weeks, late fall could still bring ice rain or snow.

Was traveling into Ebra so late in the season wise? Possibly not, but letting Hadrenn fend for himself against Mynntar and Sturinnese lancers was even less so. And the reflecting pool had shown that Synek was safe, at least so far.

Secca took another sip from the water bottle.

32

ENCORA, RANUAK

A man holds a stringed instrument, his eyes fixed on a small ingot of copper, a short bar of iron, and some strips of tin, all set on a polished circle of marble perhaps two spans in diameter. He sings, his fingers deft on the strings of the instrument.

> *". . . a rose, in bronze and hued to the white,*
> *its petals in ovals and catching the light,*
> *its stem both firm and arched in iron so dark . . ."*

As the notes of the song die away, a circle of blue light enfolds the marble and the objects upon it. Then, with the faintest of chords, unheard except to the singer, all the objects vanish to reveal a perfect white bronze rose upon an iron stem, lying upon the marble.

The door opens behind the singer, and the Matriarch enters, alone.

The man bows.

She steps forward and studies the rose. "It is truly beautiful, Alcaren."

"I am glad that it pleases you, Matriarch, seeing as little that I do is pleasing these days." The man who holds the small instrument, larger than a mandolin, yet smaller than the lutars introduced by the sorceress of Defalk, is broad-shouldered but narrow-waisted, too short for his breadth to be handsome, but not exactly stocky either. His hair is a nondescript brown, cut short, as if he were a lancer, which he is not. His eyes are gray-blue, penetrating, but not piercing.

"Certainly, the self-pity of your words is less than pleasant," counters Alya.

"What would you have of me?" Alcaren lowers the instrument.

"What do you call it—the instrument?"

"A lumand, I suppose. It's between a small lutar and a mandolin."

"Are there others like it?"

"I do not know, but I would doubt such. It is made for my voice."

"You have a voice both pleasant and true, and most effective. Yet you seem to lack the wisdom as to when it is wise to use it."

Alcaren waits, not replying.

"Using sorcery to enchant the daughter of the Exchange Mistress was scarcely wise."

"I did not use sorcery. I sang her some songs. I wrote them most carefully. There were no suggestions, and no commands. One was about a rose." Alcaren gestures toward the white rose on the marble. "But not sorcery as you just heard."

"When a sorcerer sings, it is considered sorcery." Alya's voice is dry. "Whether it be so or not. You should have known better."

"A mere man, and I am supposed to know such?"

"A cousin of the Matriarch, raised in this family and taught all we know, and you refuse to use that knowledge wisely or acknowledge it." Alya shakes her head gently. "What am I to do with you?"

Alcaren shrugs. "I am good with a blade, and I ride well. You would not let me be a lancer."

"The men's companies will not accept an officer who is a sorcerer," Alya points out.

"And the women's won't accept a man," Alcaren finishes. "I know. Why did you train me, then?"

"I had no choice. You were already making up songs

and spells. You could have hurt yourself or others."

"Better you had killed me."

"The Harmonies have a use for you."

"What? In more than a score and a quarter years, I have not seen such."

"Be patient."

"You came to tell me *that*?"

"No . . . I came to tell you that you are to be one of my personal guard chiefs. As you said, you are skilled with a blade, and I will give you leave to use two or three spells to protect me, as and if necessary."

"You are more accomplished than I, Matriarch."

"The times are changing, and I fear that the demands of being the Matriarch will mean that I can no longer be as watchful of myself as before."

"The Sturinnese will maintain their blockade?" A glimmer of interest appears in the gray-blue eyes.

"More ships have left Sturinn, and they carry far more armsmen and lancers, and those of ours in the harbor are not armed to take the fight to those already arrayed to the south."

"And you trust in the Harmonies?"

"Not totally." Alya smiles. "Best you gather your belongings. I have a wagon." After a pause, she adds, "Do not forget the rose. You may need it." She turns.

Alcaren glances from the departing Matriarch to the rose, frowning, then slips the lumand into its boiled leather case. After a long moment, he lifts the rose.

33

The day before, snow had blown out of the west, in sheets thrown almost horizontally by a wind so fierce and cold that Secca's back had been numb for deks. The sky had been clear that morning, with no sign of a storm, not even a wind, when the column had begun the ride through the Sand Pass to reach the eastern side of the Ostfels—and Ebra.

They had found some shelter in a waystation, and waited out the storm through the night.

Now, on the morrow, as they rode eastward toward Ebra, the sky remained gray, although the snow had stopped, and the wind had died away. Secca glanced over her shoulder, but the bulk of the Ostfels and the eastern end of the Sand Pass lay shrouded in clouds, perhaps five deks behind the end of the column of riders. On the left side of the narrow road—half the width of that in Defalk, but still paved—were grasslands, seemingly like those around Mencha, if covered with a thin layer of the heavy snow.

By contrast, perhaps five deks to the south lay a long beige ridge of sand untouched by the snow—the westernmost part of the Sand Hills. The air above the dunes was filled with a shifting fog from the snow that had fallen and immediately melted.

As she studied the Sand Hills, Secca shivered inside her leather riding jacket. Supposedly, more than a generation before, the sand had blocked both ends of the Sand Pass, so much so that it had spilled out of the pass above the Sand Pass fort, and isolated Ebra from Defalk. The sand had remained until the dark Evult had shifted the dunes so that he could move his Dark Monks into Defalk and begin his conquest of the rest of Liedwahr. Then Anna had arrived, and everything had changed.

Secca frowned. Someday, would the sands shift again? There were stories about how the Sand Hills had been created by ancient Spell-Fire Wars between Ranuak and the vanished Mynyan lords, but legends only—not one word in any book she had ever seen.

She dropped back to ride beside Palian and Delvor. "How are the players doing?"

"Since none have embarked on such before, save the

two of us," Palian said with a crooked smile, "they still listen when we say that they are fortunate."

"They do not believe us," Delvor added, "but they listen."

The three laughed.

"Was it this bad with Lady Anna?" Secca asked.

The two exchanged glances. Finally, Palian spoke. "It was far worse in Dumar, for the rain never seemed to stop from the time we entered the land until we passed the Falche. In Ebra ... the weather was better."

"But not the battles," offered Delvor. "Bertmynn had thunder-drums, and the sorceress knew it not. We lost many in the first encounter, and I thought I would not walk again, so exhausted was I."

Secca nodded somberly. That was a side she had not heard ... or perhaps not listened to when it had been told. "We have spells for thunder-drums, and for other possibilities."

"It will be different when you go into battle, lady. Let what you have learned sing for you," said Palian, not unkindly.

Left unspoken was the reminder that Anna had been older and wiser, and fought battles in two worlds.

After a nod to the two players, Secca urged the gray mare forward, past Richina and up beside Wilten. "How are the men doing?

"Cold and wet, and muttering under their breath, as have lancers ever." Wilten also offered an off-center smile. "This was an early storm. It passed quickly, and they will forget."

"I used the glass to check the road, and there are no lancers or armsmen ahead." Secca paused. "The stone paving ends only a few deks ahead. The road does not look muddy, but ..."

"After four companies of lancers pass, it will become so, and doubtless the local peasants will call down dissonance upon us."

"So long as none use sorcery, we'll be fine."

"Aye . . ."

Secca's eyes drifted to the left, at the fog-veiled Sand Hills, then back to the road ahead, the long road to Synek and beyond.

34

By midday two mornings later, Secca and her force had traveled far enough east that only the top of the road was damp, the clay only slightly slippery, so quickly had the late fall storm swept out of the Ostfels and then dissipated. The sky remained slightly hazy, and the sun offered little warmth. A thin layer of slushy snow covered any area where there was grass or low vegetation, but the spots of bare ground and the tree limbs were barely damp.

Richina rode on Secca's left, the side closest to the River Syne, a thin line of blue water between and below the low hills. The hills were covered mostly with snow-dusted brown grass. Smaller woodlots were dotted across the hills, generally close to the cots that appeared scattered almost randomly.

"What is Lord High Counselor Hadrenn like?" asked Richina.

"I have never met Lord Hadrenn. I have seen his image in the reflecting pond, but he preferred to deal with either Lady Anna or Lord Robero. He is said to be well-mannered and would like to do the best he can for Ebra. His arms commander is named Stepan, and Lady Anna said Stepan was most capable." Secca smiled. "He was once a most handsome man, Stepan was."

"How did you know him?"

"He is from Synek, but when the Evult conquered that land, Stepan fled to Defalk and served my father. After my father's illness, and when Hadrenn reclaimed his patrimony, Stepan and Gestatr returned to Synek."

"You know him well, then."

"I was but eight the last time I saw him," Secca said with a laugh. "Doubtless he remembers me as but a child."

"It sounds like Stepan is the reason Hadrenn has remained Lord High Counselor," ventured Richina.

"I have had surmises along those lines," admitted Secca, "but we shall see." Not that they had much time to see, she feared, since her use of the glass that morning had shown that Mynntar was almost at the end of the road bordering the River Dol and within twenty or thirty deks of the River Syne road that led westward to Synek.

When the riders reached the next hill crest on the slippery clay of the road, Secca could not help but smile at what she saw—a stone bridge with a level roadbed supported by a graceful arch that spanned the narrow River Syne, with a style that could only have been created by the sorcery of a single individual.

Richina glanced from the bridge to Secca, and then back to the bridge, before asking, "Did you know of this?"

"No. She must have done it in the early years, when I was still in Defalk. I can see why she did." Just how many other bridges, buildings, and accomplishments would Secca find in the years and deks before her? And how long before the emptiness within her healed?

"So that any forces she had to send would have an easy crossing?"

Secca nodded. "There won't be others to the east of here, I don't think. They could be used by anyone opposing Hadrenn."

Both glanced up at the sound of hoofs coming over the low rise on the road ahead. One of the lancers who had earlier been sent out as a scout rode back toward the column. With him was another rider, wearing a dark green sash over his riding jacket, and a shoulder harness for a blade far longer than the sabres used by Secca's lancers.

As Secca stood in the stirrups, she could see a half-score of riders farther back along the muddy road.

"Welcome!" called the Ebran lancer. "Sorceress-Protector, Lord Hadrenn bids you welcome."

"Our thanks to you and to Lord Hadrenn!" Secca called back.

Half-bowing in the saddle, the young brown-haired lancer pointed toward the bridge. "Lord Hadrenn's hold lies beyond the great bridge, and to the north."

"You may lead on," suggested Wilten. "The way has been damp, and we would welcome a dry holding."

"Dry and welcome you shall be," called the young lancer, grinning mostly at Richina.

As Hadrenn's lancer turned his mount, Secca glanced at her apprentice. "He was looking at you."

Even from more than a yard away, Secca could see Richina flush.

"Enjoy it. Just don't take it too seriously." Secca looked over her shoulder at the oiled case that held her lutar, then at Palian.

"We will be ready, lady," answered the chief player.

Behind the second players, Elfens stood in his stirrups and grinned at Secca. Secca grinned back at the irrepressible and cheerful head archer, then turned her attention back to the front of the column where the Ebrans rode. None slowed as they neared the stone-paved causeway leading to the bridge.

Once beyond the bridge, the road began to climb gently and followed the riverbank, more westward than north. Below, along the river, was a thick growth of bushes and trees, a few still bearing traces of tattered yellow leaves.

A good glass passed before Secca finally saw Synek to the northwest. Smoke rose from the chimneys of the town. From the dwellings on the river and from those on the hills above, Secca judged it to be perhaps a third the size of Falcor, and yet older, with no new structures that she could discern.

"We near Lord Hadrenn's hold!" called one of the Ebran lancers.

Secca looked from the town to the right, past a small

orchard. The hold for the Lord High Counselor of Ebra sat on a gentle rise, surrounded by a low wall constructed of ancient yellow bricks, no more than two yards high. An iron gate was set in the middle of the wall, and the lane running from the hold to the gate stretched almost a dek, Secca judged. The structure itself seemed to have been built at two different times, with the left side, of tan stone and yellow brick, seeming far older than the more smoothly dressed marble of the right side. Even so, the entire structure seemed only slighter larger than Loiseau. Out from the hold—more of a hulking mansion than a liedburg—stood a double handful of outbuildings of assorted sizes, some built of yellow bricks, some of a tan sandstone, and several of brick and wood.

As Secca and her escort neared the gate, a full company of Ebran lancers rode down the cobblestoned lane from the hold, splitting into two lines and turning their mounts to present an honor guard to Secca and her lancers.

A fanfare from a single trumpet echoed across the afternoon. The Ebran lancers held ranks until all of the Defalkan lancers had passed, then swung in behind the last of the column.

Secca, Wilten, and Richina reined up in the paved courtyard at the rear of the main structure.

The man who stood on the balcony above the rear courtyard was blocky, bald, and beamed down at Secca from above a large paunch. A purple scar ran from the side of his nose to below his right ear. Secca recognized Hadrenn from her efforts at scrying him.

"We welcome you, Sorceress-Protector of the East."

"We bring greetings and aid from Lord Robero of Defalk," Secca replied.

"His and your greetings are even more welcome than your assistance, although we are grateful for both." Hadrenn gestured toward the entrance below him. "Once you have taken care of your mounts, I would meet you below."

"We will be most pleased." Secca offered a smile she hoped was warm enough.

35

Encora, Ranuak

Standing in the formal receiving room, the silver-and-blonde-haired Matriarch glances toward the clear blue crystal chair of the Matriarchy, set upon the low dais at the far end of the long room half-walled with floor-to-ceiling windows. Then she looks back at Alcaren, who waits just inside the doorway, and speaks. "A lady in a black cloak will be arriving shortly. You will wait outside the door and announce her. You will not escort her inside, but let her enter by herself. You will let no others in to see me, should they accompany her. If she will not enter by herself, she may not enter."

"Should I not . . ." Alcaren stops. His eyes drop to the blue stone floor. "I am sorry."

"You are right to worry about me, but this is one room where I am secure by myself." A wry smile follows the words. "Unless I must face more than one other."

"You are the Matriarch." Alcaren inclines his head. "I am still learning. Yet . . . might I ask? One of the Ladies of Shadows?"

"Yes. I am certain that they wish to warn me about something sorcerous. I may already know it, or I may not, but it is better to listen and hear again what one knows than to ignore the request and fail to learn something that I should know." Alya nods. "You may go and take your position without."

"Yes, Matriarch."

Once the door shuts, and the Matriarch is alone, she walks to the dais, where she seats herself in the crystalline chair, upon the blue cushion that is the sole softness within the formal receiving room. She straightens herself and waits, thinking, oblivious to the cold autumn sunlight that angles through the clear glass of the closed windows and falls upon the shimmering blue stone floor.

Before long, there is a knock on the door, followed by Alcaren's voice. "A Lady of the Shadows to see you, Matriarch."

"Show her in," replies Alya.

The door opens. In walks a figure of height neither small nor exceedingly tall, but wearing a black cloak that covers all from the crown of the head down to just above the tops of the mid-calf black boots. The door closes. The hooded cloak of black shadows the face of the figure standing in the receiving room, but the shadows are not deep enough to conceal the gray hair and the age-sharpened jaw. Nor is the cloak bulky enough to disguise that the caller is a woman.

The Matriarch sits erect upon the clear blue crystal chair of the Matriarchy. "You requested an audience?"

"I did, Matriarch." The woman bows gracefully. "We appreciate that you are willing to hear us."

"What did you wish to bring to my attention?"

"We understand that two sorceresses of Defalk are traveling eastward into Ebra to deal with the rebellion of Lord Mynntar, and that a third is in Neserea. Further, there is a renegade sorcerer in Neserea who has been partially trained by the Sturinnese. He has already used sorcery to slaughter a company of Mansuuran lancers."

"For women who abhor sorcery, you know a great deal."

"We have never opposed sorcery for knowledge and communications, only its use as a tool for changing the world and weather or for warfare."

The Matriarch waits for the Lady of the Shadows to speak again.

"Last, you have trained a man in sorcery, armed him as one of your guards, and set him before you." The dark eyes under the hood fix on the Matriarch.

"That is true. He is where I can watch him, and he can protect me in these disturbing times."

"Not in generations have there been so many sorceresses—and sorcerers—in Liedwahr trained for war." The Lady of the Shadows pauses. "There are two other sorceresses yet in Falcor who may yet bring their evil arts into play, and several apprentices."

"All that is known."

"Matriarch, we exist because of the horrors of the Spell-Fire Wars. We would not see sorcery such as that ever unleashed again."

"Ranuak would not be here today without the Spell-Fire Wars," Alya points out. "All our ancestors would have died under the yoke of the Mynyan lords."

"That was a price we cannot pay again, Matriarch, and well you know that. Ebra is yet a blighted and poor land, and Wei remains so, and cold as well. We must trade, for much of our land remains boggy and wet, and far too many of those bogs poison the land around them." The shadow lady waits within the black cloak.

"All that is true. What would you have me do? I have trained none in battle sorcery, nor have I used such sorcery. Yet the Sturinnese have used sorcery to flatten most of Narial. Their vessels swarm around the coast. They are blocking our trading vessels, and they support the rebel Mynntar in Ebra. Defalk sees itself threatened."

"You must insist that Lord Robero turn from sorcery."

The Matriarch laughs, ruefully. "Defalk has perhaps thirty full companies of lancers. Dumar has less than that—or had less than that. We have twenty. The Maitre of Sturinn can bring ten times that to our shores, should he wish. Do you think my words will sway either Lord Robero or the Maitre?"

"Then close the Exchange to the Defalkans and their allies. You must. This poor land cannot bear another set of scars like those of the Spell-Fire Wars."

"We are already losing trading vessels to the Sturinnese. Before long, few or none will port here. Then . . . we will need trade from Defalk and Ebra far more than they will need it from us. Do you wish me to condemn our people to starvation?"

"Better that than death in fire and flame."

"It has not come to that. It may well not. I will do as I can."

The Lady of the Shadows bows. "Thank you, Matriarch. We have offered what we know, and what we fear from another excess of sorcery. We have warned you."

"I do hope that is not a threat," Alya says.

"The Ladies of the Shadows do not threaten, Matriarch."

"I have heard you." The Matriarch smiles coldly, formally. "As always, I must act for all in Ranuak. As always, I will not use battle sorcery. But . . ." She pauses, then utters the next words slowly and deliberately, "I will not stand by and let all that the pain and suffering of the Spell-Fire Wars produced vanish from Erde because of fear. Suffering—and sorcery—are to be preferred over slavery." Alya's eyes blaze before the fire in them is shielded once more, and she speaks her last words to the figure before her. "You may depart."

Once the door to the formal receiving chamber closes, another kind of darkness passes over the Matriarch's face, a face that has become more angular with the years, like that of her father, rather than round as her mother's had been. She looks toward the door, not seeing it, her eyes fixed somewhere else, and her face is drawn.

36

Secca carried her lutar case in her right hand and the saddlebags over her left shoulder as she stepped up the stairs and in through the marble archway of Hadrenn's palace, for it was far more a palace than a walled liedburg capable of withstanding an attack or a siege. The entry hall was perhaps a third the size of that of Loiseau, and the ceiling was less than a yard above Secca's head.

Flanked by two guards in green, blades still in their scabbards, Hadrenn bowed in greeting to those entering, although his eyes did not leave Secca.

"Welcome, sorceress. Your grace and beauty have been understated," offered Hadrenn. "Most understated."

"As has been your hospitality and warmth." In a damp riding jacket, hair tied back, with road mud splattered all over her, Secca had strong doubts about her present beauty. "Might I introduce those who have accompanied me." She motioned. "My chief of the first players, Palian. My chief of the second players, Delvor, and my overcaptain of lancers, Wilten. This is my assistant sorceress, Richina." She paused as the long-faced Elfens stepped forward and bowed deeply. "And my chief of archers, Elfens."

Elfens managed to look suitably somber as he stepped back.

"We are most pleased to see you all. We appreciate your support of Ebra in this time of change." Hadrenn bowed his head slightly. "But now is not the time for such serious stuff. You have traveled far and swiftly and need refreshment."

"I also bring gifts from Lord Robero, and will have them unpacked and ready for you shortly." Secca inclined her head.

"For such graciousness on your part and that of your lord, I am most thankful, and we will look forward to beholding such."

A thin, harried figure slipped out from a side corridor in response to Hadrenn's beckoning finger. "This is Frengal, the assistant saalmeister. He will show you to your chambers, and once you are refreshed, we shall dine." Hadrenn beamed even as he gestured a second time, and a lancer stepped forward, an older man with hair half sandy, half silver, and a crinkled smile. "You may recall my arms commander."

"Stepan!" burst from Secca's lips. She couldn't help offering a wide grin to the former armsman from Flossbend.

The arms commander laughed. "You are older, Lady Sorceress, and more beautiful, but not much larger."

"And you are older, and more handsome," Secca replied.

The arms commander grinned, then shook his head.

"Stepan will help your overcaptain settle your lancers." Hadrenn nodded to the arms commander. "Your chief players and their players shall have rooms in the north wing. Frengal's assistant will see to that."

"You brought what . . . four companies?" asked Stepan.

"Yes. They're mine, not Defalk's."

"I had thought such from the green tunics."

Secca inclined her head slightly. "How many companies have you raised here?"

"We have ten companies, and some levies from the holders—two companies worth."

The trace of a frown flitted across Hadrenn's face, but vanished so quickly Secca could have imagined she had not seen the expression. The heavy lord said smoothly, "Frengal . . . if you would see that everyone is settled?"

"Yes, lord."

Secca and Richina—and two of Secca's lancers—followed the slender assistant saalmeister up the wide stone steps that curved up off the entry foyer. Frengal continued along the corridor a good forty yards, halting before a set of half-open double doors.

"There are chambers to each side of yours, Lady Secca, for assistants."

"Richina is my only assistant."

"Then I would suggest the chamber to the left, lady. But let me show you your chamber first, as your assistant should be familiar with it as well."

Secca nodded, and the two followed the functionary into the chamber. The two lancers—Dyvan and Easlon—stationed themselves at the door.

The guest chamber was comparatively luxurious for Liedwahr—despite the seeming modesty of Hadrenn's holding—and far more elaborate than anything in Falcor.

A large desk was set before two wide windows, the glass comprised of leaded diamond-shaped panes. The window casements were draped in green velvet hangings, tied back with golden velvet ropes.

Secca set the saddlebags on the chest at the foot of the broad bed, but continued to hold the lutar as she followed Frengal through the arched doorway beyond the desk.

"And . . . here is the bath chamber." As Frengal spoke, two serving women in gray eased into the room with heavy steaming kettles, pouring the water into a tiled tub built into a dais in the rear corner of the bathing chamber. "The previous sorceress . . . suggested it."

"She and I appreciate that," Secca said quietly.

Frengal bowed. "If you need aught, there is the bell-pull." He pointed to a narrow crimson hanging running down from the ceiling on the wall beside the headboard of the canopied bed.

"Thank you very much, Frengal."

"My pleasure, ladies. My pleasure."

With a bow, the man departed.

The young lancer and standard bearer Dymen stood in the doorway with a leather-covered bundle. "Lady?"

"Thank you, Dymen. If you would just set that on the desk."

"Yes, lady." With a bow the young man crossed the room and set the bundle on the desk, then bowed again before slipping out and closing the door.

"You said I was your assistant," murmured Richina.

"Apprentices are assistants," Secca murmured back. "That was for your protection and to let Hadrenn know how seriously we take this."

"Will you let me do sorcery?"

"If necessary and it is something you can do." Secca smiled. "Now . . . go get cleaned up. I'm sure you're as hungry as I am."

"Yes, lady." Richina bowed and slipped out, carrying her own gear and lutar.

Secca walked around the room—dusty and not so clean

as she would have liked despite its opulence, then stopped to look out the windows. The sky remained clear; she hoped that would continue.

After taking out the lutar, and using a spell to clean and reheat the bathwater, which had already chilled, she slipped into the tile tub for a bath that was briefer than she would have liked, but welcome all the same. Dressing for dinner was not a problem, since all she had was the not-quite-clinging high-necked deep blue gown that offset her hair. It was the only non-riding habit she had brought and one that rolled into a compact cylinder.

She was brushing her hair—always unruly, long or short, not quite straight, but with not enough curl for that fashion, either—when there was a knock on the door.

"Lady Secca?"

"Come in, Richina."

The apprentice slipped into the room. Richina wore a gown similar to Secca's in cut, but of a rich green more suited to her unfreckled fair complexion and sandy hair. "Do you need any help?"

"I doubt that even the most forbidden sorcery could do much." Secca laughed. "We might as well go down. I'm famished. Then, I was famished when we unsaddled our mounts."

Some functionary must have been watching, Secca decided, because Hadrenn was waiting below. So were Wilten, Stepan, Palian, and Delvor, as well as several others from Hadrenn's household or retinue.

Easlon was the guard who followed the two sorceresses and who carried the leather wrapped gift from Robero.

Stepan favored Secca with a knowing smile, even as Hadrenn stepped forth and motioned toward the dining hall. Through the open double doors Secca saw a long room paneled in age-darkened oak, and lit inadequately by candles in wall sconces.

"Before we eat, here are Lord Robero's gifts." Secca motioned for Easlon to step forward.

Hadrenn did not quite frown as he took the bundle and

slipped off the leather covering. Under the covering was an ebon-black chest, chased with inlaid silver arcs and curlicues. He glanced at Secca.

"There is more inside," she said.

Secca did not peer, as did those around Hadrenn, for she had already seen the heavy gold chain with the pale green stone, and the golden seal ring circled with small diamonds.

The Lord High Counselor of Ebra did smile as he saw the objects on the blue velvet inside the chest. "Your lord is most generous. Most generous."

Secca had thought Robero had been far too generous. "He is known for that, especially for those who have been fast friends."

"We have always endeavored to be such." Hadrenn presented another smile.

"Lord Robero recognizes that." Secca inclined her head slightly, but did not bow.

"Ah . . ." Hadrenn paused, as if he had forgotten something, then turned to the woman in green silk gown and jacket beside and slightly behind him. "This is my consort, Belvera," Hadrenn said. "Dear, this is the Lady Secca, Sorceress-Protector of the East."

"I am most pleased to meet you," Secca offered.

"And I you, Lady Sorceress." Belvera did bow to Secca.

Hadrenn led the way into the dining hall and the long table, where Secca found herself at Hadrenn's right, across from his consort. Wilten was beside Belvera, and Stepan to Secca's right. Then came Richina, Palian, and Delvor.

The gray-haired and ample woman in the shimmering green tunic smiled warmly across the table at Secca. "It's so good to see you." Her smile broadened. "You are a mite of a thing for such a large title, but then, your predecessor was as thin as a twig, and it made no difference there, either."

"It is hard for sorceresses to be other than thin," Secca said with a laugh. "No matter what we eat and how often."

"So I've heard. My father said that Lord Brill was a

slender fellow too, and all the drawings of the Lady Asentar show her as thin."

"Asentar?" asked Secca.

"Ah . . . yes. She was the grandmother of that evil man, the Evult. It's been said that he buried her alive in her tower, but we'll never know, not since all of Vult lies yet under steaming rock. You know, the Zauberinfeurer yet pours molten rock over the valley. A shame. It was once a pretty place."

"Dear . . ." Hadrenn coughed.

"Oh . . . I suppose you want to offer an invocation so that everyone can eat. I'm sorry. Please do."

Hadrenn cleared his throat again, then intoned in a voice an octave lower than his speaking voice, "May Harmony grace this table and all those around it, now and in the days and seasons to come."

"Aye, Harmony," came the murmurs from lower on the table.

When Hadrenn looked up, his eyes met Secca's for a moment, and she noted that his orbs were deep and brown, almost cowlike except for the dark rings around them and the intentness they held. "Let us be served!"

Serving girls, each wearing a green apron trimmed in yellow, appeared with large platters, and with baskets of bread. A youth stepped to the table with a ewerlike pitcher, but the contents were a golden wine which he poured first into Hadrenn's pewter goblet.

Hadrenn leaned toward Secca, ignoring the goblet. "Having learned some of the habits of sorceresses over the years, I will not long defer to meaningless chatter." A bright and false smile followed the words, indicating to Secca that Hadrenn would have preferred a more leisurely approach.

"Were times more settled, Lord Hadrenn, I would welcome such," Secca said politely. "Perhaps upon my next visit."

"I sense as much. Your presence and that of your lancers bears an urgency not mentioned in the message I received from Lord Robero announcing your imminent arrival. Ah . . . but a moment." Hadrenn looked up and waited until the youth serving the wine had filled the goblets of Belvera, Secca, and those at the head of the table before lifting his own. "To our most honored guests."

Secca took the slightest of sips, knowing she dared little else until she had eaten. The wine was passible, better than what the vineyards around Mencha produced, but not so good as the barrels she regularly had carted from Flossbend.

"I do wish Haddev could have been here tonight," offered Belvera. "He always says that sorceresses must be ugly old women."

"Your son?" asked Secca.

"Our eldest. He will reach his score at the turn of spring. He and his brother Verad are visiting my parents' hold. It is strange, in a fashion, for I grew up not so far from your holding."

Something tugged at Secca's memory, but she could not remember, and smiled encouragingly.

"Being the youngest daughter at Silberfels . . . so much younger than Selber—that was strange, too."

Belvera was Lord Selber's younger sister? Then, Hadrenn would have had to have taken a consort from a lordly holding in Defalk. Where else could he have gone? "I was the youngest, also," Secca said.

"For a sorceress, does it matter, dear?"

"Ah . . . lady . . ." Stepan said gently. "Lady Secca holds Flossbend by birth, and Mencha by right of sorcery."

Belvera smiled. "So . . . she is doubly-landed, and beautiful. Haddev will indeed be regretful."

"You may convey my best," Secca offered her own smile before taking another small sip of the wine.

"Your urgency?" prompted the Lord High Counselor of Ebra, an almost amused tone in his voice.

"Lord Mynntar has assembled twenty-score lancers or more. He rides westward toward Synek." Secca broke off a chunk of the crusty and flaky warm bread, taking a quick mouthful.

"I had heard tales that he might, and Stepan has already raised some of the levies, and readied our own lancers. How soon might he arrive?"

"I would guess four days, if he presses and we remain here."

A server eased half a fowl of some sort onto Secca's platter, then ladled a golden glaze over it, while the second server added what looked to be potato dumplings.

"You do not sound as though you wish to remain near Synek."

"Synek is not the best place to fight," interjected Stepan gently. "As I have suggested, ser. Even a day's ride east would provide better terrain, especially for a sorceress."

Hadrenn nodded. "It is true. You have said such. So did the great sorceress when she was regent, and she destroyed Bertmynn." He shrugged. "I am not one to challenge success, and I am not an armsman. So I will leave the details to you two, saving I wish to know the how and reasons therefore."

"We will be most certain to offer our plans." Stepan's eyes twinkled for a moment.

"Do try the squab, dear," suggested Belvera to Secca. "After all that sorcery and riding, you must be famished."

"A bit," acknowledged Secca, taking Belvera's suggestion and slicing off a chunk of the bird. The pearlike glaze helped cover the slight dryness of the meat. Secca hadn't realized exactly how hungry she was until she found herself looking at a small pile of bones.

Belvera gestured, and before Secca could demur, a second squab and glaze appeared on her platter.

"Hungry these sorceress are." Hadrenn nodded, and then bent toward his consort to murmur, "You were right about the honeycakes . . ."

Stepan leaned toward Secca. "Could you tell me how fare Markan and Fridric?"

"Markan remains as the arms master of Suhl, where he

is greatly respected." Secca nodded toward Richina. "Richina is the daughter of the lady of Suhl, but is better suited to sorcery. Her elder brother is the heir. She could tell you more, since she has seen Markan far more except in the last few years."

"Fridric?"

"He was killed when his mount put a foot in a marmot hole, perhaps eight years ago. Many mourned his death. He was a good man."

"I had not heard." Stepan fingered his chin. "You have no consort, it is said. Is it true that sorceresses in Defalk may not consort?"

"There is no reason I could not. Were I to bear children, for a time, at least, I would not be so effective as a sorceress."

"But . . . the Lady Anna."

"She had children in the Mist Worlds, and she raised me, as well."

Stepan nodded. "I had wondered."

"What do you know about Mynntar?" Secca asked, cutting off another chunk of squab.

"Little save through the words and tales of others . . ."

Secca raised her eyebrows, but continued to dismember the second squab, listening.

". . . said to be most generous to those he favors . . . accepts the Free City most grudgingly . . . has spent much of the golds from his lands in hiring and training armsmen . . . Like his sire, vengeful . . . but unlike him in that Bertmynn was calculating, while Mynntar has been known to fly into black rages . . . will not ask any man to do what he will not do, and all his officers and lancers and armsmen know such . . . said that he and his brother be close . . ."

As Stepan talked, once again, Secca realized how little she knew. Still, Mynntar had not faced battle sorcery, and she could but hope that her spells and players would be enough.

37

Secca glanced at the road ahead, a road half-filled with puddles of icy water, then at the dark gray clouds that had rolled in out of the north in midmorning. For the last glass or so, the rain had come and gone in gusts, drizzle followed by sheets of water, but the darkness ahead and the steady downpour looked like it was not about to let up. Again, she wiped the water off her forehead and blotted it out of her eyes with the back of her sleeve.

"With this much rain, the players will be useless, even the lutars," said Richina.

"Unhappily." Secca urged the gray forward toward the two officers riding directly in front of her.

Wilten and Stepan eased their mounts apart.

"Traveling in this is foolhardy, and we certainly cannot do battle in this weather." Secca looked at Stepan. "Is there someplace nearby that would afford us shelter, yet where we would not be surprised?"

Stepan shook his head. "There are just hills and fields and hedgerows. Not until Rysl, and that is another fifteen deks."

Out of the rain came one of the scouts, his mount's hoofs spraying water and mud.

Secca didn't like the man's haste. In the rain, it augured for nothing good.

"Sers . . . Lady Secca . . . the lancers of Dolov are riding toward us. Mynntar's vanguard is less than five deks to the east—on this road."

"They're in the rain?" asked Secca. "And riding toward us?"

"Yes, lady. Twenty companies, mayhap more."

More than twenty companies against sixteen and some levies, and with no sorcery possible—or little, since she couldn't fit all the players into the single small tent. Even Elfens' archers would be useless for more than a shaft or two.

"We'll have to retreat," Secca said, almost shouting to make herself heard over the wind and rain. "We can't do sorcery in this weather."

Stepan nodded. "The rain cannot last forever, but men lost in a poorly chosen battle do not fight again."

"I will tell our captains," Wilten forced his voice over the rain and the wind.

Secca glanced ahead, but could barely make out the road. Why was Mynntar riding through the muck and the rain? To try to surprise Hadrenn? Or because he knew that Secca's sorcery would be greatly limited by such weather? If so, how had he known she was on the road, unless he had seers or sorcerers himself?

As she turned her mount, Secca tightened her lips.

38

The rain had continued throughout the night, and remained cold and steady the next morning as Secca's force was gathering itself together on the south side of a hillside meadow below a woodlot where they had been able to find some shelter for men and mounts—little enough, but the best they had been able to do, given the rain and the exhaustion of men and mounts the day before.

Stepan, Wilten, Palian, and Delvor had joined Secca and Richina in the small tent—leaving almost no room for any of the six to move. Outside, the rain continued to fall through the grayness that had never broken.

"According to the scouts," Stepan said slowly, "Lord

Mynntar broke camp early and is riding west once more on the main road. They are doubtless less than five deks from us, perhaps closer to three."

"They seem to be doing better in the rain. Do we know why?" asked Secca.

Both the Ebran and Defalkan officers shook their heads.

"His men are wearing oiled leathers," Stepan mused, "not winter jackets. Perhaps he had hoped for rain. Or the Sturinnese drive the rain with their drums."

Not liking the implications of that idea at all, Secca looked through the narrow opening in the tent flap at the still-falling chill rain, then at the road. After a moment, she asked, "Stepan . . . what would happen if we tried to leave the road?"

Even through he tried not to react, the wince of the older arms commander was obvious.

"Would that be true of Mynntar as well?"

"Yes . . ."

"Isn't there a dip in the road, and a small bridge another one or two deks back toward Synek?"

Wilten and Stepan exchanged glances.

"Well . . . if there were no road, and that were turned into a swamp?" asked the redheaded sorceress.

That got a slow nod from Wilten.

"We could not move eastward after the rain lifts," pointed out Stepan.

"I've used sorcery to build many roads and bridges." Secca laughed mirthlessly. "When we rebuild it, it will be better than before." *If you get the chance.*

"You are the sorceress." Stepan's tone was measured.

"We need to break camp and ride west, beyond the bridge. Then, we'll gather the best players under this tent . . ." Secca glanced at Palian. "We will have a single spell to do, and it must be done quickly. The short building spell."

"If we are out of the rain, we can do it," Palian affirmed.

"Delvor, you need to go back with the lead lancers.

We'll need the second players later, and I don't want anyone hurt or getting left."

"Yes, lady." Delvor pushed back the overlong lock of damp and limp brown hair, using the same gesture as he had ever since Secca had known him.

As she mounted the gray mare, Secca was still trying to work out the last of the words for the spell. ". . . move the rocks and ground . . . turn to mud all around . . ." she murmured as she rode through the downpour.

The bridge Secca remembered seemed much farther than the one or two deks to the west she had recalled, but that might well have been because she was unused to riding wet and sloppy roads. Most of the major roads in Defalk were now stone-paved, even if it had taken Anna and the three sorceresses she had trained more than a score of years. The first road completed had been the route between Mencha and Falcor.

Riding through the mud and muck, Secca was getting a new appreciation of why Anna had insisted so much on paving roads in Defalk.

Already, the small creek that ran beneath the small timber bridge was almost to the base of the roadbed as Secca and the last of the column crossed and began to climb the gentle slope, a slope that had gotten slippery with churned mud. Secca concentrated on riding until she was almost to the top of the rise, when she guided the mare to the north side of the road.

"Up there . . . on the grass just above!" Secca motioned to the two lancers who were leading the pack horses with the tent.

"Keep moving!" called Wilten. "All but the purple company. The rest of you, keep heading back to Synek!"

On the slope just above where she wanted the tent, Secca turned the mare, squinting into the rain, then pointed. "Just the canopy and side walls. Leave the front open," she told the two lancers struggling with the wet silk and canvas of the tent.

Because most of the force had been behind Secca when

she had decided on the retreat, only the purple company and the players were left—and Wilten—waiting for the tent to go up.

Secca kept glancing eastward, but she could see nothing beyond about half a dek, and certainly she heard nothing.

Despite the thick green felt hat she wore, Secca felt soaked all the way through, but she watched . . . and hoped, and began to warm up, hoping the vocalises would work amid all the rain and chill. Anna hadn't mentioned doing sorcery in the rain, Secca reflected.

"Lady Secca! The tent is up!" called Wilten.

"Players, into the tent and quick tune!" ordered Palian.

Secca dismounted and handed the gray's reins to Richina. "Just listen and watch."

"Yes, lady." The apprentice wiped more water off her face.

Secca finished another vocalise before Palian tapped her on the shoulder.

"We are ready with the short building spell, lady."

"So am I." Secca moved slightly to the side, so that she could see, peripherally, the players.

"On my mark . . . Mark!"

Secca waited through the unused first bar, then launched the spell.

"Move, move the rocks and ground. . . ."

The wind began to pick up with each bar of the spell. Before Secca finished the last words, a bolt of lightning flashed through the falling water, followed by a hiss of steam. Deep slurping sounds came fast after the lightning, and the damp ground rolled under Secca's feet. One of the younger violino players—Bretnay—staggered and went to her knees, but kept her violino up and out of the rain, which now thundered down in sheets. White fog rose from where the small bridge had stood.

"Pack up and remount!" Secca ordered Palian.

Before Secca could reach the gray mare, the sheets of water and gusts of wind buffeted the tent, threatening to rip it out of the unsteady ground. Secca struggled back to help the lancers.

Wilten rode along the shoulder of the road, even closer to where Secca and the two lancers struggled to reroll the soggy tent sections. As the overcaptain reined up beside them, he called out, except he was yelling at the top of his voice to make himself heard over the wind and rain, "Lady Secca . . . you and your players need make haste, for the road is washing out even in the lower spots to the west of us."

"Palian! Take the players and ride!" Secca snapped, still holding the end of the wet rolled cylinder as the taller lancer struggled with the damp hempen rope.

"We have it, lady," the lancer said.

"Thank you." Secca slogged through several yards of mud to where the gray mare waited, and pulled herself into the saddle, banging the sabre on her leg as she did, but ignoring the dayflashes before her eyes.

After she had turned the mare, she glanced back in the direction of the swampy lake that had begun to cover what had been a bridge and road, but she could not even see that quarter of a dek through the heavy downpour. Until the rain ended, neither force was going to charge into battle. At least, that was what she hoped.

She urged the mare closer to Wilten. "We might as well go all the way back to Hadrenn's hold. At least there, everyone can dry out."

"Yes, lady," Wilten replied.

What had she gotten herself into? Was this what war was all about? Riding back and forth, trying to find a place to fight where she might have some slight advantage? Where the land and weather could be enemies as well?

Secca kept the frown to herself.

39

Outside the windows of the first-floor study in Hadrenn's palace, fat and moist flakes of snow drifted out of a gray sky, flakes that melted the moment they struck the soaked and far warmer ground.

Inside, as Hadrenn, Stepan, and Wilten watched the scrying glass laid on the table, Secca fingered the chords on the lutar for the third spell of the morning.

"Mirror, mirror, where on the ground,
show us where Mynntar's scouts are found . . ."

The mirror on the broad table silvered, then showed four lancers riding along a lane beside bare-limbed trees.

Secca glanced at Stepan.

"They are scouting the lane they may use once the rain and snow stop," Stepan observed.

"That won't be long," suggested Hadrenn. "The sky is lightening with every glass."

"The roads are still mud-clogged, and they must find a way around Lady Secca's swamp."

"So must everyone," retorted Hadrenn.

Secca ignored the bitterness in the Lord High Counselor's words. "Do we know where this lane he scouts may be?"

"Can . . . might you see if he scouts through peach orchards?" asked Stepan apologetically.

Secca released the image, and thought, finally coming up with a modified spell.

"Mirror, mirror, where peaches are by tree,
show us Mynntar's scouts and what they see . . ."

The image was almost identical to the first.

Stepan smiled. "I can show you where they are on my maps."

Secca released the spell. Richina moved the glass, and both sorceresses waited while the silvering arms commander unrolled a cylindrical map and laid it out over the table.

"You see. Your glass showed his camp there, and his scouts here. He is looking for a way to avoid the swamp . . ."

Secca was far more worried about why Mynntar had pushed so far westward than about replacing the road through the swamp lake she had created. What was happening elsewhere that Mynntar felt confident enough to ride out of Dolov and into Synek?

". . . and he will try to move his lancers swiftly back to the road." Stepan looked up.

"There's one other matter we should look at," Secca said quietly. She took the mirror—warm to the touch—and set it gently on the map, then picked up the lutar and offered another spellsong.

"Show me now as best in sight,
where else the Sturinnese may fight . . ."

The mirror flickered, then settled on a harbor, empty except for a single trading vessel.

Secca frowned, partly because her head was beginning to throb and partly because she'd never seen the city or the harbor. From what she could tell, it faced south—but most did. Still, it wasn't Narial or Encora. She'd scried them enough before. "Do you think that might be Elahwa?"

Stepan pursed his lips. "It is not Encora, nor Sylwa."

Secca released the image.

"Why matters this?" asked Hadrenn.

Secca was beginning to understand why Anna had been less than praiseful of the Lord High Counselor.

"He has at least five companies of Sturinnese lancers. He is riding fairly far from Dolov, and he has decided to ride against me—and you—in the rain. I'd like to know why."

"And a harbor shows that?"

"If the Sturinnese are about to attack Elahwa, the FreeWomen aren't about to come to your aid, even to hold off Mynntar," Secca pointed out.

"They have little love of me," Hadrenn said.

"They have far less love of Sturinn or Mynntar. They would at least defend their borders against Mynntar and perhaps raid his lands to help you."

Hadrenn nodded slowly, as if not totally convinced of Secca's logic. Then, he glanced at the red-haired sorceress. "All you have used your sorcery for is to destroy a road?"

"Yes," Secca admitted. "If I had not, they would have overrun us, and whether we had won or not, we would have lost too many lancers."

"But had you won . . ."

"It would have been a victory worse than many defeats," Stepan interjected. "Mynntar has fifteen companies of his own and five companies or more of Sturinnese lancers. If we cannot use sorcery to destroy Mynntar's forces and preserve most of our own, then who will stop the Sea-Priests?"

"Best it be that way, then." After a last nod, Hadrenn turned.

Secca watched as the Lord High Counselor walked from the study.

Wilten glared at the departing Lord High Counselor, then at Stepan.

"He is most worried," said Stepan.

"I'm sure he is," Secca said. "But he'd be in much worse shape if we weren't here."

"I fear, Lady Secca," Stepan pointed out gently, "that such is of little consolation to rulers . . . as you may well know."

Secca could not help but smile at the gentle and ironic reminder. "We will have to ensure he has less to worry about." She looked at Richina. "You'll have your part to do."

"Yes, Lady Secca?" A puzzled look crossed the younger woman's face.

Secca smiled. "Who do you think is going to rebuild the road and bridge?"

"But . . ."

"You know the spells; you've watched me do it. It's a simple bridge. And . . . you need to do it because the lancers will need me fresh to deal with Mynntar's forces."

Stepan nodded.

"You will need to spend a little time with the players to make sure they don't play anything too high. Your voice is lower than mine."

"Lady . . ." Richina's voice was tentative.

"Bring your lutar and come up to my room. We'll go over it there." Secca inclined her head to Wilten and to Stepan. "If you will excuse us . . . best we be ready on the morrow of the day after."

Both officers nodded.

Secca reclaimed her own lutar before leaving the lower level study. A glance out the window showed that the light snow had stopped.

Once upstairs, Secca sat on the footchest beneath the canopied bed and looked at Richina. "You'll need a sketch . . . so that you know exactly what you want to visualize. This is a simple bridge—one arch, and make it small—and the road above can just be packed gravel and dirt and rock. Don't worry about the swamp. If you do the spell and concentrate on a solid rock base for the arch, the road and bridge will hold."

"Why did you decide I could do this now?" asked Richina.

"When I realized that Anna had done me no favors by not taking me into battles." Secca shook her head.

"That's not fair. There were no battles by the time I was your age and that far along in my training." She cleared her throat. Despite its opulence, and the dampness outside, the room was dusty. "We need the road replaced. That way, we can strike Mynntar with some advantage because he will not expect us there. I will need everything I have for dealing with Mynntar's forces. That is because, just like you, I am not experienced in full battles." Secca looked directly at Richina. "Do you understand?"

Richina nodded gravely.

"I am asking much of you, earlier than I would like, but if I ask too much of myself . . ."

"Then all could be lost," Richina said.

"All would not be lost for Defalk. There are other sorceresses, but I would rather not prove that Lord Robero could survive without us." Secca offered a wry smile. "Now . . . go write the spell you wish—but use a building spell, and then let me see it. Then you will seek out Palian. After you practice . . . just the notes, not the words, you should start your sketch."

Richina nodded and stood. "By your leave, lady?"

"By my leave."

Once Richina closed the door, Secca walked to the window closest to the bed and looked out across the wet grounds. She stood there, thinking, hoping, planning . . . and worrying.

40

In the midafternoon, Stepan gestured at the map spread on the study table. "Mynntar has scouted the back roads that circle the swamp where the road used to be. He is camped here on this hilltop. The one to the south is higher, but he would have to backtrack to reach the roads. As soon as the ground dries enough to support his horse, he will take this road past these orchards and either come back to the main road or continue on this lane and strike here. With the warm wind from the southwest, that could be soon. Already, the fields here are drying."

Secca studied the map. "If we repair the road, and then follow this . . . we would have the high ground."

"If . . ." Stepan said. "There is brush on the hillside. It would prevent a charge . . ." He cocked his head. "But low brush is no barrier to sorcery, is it?"

"No." Secca hoped not.

"Then they would have to circle . . . if the sorcery did not complete the task." Stepan looked to Secca.

Wilten nodded almost imperceptibly.

"How long before he can move?" asked Secca.

"The ground is drying, but it won't be firm enough for two or three days," offered the graying arms commander.

"What about the main road?"

"Two days."

"Then we should repair the swamp bridge on the morning after next, and take the hill overlooking his force and strike from behind." Secca studied the map once more. "Is not this ridge harder ground?"

"So hard that it will not grow trees. Some say it was once a hold, generations into the past."

"The wind has been blowing out of the southwest, instead of from the east. So we should get drier and warmer air, and on that ridge the wind will be at our backs, or mostly so."

"So it will carry your spells?" asked Wilten.

Secca nodded.

"What if there is more rain?" questioned the over-captain.

"Then we wait. He won't be able to move either," Secca pointed out. She just hoped she was right. Then, she was hoping far more than was wise.

41

Under a clear sky, a strong and warm breeze blew from the south. The air was almost springlike as Secca and Richina rode eastward, near the head of the column of lancer companies from Loiseau and Synek. The day smelled clean, fresh, and Secca could not help but compare the brightness of the sky and the sunlight to what she worried lay before them.

"How do you feel?" she asked Richina.

"Good, but uneasy."

"You are just going to repair a road. That's all. That's one of the things you've been trained for. You will do well. I wouldn't ask you if I did not think you would." Secca kept her voice light and cheerful. "You're ready for this."

"Yes, lady." Richina did not quite meet Secca's eyes.

Stepan eased his mount up beside Secca's, riding on the shoulder of the road, far narrower than any major roads remaining in Defalk. "The scouts say that Mynntar has not broken camp, but that the lancers are sharpening blades." He smiled. "I know your glass showed that earlier, but I am an old armsman, and I prefer to confirm what I cannot see myself."

"He had planned to move tomorrow, you think?"

"I would guess so, although, if he finds we are riding, that all could change. And most suddenly."

"Best we repair the road and move more quickly," Secca said.

"As you can, sorceresses," Stepan replied, "there is no hurry until the road is replaced. Then, speed becomes most necessary."

As if on cue, the sandy-haired assistant sorceress began a soft vocalise.

In between her own vocalises, Secca went over spells in her thoughts as they continued to ride through a morning that seemed too bright and too fresh for the battle that lay ahead. First, they needed to repair the road, then deal with Mynntar. She pushed back the thought that the battle with Mynntar might well be only the first of many, if indeed the Sturinnese had decided to attack and conquer Liedwahr. She could only fight one battle at a time.

In less than a glass, Secca and the column had reined up and looked eastward from the hilltop. Fifty yards downhill, the old track, now corraded with miniature gullies from the rain, ended in churned mud, and ten yards below that the brown water of the small lake began.

To the east, the hilltop where the road resumed was empty, showing not even a scout.

"They have no scouts near here," Wilten said.

"That may be," offered Stepan, "but if the sorcery works, then there will be no swamp to stop them, and we must be ready to ride quickly."

"Our lancers are ready," Wilten affirmed.

"As are those of Synek." Stepan glanced to Secca. "Once your assistant is done . . ."

"The road can be used at once, but the players will have to pack their instruments and remount," Secca pointed out.

Richina dismounted near the top of the road crest. She handed the chestnut's reins to Albar, the young lancer Wilten had detailed to care for her mount and Secca's while they were engaged in sorcery. Richina walked downhill several yards, studying the ground and the swampy lake below before turning and walking back to her mount, where she extracted a sketch from the top of her saddlebag.

While Richina studied the sketch, comparing it to the land, to the south of her, the players dismounted, and shortly the discordant sound of tuning began.

Secca kept studying the eastern side of the ravaged road cut, but could see no scouts. The wind remained steady from the southwest. Finally, she dismounted, also handing the reins of her mount to Albar, before walking forward, so that she stood perhaps three yards uphill from Richina.

As the tuning died away, Palian looked directly at the younger sorceress. "We stand ready, sorceress."

Squaring her shoulders, Richina offered a faint smile, then cleared her throat. "You may begin, chief player."

"On my mark. . . . Mark!"

Standing behind and to the south of her apprentice, Secca forced herself to take a slow deep breath as she watched Richina and listened to the younger woman's spellsong.

> *". . . replicate the earth and stones.*
> *Place them in their proper zones . . .*
> *Set all firm, and set all square,*
> *weld them to their pattern there . . ."*

While the last words of the spellsong faded, an intense bluish glow blossomed over the swampy lowland that had once held road and bridge, a glow so bright that Stepan and Wilten looked away, as did most of the players.

The glow faded, revealing a causeway, one with a single archway for the stream, and faced with stone rip-rap and paved with the even stones of Defalk. The newly created causeway barely dipped between the two hills, while a deeper gorge had appeared between the hills and the arch of the bridgelike causeway.

Secca blinked. The hilltops on each side were lower, and the roadway was definitely stone-paved. She turned to Richina.

A broad smile crossed the sandy-haired young woman's face. "I . . . did it." Then, her face went blank and she began to crumple.

Secca rushed forward and grabbed Richina, managing to keep her from pitching forward despite the younger woman's considerably greater height and weight.

Richina was breathing . . . but she was pale.

Stepan and Wilten had their mounts beside Secca almost immediately.

Secca glanced at Wilten. "She did more than was necessary. She will be all right, if she has rest. I'll need someone to take care of her. She'll need water and biscuits as soon as she wakes . . ."

Wilten opened his mouth as if to complain.

"She saved more men than will be needed to care for her!" Secca snapped.

"My personal guards will serve her, lady," offered Stepan.

"Thank you."

"My lady . . . I meant no ill," Wilten pleaded.

"I'm sorry, Wilten," Secca apologized. "I was worried about her. She did more than I wanted because she wanted to make sure it was right." Secca hoped she hadn't upset the overcaptain too much.

Even before Secca could turn, two armsmen in Ebran green had appeared, apparently in response to a gesture Stepan had made and Secca had not even seen.

"We needs must ride now, Lady Secca," Stepan said.

As the two guards carried Richina to the side of the road and laid her on a cloak of some sort, Secca remounted, glancing back to see another pair of Stepan's guards riding up behind the exhausted apprentice.

"They will keep her safe," Stepan said to Secca.

"Thank you." Secca turned to Wilten. "Are your lancers ready?"

"Most ready, lady."

"We are almost ready to ride," called Palian. "A moment only." Her head turned. "Move, Bretnay!"

As the errant violino player scrambled into the saddle, Palian nodded in the direction of both Stepan and Secca.

"Where are the special archers?" asked Secca.

"Here, lady." The lead archer, Elfens, raised a graygloved hand from his mount on the shoulder of the road behind the mounts of the players. "We are ready to let fly any and all shafts that you require." The twinkling in his light brown eyes belied the somber tone of his words.

"We may require many shafts, Elfens. Stay close to the players."

"Yes, lady."

Even before Secca, Wilten, and Stepan reached the causeway, four scouts had quick-trotted out before the van and were riding swiftly eastward. One turned north and began to cross a brown-grassed meadow, while the others followed the road, drawing away from the main force.

The clop of hoofs on the stones of the causeway seemed almost reassuring.

"A solid road," Stepan said. "Would that we had more."

"You can see what it takes out of a sorceress," Secca pointed out, glancing to Wilten. "Had you seen such before, Wilten?"

"No, Lady Secca."

"Did she ... Was that because she is not experienced?" asked Stepan.

"She lacks experience. That is true, but we all have to start somewhere."

Stepan nodded. So did Wilten.

The standard bearers and then Wilten, Secca, and Stepan came to the end of the new causeway and continued eastward.

"Another half-dek," Stepan called. "We take the lane past the apple orchards to the north, and along the ridge line."

The lane was but wide enough for three riders abreast, and that with the shoulders of the outside riders brushing the bare twig-ends of the tree limbs.

Stepan glanced ahead. Wilten glanced back. Secca began a vocalise.

Outside of the breathing of mounts moving across

damp ground, and low murmurs, the air was silent, and
even the wind seemed fainter.

- At the sound of hoofs on the damp ground, the two
officers stiffened, and Secca broke off the second vocalise.

A scout rode toward the officers and the banner, reining up.

"They must have seen us, sers," panted the bearded
Ebran scout. "Like an anthill turned by a plow, everyone's yelling and trying to mount. They'll be riding out
real short like."

Secca turned in the saddle. "Palian! Delvor! We need
the players ready to play when we reach that ridge
ahead."

Stepan motioned to a lancer. "Have the first company
forward. To me."

"Yes, ser."

Secca and Stepan had not traveled more than a hundred yards farther when, from the the north, came the
sound of mounts, and charging uphill were a good score
of lancers in white, although they were still half a dek
away, and barely visible because of the curve in the
lane.

"Lady Secca . . . best get your players in place." Stepan turned his mount and rode to the side of the lane.
"To me! First company!"

Ebran lancers formed and simultaneously charged
downhill after Stepan. Mud flew into the air, striking
mounts, grass, ground, and tree trunks.

"Players! Players after me!" Secca urged the gray
mare toward the open ridge line that lay less than fifty
yards ahead. "Players!"

Riding alongside Secca was young Albar, bearing her
banner.

Secca reined up and turned in the saddle as the
mounts of the players appeared behind her.

Palian was already out of the saddle, uncasing her

violino with one hand and motioning players into place with the other.

Not far behind were Elfens and the archers, and they were scrambling to string bows and uncover the quivers that had shielded their shafts from the weather.

"Here!" snapped Secca. "Stand and play! The short flame song!"

The dissonance of tuning rose, and then fell.

Downhill to the north, and even to the sides, Secca could hear yells, the sound of metal on metal, horses crashing through underbrush. She cleared her throat, trying to call up the spell, facing toward the enemy camp a good two hundred yards below and to the north, her back to the wind—or to what had been the wind.

In the distance, thunder rolled. Secca glanced up, saw the sky was yet clear, and realized that the low rumbling was from the Sturinnese thunder-drums. The wind, which had been blowing out of the south, began to die away with the rising volume of the rhythmic drums.

A gust of wind whipped through Secca's hair—cold but dry, and from the north—blowing hard and into Secca's face. She turned. "Chief players?"

"Ready!" answered Palian.

Delvor merely nodded.

Secca waited for the second bar, and then began the spellsong.

"Turn to fire, turn to flame
all Ebrans who follow now Mynntar's name.
Turn to ashes, turn to dust . . .

As the sounds of the players rose, so did the wind, whistling, and seeming to carry Secca's words back at her.

A thin line of lightnings flashed out of the cloudless sky, but only at the base of the ridge, just beyond the underbrush, cutting through a score or so of the burgundy-clad lancers, but those behind, and those in white, kept fighting, moving toward the side approaches to the ridge, and to Secca and the players. More lancers from Loiseau surged in behind Stepan's companies, but the enemy forces continued to push uphill, if more slowly.

The rolling thunder of the Sturinnese drums intensified, and a greenish haze began to creep across the sky.

"The arrows, lady! The arrows!" Elfens' voice barely carried to Secca, so strong was the wind, for all that he was less than five yards behind her.

The arrows? What arrows? Secca blinked, trying to connect the words to what she was supposed to do, attempting to think as the thunder from the drums buffeted her and the players.

"The arrows. For the drums!" Elfens yelled.

For the drums?

Below and to the north, the groups of burgundy-clad lancers, untouched by either Defalkan blades or those of Stepan's lancers, or by Secca's spells, began to cut their way through Stepan's first company.

Arrows whistled toward the hilltop.

Secca shook her head. Her thoughts were as congealed as molasses in midwinter, but she turned to Palian. "The arrow song. The arrow song."

"The arrow song on my mark. On my mark . . ."

"Archers! To the sorceress! Nock and fire from right behind her!" Elfens voice was barely a whisper against gale that seemed to sweep out of the greenish northern sky.

The melody was ragged, but the pounding beat of the lutars of Delvor's second players seemed to steady the strings and horns, enough so Secca could think and sing.

> *"Heads of arrows, shot into the air,*
> *strike the drumskins, straight through there,*
> *rend the drums and those who play . . .*
> *for their spells and Darksong pay!"*

Even before Secca finished the last syllable, Elfens' voice burst forth from right behind Secca. "Again, lady! Again!"

"The arrow song once more!" Secca ordered.

"As many shafts as you can loose while she sings!" demanded Elfens.

The repetition of the arrow spell was stronger.

Abruptly, or so it seemed, the thunder died away . . . and so did the wind . . . only to resume with gusts from the south, from behind Secca.

"The flame song! Strong as you can make it!" demanded Secca.

"The flame song!"

As the players began the fourth spell, another set of arrows whispered by Secca. She heard a dull thud, but concentrated on the spellsong, knowing that she must finish the spell strongly, above all else.

"Turn to fire, turn to flame
all Ebrans who follow now Mynntar's name . . ."

This time, lightnings flashed all across the lower land below the ridge, so many that, momentarily, Secca could not see.

Her legs were shivering, and dayflashes sparked all through her vision. She slowly sank to her knees, hoping she had done enough. She could see at least two players were down, but whether they were wounded or prostrated from their efforts she could not tell.

Someone was urging water on her, and she drank slowly. The figure in green was an Ebran from Synek, but it didn't matter as she took another swallow and then a mouthful of dry biscuit. After a time, she slowly stood, and surveyed the ridge area.

Numbly, she looked down, to see Albar, the young standard bearer, his eyes open, unmoving, a heavy war arrow through his chest. One of the Ebran guards was easing a shaft from the arm of a comrade.

Elfens was kneeling beside a fallen archer, and Secca tottered several steps, her sabre striking her leg, so unsteady was her gait. The chief archer looked up. "His leg. Won't be dancing soon, but with the alcohol elixir, he'll recover."

"Thank you," said Secca quietly. "For the reminder about the arrows."

A brief smile flitted across the long face. "Be a poor archer who didn't know when he was needed, lady."

"But a wise one to know when to speak." Her smile was as fleeting as his.

Secca turned. Below, beyond the brush, the only moving figures were those in green.

"Lady?"

Secca glanced up as Wilten reined his mount to a halt.

"They are riding away, like the wind."

"After all that . . . ?"

"When the drums fell silent, all those in the rear of Mynntar's force turned and fled, as if hot irons had been applied to their mounts, especially those in white."

"The Sturinnese." Secca nodded.

"Your fires . . . they slaughtered more than five companies of the enemy," Wilten said slowly. "And the thunder-drums are no more."

"Have them burned—the drums—or what remains of them." Secca paused. "How many did we lose?"

"More than a company's worth, Lady Secca."

Secca winced. She wasn't supposed to lose one part in four of her own force in the first battle.

"Arms Commander Stepan . . . he turned them back . . . or they would have overrun the ridge from the east before you could use your spells. Two companies came and circled behind us." Wilten shook his head. "Fought like demons, they did, but we pushed them back."

"Wilten . . . I appreciate deeply all you have done. Had you not held our rear, all would have been lost." Secca hoped this would help against her earlier outburst.

"I fear I still have much to learn, and I appreciate also your patience."

"I could not have stood before all those shafts with naught but a song, lady. We each must do as we can." Wilten nodded, both accepting and dismissing her words. "Still . . . without Commander Stepan . . ."

"It took all of us." Secca paused as the older arms commander rode tiredly onto the ridge and toward Secca and Wilten.

Stepan slowed his mount and then halted before the sorceress. His trousers were smeared with mud, blood, and other stains. He wore a grim smile. "They have turned back, and they ride eastward, taking a lane back toward the main road. We should move to hold the road at the causeway."

"So they don't get behind us and have an open course to Synek?" Secca began to trudge toward her mount.

"Aye. They have half again as many lancers as do we, and with half they could hold the causeway."

"I understand." Secca forced herself to climb into the saddle. "Players! Prepare to ride!"

"Prepare to ride!" echoed Palian, and then Delvor.

Secca watched for a moment, as several players had to be helped into their saddles. Elfens simply lifted his injured archer into the saddle of his mount. Then she eased her mount back along the trampled track her force had rutted into the damp ground, riding silently beside an equally silent Stepan.

Her first battle, and another like it would be her last.

How had Anna done it? It had sounded so easy. She had sung spells, and the enemy armsmen had died. Secca had known it wouldn't be that easy . . . but the sheer confusion and speed of what had occurred still had left her numb.

It was yet before midday, and close to fifteen score lancers from both forces were dead. Richina was exhausted. Secca was exhausted, and few of the players would be able to play in even rough tune or rhythm before the morrow.

Then . . . she had no commanders who had ever fought a pitched battle. She had never been in one. Only Stepan had that experience, and without his calm, and that of Elfens, she doubted that they would have managed the victory they had, such as it was.

42

The silken walls of the tent billowed in a brisk morning breeze as Secca handed a soft apple, a wedge of cheese, and a chunk of stale bread to Richina, who sat, pale and shivering, on the small cot in the tent she shared with Secca. Secca took another apple and began to eat, alternating between fruit and bread, with an occasional bite of the cheese she disliked but knew she needed to keep up her strength.

The younger sorceress ate the bread and some of the cheese, slowly, followed by several swallows of water, before speaking. "I feel so weak. All I did was one little spell," Richina murmured. "Just one little spell, and . . ."

"It wasn't such a little spell. You built a solid bridge and a causeway, and created and paved almost a half dek of roadway. Do you see why I wanted you to keep the visualization simple?" Secca asked.

"Yes, lady." Richina massaged her forehead. "It still throbs so much. Does your head ache?"

"A little." Secca lied. Her head was splitting, and everywhere she looked, she saw dayflashes, or, at times, nothing at all, or scenes with huge holes in them.

"You ought to eat more."

Rather than admit she needed more sustenance, Secca broke off a chunk of bread and chewed it, ignoring the dryness and the lack of taste. By the time she had gone through several more chunks and a wedge of cheese, she could feel the worst of the headache subsiding, and the dayflashes were gone.

"You still need to eat more, lady," said Richina.

"I was worrying about Mynntar, and it's hard to think about eating when I'm worrying."

"You will have more to worry about if you cannot call upon your sorcery," Richina pointed out with the practicality that recalled the younger sorceress's mother to Secca.

Secca smiled briefly. "There is that." She extended another wedge of the dry white cheese to Richina. From outside the tent came low murmurs, and Secca repressed a sigh.

"It was a good bridge and causeway, wasn't it?" asked the sandy-haired young woman.

"It *is* very good, perhaps too good for Lord Hadrenn, and once he sees it, he will complain that he has none such."

"Was that why—"

"No. You saw what it did to you. You still do not know how much energy a spell can take from you."

Richina nodded slowly. "It felt good . . . until afterward."

"As do many things unwise in life." Secca stood. "Finish the bread and cheese. I hear a few voices." She stepped from the small tent.

In the morning light, Palian, Delvor, Stepan, and Wilten were all standing outside the tent when Secca emerged.

"Mynntar remains bivouacked ten deks east of here," Wilten said immediately, inclining his head to Stepan.

Secca felt guilty that she hadn't used the glass to find that out, but the way her head had felt the night before she wasn't sure she could have called up her own reflection in a mirror, much less discovered what the rebellious Ebran lord was doing. "He's probably waiting for another rainstorm."

"The wind has shifted, and there are clouds forming in the northeast," Wilten pointed out.

"How many lancers has he?" Secca asked warily.

"The scouts think seventeen companies—thirty-four score," offered Stepan.

Nearly half again what Secca and Stepan had between them, and that was after losing perhaps four or five companies to Secca's flame spell.

"Still?" blurted Secca. "I had not realized so many had escaped."

"He had far more lancers than the scouts saw," Stepan replied calmly.

With seventeen companies, and if another rainstorm like the last arrived . . . Secca shook her head, then asked, "How are the players?"

Palian and Delvor exchanged glances.

"They could play one or two spells—if everything went perfectly?" the small sorceress pursued.

"Bretnay and Elset cannot play," Palian said. "Tomorrow, perchance."

"Woryl is unlikely to offer much," Delvor added. "Nor Hyell."

Secca nodded slowly. "I suppose the lancers are tired."

"They will fight as they must," Stepan said.

"Your lancers will support you with all they possess," added Wilten.

Secca bestowed a crooked smile on the overcaptain and the commander. "What you say is that they will fight, but they cannot do their best, and we are outnumbered."

"There is that," admitted Wilten.

"I need to get close to Mynntar's camp," Secca finally said. "There may be something that I can do."

"He has scouts and pickets everywhere," Wilten pointed out.

"Not that close—just within a half-dek, or even a dek." Secca glanced to Stepan. "Your scouts know this land best. Can they get me within a half-dek of Mynntar's camp, perhaps on a hill or across a gully—sometime just before

sunset? Being close is more important than being able to
see."

"You plan some sorcery?" Stepan frowned.

"Some small sorcery, with the lutar, not the players,"
admitted Secca. "Perhaps it will give us some small advantage."

"It *may* be possible. Best I talk to the older scouts. If
you would excuse me, Lady Secca?" The Ebran arms commander stepped back, bowed, and turned.

"Would practice hurt or help the players?" asked Secca.

"Help, if we support no spells," replied Palian.

"Unless we are attacked, I plan no spells for the players."

Both Delvor and Palian nodded.

"It has been long since Defalk has sent armsmen to fight
battles such as this," Secca said. "Or players. But I do not
think that this will be the last battle, nor will the next. Nor
the one after that."

"Nor I," observed Palian. "We stand ready to do what
we must."

Secca only hoped she was as ready as Palian and her
players.

43

The late afternoon sun hung barely above the hills on
the southern side of the River Syne, its light diffusing
through the silken walls of the tent, when Secca glanced
at Richina. "Could you get me some bread and some
cheese? I'll need to eat before I go."

"Of course, lady." The sandy-haired young woman, who
was learning to be more than an apprentice, with so much
more to learn before she would be a full sorceress, slipped
from the small tent.

Secca's wry smile was for herself. She was discovering that there was much yet that she had to learn about applying sorcery to battles. She could but hope she understood how much and what before it was too late.

She lifted the second saddlebag—the one without clothes, but which contained a score or more of small bottles, and other items taken from the sealed storeroom. After unfastening the bag and laying out almost twenty bottles, she studied them, then reordered them, leaving five bottles filled with yellow-green tinted crystals on the top where she would be able to reach them easily. Then she refastened the saddlebags and laid them on the foot of the narrow cot.

Next came the lutar. She checked the strings and the tuning, strumming several chords before replacing it in its case.

The tent flap opened, and with it came Richina and a gust of dry and cold air that reminded Secca that winter was fast approaching. Through the momentarily open flap, Secca had seen that the sun had set.

"Here you are, lady." Richina extended an entire loaf of bread, and a large wedge of white cheese.

"Thank you." Using her belt knife, Secca sliced off the layer of green mold on what had been the outside of the cheese wheel.

"You plan sorcery tonight, do you not?"

"I do. I wish it were not necessary, but I cannot risk any more losses in open battles. There is a Sturinnese fleet sailing northward to create more mischief—probably at Elahwa, but possibly at Narial or even Encora. The glass does not show where those vessels go. Neserea may be on the brink of a civil war. If that fleet goes to Narial, Jolyn must go to Dumar. That means that we will see no lancers coming to reinforce us, nor other sorceresses." Secca broke off a chunk of cheese and took a bite from it.

"What will you do?" asked Richina.

Secca finished the mouthful of cheese and some bread,

washing it down with a swallow of water before she replied. "What I can. What I must."

"Might I help?"

"Study your spells, the battle spells. You may have to use them before we are done. Sooner, if I cannot do what I plan."

Richina frowned.

Secca smiled faintly. "What I plan is easier than battle spells, but one never knows." She continued to eat, although she had to force the last of both bread and cheese down. Yet, if what she tried tonight failed, she would need all the strength she possessed on the morrow. Even if her planned sorcery worked, she might be called upon.

After she finished eating, Secca began a vocalise. She couldn't very well warm up her voice anywhere close to Mynntar's camp.

Her throat and cords felt slightly raw, and she coughed up mucus on the second vocalise, something that usually didn't happen to her.

"Should you do this . . . tonight?" asked Richina when Secca took a long swallow of spelled clean water to clear her throat.

"If I do not act tonight, then more will die tomorrow." Secca took another swallow, then corked the bottle and began another vocalise.

After a time, the rawness seemed to subside. Secca fastened the green leather riding jacket and picked up saddlebags and then the lutar.

Richina followed Secca from the tent.

Outside in the deepening dusk, alerted by Secca's warming up, Wilten and Stepan stood waiting. Farther away— to the east—a score or so of Stepan's lancers were mounted and waiting, their green tunics appearing almost gray in the twilight that was fast nearing full darkness.

Wilten stepped forward. "I would feel better if we accompanied you, lady."

"As I told Richina, it is best that we do not hazard all when we need not. Stepan and his men will do their best."

A wry expression crossed Secca's face. "They have far more to lose than do we, and he has more lancers than do we."

Wilten nodded. "Still . . ."

"I know, and I appreciate your concern for me. There will be much left, much left, for you and your men. This is just the beginning. I am most grateful for your care." With as warm a smile as she could manage, Secca turned and walked toward the gray. She fastened the saddlebags in place, then the lutar, and mounted.

"Like this not . . ." Wilten's words to Richina carried as she turned the gray mare toward the waiting lancers.

"Your overcaptain is not pleased," offered Stepan as he eased his mount beside Secca.

"I know. But I would not hazard both senior commanders and both sorceresses. And you and your men know the land far better than do Wilten's."

"That is true." Stepan laughed softly. "But he knows not me, and all officers distrust that which they do not know."

"You guarded me once, and did so well," Secca pointed out. She paused. "Did you counsel father to send me to Falcor?"

"No. That was his decision. I agreed with it, but then I was only a lead armsman in a small holding, and no one asked me. And you were a girl child to be married off to some old lord when the time came. Now, you are a powerful lady and a sorceress, and I am an old arms commander."

Secca shook her head. "Not so old."

"Then why do I feel old?" asked the silver-haired man.

"Because you remember me as a child, but that does not make you old."

Stepan was the one to shake his head.

Secca smiled faintly.

"Yusar, lead on," Stepan ordered as he and Secca neared the front of the line of lancers. "No words, no torches."

"Yes, ser."

Secca glanced over her shoulder, back at the camp that

seemed so small for an effort to stop a revolt and whatever else might be brewing. Clearly, she wasn't the battle sorceress that Anna had been. Just as obviously, she had to stop Mynntar. With the players in the shape they were in, they couldn't take another battle like the last—not soon.

Spell-singing and battle-spell-singing were definitely different.

Yusar led the column along the main road for less than a dek before turning northward on a trail so narrow that there was barely room for a single mount in the space between an ancient hedgerow and an empty ditch, partly filled in places with a few patches of slush and dark and stagnant water.

They followed the hedgerow for only about half a dek, before turning eastward again, across a sodden meadow where each hoof seemed to *squush*, but the meadow was narrow. On the far side, there was a wagon path beside a rail fence that led up a long and gradual incline. A dek farther on, and Secca could see a dark mass looming to the east.

Overhead, high in the sky by itself, hung the tiny disk of Darksong, surrounded by starpoints of white that almost seemed redder with Darksong nearby. Superstition or not, Secca didn't care for doing the kind of sorcery she had in mind under the red moon. Then, perhaps the red moon was chastising her. She shook her head.

Stepan eased his mount back toward Secca and said in a low voice, "Their camp is on the far side of the woods, only about half a dek. On all other sides are open fields, and their sentries look down."

Yusar reined up where the path turned back south beside the woods, and the lancers reined up as well.

"This is as close as we dare go . . ." Stepan said quietly.

Secca dismounted.

The arms commander eased his mount toward Secca and silently took the gray's reins.

Secca unfastened the lutar and set the case on the damp grass beside the narrow path, in front of the gray, before turning back to her mount. She opened the top of the right saddlebag and took out the five bottles, setting them in a row on the clay and opening each in turn. Then she removed the lutar from its case and checked the tuning, as quickly and as quietly as possible.

Finally, she took a silent deep breath and faced eastward, toward the camp that she knew was on the far side of the small forest—or overly ample woodlot.

Two chords to get the feel, and then she sang the spell, trying to visualize what she needed to happen.

> *"Seek and carry through this night's air*
> *crystals strong to Mynntar, camped o'er there.*
> *Take this heavy stuff; infuse through song,*
> *within the blood and sinew strong,*
> *within the brain and heart to dwell*
> *so no other battles will he live to tell . . .*
>
> *Then distribute all the rest*
> *through the blood of his captains best . . ."*

As the words and chords died away, Secca swallowed, then quickly recased the lutar in the darkness. She could hear nothing, nor had she felt either harmony or dissonance. She bent down and glanced at the bottles, lifting one in her gloved hand. It felt lighter. Leaving the bottles, she remounted.

"We can go," she whispered to Stepan.

"Good . . . hear voices coming," he hissed back.

Secca wasn't sure that she did, but was more than happy to ride back down the path, and then along the hedgerow until they were on the main road, headed westward toward their encampment.

A good half-glass passed on the return ride before some murmurings of the lancers who escorted her were loud enough for Secca to discern.

"What she do . . . ?"

"Doesn't seem happy . . ."

"Mayhap . . . didn't work . . ."

"Mayhap it did . . . and tomorrow we'll be paying for it . . ."

Neither Secca nor Stepan spoke until the lights of the cookfires of the camp were again visible.

"Might I ask . . . ?" ventured Stepan.

"I used sorcery to try to slay Mynntar and his captains. The spells took far less effort than calling forth flames or lightnings or directing arrows against thunderdrums."

"If it works . . . then his lancers might retreat." Stepan sounded dubious. "Or they might attack from anger."

"One way or another, it should help, if only to remove good leaders." Secca hoped for more than that, knowing the players would not be at their best on the morrow.

"His brother might follow the same course, a season hence."

"We'll have to go to Dolov, one way or another," Secca pointed out.

"You would slay both?"

"If need be," Secca admitted. "If I can."

"You seem displeased, Lady Sorceress."

"I am. Not at you, but because of what I must do."

"Ever always was war such," Stepan replied. "And failing to act soon has always meant more who die and more who suffer."

"So it is said." Secca wondered, but did those who began wars, like Mynntar, or his father before him, rationalize their actions in the same way?

Was war always like this? Where each side used what it could, Mynntar pressing and slaughtering under weather that inhibited sorcery, and she, using sorcery and poison under the cloak of night?

Did it have to be? In Anna's later years it had not, but had that been because she had used such overwhelming force in the early years that none wanted to displease her and provoke her to call forth such again?

Secca took a deep breath.

Stepan glanced at her, but did not comment.

44

MANSUUS, MANSUUR

The snow drifts past the study windows, almost lazily, and so infrequently that none has collected on the railings without, nor on the meadows or bare fields across the gray waters of the Toksul River from the palace. Chill radiates from the glass panes, and heavy maroon hangings have been drawn across all of the windows, except for the two wide frames behind the Liedfuhr's desk.

Kestrin stands before the desk, and the papers on it, reading the scroll that Bassil has just placed in his hands.

"What does your sister write that no one else will?" asks Bassil after a time.

"How—because there would be no one else who would wish me to know the morass in Neserea?"

"Exactly, sire." Bassil bows slightly.

When he finishes rereading the lines again, Kestrin shakes his head. "She suggests that this Belmar bribed the armsmen, and then he ambushed them, to prove the need for a strong Lord High Counselor . . . or, more likely, a return to a Prophet of Music. There are rumors that he knows sorcery, but no one is willing to say such." He turns and looks out at the intermittent snow flakes. "Belmar himself cannot have the golds to bribe an entire company and two levels of officers . . . and that means the Sea-Priests. What a disaster . . ."

"And what of Captain Cyrn and Overcaptain Tein?"

"I can't believe that they thought I wouldn't find out." Bassil clears his throat.

"They knew that I would, and they still . . . ?" Kestrin swallows. "They don't think I will punish them because they think it will look like I'm covering up my own incompetence?"

"Captain Cyrn is dead. You cannot punish him more," Bassil points out. "And if you punish Tein . . ."

"All my officers will think that I'm making him the scapegoat. If I do nothing, then it will appear as though I am weak-willed." Kestrin smiles coldly. "Better I be considered vicious and spiteful than weak. Continue with the plans for a public execution. Oh . . . and even if we have to plant the coins, make sure someone finds a hoard of golds somewhere in the overcaptain's possessions."

"I think we can do that, sire, and it is probably the best that can be done at present." Bassil bows and waits.

"So . . ." Kestrin draws out the word. "We have the Sea-Priests trying to weaken me, and to foment discord and rebellion in Neserea . . . and who knows what else in Liedwahr. The lord holders of Neserea are petitioning that Annayal consort to someone suitable—immediately. They fear that if she does not, the rule of Neserea will go to a scion of Dumar . . . or worse, that I will move armsmen into Neserea, and that, in time, I will annex the land." Kestrin snorts. "As if any of the three sorceresses would allow it."

"Are they strong enough to stand against Mansuur?" asks Bassil.

"Who knows? That is not the question, and you know it, wise overcaptain Bassil. How many lords of Defalk have died of accidents, strange fluxes, or otherwise in their beds, who went to sleep in the flush of health?"

"You think they have stooped to such? Those most honorable ladies?" Bassil's eyes contain a grim glint.

"Honorable? That is such a noble-sounding word, and it conceals more violence and dishonesty than any other. As for them, I doubt there is little to which they would not stoop to save Defalk—and Liedwahr—from a bloody and prolonged war." Kestrin smiles. "Just as you—or I—

would find it difficult not to do the same were Mansuur so threatened."

"And what will you do?"

"What I must. As will you."

Bassil nods slowly.

Outside, the first flakes of snow that foreshadow winter drift by the glass.

45

The sound of a trumpet echoed through the thin silk panels of the small tent. Secca bolted upright, barely managing to keep from tipping over the narrow cot on which she had been sleeping, fitfully and far from easily.

She blinked, rubbing gummy eyes. Outside it was barely light, a good half-glass or more before dawn, she judged, as she fumbled for tunic and trousers and boots.

"Lady . . . that was the alarm." Richina said.

"I know. Get dressed." Secca finished throwing herself into her riding clothes and green leather jacket. After belting on her sabre, she scrambled from the tent, past the pair of lancer guards.

Wilten was half-running, half-scurrying through the grayish gloom toward her. "The Ebrans . . . those under Mynntar, that were under Mynntar . . . they're forming up and preparing for battle . . ." stammered the overcaptain.

Forming up? How could they, without officers? Secca's hand went to her mouth, recalling the exact words of the spell. She had killed the best of Mynntar's officers, not all of them. While she had wanted to spare as many as possible, the effect was likely to be the opposite.

"How did you find out?"

"Arms Commander Stepan's scouts."

Richina staggered from the tent into the predawn gray, glancing at Wilten, then at Secca.

"Richina . . . find Palian and Delvor, and tell them we need to have the players ready to ride and play."

"Yes, lady."

"Don't forget your sabre!"

Richina nodded and turned.

"You intend to give battle?" asked Wilten.

"Why not? It will take them a glass or more to reach us, and we can take the hill to the east long before that. The wind will be at our back."

"Then why do they attack now?" questioned Wilten.

"To catch us by surprise, I'm sure. It isn't even dawn."

Palian and Delvor walked swiftly toward Secca and Wilten. Trailing them was Richina.

"They are attacking, lady?" asked Palian.

"It looks as such," Secca admits. "Are your players able to play a strong flame song?"

"Once, perchance twice."

"That may suffice." Secca turned to Wilten. "If you would form up our lancers. Leave the camp. Just form up."

"Yes, lady."

Secca ignored his dubious tone, turning to retrieve her lutar in case more was needed than the players could provide. Then she hurried to the tieline behind the tent where she began to saddle the gray. When she had finished, and as she was mounting, Richina scurried up with cheese and bread.

"You must eat as you ride, or you will not have the strength you need."

"Thank you." Secca looked down. "Get some for yourself and then join me. But eat."

Richina grinned and held up another loaf. "Yes, lady."

Secca smiled, then glanced to the south where the players scurried to and fro, almost like ants.

"Just your instruments!" snapped Palian. "Now!" The chief player glanced up. "Lady?"

"Join us at the banner when you are ready."

Palian nodded, then turned to her players. "Lances and shafts don't wait until you're ready! Mount up now."

Secca eased the gray forward toward the column where Stepan's lancers seemed to be forming. Behind them, in less ordered array, were the lancers of Loiseau. Secca frowned, but said nothing as she rode along the column toward the standard bearer, another young lancer. This one she knew, although it took her a moment to come up with the lancer's name. "Good morning, Achar."

"Good morning, lady." Achar bowed his head.

"Greetings," offered Stepan. "I see your players are preparing to follow you."

"And you," said Secca as she reined in the gray, who promptly side-stepped before halting. "Thank you for the warning."

Stepan nodded. "I set scouts last night."

"You thought this would happen, didn't you?"

"I had fears." Stepan looked through the gray light. "Those armsmen who have no qualms about striking a man down from behind in battle muster great anger when they see their officers and comrades struck down by what they cannot see."

Secca paused, not sure what to say for a moment, before replying, "Each side says its cause is just, and that justifies any weapon and tactic, but it is unfair for the other side to use such tactics and weapons?"

"Of course," Stepan said dryly. He glanced back at the lancers forming up. "You think this is wise?"

"No battle is wise, I'm learning." Secca shifted her weight in the saddle. "Some are less unwise than others. Whoever is leading their forces is doing it to try to take command of the forces or for revenge. He's also not going to be their best commander." At least, Secca hoped that had been the result of her spellsong of the previous night. "It's dry, and the wind will be behind us, and we can take the high ground."

"If they do not attack?"

"Then we wait and see."

Stepan nodded slowly, then turned and stood in his stirrups. "First company forward!" He reseated himself. "Best there be a van."

"You have more experience than do we, and I defer to you."

Stepan laughed. "Most of it is more than a score of years behind me."

"Better than none," Secca suggested.

"You will have more than you wish before this is over, I fear."

"So do I."

Stepan glanced over his shoulder. "Your players are riding this way."

"Palian has experience. She was with Anna through all the early wars."

"She sounded like a most irate officer."

"Players do have a feeling that they are . . . not common," Secca ventured.

"In battle, all are common." Stepan gestured. "Hold for the players, then follow!" He turned back and eased his mount, a gelding that was neither smooth-coated nor shaggy like a raider beast, forward toward the road.

Secca looked back, but Palian and Delvor led the players behind Secca and her four guards. As the entire column began to move, a single figure cantered along the shoulder of the road. Richina slowed her mount and eased into the column behind Secca and Stepan.

The combined forces of the players, Secca's lancers, and those of Stepan were formed up in an arc on the rise to the south of the main road in less than half a glass from the trumpet alert. In the center of the arc were Secca, Richina, and the players.

Palian and Delvor had the players running through warm-up melodies, while Secca and Richina worked on vocalises. After finishing a vocalise, Secca paused and cleared her throat, then took a swallow from her water bottle.

Stepan rode across the low crest of the hill and reined

up. "They are less than a quarter of a dek to the east, just beyond the curve in the road."

"Will they attack immediately?"

The older arms commander shrugged. "I would not. What this officer will do, I could not say."

"I will try to use the spells before your men must use their blades . . ."

"I understand, lady, but they cannot stand and wait, not against a full charge."

"How far . . . ?"

"No less than a hundred yards."

"I will do what I can," Secca promised. She turned. "Chief players!"

"Yes, lady?"

"Have your players stand ready. The flame song."

"The flame song," Palian acknowledged, her voice strong but flat.

Secca watched as the burgundy-clad lancers appeared, then rode forward and wheeled off the road, smartly moving into three masses—one opposite the right side of the rise where waited Secca's forces, one mass for the center, directly downhill from Secca and the players, and one for the left.

"Stand ready!" Secca called.

"Stand ready!" echoed Stepan and Wilten, Stepan on the left, Wilten and Secca's lancers on the right.

"A direct assault—up the hill and against the wind," murmured Richina. "Stupid . . . against sorcery."

Only if such an attack failed, thought Secca. "The flame spell!"

Palian swallowed, then repeated the command. So did Delvor.

"At my mark!" Secca watched, then, as a trumpet call bugled across the orange-lit dawn, the burgundy lancers charged, three masses moving together. Secca dropped her arm and waited for the notes to rise through the cool crisp air, air that would carry her words over the advancing lancers.

"Mark!" echoed Palian.

Compared to the efforts in the rain and of the night before, the flame song seemed almost effortless, the wind at her back, the rising sun to her right.

"Turn to fire, turn to flame
all those who stand against our name,
turn to ashes, turn to dust . . ."

Even halfway through the words, lightnings began to flare across Secca's vision, line after line of flame and fire. Thin streaks of black greasy smoke stretched northwest, almost in straight angled lines.

As the music of the players and Secca's words died away, the hillside ground rumbled once, then again, and Secca had to shift her weight to keep her balance. A single chime, harmonic but harsh, reverberated through her, a chorded chime that only she and Richina and perhaps a handful of players might have heard.

Not a figure stirred on the browned and blackened grass and damp clay below the rise. The thin lines of black smoke continued to rise from the heaped and blackened figures that lay strewn everywhere Secca's eyes looked. Her stomach twisted upon itself with just the hint of the stench of burned flesh—only a hint because the wind remained at her back, the wind that had carried her words and the accompaniment of both first and second players.

Then . . . why did she smell anything? She swallowed again.

The dark cloud that had momentarily shrouded the sky above the battle already had begun to dissipate, torn apart by the brisk dry wind out of the southwest.

Secca turned toward the players. "You may stand down." Her voice was suddenly hoarse, suddenly rough, but not because of overuse. This . . . this was not like the first battle, where the deaths had fallen on both sides, and been concealed by rain and thunder-drums and brush and trees. Nor like her stealthy efforts of the night before, where she had seen naught of what she had wrought.

Her eyes went back to the blackened corpses of men and mounts. A few moments ago, all had been alive, and vital. Now . . . they were dead. Yet, two days previous, they and their Sea-Priest drummers had attempted to do the same to her and her forces.

She shook her head, swallowing back bile.

After a last look at the sudden carnage, Secca walked slowly back toward her mount. Richina, pale and almost green-looking, handed back the reins to the older sorceress wordlessly. Just as silently, Secca took them and slowly mounted the gray.

Both Stepan and Wilten rode from the flanks of the lancers who had never even needed to charge.

"None survived, lady," Wilten said slowly.

Stepan rode up, nearing and reining up to the left of Secca somewhat later than Wilten. "I must also ask . . . what spell did you use, Lady Secca?"

"A spell that flamed all disloyal to Lord Hadrenn and Defalk," Secca admitted.

Stepan took a deep breath. "Your spell flamed a score of my lancers, lady."

Secca bowed her head. "For that I am sorry, arms commander, but last night, I tried to spare those who were not to blame. This morning, I could not risk sparing any who might prove disloyal."

"More than sixteen score lancers and officers lie dead on the hillside," Wilten said. "Surely . . . some . . . might have . . ."

"That would have been Darksong. What would you have me do?" she replied tiredly. "Have the rest of our lancers slaughtered in the next rain or snowstorm? Or lose more lancers when we must still take Dolov?"

"Dolov?" Stepan's eyebrows rose.

So did Wilten's.

"He has a younger brother, has he not? If we do not

finish this business, what is to keep the Sturinnese from doing the same a season or a year from now?" Secca laughed, without mirth. "We can spend a day or two making ready for the trip, but we cannot tarry longer." She looked at Stepan. "Lord Hadrenn always wanted to be uncontested lord of Ebra. If we take Dolov, that he will be."

"He did not wish that so much as he wished no other to be lord above him," Stepan suggested.

"What of Haddev?"

"He will be a stronger lord."

Secca wasn't certain whether that would be good or bad. Then, there was little about which she was certain, save that any sorcery that would allow her to prevail would create more deaths—or that any Sturinnese foothold in Liedwahr boded great ill and dissonance.

46

WEI, NORDWEI

Snow has fallen across Wei, but the sun is out, and beyond the window, the light is corruscatingly brilliant. Ashtaar must squint as she looks down the hill toward the river and the harbor piers she cannot actually see. After a moment, she draws the shutters to reduce the glare, but leaves them positioned so that the remaining light falls across the straight-backed chair facing her and the desk. Then she reseats herself at the desk, picking up the first scroll from the pile on the left side.

She has read four scrolls when there is a knock on the study door. "Yes?"

"Escadra, Leader Ashtaar."

"Come in."

Escadra steps inside the door and immediately bows. "You asked for reports . . . some matters of interest."

Ashtaar gestures toward the chair across the table desk from her, set at a slight angle.

The chunky seer eases herself down into the chair and into the line of sunlight that strikes her face. The seer squints against the glare.

"Go ahead," prompts the older woman.

"You may recall that Lord High Counselor Clehar was killed in the battle east of Narial . . . ?"

"That was last week. Is there something new?" Swallowing as if to stifle a cough, Ashtaar picks up the large square of green cloth from the desk, holding it in her left hand. "Something that affects us?"

"His brother Fehern has assumed the title and position of Lord High Counselor," Escadra announces. "Without even notifying Lord Robero, from what we can scry."

"In a time of invasion and trouble, that is understandable," Ashtaar replies dryly.

"We do not believe that the Sturinnese killed Lord Clehar. There is a partly trained sorcerer who remains close to Fehern all the time." Escadra moistens her lips nervously. "His demeanor is like unto that of the Sea-Priests. Fehern consults him often. Since the death of his brother, Feharn avoids battle, and towns in Dumar are falling quickly to the Sea-Priests."

Ashtaar nods. "What else?"

"Yesterday, the Sorceress-Protector of the East destroyed Mynntar and his forces, and close to ten companies of Sturinnese lancers. They were marching toward Synek. She also used a smaller sorcery the night before."

"Do you know what that was?"

"No, your Mightiness."

Ashtaar frowns.

Escadra shifts her weight uneasily in the hard straight-backed chair.

"I have yet another charge for you, Escadra."

"Yes, Leader?" The seer's voice is somehow subservient yet wary.

Ashtaar laughs but once before she speaks. "I am not

that unobservant, even approaching my dotage."

Escadra waits.

"As you can, watch the Lady of the Shadows and her followers."

The seer's eyebrows lift.

Ashtaar coughs, harshly, then covers her mouth with the dark green cloth. After several more violent coughs, she sets the cloth by the black agate oval and takes a slow deep breath. Finally, she speaks. "We have a Sea-Priest sorcerer in Neserea, aiding or teaching a Neserean holder who claims descent from the Prophet of Music. There is another Sturinnese sorcerer in Dumar. There are thunder-drums in Ebra, and two Sturinnese fleets. There are three powerful sorceresses in Defalk, and they have at least two strong assistants." She pauses. "And Lord Robero cannot best the Sea-Priests without those sorceresses."

"That is most likely so, your Mightiness." Escadra shifts her weight in the chair, as if trying to escape the glare without seeming to do so.

"What do the Ladies of the Shadows most oppose? Is our Lady of the Shadows any different?"

"I understand, Leader."

"Good. I need not tell you more. But do not neglect the sorceresses."

"No, Leader Ashtaar."

"You have done well." Ashtaar smiles, then nods as she picks up the scroll she had been reading. "You may go."

Escadra stands and bows, then turns and slips from the study.

Once the door is closed, Ashtaar turns and closes the study shutters all the way, cutting off the glare from sun and snow.

$\int$ ecca took another bite of the hard white cheese as she sat on one side of the table in the dining hall of Hadrenn's palace and listened to Palian. A single set of candles in a double sconce offered the only illumination in a room seemingly as chill as the cold and clear day beyond the dark wood-paneled walls.

"Yesterday . . . it was a blow to some of the players. Bretnay woke sobbing this morning, and Rowal would speak to none," Palian said.

Secca glanced at Delvor.

The chief of the second players nodded. "More of mine are like stunned bullocks. It is one thing to see a pit open in a hillside, and another to see scores upon scores of men and mounts turned into charred flesh."

Behind Delvor's shoulder, Richina winced at Delvor's words, then took a long swallow of the light and bitter ale that Secca had trouble drinking, but was swallowing slowly because she didn't wish to spend the effort to sing a spell to provide clean water. Although Secca did not voice it, the sights and smells of the carnage had indeed forced a relocation back to Hadrenn's palace, both for a day or two of rest and resupply, and for some better planning for the campaign that lay ahead. All were clearly needed.

After the battle—or slaughter—Secca understood why Anna had preferred shadow sorcery. Fewer died, and usually the guilty, while in a battle all too many died who were at most but guilty of following the wrong leader. Yet people thought she and Anna were cold-blooded? What was kind and humane—or honorable—about sending scores upon scores to certain death in massed battles?

At a cough from the door, Palian turned, then stood as Hadrenn walked into the hall. So did Delvor and Richina. Out of form alone, so did Secca.

"Frengal said that you might be here, Lady Sorceress."

"We are here," Secca replied.

Hadrenn glanced at Palian, then Delvor.

Secca nodded at the players, then at Richina, and the three slipped out of the hall, leaving the Lord High Counselor and the Sorceress-Protector of the East by themselves in the dimly lit hall.

"Stepan informs me that your sorcery cost us a score of lancers." Hadrenn's voice was bland.

"It did. That was far less than a battle would have."

"And ensured that none survived who would be hostile to Defalk."

"That was not the intent," Secca pointed out, "although I doubt that Lord Robero would be greatly troubled by it, nor should you be."

Hadrenn frowned, fingering his chin, then studied Secca for a long moment. "You are much like the Lady Anna."

Secca waited to see if Hadrenn would add more.

"If my lancers do not accompany you, will you still travel to Dolov?" asked Hadrenn.

"I must, if only to assure Lord Robero that Dolov remains loyal."

"You do not believe it will. Nor do you believe I will do what is necessary to ensure that." Hadrenn offered a single short bark of a laugh. "And you would be right. Synek, even after a score of years without wars, remains poor. In just Synek, I rule a demesne nearly a third the size of Defalk, and yet perhaps twelve companies of lancers are what I can muster without prostrating the merchants and peasants." Hadrenn tilted his head. "What say you to that?"

Secca laughed gently. "That it behooves you even more to send your lancers with me, for you can display your power with far less cost than in any other fashion."

"You are so like her, though you look not in the slightest the same."

Like Anna? Secca strongly doubted that.

"A strong north wind would seem to blow you into the next holding, yet the wind passes, and all is changed, and you remain." The heavy-set and balding Lord High Counselor of Ebra fingered his chin again before speaking. "The new part of the road . . . it makes what was there before seem poor indeed. I had heard that you sorceresses had created stone roads all across Defalk and for but a short way into Ebra. Would it be possible . . . ?" Hadrenn did not finish the question.

"There are only so many sorceresses, Lord Hadrenn," Secca said tiredly. "Richina replaced and paved a section of road that was perhaps a half a dek in length. It took all her effort, and she will not be able to do much sorcery for another day or so yet, perhaps longer. That was all she could do for a week, and she is a strong young sorceress. There have been four full-fledged sorceresses in Defalk, and we have been working on the roads there for more than a score of years. We now have perhaps one highway in each direction from Falcor to the borders of Defalk. You are more fortunate than other neighbors, for Lady Anna esteemed you," Secca exaggerated, "and used her sorcery to pave the road through the Sand Pass and for another fifteen deks into Ebra."

"Your roads benefit you more than others, for now traders flock to use your roads," Hadrenn pointed out.

"That is true, but however it benefits us, a sorceress can only do so much sorcery in a day or a week, and sorceresses are called upon to do more than build roads. Anna did also build you the bridge across the Syne to the west." Secca smiled. "Once we have settled the current . . . situation . . . perhaps, if there is another bridge . . ."

"If there were one across the Syne perhaps thirty deks to the east . . . that would save much travel, and make the folk on one side closer to those on the south."

"We will see, and I will not forget."

"Neither did she, for good or for evil." Hadrenn laughed.
"And you are much like her."

Secca offered a smile she wasn't certain she felt.

48

ENCORA, RANUAK

The man and the woman sit across from each other,
platters empty but still on the table. In a smaller and
higher chair sits a daughter, with the blonde hair of her
mother. The Matriarch sips a glass of an amber wine, while
her consort glances at their child.

The child leans forward in the chair to take one of the
glazed almonds from the dish on the table.

"Just a few," says Alya.

"Yes, Mother."

A half-smile crosses the man's face before his eyes return to Alya. "You are disturbed by the news from Synek?"

The Matriarch frowns. "I would have been surprised if
Mynntar had prevailed, even with the aid of the Sturinnese.
I worry greatly about the use of Clearsong to poison
Mynntar."

"Did he not deserve it?" asks Aetlen.

"He did. That is not the difficulty. I fear we shall see
much more and different uses of spellsongs in the seasons
ahead. Now is not the time for shadow sorcery. Not with
the Ladies of the Shadows visiting me, and recalling the
horrors of the Spell-Fire Wars."

"You worry about them?"

"Their worries are the same as mine—but they will not
see that the evils of not using sorcery may be even worse
than the horrors of using it."

"You expect the new Sorceress-Protector to abandon

what has worked so well for more than a score of years?" asks Aetlen.

"No. She acted then as she needed, but I fear she will yet try more subtle shadow sorcery," replies the Matriarch, smiling at her daughter even while she eases the dish of almonds out of reach of her youngest.

Alcaren—wearing the pale blue of the Matriarchy, but with insignia neither of an officer nor a ranker—sits in the straight-backed chair by the door, eyes flicking from the Matriarch to her daughter and then to her consort. He stands and slips to the second-story window, studying the way below, then the dark clouds beyond the harbor. His fingers curl around the hilt of the sabre, then uncurl, as if willed to do so.

"Because she does not understand that shadow sorcery is fully effective only after great power has been displayed?" Aetlen's voice is dry as he brushes back white-blonde hair that shows neither the white nor the silver of aging.

The Matriarch nods.

"Mother?" asks the girl, who would stand perhaps to the Matriarch's shoulder, "why couldn't you bring another sorceress from the Mist Worlds, the way they once did in Defalk? One who had great power?"

Alya frowns. "It is not that simple, Verlya. Knowledge is a form of Harmony. The great sorceress Anna was not a sorceress when she came to Liedwahr. She was a singer of songs, for songs do not have the power in the Mist Worlds that they do here. Even so, she was most fortunate to have survived the trip. Such a trip would kill a knowing sorcerer or sorceress." The Matriarch smiles. "We were most fortunate that she was who she was. I would not gamble on such. I could not."

"Are the other sorceresses like her?"

"No. No person is like unto another. Nor are sorceresses. There are three, and they are all powerful, but most different. The eldest is the Sorceress of Defalk, and she is most like the sorceresses of old, and finds herself in a world where such is most dangerous. The second would be a sorcerer, for she uses men as men have used women, and she feels the currents of power among the lords. The third, and the youngest, she is the shadow sorceress, much as the great sorceress was, and should she ever emerge into the full light of Harmony, she also will change Liedwahr, perhaps far more than the great sorceress. Yet she would hug the shadows close."

"Why does she stay in the shadows?"

"Because for many years, the shadows have allowed her and the one who taught her to shape the future of Defalk and of Liedwahr unseen and more gently."

"I would not like my future changed from the shadows," states Verlya. "Not by a sorceress."

"That will change, for a time." The Matriarch sighs. "It will change so much that all will yearn for the shadow days."

"I won't," avers the girl.

"We shall see," temporizes the Matriarch.

"Indeed we shall," adds Aetlen.

By the window, Alcaren frowns, ever so slightly, as his gaze returns from surveying a harbor far too empty of vessels.

49

Secca walked to the window, where she stared out into the cool and clear early morning, a day bidding to be warmer than those just previous. How long would the weather hold? Did she dare cross Ebra to Dolov? Did she dare not?

A dull thump filled the room, and both Richina and Secca turned.

On the desk where Secca had been studying the maps

was a tarnished bronze cylinder. From it rose the odor of hot and oiled metal and the smell of parchment being heated.

"Who sent it?" asked Richina. "Lady Clayre?"

Secca pulled on the leather riding gloves that she had laid on the corner of the dressing table, then swiftly lifted the bronze tube off the maps, but not before a rectangular browned shape had darkened the parchment.

Quickly, the small sorceress pried open the copper tube, and extracted the parchment, and then a second sheet, sealed in blue, and a third—with its seal and blue ribbons slightly scorched. All three were browned from the heat, but not so much that she could not read the words of the unsealed one.

Dearest Secca—

I would not send these such were matters not most amiss. Clayre already has been required to use the flame sorcery against one rebellious holder in Neserea in order to support Annayal. Many of the Neserean holders have pledged to restore the Prophet of Music—yet without revealing their names . . . or who they would install as prophet.

There are two fleets from Sturrin. One has already landed lancers and armsmen in Dumar, east of Narial, and they are moving toward Dumaria. As you know, Narial itself lies prostrate from the massive wave we think the Sea-Priests created through sorcery . . .

Secca shook her head, recalling the anguished chord that had awakened her in the night. Why hadn't she used the reflecting pool sooner to seek out the cause? Because she'd been so exhausted? It had only been a day later, and she had sent a message to Lord Robero. She moistened her lips, hoping her carelessness would not come back to plague her, not any more than it already had.

> Lord High Counselor Clehar is raising all his armsmen and lancers. There is no way I can reach Dumar in time, and you and Clayre are already well away from Defalk. So Lord Robero has requested I remain in Falcor . . .
>
> The second Sturinnese fleet appears to be sailing toward Elahwa. Lord Robero would suggest that you offer your assistance to the Free-Women, once you have dealt with the last of the threat from Mynntar. He and I feel that Ebra cannot stand if Elahwa falls to the Sea-Priests . . . not unless all of us go eastward . . . With Sturinnese lancers landing in Dumar, and rebellion in Neserea . . .

The writing seemed to blur for Secca, but she knew the letters had not blurred. She looked blindly toward the closed window, as the dark wooden walls seemed to press in upon her.

"Lady! What is it?"

Rather than speak, Secca extended the message to Richina.

While Richina read the first, Secca unsealed the second, the one with her name on the outside, and with Robero's seal.

> Most honored Sorceress-Protector of the East,
>
> The Assistant Sorceress of Defalk has informed me that a Sturinnese fleet is nearing the Free City of Elahwa. She has also informed me that you have removed the vast majority of the would-be usurper's forces. Therefore, I would request that you ensure the loyalty of Dolov, as you see fit to do so, and with the support of the Lord High Counselor Hadrenn. I have enclosed

a sealed scroll strongly suggesting that he offer
you all support within his power.

Secca's lips turned up in a faint smile. That wording
read of Jolyn's not-so-light hand. The half-smile vanished with the next words she read.

> Upon completing that task, I would suggest
> that you offer your assistance to the FreeWomen
> of Elahwa, should they still be resisting the Stu-
> rinnese. If the city has fallen, it might be best to
> see what can be done to dislodge the Sea-Priests
> before they can reinforce their position . . .

In short, approaching winter or not, bad weather or
not, she was headed eastward in an effort to stop matters
which were already less than wonderful from turning
into a complete disaster, if they had not already.

"I should have known. I should have used the glass
more." Secca shook her head. "Yet looking at the memories of reflections will not suffice."

"What are you going to do?" asked the younger sorceress.

"Take Lord Robero's scroll directly to Lord Hadrenn."

"He will not be pleased."

"I'm not sure Lord Hadrenn has ever been pleased."
Then, she reflected, in his position, she supposed she
would not have been either. Hadrenn was a local lord
who was not fitted for more, in a time when a greater
man would have been welcome. Except all those who
would have been greater had opposed Anna, and now
Secca had to find a way to rescue a weak land with a
weak lord. Without sorcery and without Stepan, it
would have been impossible from the beginning.

Secca picked up the scroll, then glanced at Richina.
"You need to practice the vocalises, the ones with the

'eees,' because you're still swallowing your voice too much. I hope I won't be long."

"Yes, lady."

Secca stepped from the guest chambers, and Mureyn, an older lancer, followed her down the corridor. Duryl, the other lancer, whom Secca did not know except by name, remained at the door.

The pair of guards standing outside Hadrenn's study stiffened as Secca marched toward them.

"Lady Sorceress . . ." The taller guard began.

"Tell Lord Hadrenn that what I bring him will not wait long."

The two exchanged glances, then the taller guard rapped on the door, and eased it open a fraction. "Sire . . . the Lady Secca. She says that it requires much haste."

Apparently, Hadrenn said nothing, but only gestured, for the guard opened the study door, bowing to Secca as she stepped inside and closed the heavy oak door behind her.

Hadrenn did not stand from behind the ornate and ancient desk, its wood so darkened by age that it appeared almost black. The dark green velvet hangings framing the tall windows behind the desk were drawn so closely together that only a slit of light passed into the study, and the four branched candelabra on the corner of the desk dropped only a small pool of light across the ledger before the Lord High Counselor.

"I was reviewing the liedstadt accounts. There is little to spare. It was not the best of harvests, and the need to use the lancers has cost more than we had set aside. Then there are the death golds for those men you flamed . . ." Hadrenn gave a dramatic sigh.

"You will need to find more golds, I fear, Lord Hadrenn." Secca extended the sealed scroll.

Hadrenn studied the blue wax of the seal and the blue ribbons, whose edges were browned by the heat of its sorcerous transmission. "How did you come by this?

And why did you not present it sooner?" He scowled.

"It was sent by sorcery," Secca stated. "In a bronze tube lined with special fabric. It appeared in my room moments ago."

"You can send such? Why then do any use messengers?" Hadrenn shook his head.

Secca took a slow breath. "It takes a sorcerer or a sorceress. Sending one small tube will take all the sorcery she can muster for a day, perhaps two. Would you prefer the battle won? Or the road built?"

"For such as you do, we would do better with more sorceresses," Hadrenn offered, not quite growling.

"Defalk has more sorceresses than ever it has had, and we have worked hard, but four could not send all the scrolls a ruler would need, and then we could do little else."

"So . . . this scroll is most important?"

"I would judge so."

"You know what it states?"

"Not the words, Lord Hadrenn, but I believe Lord Robero makes a request for your support against the Sturinnese and in securing eastern Ebra under your control."

Hadrenn studied the scroll again, still not breaking the seal. "It has been scorched."

"That happens when sent by sorcery, even within bronze. Some messages, if sent when a sorceress is too tired or sent too far, arrive as little more than cinders."

"Sorcery . . ." After a brusque headshake, Hadrenn broke the seal and began to read, his lips mouthing the words. Finally, he looked up, his head outlined by the light from the windows, but his face in shadow.

"The Sturinnese are about to attack the Free City— or so your lord says,—and I am to offer all that I can in your support, excepting levies." The Lord High Counselor lifted his hands. "I am recalled as to why I dread the visits of sorceresses. What choice have I? If I support you not, then I will have neither the backing of Defalk nor my lands. Yet . . . in supporting you, at the least I impoverish my folk and risk losing what it has taken long years to build."

Secca could not find much sympathy for Hadrenn within herself, even as she spoke. "We of Defalk did not foment this, Lord Hadrenn. Nor does Lord Robero desire your lands."

"Both I know. Both I understand. Yet . . ." The balding lord twisted the scroll in his hands, then glanced down at the desk before looking up at Secca. "Stepan and the lancers will accompany you until you need them not, and you may request aught that you need from Frengal and him." A ghastly pale smile crossed the Lord High Counselor's face. "Let us devoutly hope for the support of the Harmonies as well."

"Thank you." Secca understood how little Hadrenn wished to be where he sat. She doubted he understood how little she wished to be where she stood. "We will depart tomorrow, the weather permitting."

"As you will, Sorceress-Protector. As you will."

"As we must," Secca replied, bowing slightly before she turned and left.

50

ENCORA, RANUAK

The mother and the father and two daughters sit around the oval dining table that could seat at least another four people. The table is lit but by a single candle. Outside, the cold rain pelts on the windows and the roof.

"You're worried about Veria?" asks Aetlen, finishing the last bite of a stew that had filled but half the small bowl before him.

"Veria . . . and Encora," replies the Matriarch. "We know that the Sturinnese will lay siege to Elahwa, yet we're still losing trading vessels. Even ships from Wei are no longer porting here. Prices of all goods are going up, and there are some grain futures that the Exchange will not trade, at any price."

"Mother, why will you not send more lancers to help the FreeWomen?" asks the thin and older dark-haired girl.

The blonde daughter—Verlya—pauses in lifting a goblet. Her eyes flicker from her mother to her older sister.

"We have already sent ten companies, Ulya. What am I to do if the Sturinnese turn their ships south and sail to attack Encora? They can reach us in less than a week if the wind is right, and if their fleet is in the channel. The lancers will need to ride back, and it will take almost twice that for them to return. And they will not be fit for battle for another week if they make such haste."

"You could send Alcaren," Verlya says. "The SouthWomen would go with him."

Alya's mouth opens, if for but an instant. "Where did you hear that?"

Verlya flushes. "I shouldn't say, I guess. Should I?"

"You overheard Alcaren talking to someone?"

"No, mother. It wasn't Alcaren. He wouldn't do that."

"I'll bet it was Scyda," suggests Ulya. "She was complaining the other day that the SouthWomen could make a difference."

Alya cocks her head, as if in thought, then glances at her consort.

"Do you know what the Sorceress-Protector will do?" asks Aetlen.

"Whatever is best for Defalk, I am sure. That may not be best for Elahwa or us." Alya's lips twist. "Then it may be, but it is not something we can count upon, not in these times."

"She will not harm us, will she?" questions Verlya.

"That is most unlikely, but she is young, as sorceresses go—"

"Like Alcaren?" interrupts Ulya.

Alya laughs. "In a way. In a way. But he would rather

use a blade or a lance, while she prefers indirect spells."

"That's why he's the head of your guard," Verlya announces.

Aetlen and Alya exchange a quick glance before smiling at each other.

Alya laughs, ruefully. "Why not? If the SouthWomen would have him . . . then . . ."

Aetlen nods. "One way or another . . . it will solve the problem. Or one of them."

The brief light fades from Alya's face as she looks at Aetlen's somber countenance. She forces a smile as she turns back to her daughters. "We do have a little rice pudding."

"It's been sooo . . . long since we had sweetcakes," Verlya says.

"That's because the ships haven't come with molasses and sugar," Ulya points out. "We're lucky to have rice pudding. Most people don't have that."

"I know." Verlya sighs.

Aetlen rolls his eyes at the dramatic statement and sigh, but manages to keep a straight face.

"I could give it to someone else," Alya suggests.

"Please don't, mother," Verlya says quickly. Then she pauses. "Perhaps you should. If it's someone who doesn't get any."

"You may have some," Alya says. "I already had most of it given to some of the families of the lancers of the third company."

"The ones in Elahwa?" asks the older daughter.

"One of the companies in Elahwa. There was only enough for four families, but they have children your age." Alya stands and slips from the dining chamber.

"I can eat mine, then."

"Yes, you can," Aetlen says with a smile. "Your portion is small enough that you may enjoy it."

The Matriarch returns with two dishes, one for each child, each portion but two small bites. Neither child leaves a grain of the rice or sauce.

Neither parent smiles.

51

In the entry hall of Hadrenn's shabby palace, Secca adjusted her leather riding jacket, and then the heavy green felt hat. Lifting her saddlebags again, she prepared to step out into the clear but windy dawn, when there was a cough behind her.

Secca turned.

Wearing a green tunic thrown on askew and above purple trousers with dark splotches, Hadrenn stood and looked at the redheaded sorceress. "I wish you well, Lady Secca, in this venture . . . for the sake of all within Defalk and Ebra. Particularly for Haddev."

"Perhaps, when he returns, you should send him to join us," Secca found herself saying. "He might find the journey to be useful."

"Perhaps I should." Hadrenn cocked his head. "Perhaps I will."

"I do not know if I will be returning this way," Secca said after another period of silence, "but I thank you for your hospitality and support, and especially for the use of Stepan and your lancers."

"Your sorcery—and that of your predecessor—has made possible the restoration and preservation of my patrimony. For this, I thank you, and wish you well."

"Thank you, Lord Hadrenn." Secca inclined her head, then straightened with the warmest smile she could muster before turning.

Mureyn followed her, carrying the portable scrying mirror.

The gray mare was standing by the doors when Secca stepped into the courtyard, the reins held by a lancer. Richina was already mounted, waiting for Secca.

"Thank you, Duryl," said Secca to the lancer who tendered her the gray's reins.

"My pleasure, lady."

Secca fastened her saddlebags in place, then the mirror and lutar, before mounting.

Once mounted, she eased the mare toward the south side of the courtyard to where she spied Palian.

The chief player nodded as Secca reined up. "Lady Secca."

"Palian. How fare you and the players?"

"All are ready. The respite has done them well," Palian replied.

"Good." Secca hoped the respite hadn't cost them too dearly in dealing with Dolov, but particularly with the Sturinnese.

"Lady Secca," called Wilten, easing his mount around Delvor, who was adjusting the straps holding his lutar behind the saddle of his mount, "the lancers stand ready."

Behind Wilten, Stepan merely offered a nod that his men were also ready.

"Then best we ride," said Secca.

Slowly, order emerged from the chaos of milling mounts and players, and Secca rode down the lane toward the main road.

While the sun of previous days had melted away the thin layer of snow, the cold night had frozen the ground almost as hard as the stone of the highways of Defalk. Every rut in both the lane and the ground beside it was sharp-edged, and often outlined in frosty rime.

Once beyond the stone gates, the column turned eastward toward the bridge that led to the south side of the River Syne and the main road eastward toward Dolov—and Elahwa.

"I was a little nasty," Secca confessed. "When Lord Hadrenn thanked me for ensuring his patrimony and Haddev's, I suggested that Haddev might be well-advised to join us."

Richina grinned. "Do you think he will send Haddev?"

"I do not know."

"He will," offered Stepan, easing his mount up beside that of Secca. "The Lady Belvera will protest, for she would protect Haddev from all. But Lord Hadrenn is not unperceptive. Haddev will spend many years dealing with you two, and it would not be wise for him to be perceived as less than brave." Stepan laughed. "You fight his foes, Lady Sorceress, standing as you do but to the lord's shoulder, and with an assistant who is most young, and you ride out to battle, asking naught of him or his heir personally. If neither he nor his heir should take the field . . ."

"Haddev will have trouble in later years?" asked Secca.

"Also . . . few battles are safer than those with a sorceress on one's side," Stepan pointed out.

Secca doubted that.

"And he could well use the understanding and the experience," Stepan continued, adding dryly, "Young Haddev will gain much renown by fighting for his land."

"What is he like?" asked Secca.

"He is much like I imagine Lord Robero was at his age, though I but saw your lord when he was somewhat younger." Stepan smiled blandly.

Secca managed not to wince, and offered a smile as innocuous as that of the arms commander. "Then we will but follow the example set by Lady Anna."

"I thought as much, and so would Lord Hadrenn, within his heart."

Both Stepan and Secca smiled and nodded, near-simultaneously. To the side, Richina suppressed a frown.

52

ENCORA, RANUAK

In the formal receiving room, the Matriarch sits upon the clear blue crystal chair of the Matriarchy. The room is empty, save for her and Alcaren, who stands just before the dais. Gray light seeps through the long windows.

"You have often wished to use your blade as well as your sorcery," the Matriarch says deliberately. "Do you still desire such?"

"Only if it serves a good cause, Matriarch," replies the young chief of guards.

"Would you be willing to be overcaptain of two companies dispatched to Elahwa to help the city against the Sturinnese?"

"I might be." Alcaren studies the Matriarch. "Even if the Sturinnese threaten to overwhelm such an effort from its inception with their dissonance and thunder-drums."

"You had asked," Alya points out.

Alcaren laughs, if softly. "Now you would trap me by my own words."

"I would not trap you." The Matriarch smiles, if faintly. "You wish what in return?"

"*If* we are successful in breaking the Sturinnese, by whatever means, I would wish to remain an overcaptain in a useful position." He squares his shoulders, as if expecting a denial.

"I can only offer a useful position of stature." Alya pauses. "The companies are those raised and trained by the SouthWomen."

"You cannot send them under their own captains?"

"Under their own captains, yes, but not without an overcaptain known to be loyal to the Matriarch."

"And one whom the men of the Free City would accept?" asks Alcaren.

"Ranuak cannot afford to have it said that it would use any stratagem to strengthen ties between the Free City and the SouthWomen. A man as overcaptain, and one known to my sister as a possible sorcerer, would certainly dispel that notion."

"Especially one known to have strong views?"

"That will not hurt."

"And you will be sending me away from the Ladies of the Shadows."

Alya raises her eyebrows. "But out of my control, and that will trouble them."

"What about the Sorceress-Protector of the East?" Alcaren inquires. "She may pursue those Sturinnese lancers in Ebra into the lands of the Free City."

"I would not oppose her doing so. She is the child in soul of the great sorceress, who forced Hadrenn to accept the Free City. The younger sorceress may not choose to help Elahwa, but she will not harm it, not unless it has already fallen to the Sturinnese."

"Do you think she will come to the aid of Elahwa?"

Another faint smile plays across the face of the Matriarch. For a time, she does not speak. "My mother always said to trust in the Harmonies . . . but not without working to create one's own harmony. So long as the young Sorceress-Protector follows the Harmonies, who knows what may happen?"

"You think she might?"

"I do not know. Whatever happens, Elahwa will need all the aid we can send. Even the young Sorceress-Protector may need aid, for sorcery can exhaust the strongest. That is why you carry the brew packets. Should you chance to fight with her forces, you may offer aid such as the brew packets." Alya nods at Alcaren. "But you are not to attempt any battle sorcery, or any sorcery at all where it can be seen. You are not to tell anyone about your abilities. While many in Encora know of them, few elsewhere do. It should remain that way." Her eyes chill as she beholds him. "Do you understand?"

"I understand." Alcaren bows.

"I am most certain you do."

He bows again before speaking. "These two companies are all you can afford to send because of the Sturinnese fleets?"

Alya nods again . . . once.

"I will go, Matriarch, trusting in both you and the Harmonies." Alcaren inclines his head.

"You leave in the morning. We have two fast coastal

schooners of shallow draft, and the winds are out of the southwest. They can take you and some mounts to the north end of the Sand Hills. There, other mounts will be waiting. When you leave here, you will go to meet with Arms Commander Wyendra. She will provide all you need."

Alcaren raises his eyebrows.

The Matriarch ignores the implied question, instead standing to signify that she has said what she will say.

Alcaren conceals a smile and bows deeply. "At your will and command, Matriarch."

"And with my best wishes, Alcaren."

"Thank you, Matriarch."

The Matriarch shivers slightly, but not until the door has closed behind the new overcaptain and she remains alone in the formal receiving chamber.

53

The afternoon was quiet, the road empty, and but a handful of cart tracks marked the clay of the road that ran along the south side of the River Syne. Stepan rode to Secca's right, Richina to her left. Ahead rode Wilten, with the standard bearer Dymen, and immediately behind the sorceresses rode Delvor and Palian.

After nearly a glass of silence, Stepan cleared his throat. "More than a score of years ago, since last I traveled these roads with so many armsmen." He chuckled. "One would think that times change, but betimes I wonder if only we change, and each of those who follows us must discover anew what we have found."

"Some don't, it appears," Secca pointed out, shifting her weight in the saddle, then reaching up and adjusting the green felt hat.

"Each generation has its fools, though I was young and foolish then, as well."

"You seemed wise enough in battle. That was what Lady Anna said," Secca prompted.

"In battle, and in training lancers . . . in advising Gestatr and Lord Hadrenn." A twisted smile crossed Stepan's lips. "Two consorts I lost to being headstrong, and almost a third. Not that you young women wish to hear of an old warhorse's foibles." He glanced overhead at the clear sky, marked by but a single wisp of a white cloud to the north. "Too fair a day to talk of foibles and war and the evil that well-meaning men can do."

"There is always malice among those in power," Secca temporized.

"Why have those who opposed you and the Lady Anna been so filled with malice and so foolish?" asked Richina. "Even Lord Hadrenn and Lord Robero are less than pleased. From the foot of the table, that I can see." Abruptly, she flushed and turned to Stepan. "Begging your pardon, honored arms commander."

Stepan laughed, generously. "No offense taken, sorceress. What you have seen so have many others. It is scarce a secret."

Secca decided not to speak, but glanced at Stepan.

"Malice?" mused the older man. "I think not. Those who opposed the Lady Anna acted by their beliefs and to preserve their power." He raised his eyebrows. "Would you wish to be bartered off to whatever lord pleased your sire, for perchance a promise of friendship, some kegs of good wine, and the thought that another lord would be pleased to accept your daughter in the same fashion?"

Richina glanced down at the mane of her mount.

Secca smiled briefly, then asked, "Would you, Richina?"

"No . . . you know that." Richina's face screwed into a puzzled expression.

Stepan nodded. "Because of Lady Anna, you—and your mother—have some say over your body and your life. You would not give that up willingly, would you?"

"Of course not."

"Would you use your sorcery and all at your beck to hold to the right to defend your control of your own body?" pursued Stepan.

"Yes."

"Well . . . before Lady Anna, the Lords of Defalk had the right to control all women within their demesnes, and they saw what she did as taking away their rights, and they fought with all at their beck to keep their rights. What is the difference?"

"It is not fair . . . to ask of a woman what they will not ask of themselves."

Stepan did not speak, and Secca realized he would not push the matter. "What is the difference?" she asked Richina.

"It's . . . different . . ."

"Is it, do you think?" Secca asked Stepan. "Different?"

"Different . . . that is a matter that men and women will argue over in all times and all worlds." He shook his head. "This I will say. Those who opposed Lady Anna were neither foolish, nor were they malicious. They would have said—they did say—that the lady was the malicious one. She took away many of their powers, and gave some to women, and some to sorceresses. They said she was foolish, for women could never wisely hold such."

Richina shook her head. "I do not understand how anyone could think so." She paused, then looked at Secca. "What do you think? Were they right by their lights?"

Secca laughed harshly. "I would say not. They tried to kill me when I had less than half a score of years. Yet one must understand why people act as they do. Why do the Sea-Priests attack all of Liedwahr? Is it because they are stupid? Or thoughtlessly evil? And why do they so do in this season of this year?"

Richina shrugged.

For several moments, the only sounds were those of hoofs on the road, the breathing of mounts, and the low murmurs of the lancers and players in the column behind the three.

"I would hazard," Stepan said slowly, "that it is because what the Lady Anna began, if not halted, will change all of Liedwahr, and perhaps the world. The ladies of Defalk were servants of their lords. Perhaps some still are. But they were far less constrained than those in Ebra or in Mansuur, and never were they chained by custom, as in Sturinn. Nor had they their tongues removed if they essayed sorcery."

Richina shivered.

Secca frowned—the business with tongue-removals was not something she had heard.

"Yet the Sea-Priests believe such is the way all should live," continued Stepan. "To see a woman unchained, to know that a woman practices sorcery—to them, those are abominations far worse than dancing or Darksong. They believe, as do most folk, that the world should live as do they. Unlike most folk, they have the sorcery, and lancers, and fleets of ships, to try to make the world live in the way they think best." The arms commander shrugged. "The Lady Anna once told me, when I was not a great deal older than the young sorceress, and I protested, as you now protest, that seldom is power ever surrendered willingly, and great power surrendered even less willingly. The Lords of Defalk had great power and privilege, and they did not wish to lose such. You two—and I as well—have less power, but far more than most folk in all of Erde. We will fight to hold that. We can also tell ourselves that it is better that we hold power than others. Is it?" Stepan laughed, once more ruefully, yet gently. "We judge ourselves more kindly than might others judge us when we speak of our honor and duty."

Judge ourselves more kindly? Secca frowned.

"Each man—or woman—does as he senses best," Stepan said. "Few indeed set out to do what they see as evil. We—or others—may see it as such. That is our judgment, but they may see what we do as evil to their way of thinking." He laughed. "What I say is simple. So simple any child could grasp it, and yet . . . generation after generation, lands and men fight because they cannot agree on what way of life is good."

Somehow, with Stepan's gentle words, the afternoon felt even colder, although no clouds covered the sun, and the wind remained less than a vagrant breeze.

54

In the late afternoon, standing before a tent fluttering in a cold but light wind, under a sun whose fading light provided little heat, Secca glanced at Richina, then at Stepan and Wilten, and finally at the two chief players. She felt as though each waited for her to speak, and as though whatever she said would be faulted, if silently.

Secca moistened her lips before beginning. "I've been worrying about what the Sturinnese are doing. There wasn't much point in following them day by day until we had to decide. Stepan tells me that late tomorrow or early the next we should reach where the River Dol and the River Syne join together. We can go south to Elahwa or north to Dolov. Before I decide, I'm going to try to see what faces us in each place."

Wilten nodded, as did Palian and Richina. Stepan's face was impassive. A faint smile creased Delvor's lips.

Secca picked up the lutar and began the spell.

"Show me now and in this glass
what in Elahwa has come to pass,
with ships of Sturinn on the sea . . ."

As the last notes of the spell died away, Secca looked down at the mirror, where an arcing line of ship masts appeared in the silvered surface. Two ships were moored at the stone pier in the foreground, but there were no figures on the pier, and apparently not on either ship.

Secca frowned, wondering why the Sea-Priests were blockading the port, and why they had not used sorcery to flatten Elahwa. Was there a reason why sorcery would not work in the eastern part of Liedwahr?

After a time, she released the spell.

"You say the Sea-Priests raised the waves to destroy Narial?" asked Stepan.

"They did."

"Yet they have not done so in Elahwa," pointed out Wilten. "Perhaps they wish the port?"

"Narial is a far better port. The waters are shallow off the Shoals, and the channel is narrow and goes on for deks through those shallows." Stepan frowned. "And the FreeWomen will fight to the death, perhaps beyond."

"Why would they have ships so close to the port, if the channel to deep water is so long?" asked Palian.

"Smaller boats, perhaps?" suggested Delvor. "They wish to starve the city?"

Secca nodded slowly. That sounded like what she had heard of the Sturinnese.

"They are blockading the city. They must have lancers somewhere," suggested Stepan, glancing at Secca. "If we could see . . ."

That made sense to Secca, but she had to think for a time before she came up with the spell words she needed.

> *"Show us now and as you will*
> *if and where lancers battle still*
> *near Elahwa and by the city's sea . . ."*

The mirror showed a battle—or a skirmish.
A line of lancers in white charged up a gentle incline.

Another force met them a third of the way down the incline. Most of the defending lancers were women who wore tunics of a brilliant crimson. Scattered among them were other lancers—both men and women—whose colors were a pale blue.

"The blue—those are the colors of Ranuak," Richina blurted.

As she spoke, the attackers fell back, but not before leaving bodies in crimson and blue strewn on the hillside.

"Would one expect less?" asked Stepan. "The Free City is supported in part by the Matriarch, and it is said that one of the councilwomen is her sister."

"They are losing," offered Wilten.

Stepan nodded, and Richina looked to the overcaptain.

"The defenders have repulsed this attack, but they have lancers from three units together," Wilten said. "One does not mix lancers from different companies in a battle unless none have enough to stand alone."

"The Ranuans have companies of male lancers and women lancers, but they do not mix them. The women are the armsmen and sailors of Elahwa, while the men are the artisans and crafters," Stepan added. "Here all three groups fight in the same place."

Richina looked at Secca, as if to ask what she planned.

Secca released the second scene. She felt tired, almost light-headed, and one or two more quick scrying spells were about all she was ready for without eating and refreshing herself. "Let us look at Dolov," she temporized. Perhaps she should leave Dolov until later.

"Show us now and show us fair
the keep at Dolov and lancers there . . ."

The mirror split into two images, one displaying a keep on a bluff overlooking a river, the other side showing lancers in white in the courtyard. In fact, the entire rear of the courtyard held tents with white banners.

"They must have landed off the coast and ridden overland," Wilten said.

"They could have landed just beyond Elahwa and taken the road on the east side of the river north," suggested Stepan.

Secca shook her head. There looked to be at least ten companies of Sturinnese lancers garrisoned yet at Dolov, and that didn't even count whatever lancers Mynntar had left in reserve, lancers that his brother might well use against Secca and Stepan's forces.

After a moment, as dayflashes appeared before her eyes, she released that image.

She had enemies in both places. Which way should she lead her forces? And why?

Somehow, she had the feeling that either decision would be wrong. Four or five days upriver, possibly a battle and sorcery, and then five or six days back to Elahwa—if the weather held. If Wilten and Stepan were right . . . She looked at Stepan. "The FreeWomen cannot hold for two weeks."

"Not if that battle shows their strength."

"They cannot last . . ." Stepan murmured. "Not without reinforcements."

Robero had ordered Secca to secure Dolov—except he hadn't. He'd requested. That meant that it was all on her head. If she went to Dolov, then she'd face an entrenched enemy by the time she returned to Elahwa—and one doubtless reinforced by the blockading ships.

"We'll have to go to Elahwa," she finally said.

The hint of a momentary frown passed across Wilten's forehead.

Stepan said quietly, "If you attack the Sea-Priests from the north, the city forces can help you. If you go to Dolov, then you must face both enemies without aid."

At that, both Wilten and Palian nodded.

Secca could only hope she was making the right decision.

55

The tall and muscular woman who steps into the Matriarch's formal receiving room wears the hooded cloak of black that shadows her face, as with all the Ladies of the Shadows, and the black trousers and calf-length boots. Despite the winter gloom and the cloak, her dark brown hair and clean hard jaw betray that she is neither in first youth nor old, and that she is a different lady from the last who had visited Alya.

"You wished me to see you?" The Matriarch's voice is pleasant, but not warm, as she looks down from the blue crystalline chair on the dais.

"We did. We offered a warning before, and you have chosen to ignore it."

"I took your warning, and I did not ignore it. I have not used sorcery, save for information. There is nothing against what you believe in dispatching lancers to support Elahwa."

"We are deeply concerned that you have sent . . . that you have sent a . . ." The brown-haired woman shakes her head as if she cannot bring herself to utter the next word. ". . . a sorcerer to Elahwa."

"He is not a sorcerer, not like those you have in mind. He was trained in sorcery, as well you know, so that he would not misuse those talents." Alya offers a scornful snort. "What would you have me do? Murder every child who shows the ability to truly sing? Or lock them away in a prison?"

"You could have sent the SouthWomen without him. There are other overcaptains."

"Who would you have had me send? There are no others of ability that Elahwa could spare, not that either the Free

City or the SouthWomen would accept as overcaptain."

"Those who receive aid should not be that choosy, Matriarch."

Alya's lips tighten, and for a moment she is silent. Then she takes a slow breath and smiles, almost lazily. "As I understand your words, and those of the lady who came earlier, you feel so strongly about what you believe that you would risk the destruction of Ranuak and the sacrifice of all those who died in the Spell-Fire Wars to hold to your beliefs. Yet you think that the FreeWomen should relinquish their beliefs for two companies of lancers?"

It is the turn of the Lady of the Shadows to be silent for a time. Finally, she replies. "It is not the same."

"It is the same," Alya replies, adding more gently, "Besides, the overcaptain does not know battle sorcery. He has never been trained in such, and there are no players to support him."

"He is a sorcerer, and a man."

"Sorcery is like any other tool," Alya points out. "It can be used or misused. Without the Great Sorceress of Defalk, we would have the Sturinnese as our neighbors already, if not as our masters."

"The great sorceress was a woman, and she had suffered. She was older, and she had some idea of the powers of sorcery and what they could do to our world. As she discovered her powers, she used them less, not more. Even as an outlander, she had some understanding and remorse. Your overcaptain is a man, barely more than a child, and no man in this world has ever restrained such powers."

"What would you have me do? Recall him? Tell the Free City that because you fear the disasters of the past, in which he took no part, they may not have his abilities?"

The Lady of the Shadows shakes her head within the dark cloak. "If, if all is as you say, and if he acts as an overcaptain should, then all will be acceptable . . . but only because of the respect we have for the office of the Matriarch."

"You wish Ranuak to fall into the hands of the Sea-

Priests?" Alya's voice remains low, almost gentle.

"It will not come to that. The Harmonies will not let that occur, not unless we fail in our duties to restrain the evils of song-sorcery."

"The Harmonies do not seem to be restraining the evils of the thunder-drums, nor of the Sturinnese song-sorcery. Nor did they restrain the sorceries of the Mynyans."

"That is because Liedwahr has not rejected its evils," replied the Lady of the Shadows. "How can the Harmonies protect us when we embrace evils such as song-sorcery?"

Alya nodded politely, although the nod was scarcely of agreement, but of resigned acknowledgment. "We will see."

"Indeed we will, Matriarch, and we will be watching. We cannot ever accept the dissonance and destruction of song-sorcery. Not ever again." The woman in the black cloak bowed. "By your leave, Matriarch?"

"By my leave." Alya nods once more.

The hooded figure bows a last time, turns, and departs.

Looking to her left, toward the closed windows that hold out the wind and the cold winter mist, Alya shakes her head, slowly, sadly.

56

A lancer rode almost to where Secca stood with Richina as the two sorceresses were adjusting the ties on the tent that they had helped set up on the knoll to the south of the river road. Secca had tucked the green felt hat into her belt, because it kept threatening to blow away, and brushed back a strand of red hair disarranged by her efforts and by the light, but occasionally gusty wind that remained cold, but not quite bitter.

She waited as the lancer inclined his head.

"Lady Secca, Overcaptain Wilten sent me to tell you that young Lord Haddev is nearing. He is less than a dek away."

"Thank you, Duryl. We will await him here."

The lancer nodded and turned his mount back toward the road.

"So Hadrenn did send him," mused Secca, retying one of the tent's tie-strips.

"I wonder what he looks like," added Richina.

Secca glanced at the younger sorceress. "I doubt you'd be happy in Synek, especially with your powers to do sorcery greatly diminished. And they would be, with the need to produce heirs quickly."

Richina flushed.

"Sometimes, love does triumph. But usually, it's lust, and that's a defeat for most women."

"Most?" Richina raised her eyebrows. "Were you thinking of someone in particular, lady?"

"Not necessarily," evaded Secca, since she had been thinking of Jolyn, who seemed, from Secca's vantage point, to use men as some men used women.

"Do you think a sorceress can ever truly love, lady?" ventured Richina.

"Lady Anna did."

"But Lady Clayre hasn't, has she?"

"I don't know," Secca confessed. "Clayre and I are friendly, but . . . she came to Falcor when I was barely nine. She was more than six years older and trying to avoid being consorted to anyone who was available. By the time I was just a few years older than you are, Lady Anna brought me to Loiseau. Clayre and I have spent more than ten years apart from each other except for a few weeks a year, and we have seldom talked about such matters."

"Oh . . ."

Secca smiled faintly. "Very few lords anywhere—or their heirs—wish a consorting with a woman more powerful than they."

"But there aren't any sorcerers left in Defalk—not since Lord Brill died."

"There is one in Neserea."

"Is that why Lady Clayre . . . ?"

"No." Secca shook her head. "Lord Belmar is not her friend. I fear he is in league with the Sea-Priests. At best, he wishes to use sorcery to become the Lord High Counselor of Neserea."

"Or the Prophet of Music?" asked the sandy-haired young sorceress.

"That is possible."

After a slow nod, Richina slipped into the tent—to brush her hair and make herself more presentable, Secca suspected.

Rather than worry about that, Secca rummaged through her provisions bag and finished off the last chunk of stale bread and some white cheese that was getting soft. Swallowing it took several healthy swigs of water from her bottle.

Before long a column appeared on the road to the west, consisting of perhaps a company's worth of lancers—not in the green of Ebra, but in mottled black tunics. At the head rode Stepan, along with a younger, clean-shaven man. The column turned off the road and halted, and Stepan and Haddev rode slowly past the tethered mounts toward the single tent that was Secca's.

Haddev was taller than his father, and had a full head of reddish-brown hair. His smile was warm and friendly as he reined up and dismounted simultaneously with Stepan.

"Haddev," Stepan said warmly, "this is the Lady Secca. She holds both the lands of Mencha, as her right as Sorceress-Protector of the East, and those of Synope, as her birthright."

The tall young heir bowed deeply and directly to Secca, then again, not quite so deferentially, to Richina. The smile as he rose was definitely for Richina.

In a way, that both reassured and troubled Secca.

Haddev returned his gaze almost immediately to Secca. "My grateful thanks, and those of my sire, for your efforts to protect Ebra, gracious lady and sorceress." He paused. "Lady Sorceress, I joined you as soon as I was able. I also brought another company of lancers, although they are from Silberfels . . . a token from my uncle."

"We welcome your presence, and the lancers. They are certainly more than a token, and I owe great thanks to Lord Selber." Secca also wondered why, after years of reticence, and almost isolation, one of the Lords of Silberfels was actually providing lancers. Was Selber that worried about the Sturinnese?

"I had hoped to reach you before you dealt with the rebels at Dolov, and it appears that I have."

"You will have time for that," Secca said easily. "How was your journey?"

"Cold but clear. There was a light snow through the Sand Pass, and much snow on the road until we were well into Ebra." Haddev paused as if Secca's words had struck belatedly. "You do not intend to deal with the rebels?"

"We have another more pressing problem that will not wait," Secca replied. "The Sturinnese are about to take Elahwa. They have close to ten companies in Dolov. If we ride to Dolov first, we could be caught between two Sturinnese forces. If we attack those besieging Elahwa, we have the support of the Free City."

Surprisingly, at least to Secca, Haddev nodded. "They take some of the casualties, and you obtain support and gratitude and risk less of your and our lancers."

"That is the plan."

Haddev's eyes strayed to Richina once more, and he offered another warm smile as the eyes of the younger sorceress met his. Abruptly, he replied to Secca. "I will do what I can to aid you, for the sorceresses of Defalk have always been friends to Synek."

"Indeed they have," offered Stepan, stepping up beside the heir. "Now . . . perhaps we should see to your lancers, for you have had a long and a hard ride, and tomorrow will not be easy either."

"That is most true." Haddev offered his warm smile to Secca and bowed once more. "Until later, Lady Secca."

"Until later, Haddev." Secca returned his smile with one of her own.

The two sorceresses watched as the tall young man remounted and rode with Stepan back toward the waiting lancers of Silberfels.

"He is most charming," said Richina.

"Charming . . . yes, he is. And he is far brighter than his sire, and most able to wield any tool to his own ends." Secca's voice was dry.

"You do not like him, lady?"

"I like him very well. He will be a good lord of Synek and a good Lord High Counselor of Ebra." *He just won't be very good for you,* Secca wanted to add. She did not, knowing that the younger woman would scarce listen, not with the glow in her eyes.

"You did not seem totally pleased."

"I'm thinking about tomorrow . . . and what lies before us," Secca replied. After a moment, she added, "You will need to help with the scrying. We will need some rough maps of where the Sturinnese forces are."

"Yes, lady."

Richina smiled, but her eyes flicked toward the road, and Haddev.

Secca repressed a sigh. At least, when she had been young, and in love with love, Robero's faults had been so obvious that she had not been tempted.

57

NESALIA, NESEREA

Two men sit on opposite sides of a square table set in the bay window of a large study. The window overlooks a small walled garden. The table is inlaid and contains a set of game pieces. One set is gold, and each figure is smoothly curved. The other set is black, and each figure has sharp and jagged edges.

Belmar takes a sip of the amber-tinged white wine. "A very good vintage, Svenmar. From your lands?"

"The hills to the west."

The dark-haired visiting lord looks down at the inlaid game board and the pieces upon it. "That is an old set. You don't see the gold and black onyx these days."

"It has been in the family for too long to trace."

"Old families . . . they're important in Neserea, even these days. Old families and lineage." Belmar takes a second sip of the wine. "Good vintage." He holds the crystal goblet almost carelessly. "You're a distant nephew of Lord Behlem, aren't you . . . or some such, anyway?"

"You only ask the question to raise the point that your lineage is the more direct, I would wager." Humor tinges Svenmar's voice. "What did you have in mind? If I may ask?"

"These really are beautiful pieces." Belmar picks up the black sorcerer and studies the lined face, carved centuries ago, before setting it back on the inlaid wooden table. "What do I have in mind?"

Svenmar nods politely, then sips from his own goblet, his eyes not meeting those of Belmar, though not seeming to avoid the younger man's.

"Lord Rabyn disgraced the proud heritage of Neserea,

would you not agree?" Belmar's voice is warm, yet almost indolent.

"He thought he fought to hold his patrimony." Svenmar's tone is cautious.

Belmar laughs, almost a deep guffaw, humorous and sardonic.

Svenmar's eyebrows lift.

"To this day, peasant mothers tell comely daughters that the shade of Rabyn will come for them if they raise their eyes too high," Belmar says smoothly. "In less than a year, more than a score of beautiful but poor girls were sold into his service, and most vanished into unmarked graves, and Rabyn scattered golds to their families." He shrugs. "Pleasures are one thing, but open contempt purchased with golds is neither wise nor seemly."

"That was more than a score of years ago, Belmar."

"Ah . . . yes . . . I can see that my words follow a well-worn track, one you have pondered so long it is most familiar, so familiar that . . . but I digress . . ."

"Usually . . . you are more direct, my friend. You must have had a long journey."

"It is never a long journey when those who support you are at its end." Belmar lifts the goblet once more and seems to take another swallow, a swallow that is barely a sip.

"All too true." Svenmar waits.

Belmar sits more erect, not suddenly, but gracefully. Yet the change is as if a dog had become a wolf, yet without changing its coat or markings. "You have seen the tall man in gray, have you not?"

"The one who seems like a shadow?"

"He is a Sea-Priest."

"You talk of Rabyn's evils." Svenmar shakes his head. "The Sea-Priests have not the good of Neserea at heart, if hearts they have at all."

"They do not have our good at heart. With that I agree. But their enemy is Defalk, and the sorceresses who command its lord from the shadows. And . . . well . . . one must use the tools at hand. One must also learn from the past."

Belmar smiles again. "I have not made the mistakes that did . . . say, the Lord of Dumar. Master jerGlien is the sole Sturinnese ever to set foot in my holding, or anywhere in Neserea at my beck. All my lancers . . . did you know that I now have fifteen companies?" The dark-haired lord pauses.

"No. I cannot say that I am surprised."

"Ah . . . you are perceptive. You would not be. As I was saying, all fifteen are solid Nesereans. No mercenaries. No Sturinnese. And they have been trained by the best, not for a season or so, but at least a year, and for the finest, almost five. I did not bring my archers, for this is a friendly visit, nor all of my players, nor my small corps of thunder-drums . . . Oh . . . I do have trouble following a single thought." Belmar smiles broadly. "But then, I have thought long and hard for many years about what may transpire if, perchance, young Annayal were to follow the example of Ranuak."

"Why don't you suggest that you would make a most desirable consort?" Svenmar smiles. "You are not ill-favored, nor ill-landed. Or do you worry that the Lady Aerlya did not hesitate to call in the demon sorceress against Hureln?"

"You call her lady?"

"Unlike the sorceresses you dislike, she does come from a long and noble line and has not usurped lands rightfully belonging to a brother or uncle."

"As do you," Belmar points out.

"Almost as long and distinguished as yours, Belmar."

"Distinction must be, alas, often supplemented." Belmar again picks up a figure from the board—this time the gold sorceress. He smiles, if faintly.

"Supplemented? A rather odd word, my friend."

"If a noble holder such as you were to offer a suggestion that consorting were to find favor with the noble holders of the south . . ."

"Ah . . . and what of Chyalar?"

Belmar shrugs. "He has no sorcerous abilities, and his

sire is ailing. With but three companies of lancers . . . Even you have more than he."

"Come now." Svenmar laughs. "You cannot bring arms to bear against us all."

"I would not do that to you, my friend." Belmar sets the sorceress back on the board. "Of course, if a certain letter were made public, about closing the wagon road to Sperea . . . but that was years back. And some other scrolls, perchance . . ." There is the briefest of pauses before he asks, "How is your dear consort Twyla?"

"Perhaps a letter might be just as well in these troubled times." Svenmar forces a smile. "And the lancers of Worlan might be able to spend far more time, say, near Itzel?"

"They might indeed." Belmar smiles and lifts the goblet. "This is indeed a remarkable vintage."

"I am glad you find it so." Svenmar lifts his own goblet and touches its rim to his lips, but does not drink.

58

A fine cold mist drizzled out of formless gray clouds, clouds that made it seem still like dawn, though it was a good glass past that and time for the sun to have risen. There was only the slightest touch of a breeze, and that was out of the south. Secca studied the clouds, but could see no movement.

"Richina . . . I'll be back in a moment." Hoping that the drizzle would lift, Secca walked away from the tent that Richina and the lancers were striking. The two younger lancers, Dyvan and Achar, followed her.

As Secca neared the archers, Elfens stepped forward and offered a deep bow. "Lady Secca."

"Elfens. I just wanted to see how you and your archers

were doing. There was one who took a shaft in the thigh . . ."

"Weald is riding, and can use his bow. Sore, that he is." Elfens cocked his long face. "You will need us against the Sturinnese in Elahwa?"

"I would think so. They will have thunder-drums." Secca flashed a wry smile. "I might even be able to re-member the need for the arrow spell."

"We will be ready, lady." Elfens offered another of the sweeping bows that would have been a mockery from any-one but the long-faced archer.

Another thirty yards past the archers, close to a small copse of bare-limbed birches, Secca found Stepan talking to several of the Ebran captains.

The sandy-and-silver-haired arms commander stopped and turned toward Secca. "Lady. We are almost ready to ride."

"Finish what you must, arms commander. I need but a moment."

As she waited for Stepan, Secca's eyes traversed the camp, noting that Wilten had the lancers from Loiseau forming up, as did Haddev the company in motley black from Silberfels. The tall heir made a striking figure in the saddle, she had to admit.

"Lady?" Stepan stepped toward the red-haired sorceress.

"It may seem odd, for the moment, but I wanted your opinion." When everyone else is so busy they aren't lis-tening, she added to herself. "What is Verad like?"

"Verad?" The surprise was evident in the older man's voice.

"Isn't that Haddev's younger brother?"

The older arms master shook his head, almost as if still puzzled.

"You do not have good feelings?"

"It is not that." Stepan smiled ruefully. "It is so seldom one asks about the younger son."

"I need to know."

"When a sorceress asks a question such as that . . ." He

paused, then said, "Verad is sixteen, and he is diligent. He will never be so skilled at arms as Haddev, for he is a span shorter and more slight of build, but he rides well, and can hold his own with a blade. I am told he writes well, and is more skilled with his calculations. He is the one who has come to assist his sire with the accounts."

"Do people like him and trust him?"

"After they come to know him. He is less outgoing, and slow to warm to those he does not know."

Secca nodded. She understood that.

"I will not ask why you inquire."

"It's not that important." *Yet*, Secca added to herself. "I have met Hadrenn and his consort. I have exchanged a scroll or two with his consort's brother, but about Verad I know nothing, and, as Sorceress-Protector of the East, I thought I should. Lady Anna greatly valued your judgment, and so do I."

"Lord Hadrenn is fortunate to have two sons so able," Stepan pointed out.

"Does he have any daughters? I didn't see one."

"That you might not have. Seryla is but nine. She also is said to be favored by the Harmonies, but only have I seen her ride. She rides well for one so young."

"And Haddev?" she finally asked.

Stepan shrugged. "You have seen him. He smiles easily, rides well, and is well trained in the blade and with a bow. He speaks with a fair tongue."

Secca laughed softly. "I see."

Stepan raised his eyebrows. "Perchance you do."

"He may make an effective lord, but not precisely one like . . . say, my father or Lady Anna?"

"Well said, Lady Sorceress."

"Let us hope this journey will offer him new insights."

"I fear his eyes are on other conquests."

"I have noticed that, too."

Stepan laughed. "I have noted your notice. You missed little as a child, and you miss less now."

"You're still a most charming man, Stepan."

"Charm counts for little in battle or in planning for one." Stepan glanced toward his lancers, who were mounting and forming into a column.

"Or many," Secca added. "But we have one more day. That's what the glass shows."

"Will they see us in their glasses?"

"They may," Secca admitted, "but we have not turned south."

"Until a glass from now."

"I will watch what they do," Secca promised. "I'd best leave you to your men and duties. Thank you."

"Once we are in formation, I will join you." Stepan bowed, then turned.

"Thank you."

Secca walked quickly through the mist, a mist that seemed finer, and perhaps lifting, back toward where Richina waited with their mounts.

"The tent is on the pack horse, lady, and we are ready to ride," said the sandy-haired younger sorceress.

"Thank you, Richina. I was checking with Elfens and Stepan." Secca picked up her own saddlebags.

"Ah . . . lady?"

"Yes?"

"Haddev would ask your leave to accompany us for a short time, before he returns to his lancers."

"He may, for a bit." Secca nodded. "You may tell him."

"Thank you, lady."

Secca watched as Richina swung into the saddle of her mount with a long-legged grace. Secca's legs were far too short for such grace, except on a very small mount, and Secca envied those who possessed it, as she had once envied Anna's grace, for all of Anna's protestations that she was not graceful.

For but a moment, Secca's eyes burned, and she felt empty inside.

Then, she shook her head and straightened. She watched Richina ride toward the lancers in black motley, and a faint smile crossed the lips of the older sorceress, a smile of amusement tempered with concern . . . and regret. Then she began to strap her own gear in place behind the saddle of the gray mare.

59

In the late afternoon, Secca and her unofficial council clustered in a circle on a low hillside in the center of the camp. The smoke of cookfires drifted across the group, along with the smell of mutton roasting, sheep purchased all too dearly. Secca was thankful she'd recalled Anna's observation that wars required coins. Yet she wondered if those she had brought, seemingly enough for a liedburg treasury, would even last another three weeks.

She forced her attention back to the mirror on the ground and the spell that held the image that shimmered on the silvered surface.

"Those are picket lines, and they have cut limbs and woven them into fences." Stepan pointed.

The image that Secca had called up in the glass also showed earthworks, spaced at intervals along the woven fir-limb fences, behind which were tents and mounts on tielines, and cookfires. Secca studied the image, as did Stepan, Wilten, Palian, and, not quite indifferently, Haddev. Richina studied Haddev, if covertly, but obviously enough that Secca could feel it.

"Those are to the north, are they not?" asked Haddev.

Stepan nodded.

"The city is on the east side of the river . . . to the south," Secca pointed out. "They have circled it."

"They don't have any forces on the other side?" asked Haddev.

"There's little point to that," replied the arms master.

"They want the port. Once they take the city, they care not if the FreeWomen flee. There is but a single narrow bridge, and if the Sea-Priests destroy it, then they cannot be easily attacked. Their ships hold the Gulf."

"They do not fear reinforcements coming across the bridge?"

"Who would come?" asked Stepan. "The Ranuans have sent what they can. We cannot reach there easily, not from the north with the river cliffs there."

"Oh . . . so that is why the bridge stands yet?" asked Haddev. "Because it is difficult for the Sturinnese to reach, and affords little more aid for the defenders?"

Secca decided she wanted to reprimand Haddev like an apprentice who tried to show off. She didn't, but sang the release spell gently, then looked up, first at Wilten, then at Stepan.

"What do you suggest?"

"The Sturinnese have the hills to the north and east of the port," Wilten said slowly, "but there are low rises that surround the city itself."

"So to get to the defenders, they have to ride down and then up?" asked Secca. "That's why they haven't broken through yet?"

"I would judge so," replied Stepan.

Wilten nodded.

"The glass shows that there are rocky hills farther to the east," Secca offered.

"It would be hard to circle the barriers and to attack from the east or the south," Stepan pointed out.

"Coming from the north, we could get close enough for sorcery, though," Secca said. "If we had the wind behind us, and their fences would make it almost as hard for them to attack us."

"Perhaps . . ." Stepan fingered his chin.

"How far are we from their camp?"

"Twelve to fifteen deks, I would say." Stepan frowned. "A half-day's ride to a camp from which we could attack."

"I'll check what they're doing in the morning," Secca said. "We should meet again then."

"That would be best." Stepan paused. "They do not look as though they had been fighting today, or even yesterday. Yet they had no scouts sent to the north."

"They do have mirror glasses similar to ours, I think," Secca said.

"We must do what we can, but I like that not."

Neither did Secca. As the days went by and winter approached, there was more and more she disliked. Yet . . . if the Sturinnese had an entire winter to fortify Elahwa— and Dolov—the problems she faced now would be insignificant compared to those of the next spring and summer.

60

ELAHWA, EBRA

Five figures stand on the low tower of logs, hastily constructed on the northeasternmost corner of the equally hurriedly created defense works. They all look out into the early morning haze that clings to the edge of the hills, and is dark gray and thick farther north, filling the lowlands to the north like a dark ocean.

"Why do they not attack?" asks the square-faced overcaptain, a stocky woman in a crimson tunic splattered with mud and blood. "Surely, they would not halt their assaults because we received another two companies of lancers, SouthWomen or not."

The taller councilwoman, whose black hair is streaked with silver and cut short, laughs, then nods toward Alcaren. "No. While the good overcaptain is more than welcome, his arrival is not what has given the white pigs pause. The Sorceress-Protector of Defalk is riding south with close to fifteen companies."

"The sorceress died half a season ago," points out the

other and more junior Elahwan overcaptain.

"This is the shadow sorceress, the one she trained." Veria continues to study the hills to the north and east.

"How will she help?" asks the overcaptain of the Ranuan companies. "She is young."

"She has already destroyed more than fifty score—thirty of the eastern lord's men and twenty score Sturinnese." Veria pauses. "She looks yet a child but holds more than a score and a half of years."

"Another unaging one?" asks Alcaren.

"No. She will age." A quick smile flits across Veria's lips. "As will we all before this is done."

"She does not come with the eager blessing of Lord Robero, I would wager," suggests the Ranuan overcaptain.

"It matters not, so long as she comes and attacks. They fear her." Veria gestures toward the heavy ground fog. "Or respect her power. That fog is not natural."

"They did not fear an entire city . . . yet an untried sorceress with half their numbers?" The senior FreeWoman overcaptain's voice carries a touch of disbelief.

"You might recall that her mentor was untried, too," replies Veria evenly. "I raised the same questions you now do. I was wrong. I survived because I was."

The muscular overcaptain's eyes elude Veria's. So do those of the other women overcaptains.

Alcaren nods. "Do you wish us to hold and wait?"

"Yes. This sorceress is strong, but she is inexperienced and untried in such a large battle. The Sturinnese have prepared and learned. They are wily. They will try to force her to exhaust herself so that she cannot attack them. They will attempt to keep her from giving any support to her lancers—and then they will attack. Perhaps then, we can also attack, with Overcaptain Alcaren's companies leading the way." Veria inclines her head to the younger overcaptain.

"When?" asks Alcaren.

"Not today," replies Veria. "They cannot attack through their own fog. They seek time to prepare spells, and perhaps to wait until the white companies at Dolov can ride to attack the sorceress from behind."

Alcaren glances to the north, his eyes narrowing ever so slightly.

61

Secca held the gray mare reined in on the edge of the rocky ridge that overlooked a valley more than two deks wide—a valley filled with fog. The hills were mainly forested, mostly with white birches and firs. To the far southwest, she could see the glint of sunlight on water, on the arm of the Gulf of Discord that formed the shallow harbor serving Elahwa. The city itself was but a blur of light and dark splotches, and the river bridge was out of sight, presumably on the western side of the hilly part of the city that Secca could barely make out.

Even in the midafternoon, under a sun that gave little warmth, Secca's breath was a white fog, and the same white fog issued from the nostrils of the mounts, blown gently southward over the valley.

Stepan pointed at a nearer hillside, close to three deks to the south. "You see . . . their encampment lies on the hills above the fog. The white banners . . ."

From her earlier looks at the Sturinnese encampment, Secca didn't recall any fog, or lakes that would create such fog. "How would we best attain a position high enough to use sorcery?" She paused and added, "If the fog lifts."

"There is a wind out of the north. It will get stronger at night," Wilten said. "That should blow out the fog by morning."

Stepan studied the valley, then drew out the maps he had drawn from Secca's scrying of the area. Finally, he pointed. "The higher ground leads to that ridge to our left.

If we follow it west . . . there . . . we will be on the rise to the north of their encampment . . . there . . . where the trees show out of the mist."

"If the wind holds," Secca mused aloud, "then our spells will carry to them. Even so, with their drums, we'll have to use the arrow spell first." She glanced back at Palian, reined up several yards to the north.

The chief player nodded.

"We can hold a charge, perhaps two, Lady Secca, but they have many more lancers than do we," pointed out Wilten.

"I know." *Everyone has more lancers than does Defalk,* thought Secca. *All Defalk has is three sorceresses and a few assistants . . . and far too many stubborn lords even yet. More lancers would have been better.* Secca still wasn't certain she agreed with Anna's insistence that the liedgeld not be raised too much at any one time, or Anna's concerns about what she had called infrastructures, rather than arms and armsmen. "We will have to sing the spells quickly."

"I will have the players warm up before we ride," Palian said. "That will help them be ready sooner."

For a moment longer Secca looked out across the foggy valley and the hills before looking back at the older arm commander. "You'll post scouts here?" Secca asked Stepan. "We can't keep using the glass if either Richina or I have to use sorcery tomorrow."

"I will have many scouts," Stepan said with a smile that faded as he added, "And so will they, I would wager."

Secca nodded, then eased the gray around, to start back to the adjoining high meadow where her forces had set up camp. She ignored, for the moment, the looks passing between Richina and Haddev, though she would talk to the girl before evening. *Well before evening.*

62

Before dawn, Secca woke with a start at hearing distant thunder, except the sound wasn't thunder, but something far more regular, more rhythmic.

"The drums . . ." she murmured to herself as she scrambled upright and pulled on her riding clothes, and jacket, and her sabre.

Not once as Secca dressed in the darkness did Richina stir.

Secca shook her head. The younger sorceress thought Secca had not heard when she had left and when she had returned. While Secca had cautioned Richina before they had eaten the night before, obviously the young woman had dismissed the cautions. Just as obviously, she had decided to try not to let Secca know.

By the time Secca was out of the tent, Stepan was already walking toward her through the darkness that was beginning to show faint graying above the firs to the east. The sound of the thunder-drums had already faded away.

"Do you know—" she began.

The older man, his face drawn and haggard, shook his head. "Fog . . . the thunder-drums have created a wall of fog. It fills all the valleys around their encampment. It is like a wall of darkness."

"Your scouts?"

"They can see if anyone leaves the fog, but no one has. Otherwise, they are useless."

Secca nodded abruptly. "Let me get my glass."

When she returned to the tent, Secca did not make any attempt to be quiet.

"What . . . is it, lady?" asked Richina sleepily.

"If you hadn't been so besotted with Haddev and gotten

some sleep last night, you'd know," Secca replied tersely, just short of snapping. "As I told you before, he doesn't understand you. He just sees you as a prize, and if you give yourself to him, you won't be. You'll either bear more heirs than you can stand, or, if he's wise, he'll discard you. Either way, it's going to hurt. If you care for him, it will hurt even more." She paused in the entrance to the tent. "Oh . . . the Sturinnese have used the thunder-drums to stop the wind and create more fog."

She stepped outside, carrying the lutar she had not bothered to uncase and the mirror, realizing she shouldn't have been so curt with Richina—and also realizing that she should have started the younger sorceress on scrying the Sturrinese. She shook her head. Once again, her nature had gotten in the way of what she should have done.

Stepan's face was grave as Secca neared. He took the mirror from her, but he did not speak, although his eyes flicked to the tent.

"I suppose I was harsh, but she doesn't understand, and he certainly doesn't." Secca laughed, without joy or mirth. "She will think I neither understand nor care."

The arms commander nodded. "Few could consort with a sorceress. Fewer still should."

The two walked through the damp chill to the campfire. To the south, wisps of dark fog swirled lazily into the graying sky, but the wind was even lighter than the afternoon before, despite Wilten's prediction that it should have strengthened.

Secca's fingers felt clumsy as she tuned the lutar, and it took her longer than usual—or it felt that way. Before she finished a pair of vocalises, Wilten, Palian, and Delvor had joined them. Haddev stood well back. Richina did not appear.

The scrying song was short.

"Mirror, mirror, on the ground,
show us where Sturinn's forces may be found . . ."

The mirror obliged with an image of the Sturinnese camp from above, a camp strangely quiet, given the drums of earlier. Cookfires were blazing with the early high flames that indicated a time before food would be cooked and served. Mounts remained unsaddled and upon tielines run from posts to trees.

Secca quickly tried another spell, one seeking the thunder-drummers. But they were clustered around a cookfire, warming their hands.

A third spell got her a Sea-Priest looking at a mirror.

As she released the last spell, all too aware of the daystars flashing before her eyes, she wondered if the Sea-Priest were watching her in his mirror. Her fingers shook on the lutar as she lowered it.

"You ate not this morning, did you?" asked Palian.

Secca shook her head, squinting against the flashes of light.

The chief player stepped away from the campfire.

"Lady . . . they wait, and they must have a reason for such," offered Wilten.

"Either they wish to force us to attack in poor conditions, or they expect aid," Secca suggested. "Or both."

"How—"

"In a few moments, I will try the glass again," Secca said tiredly.

"Lady . . . here is some bread." Palian stepped forward.

"Thank you."

After eating several chunks of bread and some yellow cheese just short of molding, and drinking nearly half a water bottle, Secca stood and lifted the lutar.

"Mirror, mirror on the ground,
show us what aid for Sturinn may be found,
whether by ships upon the sea
or lancers riding from where they be . . ."

The mirror silvered, then displayed a line of lancers riding down from a hold on a bluff. A misty fog rose from the heated surface of the glass, momentarily distorting the image presented in the cold predawn light.

"The Sturinnese lancers at Dolov," murmured Stepan, "Still, they are six days away, perhaps a week."

"But they do not expect more help from the ships," Palian pointed out.

"We have a little time for the fog to lift or be blown out," Stepan said. "If it will . . ."

"Let me think," Secca said slowly. As well as Stepan, she knew that the Sea-Priests could hold the fog for days if the weather remained calm.

She recased the lutar, and picked up the traveling mirror, then walked slowly back toward her tent.

Richina stood before the tent, fully dressed. She bowed. "I am sorry I displeased you, Lady Secca."

The formality of her tone showed more anger than contriteness to Secca. The older sorceress motioned for Richina to follow her into the tent. There Secca slid the lutar and mirror onto the ground cloth under the cot. She straightened, then sat slowly on the cot, before gesturing to the younger woman to sit on her own cot.

After a moment of quiet, Secca sighed and looked at her charge. "Richina . . ." Her voice was soft, gentle, sad. "Do you think that I am not a woman? Do you think I have never felt what you feel? Do you think that I do not see how comely Haddev is? Or how warm was the smile of Lythner?"

Richina did not reply. Her eyes were bright with unshed tears, but Secca was uncertain whether those tears were more of anger or of unhappiness.

"Do you think I do not care about you?" asked Secca.

"You sounded so angry."

"I suppose I was. I wished to spare you from what will happen with Haddev, and you did not listen . . . but we do not spare ourselves. Sorceresses and women do not." Her laugh was half-gentle, half-ironically self-mocking. "Why should you be any different from me, or from Lady Anna? Or Clayre . . . or Jolyn?"

"You . . . I thought . . ."

"You think I do not favor men?" Secca shook her head. "I do not favor men who would use me, or hide their fear of me with a smile. I do not favor men who seek me only to provide an heir or lands they could not get otherwise. And for me . . . then whom does that leave?"

"Oh . . . lady . . ." Richina swallowed. "You sounded so cold . . . I am sorry."

"You think it not, but I would spare you what I can. I suppose none of us can spare another, not as we would wish . . ."

"He is gentle, lady, and has asked nothing of me."

"That may be." Secca hoped that was true, for all of their sakes. "You cannot afford to give of yourself, not until we have done what must be done. Remember what one road spell cost you."

Richina paused. "I know."

"He is handsome, but there is more to life than handsome." Secca paused, massaging her neck for a moment.

The younger sorceress asked, "What of the thunderdrums?"

Secca leaned forward from where she sat on the edge of the cot. "They have used them to build a wall of thick fog around their encampment, and they do not prepare for battle."

"What will you do?"

"For the day, we will wait and watch. Our lancers and players and mounts can use the rest."

"If it continues . . . ?"

"I worry about that. I worry greatly." Secca massaged her forehead. "Their Sea-Priest at Dolov has seen what we do and is sending those lancers south. They cannot reach us for nearly a week, but . . ."

"But?" prompted Richina.

"If the weather remains mild, then they can continue to hold the sorcerous fog. If it should storm, then we will be at a great disadvantage. I will need your assistance in scrying and perhaps in much more. Much more."

Richina fell silent, her eyes not meeting Secca's.

The redheaded sorceress, who suddenly felt far older than she was, stared sightlessly at the time and travel-worn silk side panels of the tent.

63

From the saddle of the gray mare, Secca looked out across the valley, again in the early dawn, once more at another thick layer of fog that separated her forces from the Sturinnese encampment. Behind her were Stepan, Wilten, Haddev, Richina, and the two chief players. All were mounted and looking southward across the gray that blanketed the valley below. If the valley were narrow—like a river gorge—Secca might have considered building a bridge, but no sorceress could song-build a structure spanning nearly three deks—and even if she could . . . she and the players would be exhausted and worthless for weeks.

"The fog is thicker than before," Wilten said. "We cannot wait and wait."

"Not for long," agreed Stepan. "Yet to attack through it would be foolhardy. Even scouts would lose their way, and could be slain or captured by any Sturinnese waiting there."

Above Secca, the sky was cloudless, the air still, but cold. Clearsong's pale white disk was at the zenith, while Darksong would be at its zenith near midnight. Secca glanced again at the fog that shrouded the valleys to the south. With such weather, she feared the Sturinnese could create and hold their fog for days, if not weeks. All the scrying glass showed was that the Sturinnese forces maintained their sentries and picket lines, practiced arms and thunder-drums ... and waited.

"Let us see where the Sturinnese lancers from Dolov are. Then we will see what we must do." With a nod at Wilten and Stepan, she turned her mount and rode the gray back along the ridge and toward her tent.

Once back in the encampment, she dismounted and extended the reins to the lancer guard. "Achar ... if you would ... I won't need her for a while."

"Yes, lady."

"Thank you." Secca offered a smile, then hurried into the tent to reclaim lutar and mirror. She brought out the mirror and began to retune the lutar, going through a vocalise as she did so, hoping to be ready by the time the others had taken care of their mounts.

Still, the others had gathered and were standing in a semicircle around the mirror as Secca finished her third vocalise. She cleared her throat and launched into the short spell.

"Mirror, mirror, on the ground ..."

As her words died away, the glass turned a blank silver, then misted over before the swirling mists dissolved and revealed an image. The white-clad lancers who had been at Dolov were breaking camp, forming up into columns once more. On the left side of the image was a river.

"The river is not so wide there. I would judge another four days, three if they ride hard, before they reach the River Syne," Stepan said.

"How long can they hold that fog?" asked Wilten.

"For days," Secca replied, "if the weather remains as it has."

"There is no sign of change," observed Delvor.

For a time, no one spoke.

Finally, Secca said, "There may be a way. I will work on it and let you know." She smiled at Stepan, and then

Wilten. "If your scouts will keep us informed . . ."

"That we will."

"Yes, lady."

After all had left but Richina and the lancer guards, Secca recased the lutar.

Richina picked up the mirror and carried it into the tent behind Secca, replacing it in its case and sliding the case under the narrow cot.

Secca slid the lutar beside the mirror.

"Can I help, lady?" asked Richina.

"If you would get me some water . . . I need to think."

Richina nodded and slipped out of the tent.

Secca sat on the cot, in the middle, where she wouldn't tip it over.

The problems were simple enough. The lowlands that were filled with fog were too wide for her spells to carry across and too deep for casual winds or breezes to disperse. So she couldn't sneak up in the night the way she had with Mynntar. She couldn't get the archers close enough to attack the drums or drummers without going into the fog itself.

So . . . she had to get rid of the fog . . . somehow.

Wind? Could she raise a wind to disperse the fog? She got wind when she did the mining spell.

She pulled out several folded sheets of paper and the grease pencil and began to jot down phrases.

64

In the grayness and almost still air before dawn, Secca and Richina—and Wilten, Stepan, Haddev, and the two chief players—looked out from the high ridge at the fog below. That fog had begun to thin enough that the higher ground, such as the tree-lined rise below, was intermittently visible, although the hillside opposite them, more than a dek away, remained swathed in the heavy gray mist.

Haddev glanced at Richina, then at Secca. Richina did not look at the heir to Synek.

"If . . . if the wind blows away the fog . . ." Secca glanced to Stepan, "can we take that rise there quickly?" She gestured.

"It is closer to us than to them. If they are not waiting . . ." Stepan shrugged.

"The glass shows that they remain in their encampment," Secca replied.

"That is lower than their camp, but it is the highest ground. We could charge from there if they tried to attack." Stepan looked at Secca. "Your players will need to be ready to play."

"They can play a spell here, and then remount and ride down," Palian affirmed. "It will not take long."

Delvor just nodded at Palian's words, then brushed back the lank brown hair that always seemed to fall across his face. His eyes were clouded, Secca noted, as if he were considering a fingering, or a chord progression, the way he did before he came up with something new for his lutarists.

"There is little fog on this side of the ridge," Stepan said. "Will it harm us or disrupt your spell if we begin to ride down?"

"No. It could get windy, but that's all."

"Wind we will take, if we can gain position." Stepan glanced at Haddev. "If you would use your lancers to guard the sorceress and the players?"

"That we can do." Haddev nodded, then turned his mount back toward the black-clad lancers of Silberfels.

"We will follow Stepan, if you will permit," added Wilten. "We can offer greater protection if we are well before you."

"Thank you, Wilten." Secca offered a smile she did not feel and dismounted, handing the gray's reins to Achar.

She cleared her throat, then stepped forward to the most open point of the ridge.

"Dismount and quick-tune!" commanded Palian as she dismounted, and then unstrapped her violino from behind her mount.

"Dismount . . ." followed the order from Delvor.

The first players formed a core, and the second players drew up in an arc around them.

Only the faintest hint of a breeze flowed from behind Secca, scarcely enough to matter, one way or the other. The vagrant breeze died away even as she began a quick vocalise.

Behind her rose the sounds of tuning. To her left, the double column of riders began to angle down a narrow way that was more animal track than trail.

When Secca finished the first vocalise, Richina extended a water bottle.

"Thank you." Secca took a swallow, then glanced at Palian.

"We stand ready, lady."

Secca glanced across the valley, then at the lancers descending. All she could see moving were her forces. She looked back at Palian and nodded.

"Prepare to play. The second building spell," commanded the chief player.

"Prepare to play," echoed Delvor. "The massed harmony for the building spell."

The first bars of the accompaniment echoed out past Secca, somehow almost eerily in the lightening gray that preceded dawn, and then it was time to sing the spell, against the bright melody and the deeper chords of the heavy lutars of the second players.

"Bring us wind both fierce and strong,
to sweep this fog to the south along . . ."

A low grumbling reverberated from the ground, then passed, even before Secca was well into the words, but the sky began to darken immediately, and the wind began to build behind Secca's back.

Within moments, the light gray of the sky had turned blackish, and the wind was whipping Secca's jacket around her and her hair against her forehead and cheeks. The gusts of wind, ever growing, seemed to rip at the gray fog in the lowlands below, tearing chunks away. A faint pink-orange light began to creep from behind the trees to the southeast.

Secca stood there for a moment, half-amazed that the spell had worked. It should have, for it was pure Clearsong, but she had not known if it would.

"Lady," suggested Richina, "we need to ride."

Secca shook her head and turned to Achar, taking the gray's reins from the young lancer and mounting.

As Secca settled herself in the saddle, Richina extended a chunk of bread and a wedge of cheese. "Eat as you ride."

Secca took the bread and cheese.

"Players!" ordered Palian. "Remount and ride! Follow the sorceress."

"Silberfels!" came Haddev's order above the sound of the still-rising wind. "Follow the players! Blades at the ready. Watch the sides of the trail."

Secca and Richina were almost at the head of the second column, with only Achar and Dymen riding before them on the trail that angled downward. The wind was cold, and it half-moaned, half-howled around Secca's ears as she rode and tried to chew and swallow the dry bread and hard cheese.

Once in the birches and firs, Secca could only catch glimpses of Stepan's and Wilten's lancers. She swallowed, hoping that she could reach the rise on the far side of the valley before the Sturinnese could gather. The descent seemed to take a glass or more, with the wind moaning and howling and misty fog shreds obscuring her view, and then passing, with yet another segment of the disintegrating fog bank taking the place of the last ... and again passing.

By the time she had finished the bread and cheese, the section of the trail which she followed had eased into a gentler decline, and most of the fog seemed to have cleared from the valley.

"It's longer than it looked," said Richina quietly.

"Yes." Too much longer, thought the older sorceress. "We'll have to hurry when we get to the rise."

As soon as Secca was out of the trees and on the grassy flat, she urged the gray forward, into a quick trot. She didn't need to be caught on low ground. Neither did the players.

As she rode, she swallowed again. She hadn't realized just how much lower the valley was. Yet ... if she turned, she'd be abandoning Stepan and Wilten and their lancers. Better that she do her best from the low rise ahead. Changing even a poor plan in midstream would probably be worse than carrying it out. That's what you hope, she told herself.

A glance to the south showed no Sturinnese ... not yet.

As she rode up the gentle slope onto the rise, running through a vocalise to keep her voice ready, Secca could see that the entire north slope of the hill she faced was nearly bare of the concealing fog. She could also see movement at the top of the hill, figures in white, she thought, although the firs obscured any clear images.

A series of trumpet commands rang out from the south, echoing off the ridge behind the Defalkan and Ebran forces.

Secca glanced around the ridge, then turned in the saddle, looking back at Palian, before gesturing. "The knoll there. Set up and ready the players."

Stepan had clearly marked the area, because his lancers had left a semicircle there, and a clear path.

The sorceress reined up the gray and swung down out of the saddle, walking quickly onto the slightly higher ground on the south side of the rise.

A dull rumbling rose, and then died away.

"Dismount! Quick-tune!" Palian's voice cut through the morning air.

The players reined up, and at that moment, the sun seemed to rise over the eastern side of the valley, flooding it with an orange light. The last shreds of fog rose into the sky, dark blots that thinned and then vanished.

White specks appeared among the birch trunks, white splotches that moved downhill, almost like a breaking wave.

"They are less than a half a dek away, lady," Stepan called.

Secca shook her head, forcing her thoughts back to what needed to be done, calling up the spell she needed to use.

The quick sounds of tuning died away, and the red-haired sorceress turned toward Palian.

"We stand ready."

Secca looked back to the south, where two hundred or so yards of brown grass separated the bottom of the rise where she and her forces waited from the trees on the north slope of the hill held by the Sturinnese. The brown meadow remained empty of lancers or mounts.

Secca waited.

The fog had vanished, but wind was lighter, as if the effects of her spell had died away.

Another series of trumpet calls issued into morning air from the south, then echoed from the hillside behind the players and the lancers. Mounts *whuffed*, and someone coughed, but the air became even more still. The brown meadow to the south of the rise remained vacant.

Secca swallowed, still waiting.

Abruptly, like a thunderclap, the roll of drums began, a triplet of trumpet notes sang forth, and a sea of white-clad lancers charged from the trees, forming into four wedges as they galloped toward Secca.

Secca swallowed, then ordered, "The arrow spell!"

She shouted to Elfens. "Make ready with your shafts!"

"The arrow spell!" echoed Palian. "Mark!"

"Stand ready to nock arrows!" Elfens' voice trumpeted over the howling moan of the winds.

"The arrow spell! At my mark . . ." ordered Palian. "Mark!"

Singing as strongly as she could, yet trying to be open and not to force her voice, fighting the urge to push and strain against the thunder-drums, the spells they carried, and the wind, Secca sang the spell.

> *"Heads of arrows, shot into the air,*
> *strike the drumskins, straight through there,*
> *rend the drums and those who play . . ."*

Even toward the end of the spell, strong as her voice felt, she could hear and feel the pressure of the thunder-drums, a pressure that tried to contain, to push back the impacts of her words and the music of her players. With that pressure came a strong wind, blowing out of the south, carrying the scent of damp and moldy meadow grass to Secca, a wind seemingly directed at her, grit flaying her face and eyes.

As she finished, she watched open-mouthed as more than half the heavy arrows curved, fighting against the wind, and perhaps against sorcery, before diving into the damp grasses of the meadow near the woods.

There was a lessening of the drums, a raggedness, and a momentary faltering, but the drumming continued.

Secca glanced at the wave of white-clad horsemen thundering toward her too-small force. A second arrow spell might stop the thunder-drums totally, but would she have any lancers left?

"The flame spell!" Secca ordered.

"The flame spell! At my mark . . ." ordered Palian. "Mark!"

The tone from the players remained strong and true,

and the heavy-chorded harmony from the second players was solid.

Secca sang:

"Turn to fire, turn to flame,
all those who stand against our name,
turn to ashes, turn to dust . . ."

The drums and the wind rose, along with the pounding hoofs of the Sturinnese mounts, now less than fifty yards from the base of the rise, yet when Secca's last words died away, the sky flashed, and the flame lightnings flared—but only across the first lines of the charging Sturinnese. Horses and men went down in charred heaps, and the scent of burnt flesh flowed back to Secca, seemingly instantly. Nor did the lightnings reach all of that first rank.

The white wedge of riders to the west, toward the river and farthest to the right, seemed almost untouched as the lancers surged up the rise—and were met by Stepan's lancers, who had managed a short charge downhill.

The lightnings died away, and from the hillside to the south, the pounding of the thunder-drums rose once more, not quite so loudly. With that rhythmic thundering came fiercer winds, howling, ripping at Secca's jacket and hair, pelting fine grit into her face and eyes.

She squinted out across the lowlands. Through her watering eyes, she could see that the remaining Sturinnese lancers had turned their mounts back toward the cover of the birches and firs. Even those who had attacked Stepan's lancers on the flank were falling back and turning their mounts. But though they had turned, the pounding of the thunder-drums continued.

"The arrow spell! Again!" Secca turned and shouted to Elfens. "Make ready more shafts!"

"The arrow spell!" echoed Palian. "Mark!"

"Nock arrows!" Elfens' voice again rose above the winds.

Secca turned into the grit-bearing wind again, squaring her shoulders, then trying to relax her body. As the first bar of the players' spelltune echoed across the lowlands between the rise and the firs and birches that the lancers had retreated into, the dull rumbling of the drums intensified once more.

Secca offered the second arrow spell.

"Heads of arrows, shot into the air. . . ."

With her words, the wind rose, seemingly directed at her, more grit slashing across her cheeks and toward her eyes—and once more, the majority of the heavy arrows were turned by the winds. Not all—some must have struck a drummer or two, because the drumbeat faltered . . . but only for a time.

Secca could barely stand, daystars flashing across her vision, but the drums continued to beat, and heavy fog began to form in the lowest and dampest part of the meadow below the rising, streaming upward even as Secca watched through her dayflashed vision.

"Lady!" An Ebran captain in green rode toward Secca. "The arms commander would have us ride back to the high ridge."

"Back to the high ridge," Secca shouted back. "We will join forces there." She stumbled toward the players, stopping short of Palian. "Remount . . . we must ride back to the high ridge before they regroup."

"Players mount . . . back to the high ridge. Reform there!" ordered Palian.

"Remount! Now!" followed Delvor's commands.

Secca staggered toward the gray mare, using what felt like the last of her strength to mount. Richina, already mounted, eased her mount next to Secca's. The younger sorceress extended a water bottle.

"Lady, you must drink . . . and eat as you ride."

With a nod, and a trembling hand, Secca took the water bottle. She drank as she rode at a fast trot back down the rise, glancing back over her shoulder. Behind her, Secca could hear the near frantic pounding of the thunder-drums, and feel the cold wind die away once more as she crossed the stretch of damp and brown-grassed meadow between the rise and the trees on the south side of the ridge which she had ridden down such a short time before.

Once back amid the trees and riding up the trail, Secca could see patches of fog appearing, oozing upward out of the ground itself, near-instantly.

Richina offered some bread, and Secca wolfed that down. While the daystars did not vanish from her vision, they did diminish in frequency and intensity.

"What a dissonant mess . . ." murmured the redhead under her breath between bites of the bread. She glanced over her shoulder. All she could see through the trees were patches of fog and trees.

By the time she was halfway up the ridge trail, the drums had died into silence and the lowlands were again covered with fog.

Once back on the ridge, the sorceress reined up the gray mare, and surveyed the lowlands and the hills to the south. It was as though she had done nothing—except destroy a few of the enemy and lose who knew how many of Stepan's lancers.

She just kept looking at the swirling fog that had refilled the valley that separated her forces from those of the Sturinnese.

Stepan eased his mount up beside her.

Secca shook her head.

"It felt worse than it was," offered the silver-haired arms commander. "We lost less than a company. They lost close to three companies, perhaps four."

"They have twice our number, and they will have more soon," Secca replied, "if I cannot find a way to stop this fog."

Stepan looked down for a moment, not quite meeting her eyes, before he looked at her. "That is true. We cannot hold our position, not if we are attacked from the north."

Secca nodded.

After a moment, she said, "I must think." And eat . . . so she could think.

65

By just past noon, when she stepped out of the tent into the cold calm air under a sky that held but a trace of high haze, Secca thought she had a workable plan. She had best, she knew, for the mirror had revealed that the Sturinnese lancers from the north were no more than three days' ride away.

"Richina . . . I'll be back in a few moments. I need to talk to Elfens. Then we need to talk."

"Yes, lady." Richina's voice was polite, but abstracted, as she glanced toward the east end of the camp.

"He's all right. He's just worried."

"Who?" Richina flushed, adding quickly, "His lancers weren't attacked, were they?"

"No. Like all of us, he's worried about the battle that will have to come," Secca said, before walking toward the higher end of the camp area. Quietly, Achar followed her. Secca could only hope that Richina would see Haddev for what he was before the younger sorceress did something truly foolish.

Secca found the chief archer on the west side of the camp, working with a pot of glue, refletching some arrows on a flat stone.

"Lady . . . if you would wait but a moment . . ."

"Go ahead." Secca smiled faintly. "We will need every shaft."

After several moments, the chief archer set down the glue pot and the knife and stood. "Your wish, Lady Secca?"

"Elfens . . . you still have arrows with the large iron heads?"

"But, of course."

"How many do you have?"

"Not many . . . perhaps three score," admitted the chief archer.

"That will be enough . . . if you can get them all into the air while I do a spell."

"That we can."

"We will need them before dawn—well before dawn." Secca's eyes fixed on the long-faced man. "Can you keep your archers together in darkness and a thick fog?"

"Ah . . . that I can do . . . but how will they know where to place their arrows?"

"That is my task."

"We can get our shafts high, so that you can do the rest."

"That is all I ask."

"We will be ready."

"I will let you know more later, after I have worked out the details with Wilten and Stepan."

Elfens bowed, his long face somber.

Secca walked quickly back across the camp toward the single tent, her breath still a fog in the cold air, her boots crunching on the half-frozen ground. The ever-colder nights were yet another reason why she needed to act.

As she approached the tent, Richina stepped forward. "Palian . . . she and Delvor were here a few moments ago. So was Stepan. They looked most worried."

"I am most certain that they are." Secca offered an off-center smile. "I'll need your help, Richina. More than ever before."

"Another building spell, lady?" Puzzlement colored the younger sorceress's words.

Secca shook her head. "The flame spell."

Richina swallowed.

"You know the melody," Secca said. "I'll write out the words for you. Best you study it a while this afternoon and tonight."

"But . . . you are the stronger sorceress."

"I doubt I will be by the time we join battle tomorrow."

"The fog?"

"If I do what I must, there will be no fog, or little enough by morning. If there is, then I will disperse it, and you will use the flame spell against the Sturinnese."

"Will they then attack?"

"It matters not. We must if they do not. We cannot survive a battle where we are attacked from both sides, and if we retreat and leave eastern Ebra in the hands of the Sea-Priests, we will see women in chains across the east for generations to come."

"You do not think we could dislodge them?"

Secca raised her eyebrows. "Hadrenn is hard-pressed to raise twelve companies of lancers. Lord Robero would be hard-pressed to raise twice that in additional lancers. Few of the levies in Defalk could stand against the Sturinnese, and there are already more than fifty companies of Sturinnese in Ebra, counting those we destroyed near Synek. If they take Elahwa and hold Dolov, do you not think we will see more? And more thunder-drums?"

"We will," Richina agreed.

"And with sorcery against sorcery, then what?"

"Many will die."

"If we fail now . . . many more will die." Secca shook her head. "I will write out the two spells you must use. Then we will see Palian, and you will go over the words in your mind while the players play . . ."

As Secca explained, Richina nodded.

The older sorceress could only hope that the younger

understood . . . before she saw what would happen, were she successful.

Secca tried not to consider what would happen if they failed.

66

SPEREA, NESEREA

Belmar nods to the two guards as he steps into the white-walled private study, but the pair remains stationed on each side of the door, inside the study. Their eyes never leave him as he steps toward the man who awaits him.

In turn, Belmar bows politely to the holder with the iron-gray hair. "Cloftus, it is good to see you once more." As he straightens the fingers of his right hand pass the empty scabbard at his belt. In his left hand, he carries a leather case five spans in length, large enough for a small instrument.

"I must say that I was most surprised at your appearance—not at the force which accompanied you, however." Cloftus smiles, but does not return the bow. "You were wise to leave them well back of the walls. You know you cannot take Sperea—not without siege engines and far more armsmen than even you can afford." The taller and older holder remains standing beside the desk. The sabre in the scabbard at his side threatens to bump the pedestal leg of the desk, a leg carved to resemble a climbing rose upon a circular trestle.

"I have no intention of wasting siege engines on Sperea—even if I had any to waste." Belmar laughs easily. "Besides, I have a proposition. It might be of interest to you."

"It might. I cannot imagine why, but if you are so convinced that I would be that you would walk in unarmed . . . I should at least listen." A wintry smile accompanies the light tone of Cloftus' words. "Especially given . . . our history."

"What do you think about the daughter of the late Lord High Counselor succeeding him? Does it appeal to you?"

"You obviously do not care for that, or you would not have asked," points out Cloftus. "As for me . . ." He pauses and smiles. "Let us just say that we could do better and we could do worse. What have you in mind that would be better?"

"The restoration of the Prophet of Music in Neserea, the independence of our land from Defalkan domination." Belmar shrugs. "I cannot imagine you enjoy being under the domination of foreign sorceresses."

Cloftus frowns, fingers his chin. "I cannot say I have ever liked anyone trying to dominate me, Belmar. But little of that have I seen in the past score of years. Do you think we will see such in the years ahead?"

"When a land controls not its own destiny, that is bound to happen."

"I see. What have you in mind? Your proposition?"

"I seek your support in becoming the successor to the last Prophet." Belmar delivers the words easily.

Cloftus laughs, ruefully, but not mockingly. "As I recall, one sorceress destroyed the last Prophet, and there are three now."

"And all three together have not her power or her wit. One foreign sorceress cannot stand against three-quarters of Neserea, not with but a mere girl as Counselor and her mother acting as a Mansuuran puppet."

"I would not call Lady Aerlya a puppet, Belmar. Nor a tool. Strong-willed, even a bitch, but never a puppet."

"What we call her need bear no relation to what is." Belmar laughs gently. "Surely, you would not begin to quibble over words. I believe you called me . . . what was it . . . the legitimate offspring of an extended line of unconsorted minor holders?" Belmar shakes his head. "Your words were even less pleasant, I fear."

"Did you come all this way to insult me?" Cloftus

smiles, his eyes going to the guards, his fingers dropping to the hilt of his blade.

"Dissonance, no." Belmar smiles. "I brought something you should see . . ." He gently and slowly opens the leather case to display the instrument within.

"A small lutar, it would appear . . . a lady's toy."

Belmar adjusts the strings. "It's most similar to the one used by the Sorceress of the East. It has a beautiful tone."

"What has this to do with your proposition?" Cloftus raises his eyebrows.

"Everything." Belmar's fingers run across the strings. "Everything. You see . . ." He pauses and clears his throat, then smiles, before beginning to sing in a strong baritone.

"With their own blades, slay all here but
me . . . with their own . . ."

Cloftus lurches forward, yanking his sabre from the scabbard so violently that it bangs back into the desk.

The two guards, after a momentary hesitation, draw their own blades and edge toward the younger holder.

Belmar, still smiling, finishes the double couplet and leaps back toward the closed windows to the corner balcony.

The looks of surprise on the faces of the three armed men are short-lived as their blades take on a life of their own, and then take their owners' lives as well. After a short time, the study is silent, and Belmar remains the only figure standing.

He walks to the balcony and opens the door, stepping outside into the chill air, where his breath comes out in white puffs. From within his tunic, he takes a yellow cylinder and unrolls it—a short yellow pennant attached to a polished wooden rod.

Below the steep wall stands a group dressed in brown drab, almost invisible to the eye.

Belmar waves the yellow pennant, and is answered

by a crimson one. He pauses, holding the yellow pennant up, then drops it.

The players in brown begin to play. At the second bar, Belmar begins the spell.

> *"Within each Sperean breast, freeze each*
> *armsman's heart ..."*

67

A cough in the darkness preceded the words Secca dreaded. "Lady? It is two glasses before dawn."

"Thank you," Secca whispered back to the guard outside the tent. She slowly rolled into a sitting position on the narrow cot, took a deep breath, and began to fumble for her overshirt and tunic in the darkness.

With a sound half-moan, half-groan, Richina shifted her weight on the other cot, but her breathing returned to that of a sleeper.

Secca eased into her tunic, pulled on her boots, and then her riding jacket, slowly, for her fingers fumbled with the clothing in the darkness. The cramping in her lower abdomen didn't help, either, nor the faint nausea that came with it. She hardly needed the additional complications of the proof that she was a woman right before sorcery and a battle, but there was no help for it, none at all. She decided against wearing the hat, but stuffed it into the saddlebag in case she needed it later.

Finally, she stood, then bent to ease the leather-cased lutar and saddlebags from under the cot. She carried them outside the tent, then slipped back inside the silken panels to retrieve the water bottle and the provisions bag.

Back outside the tent, in the flickering light of the single torch, with Achar and Rukor standing back several paces, on guard, Secca began to eat, mainly the dry bread, with occasional bites of cheese. She tried to ignore the cramping and nausea, knowing that sorcery on an empty stomach would be a disaster, and also knowing that eating so early in the day in her present condition would make her even less comfortable.

When she had eaten all she could force down, she took a last swallow from the water bottle and corked it. She knelt and checked the small bottles in the saddlebag once again to make sure the stoppers were firmly in place. She was almost finished when she sensed someone coming, and glanced up as a figure walked toward her.

Stepan halted a yard away. Even in the uncertain light, Secca could see the circles under his eyes, and the haggardness in his face. She stood, wondering if she looked as tired as did the arms-commander.

"Lady, the lancers and archers are preparing to mount."

"I'm almost ready."

"Best I lead the archers with my first company," said Stepan quietly.

"You don't have to," Secca protested.

"And if aught happens to you, then how do I tell Lord Hadrenn or your lord?" asked Stepan.

"Your watch will wake the players and Richina in another glass?" Secca asked. "So they will be ready when I return."

"That they will."

"I'm ready."

"I will have the men mount." Stepan turned and slipped back into the darkness.

After another long swallow from the water bottle, the red-haired sorceress picked up her gear and walked toward the tieline fifty yards behind the tent. There, the gray mare waited, lifting her head as Secca neared. Achar followed Secca, carrying a pitch torch he had lit from the one burning outside the tent.

As Secca saddled the gray in the flickering torchlight,

she glanced to the east, but all she could see was the purpled blackness of night, and the brightest stars shining through a thin haze. To the west, Darksong hung just above the horizon. Secca shivered.

Once more, there was little wind, although the night was chill. She made sure both saddlebags were fastened tightly before strapping the lutar in place.

She mounted and rode southward toward the open section of the ridge, Achar following on his mount with the torch. They reined up at the head of the column, where Stepan waited with a vanguard of a half-score of guards. Behind Stepan and the van were the archers, and behind them a company of lancers.

In the dim light, Secca nodded to the older man.

"Douse the torches!" ordered Stepan. "Down the trail. No talking. Words carry in the fog."

Slowly, the mounts of the vanguard began to move, over the ridge and onto the narrow trail. Once into the trees the fog thickened, so much that Secca could scarcely see more than a pair of yards before her, cutting off the small amount of light from the stars.

"I'll have to send scouts out once we reach the bottom," murmured Stepan, as he leaned in the saddle toward Secca.

"I know. But the closer to the trees on their hill the better."

"Not too close. A hundred yards."

"That's fine."

In the clammy heavy grayness, the ride down the narrow trail was slow, far slower than the last time, and that had seemed to take forever. Secca listened, but all she heard was the breathing of mounts and the impact of hoofs on hard ground.

Stepan said nothing, but Secca felt she knew what he was thinking, that she risked much with such a predawn effort in fog where no one could truly see. Yet the risks of not acting were so much greater. She took a slow breath and resettled herself in the saddle, trying to ignore the dull cramps and nausea that persisted, and attempting to warm up with a series of softer vocalises she hoped would not carry, or not too far.

In time—how much later, she was not certain—the trail flattened, and then opened onto the browned and flattened grasses of the lowlands.

Stepan hissed, and eight lancers eased forward from the van and out into the deep gray that swallowed them before they were three yards away.

"Four will scout the trees, and four will form a line where we should halt. With luck we will find one of them." Stepan's soft laugh was rueful. "One hopes, at least."

So did Secca.

The meadow grasses were coated with a silvery frost, yet another sign that winter was upon Ebra, and one that told Secca that she had little enough time to defeat the Sea-Priests' forces, if indeed she could. She cocked her head, but the valley was silent except for the *whuffing* of the mounts and the occasional crackling of the more frozen and stiffer stalks of meadow grass.

Before long, Secca could make out the figure of a single lancer, shadowy, appearing out of the mist. He did not speak until Stepan and Secca reined up. "I am the third, ser. The others are at the trees. They will call if the Sturinnese near."

As Stepan quietly reordered the lancers, Secca dismounted and handed the gray's reins to Achar, then unstrapped the lutar and set it on the ground before opening the left saddlebag and extracting more than half the small bottles. She paused. She could hear nothing but the occasional *whuff* of a mount, or the creak of a lancer shifting his weight in his saddle. After unstoppering each bottle, she took the lutar from its case, and quickly ran through the tuning.

Then she began to play and started the first spell—the poison for the officers and thunder-drummers.

"Seek and carry through this night's air,
crystals strong to all drummers, camped up there.

Take this heavy stuff; infuse through song,
within the blood and sinew strong,
within the brain and heart to dwell
so no other battles will they live to tell . . .

Then distribute all the rest
through the blood of captains best . . ."

When the last sounds of the spell and accompaniment died away, Secca paused, straining to see if she could hear some-thing . . . anything.

There was not a sound beyond that of the mounts of her force, nothing, not from the encampment up the hillside, nor from the scouts.

After a moment, she cleared her throat, then called softly, "Elfens?"

The archer appeared out of the misty gray. "Yes, lady?"

"When I begin the next spell, have your archers loose as many shafts as they can, in a high arc toward the trees to the south—that's the way I'm facing. Keep lofting them up until I stop singing."

"That we can do. Give me a moment to have them ready."

"Call when you are ready."

"Yes, lady."

Secca squared her shoulders, her fingers touching the strings of the lutar, her eyes looking into the featureless gray before her, trying to visualize what she wanted the arrowheads to do.

"Archers ready!" came the soft call.

Secca's fingers touched the strings, and she sang forth the second spell, the one for the drums and drummers.

"Heads of arrows, shot into the air,
strike the drumskins, straight through there,
rend the drums and those who play . . .
for their spells and Darksong pay!"

She ran through the same spell twice before lowering the lutar and taking several deep breaths. Then she quickly recased the lutar and strapped it behind her saddle before remounting the gray.

"Are you finished?" asked Stepan.

"For now. From here."

"Lancers . . . . return to the ridge. Pass the order," the older officer called softly. "Bring in the scouts."

As the hissed orders passed through the fog, Secca and Stepan led the way back through the fog and across the brown-grassed meadow, following the traces of their earlier passage.

"You used different spells, but both were directed at the drummers." Stepan's words were not quite a question.

"Without the drummers, our sorcery should work."

"It has before," Stepan agreed in a low voice. "It must now, for I fear they have more lancers than we have counted."

"How many?"

"That . . . your glass does not show, but the smoke from the cookfires and the expanse of their encampment . . . perhaps as many as forty companies."

In spite of herself, Secca winced. "Why did you not tell me this earlier?"

Stepan shrugged. "Would it have made any difference?"

"You were afraid I would leave?" Secca could feel the anger building.

"No. I feared that too many lancers would vanish. I had seen what sorcery can do before you came. None of the lancers have."

Secca wasn't sure she believed Stepan, but, at the moment, as he had said, it made no difference, except that she would probably have to be ready to perform more sorcery later in the day. Ignoring, once more, the cramping, she forced herself to eat a few more mouthfuls of dry bread, interspersed with the cheese.

After a long silence, Stepan asked, "You have said nothing. Are you angry that I did not tell you?"

"Some," Secca admitted, "but you were right. It only means we must fight now."

In the silence that followed, Secca kept listening, but could hear nothing from the south, and that worried her more than if she had heard sounds of pursuit or trumpets of alarm. She continued to nibble at the bread and cheese she had brought while she rode upward on the narrow trail. So far, she was not seeing flashes, but she still had much to do, even more, she feared, from what Stepan had said.

The climb was slower, back up the trail, and with each yard that they covered in near-silence, Secca felt her stomach tightening more. In her condition, she needed that tension not at all. By the time the rocky edges of the ridge were visible, there was a slight graying of the sky above the trees to the east.

Perhaps a quarter of a glass later, the mare carried her onto the ridge, where in the faint gray light, the players were lined up, tuning gently. In columns behind them were the bulk of the lancers, headed by Wilten.

Richina sat in the saddle of her mount—stiffly—in front of the players. As she saw Secca, a faint smile crossed the younger sorceress's face, and Secca could see a certain relief. The older sorceress offered a smile in return. When she reined up beside Richina, Secca inclined her head to the south. "Have you seen anything?"

"Just the lights of cookfires, lady. There have been no trumpets, and no signals."

"None at all," added Wilten, glancing from Secca to Stepan. "The quiet worries me."

"It worries us all, I think," replied Secca. "Best I disperse the fog." She dismounted, handing the gray's reins to Achar, and stepped toward Palian.

"Still the second building spell, Lady Secca?" asked the chief player.

"The second building spell," Secca affirmed. "After I do a vocalise."

Her voice only cracked once, and after the second time through, her cords felt clear. She nodded to Palian, and then to Delvor. "I am ready."

"The second building song. On my mark . . . Mark!"

Secca tried to let the song come, flow out with full but unforced volume, riding both the melody and the deeper chords of the heavy lutars of the second players.

> *"Bring us wind both fierce and strong*
> *to sweep this fog to the south along . . ."*

As with the last time she had dispersed the fog, an almost inaudible low rumbling issued up from the ground beneath her feet, then passed well before Secca finished. The sky, whose dark purpled gray had begun to lighten yet more, immediately darkened, seemingly turning back the time toward night. The wind moaned, building behind Secca's back, quickly, ripping at her hair and jacket. Secca thought it was far colder than the one she had raised three days earlier—far, far colder. Colder—and stronger. Within moments, the upper layers of the ground fog were shredding like rotten cloth.

She shook herself, trying to forget the intensification of the cramps, and turned to Palian. "Best we mount up and ride down."

She and Richina and the players were ready even as Stepan rode toward them.

Riding back down to the site of the battle three days previous, Secca was still feeling slightly nauseated, but forced herself to eat slowly, mouthful after mouthful of dry bread washed down with water. Every so often, she added a bite of cheese or cold mutton taken from the provisions bag hanging from her saddle.

With each step that her mount took downhill, the dayflashes that sparkled before her eyes were subsiding, but not totally vanishing.

She could hear Richina warming up, but the notes of the vocalise sounded distant, so distant, even though the younger sorceress was but three yards behind her, riding beside Wilten, and in front of the players.

Patches of fog still clung to the lower and more sheltered spots on the hillside out away from the trail downward, but the frost that had looked a dull gray began to sparkle as the sky lightened. Secca would have appreciated the beauty more under other circumstances, and she wondered if Anna had felt the same way—or if her mentor had ever had to fight fog and huge numbers of Sturinnese. Or were Secca and the others in danger of failing because they were in a position where they had allowed the Sturinnese such a foothold?

Secca shook her head.

"Are you all right, lady?" asked Richina.

"I'm fine," Secca lied. "Just keep warming up. Don't push it, but you won't have much time when we reach the middle of the valley."

The dawn sun was touching the far western side of the lowlands when they rode from the trees, and a second misting fog was rising from the grasses touched by the sun, but that mist, too, was being whipped away by the chill north wind.

Secca kept studying the tree-covered hillside to the south, the hillside and the intermittent woven fir barriers, but she saw no Sturinnese. It was not until the column neared the rise in the center of the valley that a series of trumpet calls echoed over the lowlands, faint against the wind, but coming from the hillside to the south.

Stepan gestured, and two companies of lancers galloped by Secca and Richina toward the rise, forming a line at the southern crest.

Secca turned in the saddle. "Dismount and quick-tune as soon as we reach that knoll. The same one."

Palian gave a brusque nod.

"Yes, lady," called Delvor.

While riding along the eastern section of the middle of the rise, Secca glanced southward again. Amid the trees and the shadows, against the angled glare of the rising sun, she could barely make out splotches of white where there had been none before, and those groupings of white were descending rapidly.

"We need to hurry!" she snapped, easing the gray into a quick trot toward the knoll she had picked out. The players followed.

Once there, Richina and Secca dismounted hurriedly.

The players scrambled from mounts and began to tune.

Orders echoed around the sorceresses and players as Stepan and Wilten lined up the lancer companies.

Richina stood at the front of the knoll and began a full vocalise.

The lower section of the hillside still in shadow looked as if it were blotched with white snowdrifts under the dark trees. A trumpet triplet blasted out across the morning, and the white began to move, resolving itself into men in white spurring mounts forward across the shadowed and still-silvered frozen meadow that separated the trees from the rise.

Secca watched . . . waited.

Richina glanced from Secca to Palian, then back to Secca.

Finally, when the leading Sturinnese riders were less than two hundred yards away, Richina looked almost desperately at Secca.

Secca nodded.

"The flame spell!" Richina ordered, her voice firm.

"The flame spell! At my mark . . ." rang out Palian's command. "Mark!"

Strong and direct was the spell melody, with a solid chorded backing from the second players, and Richina's voice was unforced and true.

The first of the white riders neared the base of the rise and started up. Secca's eyes flicked from Richina to the mass of white lancers charging the rise, then back to the young sorceress.

"... *turn to ashes, turn to dust* ..."

Even before the last words, the gray morning sky darkened, and lightnings began to flash out of the sky. The first riders were within yards of the Defalkan lancers on the eastern side of the rise when, like trees struck with instant flame, they flared into instantly blackened figures.

With those first fatal lightning strokes, the white riders turned, all but the front-most ranks, and spurred their horses ... seemingly in all directions away from the rise.

A faint and low cheer issued from somewhere on the rise.

"Enough! They'll be back." Stepan's voice rode over the cheer.

Seeing Richina swaying on her feet, Secca stepped forward to be the one who tendered bread, cheese, and water.

The younger sorceress took a long swallow of water first, then smiled as she looked at Secca. "I didn't overdo it."

"Good." Secca offered a chunk of bread.

Stepan rode toward the two sorceresses, then reined up, his eyes still looking out to the south. "They lost more than five companies, but they are reforming ... and there will be another charge before long."

Secca looked to Richina. "Can you do it again?"

"Yes, lady."

Stepan glanced at Secca, eyes questioning.

"If she says she can, she can." Secca turned to Richina. "You need more water." Then she looked at Stepan. "We will wait this time until they are within a score of yards. That way fewer can flee."

Stepan nodded. "We will lose some lancers, but it cannot be helped."

"No . . . it can't." Secca's voice was both flat and firm.

When the second series of trumpet triplets wavered across the lowlands, it seemed as though no time had passed, although the unseen sun now offered the orangish light of the time just past dawn, but that light did not yet fall upon the trampled grasses of the meadow itself, and shadows covered but the eastern side of the lowland meadow. Immediately, the mass of lancers in white surged from the trees, and even from the east and west, as if they were determined to surround the Defalkan-led forces on the rise.

"Hold! Hold your line!" ordered Stepan.

Secca watched as the Sturinnese rode ever closer.

Palian looked to Richina, then Secca.

"A little longer . . . a little longer," Secca called. Not until the first of the Sturinnese were less than fifty yards did she drop her hand.

"Mark!" snapped Palian.

Richina's first note was tentative, but her voice was strong as she carried the spell out across the lowlands.

As Secca had known and Stepan predicted, the first white lancers had to be met by a short charge from Secca's forces before the sky darkened and the lightnings flashed. One seared figure crashed into the brown grass less than ten yards from the players, to the west of the knoll.

The lightnings lasted longer, and left swathes of burned bodies—of both men and mounts—across the meadow and the slope, but there were still a large number that had turned their mounts. There were also lancers in green lying at the forward edge of the rise—not many, but a good score.

Richina and Secca watched, but the Sturinnese did not turn and reform immediately.

Then Richina sat down on the ground . . . abruptly.

Secca hurried forward, and offered her water and some bread. "Eat and drink. I will do the next one."

"Next one?" Richina's voice wavered.

"I fear the Lady Sorceress is correct, young sorceress," said Stepan.

Secca hadn't seen the arms commander ride up, but she nodded.

"They will reform and attack within less than a quarter-glass," Stepan predicted. "They know that they must win or they cannot hold eastern Ebra. So they will attack and break, attack and break, until you can cast no more thunderbolts."

"Richina cannot cast more for a time." Secca gestured to Palian and Delvor. "Can you play the flame song again?"

"We must, must we not?" called back the chief player, with a rueful look upon her lips. "If we are to ride out, that is."

"Yes," Secca admitted.

"Then we will play."

"Stronger than before," added Delvor, pushing a limp lock of hair off his forehead. "We must."

Secca smiled, then let her voice run through a short vocalise, only enough to ensure her cords were clear.

She watched, her eyes on the trees to the south, where once again the Sturinnese reformed. Even as she did, she had trouble believing that they wanted Ebra so badly that they would charge a sorceress again and again, without even the support of their thunder-drums.

But the trumpet triplets, wavering more than before, echoed across the lowlands, now completely in morning sunlight, and from the trees came the white-clad lancers, seemingly as many as in any of the earlier attacks.

"We stand ready," called Palian.

"Not until they start to climb the rise," Secca returned. She had to destroy them all on this attack, because she doubted either she or Richina could handle another spell—and probably the players couldn't either.

"Hold your line! Hold till they reach midrise!" ordered Stepan.

The meadow was covered with white-coated lancers, and more appeared from under the trees, swarming toward the Defalkan and Ebran forces, and Secca realized that the first attacks had been as much to tire her and Richina as anything, with many of the Sturinnese forces held in reserve.

She wanted to shake her head, thinking about her lack of experience, but it was too late for regrets and might-have-beens. So she watched, slowly raising her arm as the Sturinnese riders neared the base of the rise and started up.

Then she dropped her arm.

"Mark!" snapped Palian.

The players began, not as strongly as before, but true. The chorded harmony of Delvor's second players seemed stronger, but that might have been by comparison. Secca pushed that thought away and concentrated, not just on the spell, but on visualizing sweeps of lightnings—from the eastern side of the lowland, all across the southern hillside and the camp above, and to the sunlit western and lower end of the valley.

As the last words and notes faded, a crystalline chord chimed through the air, a chord few heard except Secca and Richina, and perhaps Palian. Then, lightnings exploded around them, across the front of the rise, across the browned grasses before the rise, across the hillside, across the top of the hillside.

The sky darkened, and the cold wind whipped across Secca and Richina.

From the corner of her eye, Secca could see several players collapsing, and even Palian staggering, barely hanging on to her violino. Secca just stood there, trying to see through the flashes of light that put holes in her vision.

"To the rear!" Stepan's voice boomed out over the wind.

"To the north!" called Wilten.

To the north? Secca shook her head, trying to see past the dayflashes that seemed to mix with the last of the lightnings. *To the north?* She turned, shakily . . . to see riders in green swirling past to meet a wedge of riders in white.

"Mount!" snapped Secca. "Into the saddle!" It seemed to take every bit of her strength to get up onto the gray.

Richina seemed faster than Secca, but both women mounted quickly and turned their horses toward the north and the lines of white-coated lancers who charged toward the back of the rise.

Her eyes still flashing with daystars, Secca did what she could, knowing she could use no more sorcery. She drew the sabre as a Sturinnese slashed down a Defalkan lancer in green and charged toward her.

Somehow Secca parried the first slash, and used the moment of surprise on the Sturinnese officer's face—as he realized he was facing a sorceress with a blade—to half-slash, half-thrust, at the left side of his neck.

More figures in white charged past the thin green line.

Secca ducked as another slashed at her, her arm numb from the off-center parry.

Her attacker fell, cut down from behind by Richina.

Another Sturinnese appeared, glancing from Secca to Richina. Secca thrust, awkwardly, but it was enough to make the lancer defend himself, enough that Richina's sabre cut deeply enough across his upper arm to disarm him. Secca cut his throat as he opened his mouth.

Secca urged the gray forward, but Richina had needed no aid to dispatch a third Sturinnese.

A wave of black lancers appeared, but there were no figures in white left mounted.

Haddev reined up. "Ladies?" Worry filled his voice.

Despite the intermittent daystars and the cramping in

her abdomen, Secca forced a smile. "We're fine." She glanced at Richina.

The sandy-haired sorceress nodded, if tiredly.

Haddev glanced at Secca, and the blood sprayed across her trousers and vest, and at the still-bloody sabre in her hand. Then he looked at Richina, who was even more blood-splattered.

"Your guards . . . ?" asked the heir.

"They were busy," Richina said. "We did all right. Lady Secca killed their captain."

"Richina was better with her blade. I think she killed three of them," Secca said, letting the flat tiredness in her voice show.

Haddev glanced at the heavy sabre carried by the tall younger sorceress, then back at Secca. He started to speak, then stopped as Wilten rode up.

"Lady Secca?" Wilten's voice was low.

"Yes, Wilten?" Secca looked at the overcaptain.

"It's Stepan. He and his company . . . they broke most of the assault from the rear, and killed many . . . but . . ."

"But?" asked Richina.

Wilten glanced down. "He ended up fighting four of 'em. He got three."

Secca nodded slowly, sadly, feeling another kind of numbness. It had been that kind of campaign, and probably mostly her fault, or her inexperience. "There was no other like him. He will be missed. Sorely missed." More than anyone would know, she suspected. Far more. "More than any would know."

She straightened in the saddle. "Make sure that the Sturinnese are not re-forming."

Wilten shook his head. "They rode out. There were but five companies or so remaining. The scouts said not a one has turned."

For the moment, thought Secca. For the moment.

She glanced toward the north where a group of Ebran

lancers had gathered, doubtless around the fallen Stepan, and urged the gray forward, squinting through the intermittent dayflashes to make her way toward the arms commander.

68

By midafternoon, Secca could see clearly most of the time, with only occasional dayflashes, but her head still throbbed. She sat on the edge of the cot in her tent, drinking yet more water and trying to eat more bread and cheese, not knowing when she might have to do more sorcery.

Richina sat on the other cot, doing the same.

Secca also thought about Stepan, both as the handsome young man she had looked up to as a child, and as the haggard arms commander who had done his best, perhaps doomed by the inexperience of the sorceress he had served. She shook her head. She should have thought about the Sturinnese attacking from the rear. She could have visualized that, had she just thought. Had she just thought!

Was that also warfare, she wondered, realizing that she had not done all she should have, and that others had died because of her mistakes?

The scouts Secca had sent out had reported back. The Sturinnese camp was empty, and there were no signs of the Sturinnese lancers anywhere. A rough count had shown that between Richina's and Secca's sorcery and the lancers' blades, they had slain close to eighty score Sturinnese. Stepan had been right—more than forty companies.

She had tried a single scrying with the mirror, and before she had almost collapsed, she and Wilten had determined that the Sturinnese were continuing to ride to the northeast. She shook her head, and wished she hadn't as a sharp pain shot through her skull and her eyes watered. That intensified the cramping, and she just sat stiffly on the edge of the cot for a moment.

"Are you all right, lady?" asked Richina.

"I have felt better," Secca admitted. It didn't help that close to five companies, the survivors of those who had swept in from behind, had escaped. She had the feeling that they would join with those from Dolov, and once again, she would be facing a force more than twice the size of hers, and without an arms commander with the expertise of Stepan.

Still . . . there was little she could do at the moment. It would be a day before many of the players could even ride and longer before Secca could count on them for any intensive sorcerous accompaniment.

"Lady?" called Achar. "Melcar is here."

Secca slowly stood and stepped outside into the cold and clear air, into the chill of the north wind that had persisted long after her early morning sorcery.

Overcaptain Melcar was black-haired, perhaps five years older than Secca, with a blocky build and a square-jawed face. He bowed. "Sorceress-Protector."

"Overcaptain." Secca paused. "I would like to suggest that a half a squad be detached to accompany Stepan . . . back to Synek. Perhaps a few more if there are some who can ride but not fight."

Melcar bowed. "They would be honored."

Secca smiled sadly. "He was a good man."

"Synek will miss him," Melcar said slowly.

"We all will, yet . . . there is more before us."

"What plan you next, lady?"

"To ride north, to destroy the remainder of the Sturinnese, and then to ensure that Dolov remains loyal to Lord Hadrenn." Secca looked squarely into Melcar's brown eyes. "Would you suggest otherwise?"

The overcaptain shook his head. "From what I have seen of your sorcery, that is best for Ebra." A faint smile followed before he added, "And for Defalk. It may not be best for any of us."

Secca matched his smile with one also faint and ironic.

Both turned at the sound of a lancer riding across the camp.

The ranker reined up. "Lady Secca. Overcaptain Wilten sent me. He is escorting a party riding to see you. It is led by one of the Counselors of Elahwa."

"Thank you. We will be ready."

"I will tell the overcaptain."

As the lancer turned his mount, Secca said, "Best you remain, Melcar."

The overcaptain nodded.

Secca turned toward the tent. "You should join us, Richina. We're having some visitors from Elahwa."

The younger sorceress both shivered inside her jacket and squinted as she stepped from the tent into the cold brilliance of the day. "They are quick to pay their respects."

"They should be," said Melcar. He inclined his head to Secca, almost embarrassed. "Excuse me, lady. I spoke—"

"In haste, and in truth." Secca laughed, once. "I prefer that to obscurity."

Melcar's brief smile was one of relief.

At the western edge of the encampment a line of riders appeared.

The three by the tent watched as the party neared, then reined up. Wilten dismounted, and was followed by two others—a tall woman and a lancer officer in pale blue.

Wilten bowed to Secca, then turned to the two. "This is Lady Secca, Sorceress-Protector of the East, and her assistant, Lady Richina. Overcaptain Melcar of Synek."

Melcar bowed. Secca nodded. Richina offered a slight bow.

The counselor was tall, well-muscled. Her dark-brown hair was streaked with gray, and fine lines radiated from her eyes. Under a brown riding jacket, half-open, she wore a crimson tunic that bore faint splotches, possibly blood that had not been removed by washing. With her was a lancer overcaptain in the uniform of Ranuak, broad-shouldered, narrow-waisted, and far too short for his breadth of chest to be handsome. His gray-blue eyes took in Richina, then fixed on Secca for a long moment, before traveling back to the counselor he accompanied.

Secca repressed a shiver at his brief scrutiny, for it seemed as though he had seen to her core.

"I am Veria, Second Counselor of Elahwa. We appreciate your efforts, lady, far more than words can convey. We must also apologize for not being able to assist you, but . . . we did not dare abandon our defense posts with so few lancers remaining to us." Veria bowed. "A fleet and seventy companies of Sturinnese were more than we had ever expected. Nor had we expected that Lord Robero would hazard lancers and sorceresses against such a large Sturinnese force."

Secca hid a frown. Had there been seventy companies? How would she ever know? And if there had not been that many in the battle . . . where were the others? "We did what we thought best, Lady Veria—"

"Veria, please. When it is appropriate, please convey our thanks to your lord for your efforts, although we will certainly do so as well."

"That I will." In time, and only *after* she dealt with Dolov and the Sturinnese. Secca massaged her forehead, then, absently, tugged the sabre belt back into position.

The unintroduced lancer overcaptain's eyes followed the gesture, then, almost belatedly, took in the blood splotches on her sleeves and trousers. The faintest of smiles appeared, almost as if of approval, before vanishing.

"You have blade training as well, Lady Sorceress?" asked Veria, gently, apologetically.

"My . . . mentor . . . Lady Anna—she insisted that all whom she trained be as skilled as possible with knife and sabre." Secca's smile was wry. "I had not quite understood the reasons for a sorceress to know such, not until today."

"So you killed some with a blade as well as sorcery?" Veria laughed. "Good."

The Ranuan overcaptain nodded.

"There wasn't much choice," Secca pointed out, abruptly conscious that everyone around her seemed to tower over her, except for the blue-eyed lancer overcaptain who was but a head or so taller. "We lost the arms commander of Synek and many others."

"There seldom is much choice in such." Veria's tone was wry. After a moment, she asked, "What will you now?"

"Five companies of the Sturinnese are riding northward to meet with reinforcements from Dolov." Secca shrugged. "I cannot leave them to ride where they will."

The Ranuan overcaptain leaned forward and murmured something in the counselor's ear.

For a moment, Veria frowned, then nodded. She smiled as she addressed Secca. "There is little we can yet offer you, for our stores are few and our losses grievous, and the Sturinnese ships remain yet off the port. That is, for now at least. Overcaptain Alcaren would offer his two companies of SouthWomen to aid you in dealing with the Sturinnese as a partial recompense for your willingness to look beyond your own borders and needs."

"That is most generous . . . and welcome," Secca said immediately, even as she wondered at the reasons behind the offer—and her own quick acceptance.

"They would, of course, be under your direct command." Alcaren's voice was a smooth baritone, a voice that carried without effort. "Through me, but under your direct orders."

Secca understood Alcaren's offer. The SouthWomen would not accept the command of an outsider—and usually not from any male officer.

Veria smiled, as if she understood Secca's puzzlement. "Alcaren was the chief personal guard of the Matriarch."

"Just one of them," the broad-shouldered officer added apologetically. "We were the last sent from Encora to aid

Elahwa. We have suffered far less. We would not wish the Sturinnese to remain anywhere in Liedwahr."

"Neither would we," Secca pointed out.

Veria cleared her throat.

Secca turned, waited.

"We can bring some supplies," Veria said. "We have taken the liberty of sending a few wagons already so that you will not have to forage or go hungry in following the Sturinnese."

"We are most grateful," Secca said. "If the weather permits, we will begin tomorrow."

"It should be most clear," Veria suggested.

There was another period of silence before the counselor spoke again. "There is little else we can say, except that we are most grateful and that you are always welcome in Elahwa." She bowed slightly. "We will send what more we can in rations and supplies."

"Thank you." Secca inclined her head.

"And Overcaptain Alcaren will brief you on his lancers." Veria bowed again. "I should go."

"We thank you," Secca said again, not knowing exactly what else she could say.

The five watched as Counselor Veria walked back toward her mount.

As the counselor rode away, accompanied by little more than a squad of woman lancers in red, Alcaren turned to Secca. "My lancers are SouthWomen."

"I understand. Would you prefer to billet them close to me, or on one side of the camp?"

Alcaren tilted his head slightly, then smiled. "*They* would be honored to be billeted close to a sorceress-protector."

Secca glanced to Melcar and then Wilten. "That will be the way it is done."

Both of her overcaptains nodded.

"If you would not mind, I must look to my lancers." Alcaren bowed.

"Melcar and Wilten will join you in a moment," Secca

said. "That way, you three can work out matters."

Alcaren bowed, letting his eyes linger on Secca for just a fraction of an instant longer than he might have, before turning.

Once the Ranuan overcaptain was a good ten yards away, Secca turned to Melcar and Wilten. "You know that his lancers are all women?"

Melcar nodded.

"Ah . . . yes," admitted Wilten, as if he had not thought about the matter.

"Pass the word that they are not to be approached, except as allies. You might also pass the word that they are very good with blades of all sizes, and that attempting to force one . . ." Secca paused. "Most men lose what they consider most valuable, if not their lives. We don't need to lose lancers on either side."

Wilten swallowed.

Melcar smiled. "I think I can make sure that the men understand."

"Ah . . . yes, lady," stammered Wilten.

After the two left, Secca turned to Richina. "What do you think?"

"Overcaptain Alcaren is handsome, and he must be good."

"At what?" asked Secca. "Someone wants him here to watch us."

"You do not think . . ."

Secca shook her head. "I don't know what to think. If the lancers weren't SouthWomen . . . but they will certainly fight the Sturinnese. Holding them back may be more of a problem."

"He likes you," Richina ventured.

Secca shook her head. "He's interested. Why—that's another question." She had more than a few speculations, wondering if the two companies were as much a guard for her and Richina as a thank-you. As for Alcaren . . . she wasn't sure what to think, except that she knew she would have to watch him and consider his role most carefully.

And she was going to miss Stepan. That she knew.

69

The Exchange Mistress steps into the small study of the Matriarch.

Alya motions to the chair on the other side of the flat table desk.

Dyleroy eases into it. "You had requested my presence?"

"I did." The Matriarch smiles. "What do your seers and traders tell you about Elahwa?"

"That the warships of the Sea-Priests remain untouched. They have left the Gulf of Discord and sail along the north coast. Alcaren and the SouthWomen remain with the Sorceress-Protector."

"Why the north coast?"

"Either to reinforce the lancers at Dolov . . . or, I fear, to reclaim them in order to attack us."

"Because they were defeated at Elahwa? Because the Sorceress-Protector was victorious?" asks Alya, leaning back ever so slightly in the straight-backed chair.

"It was a costly victory, I fear," replied the Exchange Mistress. "Even for us. We continue to lose trading vessels, and now . . . perhaps more."

Alya nods. "The Sea-Priests failed to understand one small matter, the Harmonies be praised."

An expression of puzzlement flits across the face of the older woman and vanishes. "There may be much . . ."

"The new Sorceress-Protector of the East was willing to share power and glory—and danger—with the younger sorceress. It took two strong sorceresses." Alya nods. "You are right. That is why they will attack us next."

"Because we lack sorceresses such as Defalk?"

"Because we have not trained sorcerers and sorceresses

for war." Alya shakes her head. "The world is changing, and I fear what those changes will be. The Sea-Pigs destroyed Narial by combining Darksong and Clearsong to raise the oceans into a giant wave. The sorceress-protectors are wrenching metals from the earth and changing the weather. They are using sorcery to poison their enemies at a distance."

Dyleroy attempts to block an expression of disgust and does not fully succeed. "The Ladies of the Shadows . . . ?"

"Yes. They have been to see me twice. They seemed more concerned about Alcaren or the possibility that I might try battle sorcery if we are beleaguered. They would be even less pleased if they knew what I know." Alya's lips twist. "I should say . . . when they know, for they will discover such soon enough."

"Liedwahr . . . can we stand another Spell-Fire War?" asks the Exchange Mistress.

"I do not know. I only know that only sorcery will save us from the evils of the Sturinnese, and yet that sorcery may be almost as deadly as their thunder-drums and chains." The Matriarch moistens her lips. "There is much evil yet locked behind the iron of the keep at Loiseau. The great sorceress showed restraint, and because most feared her power, she and her restraint were respected. None believe her successors have the power that she did. They do not, although they have more than most will believe. But there are more of them, and they have the knowledge she amassed. They will need to use it to preserve what they have created, and all of Erde and Liedwahr will suffer for it."

"But . . . if no one stops the Sea-Priests . . ." Dyleroy says slowly.

"Then the suffering will be greater and last far longer. The Ladies of the Shadows do not wish to accept that. One told me that we would be saved if all Liedwahr rejected song-sorcery." Alya pauses. "As if we could ever enforce such."

Dyleroy offers a smile, partly of sympathy, and partly of condolence.

"As my mother said, we must trust in the Harmonies when it seems that it is most unwise."

"What of Alcaren? Did you give him orders?" asks Dyleroy.

"To deal with the sorceresses?" Alya smiles. "No. If I had given him orders, or even suggestions, he would have rejected them. With him, too, I am trusting in the Harmonies."

"That is a dangerous trust, with a sorceress watched by a sorcerer."

"Not so dangerous as leaving her unwatched. And who knows? Sometimes, two in sorcery are less dangerous than one."

Dyleroy nods, but barely.

70

Secca glanced around the cramped tent, which was crowded even with the cots folded up and set outside, what with two sorceresses, three overcaptains, an heir, and two chief players. The air was also close and slightly rancid, but she ignored that as she laid out the mirror and checked the tuning on the lutar.

The first day of travel—two days after the battle north of Elahwa—had been short, less than five glasses, rather than the eight to ten that Secca's lancers had averaged on their way from Synek to Elahwa. Part of that had been the late start, and part the cold wind and the intermittent flakes of snow blown out of the high gray clouds. And part had been the mixed nature of those following her. She had to wonder about the effectiveness of her force—with Melcar and the Ebrans, her own lancers under Wilten, Haddev and the company of Silberfels lancers, and now Alcaren and two companies of SouthWomen. Again, she missed Stepan's quiet way of ensuring all worked together, although Melcar seemed to be following Stepan's example.

Secca knew she was pressing her luck, but she certainly couldn't leave ten or fifteen companies of Sturinnese lancers, possibly with a Sea-Priest and thunder-drums, behind her. Even if she dared, where would she go? Back to Loiseau and through the Sand Pass in winter—just to turn around or head somewhere else when Robero found she had returned? She refrained from shaking her head.

Instead, she looked at those around her, meeting each set of eyes in turn. "I'm going to try to see where the Sturinnese lancers are. All the scouts can tell us is that their tracks are headed to the northeast."

Without more explanation, she began the spell.

"Mirror, mirror, on the ground . . ."

The silvered glass showed a campsite, much like the one outside the tent, except it was on a long flat rise overlooking the Eastern Ocean. Smoke rose from cookfires, and the darkness of the smoke indicated something was being cooked—most likely livestock taken from peasants and holders who would complain to either Hadrenn or Robero before all was done.

"They are on the coast road," Melcar said. "Not on the river road."

"Is the coast road a better road?" asked Secca.

"In winter, it is less likely to receive snow, and it is warmer," Melcar said. "But once you are more than a day north of the river junction, it heads in almost the opposite direction from Dolov."

Secca released the spell and tried a second one, one targeted at the lancers from Dolov. When the mists cleared, the glass showed the exact same image.

"They've joined up," Wilten said. "They must have arranged this before."

Secca frowned, then released the spell. She noted that Alcaren was also frowning. Palian looked at Secca intently, but said nothing.

"Let me try to see where the Sturinnese ships are."

The third image showed a formation of vessels under full sail. Although it was difficult to tell, the ships displayed in the glass seemed to be sailing northward. Secca liked that even less. Were the Sturinnese going to land more lancers and thunder-drums to fight her? Using the weather of winter to their advantage?

The fourth scrying spell was for the harbor at Elahwa. From what the glass showed, there were no Sturinnese vessels beyond the harbor.

Secca released the spell and lowered the lutar. Her head was aching, and daystars had begun to flash before her eyes.

"You look worried, lady," offered Richina.

"I should be happy for the FreeWomen, but I have to worry about what the Sea-Priests have in mind for those ships."

"Perhaps they go to meet with the other Sturinnese forces," suggested Haddev, a faint smile indicating satisfaction at determining the reason for such action.

The slightest hint of a furrow crossed Alcaren's brow, but the Ranuan overcaptain said nothing.

"They may be, but I can't do any more scrying right now. I'm not sure it would tell us anything more," Secca said.

"Perhaps they will reclaim the lancers fleeing us and then sail to Dumar to reinforce their lancers there," suggested Wilten.

"We'll have to wait and see." Secca blinked. "I just wanted you all to see what I did so that everyone saw the same thing." That was important, she felt, with all the different overcaptains and forces. "Think about it, and we'll talk later, after the evening meal."

All those in the tent just stood there, shifting their weight from one booted foot to another, or not moving at all. Secca squinted, trying to read expressions that blurred with the daystars and holes in her vision.

"The Lady Secca needs a moment of rest," Richina said politely but firmly.

As the small crowd filed out, Secca suspected she needed far more than rest.

71

The wind blew out of the northwest, a cold and steady flow of air that chilled the riders and their mounts. Secca's ever more motley force rode northward, remaining yet on the river road. By the next day, she would have to choose whether to head eastward after the Sturinnese or continue northward to Dolov.

She shook her head. That was no choice at all.

As Secca had been taking time to talk to each of the overcaptains, for the moment she rode beside Haddev, with Richina and Palian following directly behind.

". . . have you always visited Silberfels often?" she asked the heir to Synek, offering a smile that was less than she felt.

"I was fostered there for a year when I was thirteen, as was Verad three years ago when he was fourteen. We rode back together this time." Haddev laughed. "That was how we came to have two companies of lancers. My uncle did not feel one company was enough in these troubled times, and sent his own."

Secca nodded. So . . . one company of Ebran lancers, unmentioned by Hadrenn, and perhaps more, remained at Synek. That did not bother her so much as Hadrenn's insistence that he could raise but ten or twelve companies. She wondered what else the Lord of Synek had concealed.

She also wondered how much would change with Stepan's death. "What do you think of Silberfels?"

"It is a holding. The keep is much older than father's, you know, and the main section is built into the mountain. There are tunnels under the keep, from the old mines. Uncle Selber stores provisions there now. One is a cistern, with always fresh water. It would be hard to take, I would think."

Secca smiled and nodded again, trying to encourage Haddev to keep talking.

"The older rooms are dark. That is because they were built to stand off the Corians and the Suhlmorrans."

"I've heard it said that your mother's and your uncle's line predates both by many generations," Secca suggested.

"It could well be, lady," Haddev replied. "The tunnels are very old and very deep. The back parts were walled off generations back."

"What is your uncle like? Lady Anna exchanged scrolls with him, but I never have, nor have I ever met him."

"He is built more like Verad than me. He is slender, and his hair is thick and silvered. He rides well, and has made a practice of mastering all arms. He even can use a morning star." Haddev shook his head admiringly.

"Has he instructed you in such?" asked Secca.

"Not the morning star, but in all other weapons. My sire said that would be best for both of us, for he doubted we would learn from him."

"Often children have difficulty learning from their parents, or so I am told. That is one reason for fostering. Did you enjoy the time at Silberfels?"

"At times. It was lonely at first. Uncle Selber is a man of great skills and few words . . ."

When Haddev finally eased his mount back toward his company, Secca could not help but notice that while he smiled at Richina, and inclined his head, he did not pause to share a word with the younger sorceress. A smile faintly sad crossed Secca's face.

Shortly, a broader and shorter officer in pale blue rode

up from the rear of the column. "You requested my presence, Lady Secca?" asked Alcaren.

"I did," Secca acknowledged. "I have had little time to talk to you. I do not know you, overcaptain, yet you volunteered to accompany us. Just why did you suggest that you accompany and aid us?" asked the red-haired sorceress, trying to ignore the chill of the wind. "You made the suggestion to the counselor."

"There were two reasons. I wished to fight against the Sea-Priests, and I did not wish to return to Encora and to be a guard captain," Alcaren replied. "That is almost imprisonment. One is restrained by the needs of those one must guard."

"I had not thought of it in that way," mused Secca. "That is most interesting. Do you come from a family of lancers?"

"Me? Hardly. My mother is a trader, as are many in Encora, and my father is an artisan."

"Your mother trades in what?"

"Anything she can, but mostly in furs and dyestuffs, sometimes raw cotton and cloths from all over Erde."

"You did not wish to be a trader?"

"She had hoped I would be, but I was not suited for it."

The reserve in the Ranuan's words suggested a story there, but she did not think it wise to pursue that immediately. "What kind of artisan is your father?"

"A sculptor, in the main."

"So how did you become a lancer?"

"How does one become anything?" countered the Ranuan easily. "I had a skill with blades, and perhaps because it upset my mother, and because I was unruly and contrary, I pursued it. They did not encourage it, and it was some time before I was allowed to follow that road." He shrugged. "And here I am, far from Encora."

"Just like that?" Secca raised her eyebrows.

Alcaren laughed, a warm and self-deprecating sound. "It took much longer. The Matriarch finally allowed me to become a guard captain in her household. Most of those in Encora who knew my family were less than pleased at such a waste of talent."

Secca wanted to laugh at the dryness of the over-captain's tone. Instead, she said, "What changed the Matriarch's mind?"

"She said little to me except that she had decided the Harmonies had a use for me."

"She didn't give you any idea what that use might be?"

"Not until she sent me to Elahwa."

Again, with the dryness in Alcaren's voice, Secca wanted to smile. She did not. "Tell me about Encora, if you would."

Alcaren pursed his lips for a moment. "There is much to tell . . . and little."

"Start with the much," suggested the sorceress.

Alcaren laughed, this time gently. "It is a city based on a harbor that is wide and deep enough for many trading ships, yet easily defended against the Sturinnese."

"How can it be both?"

"The harbor is like a basin that is all the same depth, no less than seven yards, no more than ten, but there are rocky shoals farther to sea, except for the main channel, and that is less than a half-dek wide. Seaward of the shoals, the water is shallow, no more than three or four yards in depth, often far less, for another eight to ten deks out toward the Southern Ocean." Alcaren shrugged. "A narrow channel is more easily defended."

"The harbor at Elahwa is similar, is it not?"

"Both have long stretches of shallow water . . . it is true."

Secca nodded, wondering if that might be why the Sea-Priests had been unable to call massive waves against those ports. "How did you go from being a guard captain of the Matriarch to an overcaptain of SouthWomen?"

Alcaren laughed easily. "I had wanted to be a lancer, but the Matriarch preferred me as a guard—until there were no others to be sent to the aid of the FreeWomen except the SouthWomen, and she would not send them anywhere beyond Ranuak under their own overcaptain. They have accepted me as necessary, for they dislike the Sturinnese more than any."

"They always have, from what I have learned. Isn't that true?"

"Very true. They dislike any men who would force women to submit to their will." Alcaren smiled. "I always give orders to their captains."

After a moment, Secca said, "Tell me about the Matriarch. I know almost nothing."

"Her given name is Alya. She has a consort. That is Aetlen, and they have two daughters. Her mother was the Matriarch, and she had two daughters as well."

"What does she look like?"

"She was blonde as a younger woman, and her hair is silver and blonde these days. Unlike her mother, she is most slender, and her voice is higher, more like yours. She is most firm in a courteous but unyielding fashion." Alcaren glanced at the road ahead.

Thinking of all the rivalries in holdings in Defalk, Secca asked, "What happened to the Matriarch's younger sister?"

"The Matriarch is the younger sister," Alcaren replied with an amused smile. "You met her older sister. That was Counselor Veria."

Secca blinked.

"The story is well-known in Ranuak," the Ranuan overcaptain continued. "When the FreeWomen revolted against the Lord Bertmynn, Veria joined the SouthWomen against the Matriarch's wishes and went to Elahwa to fight. She almost died, but was saved when the great sorceress defeated Bertmynn and forced Lord Hadrenn to accept Elahwa as a Free City. Veria has been in Elahwa ever since, and is most respected."

Secca noted the reference to Anna as the great sorceress, but continued, "And Counselor Veria did not insist you return to Elahwa?"

"I doubt she would have given her sister the pleasure," Alcaren said dryly.

For all his ironic tone, and seeming straightforwardness, Secca had to wonder. "What does the Matriarch gain by having you accompany me?"

"Your good will, I would judge, and any knowledge of you I may choose to provide her."

"You seem . . . you are most polite when you speak of the Matriarch," Secca observed.

"She deserves my respect," Alcaren replied.

"How did you get to be one of her guard chiefs?"

"She respects my abilities, and she told me she refused to allow me the luxury of self-pity." Alcaren offered a laugh that contained equal parts of humor, amusement, and irony.

"And you respect her abilities?"

"How could I not? She is a most effective Matriarch."

"She must be," Secca said. "You are here."

"Of course." Alcaren could not quite conceal the frown that he tried to smile away.

Again, Secca wondered exactly why Alcaren had volunteered to aid her forces, beyond what he had said. She definitely needed to know more, but she needed to think before she inquired too deeply.

She also worried that she wanted to like the man, without knowing almost anything about him.

72

MANSUUS, MANSUUR

Kestrin paces back and forth in front of the study desk, ignoring the rattling of the windows in their casements from the northwest wind that hurtles through the clear skies above the hilltop palace.

Bassil's eyes follow the Liedfuhr for several cycles of pacing before the older man just lets his eyes rest on the window directly behind the desk.

Abruptly, Kestrin halts before the desk and turns. "Aerlya has asked for support against this Belmar. He is raising the holders of the south and the west against Annayal."

"Will you support her, sire?" Bassil's words are uttered with the barest hint of a question.

Kestrin shrugs. "Not over the protests of Defalk, or not unless he vanquishes the Sorceress of Defalk."

"If he does, would it be wise to send lancers?"

"Probably not." Kestrin's laugh is forced. "These days, nothing is wise. We have a force of Sea-Priests sweeping toward Narial. There is revolt in my sister's land, supported by a sorcerer-holder trained by the Sturinnese. The Sea-Priests are trying to wrest Ebra from the Sorceress-Protector of the East, and she receives but little aid from the lord whose lands she is trying to preserve. Yet the Lord of Defalk holds back one of his sorceresses in Falcor, where she can do him no good."

"The Sea-Priests will not succeed in Ebra," Bassil predicts.

"You think not?"

"The shadow sorceress has broken their force at Elahwa, your seers say, and slaughtered fifty score or more in two battles."

"But she has not touched their fleets," Kestrin points out. "That is where the power of Sturinn lies."

"The ships cannot be used with great effectiveness against Ebra, though the Maitre may try once more to support the heir of Dolov, if only to weaken and delay the sorceress."

"You think that they will hold Dumar?"

"Once they set a goal, the Sea-Priests always attain it, though it may take years." Bassil remains standing before the desk, but shifts his weight, as though he does not relish the words he has spoken.

Kestrin purses his lips, then nods.

"You have decided," Bassil says. "What will you do?"

"Send twenty companies of lancers to Unduval, and a message to Lord Robero saying that I am doing so, but only to support Annayal, should she need such."

"And you think he will believe such?"

"He will doubt it, I am sure." Kestrin shakes his head. "You will also dispatch another thirty companies to Deleatur."

"So that if your sister needs not your aid, you can move all to Dumar?"

"With the south in revolt, one way or another, southern Neserea lies open to the Sea-Priests once they take Dumar. I would rather fight on another's lands than mine, and I am most certain that whoever may be Lord High Counselor of Dumar will not object to our assistance."

"I foresee great conflict," Bassil says quietly.

"Do you think I am wrong?" Kestrin raises his eyebrows.

"No, sire. I fear you are right. My only advice to you would be to make sure you have more lancers to dispatch by summer. And pray to the Harmonies that the sorceresses of Defalk are most effective."

Kestrin frowns, but does not speak.

73

High and fast-moving clouds had scudded overhead most of the day as Secca's force had ridden northward. Occasionally light flurries of snowflakes had fallen, flakes that melted with the next burst of cold sunshine.

By late afternoon, when it was time to stop for the day, Secca and her forces had passed the river junction, but were still short of where the two roads split. Melcar and Wilten had recommended a bivouac site on a stream feeding the River Dol, one that had eroded away the clay on one side, leaving a low bluff on the northeast side that blocked the wind.

Once tielines had been set, and lancers organized into their own areas, Secca had summoned the overcaptains, the chief players, and Haddev. Because the wind was light, if chill, and the tent small, she propped up the traveling mirror with stones at a slight angle against the outside rear panel of the tent, so that all could more easily see.

"I'm going to try to see what the Sturinnese are doing. At midday, they were still riding the coast road, but they weren't moving that swiftly." Secca let her fingers run over the strings of the lutar. Then, abruptly, she glanced up toward Richina, and handed the younger sorceress the lutar. "Perhaps you should try, first. You have seen them enough to hold the image."

Richina nodded gravely and took the lutar, fingering the strings and clearing her throat.

Finally, she began the spell.

"Mirror, mirror, on the ground . . ."

As Richina finished the last words, Secca realized that while almost everyone crowded around the mirror watched as the image formed out of the silver mists, Alcaren had not. His eyes and attention had been totally on Richina, on her words and playing.

Trying not to dwell on that observation, Secca studied the image along with the others.

The picture in the glass wavered at first, but then seemed to steady as Richina concentrated. Most of the silvered picture showed just a wide beach, but as Secca looked more closely, she could see the ships apparently anchored in dark gray water that appeared almost glassy. White-coated figures filled several boats.

"They're landing more," said Haddev.

"Look again," Melcar said. "They're climbing nets into the ships."

As the eight watched, another boat rowed toward the nearest vessel, and more of the lancers swarmed up the nets. Secca squinted, trying to make out the strange craft on the beach, with a ramp on it. She blinked, realizing that the square boat was a barge bearing a half-score mounts, scarcely a small craft. While Secca and the others watched, the barge began to move, although there were neither sails nor paddlers.

Alcaren pointed. "They have a cable, and they are using a winch. They will lift the horses aboard with a crane."

Secca had the dismaying feeling that the Sturinnese had done just what she had watched many times before, and that they could unload mounts and lancers—perhaps even more swiftly than they were loading both. "They must have used the thunder-drums to still the sea near them."

"If need be," Alcaren said, "but that sorcery lasts only a short time, less than half a glass, and cannot be repeated often."

The image wavered again, and Secca nodded to Richina, murmuring, "You may release it."

After singing the release couplet, Richina took a long slow breath. Secca smiled.

"They would not be doing such were they planning to stay in Ebra," noted Melcar.

"Or not near where they are," said Wilten.

"We cannot reach them before they have loaded all the lancers and mounts," said Haddev. The heir flushed, seeming to have realized, belatedly, that he had but stated the obvious.

"Best we hasten to Dolov," said Secca.

Alcaren raised his eyebrows.

"Twice the keep has rebelled. There will not be a third time."

"There should not be," affirmed Melcar.

Haddev nodded.

At Alcaren's continued faint frown, Secca looked to the Ranuan. "You may recall that Mynntar's sire sacked Elahwa, and abused or killed most of the women there. There seems to be little difference in outlook between those of Dolov and those of Sturinn." She paused, before adding, "We also may well be needed elsewhere before long, and we cannot leave Dolov in such unfriendly hands."

"Elsewhere?" murmured someone, so low that Secca could not determine who might have spoken.

"Dumar . . . or even Neserea," Secca suggested. "The Sea-Priests might bring more vessels back upon Elahwa. So we must act swiftly."

If she could . . . riding against time and winter, without the most experienced arms commander, and without the experience she herself could have used.

74

By midmorning, Secca and Richina were riding northwest on the river road, well beyond the fork where the road to the coast had split off to head due east. The recent hoofprints in the damp clay of the coast road confirmed the earlier passage of the Sturinnese, and Secca's use of the glass in the early morning had shown that the Sturinnese had completed loading all the lancers and mounts. The Sturinnese fleet was sailing southeast, doubtless to skirt the Shoals of Discord. Secca but hoped that she could deal with Dolov quickly, before the Sturinnese created another situation with which she might have to contend.

Richina turned slightly in the saddle of her mount and glanced back toward the rear of the column, her eyes seeking the black pennant that served as the standard for the lancers from Silberfels.

Secca caught the quick search, but refrained from saying anything, though she wanted to offer consolation. Instead, she reached for her water bottle and took a long swallow.

Even in early winter, with the constant light but chill wind, riding was a thirsty business.

After they had ridden another dek, Richina eased her mount closer to Secca. "Was it just because he saw me do sorcery, lady?"

"I would think not," the older sorceress replied, asking quietly, "What do you feel?"

"He used to find ways to talk to me, if briefly. He used to smile more at me. Now he smiles at me in the way he smiles at you."

"He does seem a bit more removed," Secca said.

Richina snorted. "He saw me sing two spells, and protect myself with a sabre, and I am different?"

"No. What he saw before was what he wished to see," Secca suggested. "Then he saw you as you are."

Richina glanced sideways at the red-headed sorceress. "Was that why you never consorted?" She lowered her eyes. "I am sorry, lady. I should not have asked such."

Secca smiled gently. "It is difficult for any sorceress to find a consort."

"Because we are different?"

Because we have power, Secca wanted to answer. She did not, instead pausing before replying deliberately, "All folk differ, even those in the same family. Is that not true in your family?"

Richina tilted her head before replying. "I had never thought it otherwise, but . . ." Her words trailed off into the slight whistle of the cold breeze.

"The Lady Anna once said," Secca said slowly, "that a lady in Defalk had to choose between being an accepted possession or being unaccepted and respected."

"I don't think it's like that at all," Richina replied.

"We are riding to Dolov. The father of the present lord could not accept the idea of the free city of Elahwa. He sacrificed himself and scores of lancers and armsmen to keep women from being respected."

"But . . . my mother is a lady, and she is respected."

Secca nodded politely.

"You're saying she's not accepted?"

"I did not say anything," Secca pointed out, "except what Lady Anna said."

"Do you think that was because Lady Anna was an outsider?"

"That she felt that way? Perhaps." Secca wasn't so sure about that. She wondered if Anna had been an outsider in the Mist Worlds as well. "I don't see as we'll ever know."

"No, I suppose we won't."

Secca took out the water bottle again.

After another long silence, Richina spoke once more. "Alcaren is handsome, don't you think, Lady Secca?"

"I hadn't noticed." Except Secca *had* noticed the Ranuan. She wouldn't have called him handsome, but striking. He was exceptionally broad-shouldered, with penetrating gray-blue eyes, and fine brown hair, cut short, but lustrous, almost silky. He spoke little, except when addressed, and rode so gracefully that young Haddev looked gawky by comparison.

Secca still worried about the way the overcaptain watched her and Richina perform sorcery. Alcaren had not had the appearance of trying to memorize the spells or melody, nor had he pried or asked questions. He had not appeared anything but interested. He had not tried to ingratiate himself, nor to distance himself.

Secca shook her head. Not for the first time—nor the last, she suspected—she had to wonder just why Alcaren had wanted to accompany her. She wondered if she could find out while she still had time to decide what to do about the Ranuan—if indeed she would even have a choice. What seemed to be choices, she was discovering, were often illusions. Had she really had any choice about going first to Elahwa? Or pushing Richina into sorcery possibly dangerous to the young woman?

"Lady?"

"It is nothing. I was just thinking."

Had it been any different for Anna? Secca wished now that she had asked more . . . and listened much more— much, much more.

....

75

For once, the day, although cold, was without wind, and felt far more temperate than it actually was. Riding the gray mare northward on the river road that led to Dolov, Secca felt warmer than she had since she had left Synek weeks earlier. She turned in the saddle and looked at Richina, who was studying the words on the paper before her, and humming the note values to match them. "How are you coming with that?"

"It's not too hard."

"You'll have to know it well," Secca said. "We'll sing it together, and we need to match exactly."

"Together?" Richina's mouth opened. "Is that not Darksong?"

Secca shook her head. "The Evult used massed voices, but it was their use that was Darksong, not the massing of voices. The Lady Anna studied this much in the last years, and we did some building spells together. It is tricky, but much easier that way."

Richina gave Secca an off-center smile. "This spell is not for building."

"No, but it will be necessary, I fear."

"You are doubtless right, lady."

"It is part of being a sorceress."

Richina nodded slowly, as if to indicate that there were more than a few aspects of being a sorceress that were not totally to her liking.

Secca concealed a snort. Why did the young always think that a chosen calling meant that all parts of it would be to their liking?

After perhaps another dek of riding, Richina looked toward Secca. "How much longer? Another two days?"

"Three, probably, from what the maps show," Secca answered, squinting at the oblong object rising out of the winter-browned grass on the left side of the road.

"That's the first dekstone in days," said Richina, her eyes following Secca's.

"It's an old one, probably from well before the Evult." As the gray mare carried Secca toward the stone marker, the sorceress could finally make out the worn and simple inscription: "Rielte—4 d."

Secca turned to Melcar, who rode on her left. "Do you know anything about this town?"

"No, lady," Melcar replied. "I was born in Vuyoal." When Secca did not reply, he added, "That is south of Vult and north of Synek. The town was mostly destroyed by the sorceress's flood."

"I am sorry." As she spoke, Secca wondered why she happened to be sorry. That had been more than twenty years before, and she'd been less than ten years old at the time. Was it because sorcery always created hardships? "What have the scouts reported?"

"The town is quiet, and most have shuttered their houses."

"Do you know if anyone might know something about the town?" Secca pursued. "We do have some golds left, and it might be a better place to obtain some supplies."

"I will have a messenger inquire." Melcar inclined his head stiffly and swung his mount away from the column, and began to ride down the column.

Secca wondered why a simple question had offended the overcaptain, or was it that she had put him in a position of having to ask something of one of his lancers? If so, that was his problem, and if it had been his touchiness about the destruction of Vuyoal by Anna . . . well, that was his problem as well. Anna had been doing her best to save Defalk from the Evult, and, unhappily, in war the less guilty often suffered with the more guilty—and that was another reason why shadow sorcery, cold-blooded as it might seem to some, was often to be preferred over hot-blooded war that could be justified by cruelties that could have been prevented by cold-blooded shadow sorcery.

Richina half-giggled.

Secca raised her eyebrows.

"He is like all men. He dislikes not knowing something, and dislikes it even more if he must ask."

With that, Secca nodded and smiled ruefully. Perhaps Richina was right, that it was merely a man's discomfort with having to ask for information.

So far, most of the towns through which Secca and her force had passed had been little more than hamlets—groupings of houses seemingly scattered along the road, with perhaps a few craftshops or an occasional chandlery that had seen better times. But then, all of Ebra seemed to have seen better times, save perhaps for the sections of the far west where Anna had built some roads and bridges, and where Hadrenn had made some limited efforts to improve a few towns and buildings.

The ruts proliferated and deepened as they rode closer to the town, but many and deep as the ruts were, Secca had seen no sign of any riders, or of carts or wagons, or even souls on foot. Was that because word had spread that the Sorceress-Protector marched northward? She shook her head. What other reason could there have been?

The road wound between two hills, mostly covered in bare-limbed trees. Those on the upper reaches were white-barked birches, those lower on the slopes arranged in deliberate orchard-like patterns, although Secca did not recognize the type of orchard from the road.

Beyond the hills, the road passed through lower orchards—the apple trees Secca did recognize. Just past the small orchards there was a set of ancient stone columns, one on each side of the road. Beyond the columns, the road widened, and there were dwellings, but only on the eastern upslope side of the road.

"Ah . . ."

Secca turned in the saddle.

Alcaren had ridden his mount along the shoulder of the

road and eased in beside the older sorceress. "You were asking about the town, Lady Secca?"

"I was."

"Rielte is the river port for the northeast of Ebra. I was once here with my mother. In years past, the trappers would bring in pelts from the mountain woods, and they would sell them to factors here. These factors would save the best for the traders from beyond Ebra. A good golden cougar hide might fetch three silvers."

As they rode past the pillared gates, which bore no inscription, Secca could see more clearly to the right of Alcaren a row of larger dwellings, running perhaps a half a dek. All but one were finished in red-stained board siding, the exception being a larger three-story dwelling near the middle whose walls were of a faded golden-brown brick. Most of the roofs were of split-wood shingles, and each window had both glass and shutters. The shutters on the ground floor windows had all been closed and fastened.

On the downhill and western side of the road was a long expanse of brown grass—surrounded by a neat stone wall slightly more than a yard high. Within the wall Secca could see several circular briar-rose gardens, and low and trimmed yews and pfitzers. On the far side of the green were smaller dwellings, cottages, but they too were neat.

Beyond the smaller dwellings on the downhill side of the road were several large wooden buildings.

"Those are the warehouses," Alcaren said.

Secca could make out one long wharf by the river, and at least one barge with a deckhouse was tied up to the northernmost section. She gestured to the larger dwellings. "Those belong to factors?"

"They once did. I have not been here in a half-score of years or more," the Ranuan overcaptain offered apologetically.

Rielte was perhaps the size Mencha had been when Secca had first come there after Anna had left Falcor, although Mencha had almost doubled in size in the last half-score years.

Secca studied the brick dwelling as the gray carried her past it. Unlike the other dwellings on the east side of the road, which were all of two stories, the golden brick structure was of three stories and had a split-slate roof. It also had a circular carriage drive, paved in the same faded golden brick, which passed under a roofed receiving area. A brick wall nearly three yards high hid the rear grounds of the tall dwelling from view.

"Do you know . . . ?" Secca ventured.

Alcaren shook his head.

Secca thought she saw a silver-haired woman at one of the windows on the second level, but as she looked upward, the figure drew a hanging across the window.

"Lady?" called Melcar.

Secca turned and offered a smile to the Ebran overcaptain. "Yes, Melcar?"

"Captain Islanar is riding ahead to the large chandlery to see what they have."

"Good. Thank you," she added. While she could requisition food for the lancers in the name of Lord Robero, she preferred not to . . . unless it were necessary, and well it might become, she knew, before she saw Loiseau once more.

The rest of the dwellings were equally silent as Secca's force rode downhill toward the center of the town—and the chandler's warehouse. Although Secca did not look to her right, she was still conscious of how closely Alcaren rode beside her.

76

The farther north Secca had ridden, the more briskly the wind had blown, though not necessarily any colder, and the road had gotten narrower, with the ruts frozen into stiff ridges that jarred riders and slowed mounts. The white birches had slowly given way to firs and pines, and to smaller peasant fields hedged in woodlots that were more like tended forests.

"A fool's errand," she murmured under her breath, shifting her weight in the hard and cold saddle. The glass had shown Dolov with but a handful of lancers, certainly no more than two companies. If it were not for the high and thick walls, Hadrenn would have had lancers enough to subdue the holding.

But the walls were there, and the gates were shut, and there was no help but for having to ensure Dolov did not revolt again, nor become a staging point for the forces of the Maitre of Sturinn. Secca took a deep breath. Sorceress-Protector of the East?

At the sound of humming, Secca glanced sideways at Richina. "Do you have it?"

"Yes, lady."

"Sing it for me, using blank syllables."

"Now?"

"It will only be a glass—more or less—before we reach the hillside south of the hold. That is what the scouts have reported."

Richina nodded, then cleared her throat before beginning with the first "la."

Secca listened.

When Richina had finished, the younger sorceress looked to Secca.

"You have the melody, but you're swallowing the sound some," Secca said, "and you're not putting the stresses where they will fall when you use the words. Try it again."

The second time, Secca nodded. "Better. Stronger stresses would help."

"Do you wish—"

No," Secca said gently, stopping as she spoke. A pair of riders had appeared over the low crest in the road ahead.

The pair of scouts—in Ebran green—rode southward on the road, toward Secca and the blue and gold standard that preceded her. Melcar and Wilten rode forward of the van to meet the scouts. The four talked briefly, and the scouts headed back northward.

The two overcaptains turned their mounts toward Secca, then swung them around to ride alongside the two sorceresses.

"The keep is but four or five deks farther. You can see it from that second rise in the road ahead," Melcar explained. "The scouts say that the peasant cots are deserted, and that the keep is secured, as if for a siege. All the livestock is gone, and the granaries emptied."

"Did they see any sign of armsmen or lancers? And recent tracks in the road?"

"No, lady."

Secca liked none of it, and she half-wondered exactly the reason for such defiance. Was it greed for power that ran through Bertmynn's family, down unto his sons? Or was the yoke of Defalk and Synek perceived as too heavy?

She frowned. Hadrenn's small palace in Synek was certainly not the height of luxury, and from the vantage point of Loiseau, Secca and Anna surely would have seen golds or vast amounts of goods coming from Dolov or anywhere in Ebra to Falcor. That hadn't happened, and Robero, while far better off than Hadrenn, was definitely not looting the lands.

"Lady?" asked Melcar.

"Why would they do that? They have few lancers remaining, and Lord Robero's liedgeld is far from heavy. Nor are Hadrenn's tariffs."

Melcar glanced at Wilten. The Defalkan officer looked back at the Ebran. Neither spoke.

"There's no help for it. We'll press on to see the keep."

Again, the two overcaptains exchanged glances.

"Yes, Lady Secca."

Secca offered a smile. "Is there something I should know?"

After a moment, Melcar spoke. "The liedgeld be not

popular, and Mynntar told all that they would live better were it not for Defalk."

Secca nodded slowly. That meant Hadrenn was doubtless saying something similar. "It is not true, but it's far too late to dispel that feeling. Thank you."

"Our pleasure, lady. If you would excuse us . . . ?"

Secca nodded, then turned in the saddle as the two overcaptains eased their mounts away. "Chief players!"

"Yes, lady?"

"We will need to run through the first building spell when we reach Dolov. We will need you to play it several times before we sing the spell."

The hint of a smile crossed Palian's face, but she nodded.

Secca turned to look at the road ahead as it sloped gently toward the rise. She frowned as she took in the dark clouds that had appeared on the northwest horizon.

"You think we will need that spell?" asked Richina.

"What the scouts have discovered would say yes," Secca replied.

"Why . . . lady?"

"I know, but I do not know." After seeing Richina's puzzled expression, Secca continued. "Bertmynn was furious that the FreeWomen would not accept his rule. Even now, many would rather not speak of all that he did when he took the city. He used not only drums but Darksong in opposing the Lady Anna. His son invited the Sturinnese into Ebra, and the Sturinnese, you know, chain their women. All that, and a closed keep, do not speak of a lord who will ever keep faith with Defalk." *Or who will respect women.* As the words crossed her mind, she realized that Anna could have spoken them, and Secca was, again, conscious of the emptiness within her.

Richina's eyes flicked toward the rear of the column, then back to Secca.

The older sorceress did not remark upon the gesture. "We will see." Secca shifted her weight in the saddle.

It was nearly midday when Secca reined up on the rise

a good two deks to the south of the keep of Dolov. Between the rise and the bluff on which the stronghold stood was an expanse of low fields, bare brown ground dusted with snow from the night before. The clouds to the north seemed nearer, and perhaps darker.

Secca studied the stronghold, the bluff, and the River Dol to the west. As the glass had shown, and the scouts confirmed, the gates were closed. As she surveyed the land, the four overcaptains gathered around on their mounts.

"The peasants have left, or they are within the keep walls," Wilten reported.

Secca glanced at Melcar, who had just ridden up. The Ebran overcaptain was smiling.

"Lady . . . we have a message. It is from the craftspeople from the town to the south, not Rielte, but the other one . . . the closer one." Melcar paused. "Hanlis, that's it. They pledge their allegiance to you and Lord Robero. They even sent a wagonload of provisions."

"We can use those." Secca wondered how many wagonloads had gone to Mynntar or his younger brother before she had marched up the river. She also realized that she had forgotten the name of Mynntar's brother.

Secca took another look at the keep, then looked at Melcar. "Send a message. All within must surrender and walk out unarmed within the glass. Otherwise I will pull down the walls around their ears."

Melcar nodded, too agreeably for Secca. So did Haddev. Alcaren's face revealed neither approval nor disapproval.

Wilten looked at Secca.

"Lady Anna gave Dolov back to Mynntar when his father revolted," Secca answered the questioning expression. "These are the thanks Defalk gets for that generosity?"

"It is harsh for those who must follow a lord."

"It is, but it is also harsh for the lancers who have died and need not have perished because a selfish lord was not satisfied with holding what his father held. It is harsh for the mothers and lovers and consorts of those who have died and will die. And for what? Because an arrogant lord wants to revenge an evil father?"

The Defalkan overcaptain turned away from Secca's blazing amber eyes.

"Send a messenger, Melcar," Secca repeated. "We will ride to the lower ridge beyond bowshot of the keep walls."

Melcar half-bowed in the saddle before turning his mount.

Less than half a glass later, Secca, Richina, and the players were dismounting on a rise that was barely that, where they looked up to the gray stone walls of the keep.

Richina glanced from the keep to Secca and then back to the players, who were beginning to tune their instruments.

"The wind is not that strong," Secca observed, walking forward on the rise. "But it will get stronger before long." Her eyes flicked to the clouds that now covered all of the lower part of the sky to the northwest.

"You think we will need to use your sorcery?" Richina's fingers twisted around each other.

Secca did not reply, instead watching as Melcar and Wilten rode toward her, followed by a squad of lancers in the green of Synek, a green darker than that of her own lancers.

Melcar and Wilten reined up. Although the Ebran overcaptain looked down on the diminutive sorceress, his eyes avoided hers.

Secca waited.

"Lady . . . ?" Melcar's voice was almost apologetic.

"They refused."

"You do not seem surprised."

"No one who has not seen sorcery seems to believe that it exists or that it can cause great damage. That was something Lady Anna told me years ago." Secca laughed once, without mirth. "I did not believe her."

"They tried to kill the messenger with crossbow bolts, and dared you to do your worst," Melcar replied slowly.

"They have lost more than ten score lancers, and the

Sturinnese have departed. Yet they would defy you?" Wilten shook his head.

"They did not see their lancers destroyed," Secca pointed out. "Nor the Sturinnese defeated. At best, they have heard stories that they did not wish to believe." She laughed harshly. "Were I more cruel, I would leave maimed and broken bodies so all could see and hear what sorcery can do."

"I cannot believe that they would dare a sorceress . . ." Melcar swallowed. ". . . to do your worst."

Richina's eyes flicked from Secca to Melcar and back again.

"We will do our worst. We cannot risk lancers when we need not." Secca looked to the younger sorceress. "Best we act before they attempt something, and before the weather turns upon us." She had no idea what those in the keep might try, but she saw no point in allowing them the time. She turned toward Palian and Delvor. "Players. The first building spell . . . run through it so Richina and I can mark it together."

Both chief players nodded.

Richina swallowed, then shook her shoulders to relax.

Secca returned her study to the keep—gray and cold and silent.

"The first building spell," Palian called out. "On my mark . . . Mark!"

Secca sang with the players, not the words, but just the single syllable "la."

After several bars Richina joined her.

When the last note died away, the red-haired sorceress looked once more at the taller and younger one. "You sound ready."

"Yes, lady."

A dull and distant rumbling echoed from the dark clouds to the north.

Secca gestured to Palian. "When you are ready, Chief Players."

Palian responded with a curt nod, then lifted her bow.

"The first building spell . . . on my mark . . . Mark!"

The sounds of both first and second players melded into the opening of the spellsong.

Both Secca and Richina faced the keep. Secca concentrated not just on the words, but on the images of the keep crumbling into rubble.

Richina's voice was true, if tentative, but by the third measure, both voices meshed and hurled forth from the low rise toward the silent and hulking keep.

> *"Break the brick and rend the stone*
> *leave not a single course alone*
> *break to rubble and to dust*
> *all the walls in which they trust . . ."*

The sky overhead began to darken from the first words that the two sorceresses sang, and more dull rumblings drifted out of the approaching clouds.

A triplet of chimes cascaded across the lowlands, chimes Secca knew were unheard except by the two sorceresses and the chief players, and the darkening sky left the sun dimmer and ever dimmer, until it was lost behind featureless gray clouds.

With the darkness came lightnings, yellowish bolts flashing toward the keep, bright against a purpled horizon. Then a deep rumbling groan issued from somewhere deep beneath the ground. The land rippled, the waves of soil and earth beginning at the base of the rise and heading northward. With each ripple, the rise beneath Secca's feet shivered, and she had to spread her feet to keep her balance.

Secca felt as though a dull knife had cleft through her skull. She struggled to see the keep of Dolov, but unseen needles stabbed at her eyes, and tears that burned like vinegar streamed down her cheeks.

Richina's knees seemed to buckle, and the younger and taller sorceress sat down on the winter-browned and snow-dusted grass.

Behind her, several players also sat down, involuntarily, but one—Britnay—simply pitched forward. Somehow, Palian managed to break her fall and save the violino.

Still squinting through the stabbing pains in her eyes, Secca struggled to watch the results of the twin-voiced spell.

To the north, the walls of the keep began to tremble, and puffs of dust spurted forth from between the ancient stones. The walls began to shake with each set of ground waves that rippled up the bluff to the base of the keep.

Another set of lightning bolts imprisoned the structure in a momentary cage of yellow-white, then slowly, the walls buckled, stones cascading outward, seemingly in a motion as slow as winter-congealed molasses, yet as inexorable as the fall of an axed tall pine.

The impact of the stones raining down away from the bluff shook the rise where Secca watched. Another set of lightning forks flared, so brightly that Secca blinked, and dayflashes blurred her vision.

When she could once more see, only heaps of small stones and gray dust remained on and around the bluff that had held a keep but a fraction of a glass before.

". . . Harmonies save us . . ." said someone behind Secca, but she did not turn, as she still looked almost blankly at the gray devastation. While a few words had not been sung as strongly as Secca might have liked, the effect had certainly been powerful enough. More than powerful enough.

Thuruummmm . . .

At the long roll of thunder, Secca blinked and glanced upward. The clouds that had been creeping out of the north were suddenly almost overhead, and gusts of wind far colder than the breeze that had chilled all the riders earlier blasted across the rise.

With the wind came fine flakes of snow.

Secca turned toward Melcar and Wilten. "We need

to ride to that town ... the one ... sent provisions ... need shelter."

"It is ten deks, lady."

Secca gestured toward the steaming rubble and the curtain of white that had begun to fall just to the north of what had been the proud keep of Dolov. "Is there shelter here?"

Dumbly, Wilten shook his head.

"Players ... prepare to ride."

Secca winced at the tiredness and bleakness in Palian's voice. In front of the players, Palian blinked, her face tight with lines of pain. Then Secca stepped forward to help Richina stand.

Both sorceresses looked for a long moment through the fine white flakes that fell around them, then back at the lifeless gray dust and rubble that had been Dolov.

77

The snow fell in large fat flakes, just damp enough to cling to leathers, jackets, tunics, and to the skin and manes of mounts, but not wet enough to turn into slush on the damp clay of the river road. The daystars that flashed across Secca's eyes showed no signs of becoming less frequent, despite the morsels of bread she had choked down, and her headache was, if anything, worse than when she had climbed into the saddle deks back at the ruins of Dolov. Beside her, Richina rode silently, one hand on the left side of the low front pommel of her saddle.

Within less than a glass from the time they had left Dolov, everything had become covered with white. Silence swathed the entire line of riders, the snow muffling even the sound of mounts breathing and hoofs striking the frozen ground.

Cold water from the snow that had clung to her hair and neck began to trickle down Secca's back, and she wished she had brought a scarf like the one Richina was wearing. The worn green felt hat she had, nearly a copy of Anna's except for the color, was not enough protection in a heavy snow. Then, she hadn't exactly expected to be traveling in a snowstorm.

Melcar and Wilten rode up beside Secca.

"The lancers can ride for a time, but the wind is rising, and before long, we will need shelter . . ."

"How far is Hanlis? That is the nearest town, is it not?" asked Secca.

"Another five deks. That is what the scouts say."

"We will need to take shelter there." Secca didn't like the idea of commandeering a town, but better that in an area whose lord had rebelled than having lancers die from the cold. At the same time, she knew that most of the townspeople probably had little to do with the rebellion. "They are not to harm any of the townspeople, not unless they are attacked. We are taking only shelter. Any food we take, we should keep accounts." She wasn't about to promise recompense, not when what had started as a rebellion was looking more like a war that might involve all of Liedwahr.

"That we can do," said Wilten. "Will you offer payment?"

"Say I will if we can once I return to Defalk." Secca just hoped she could.

Perhaps she should have tried to craft a spell to extract any coins from the rubble of Dolov. Except how could she have done so? Half the players had collapsed, and neither she nor Richina had been in shape to sing a second spell. No matter what outsiders thought, sorcery had its limits. The sheeting snow concealed her bitter smile as the column continued on through the storm.

How long it was before they reached the town, Secca couldn't have said, but neither the headache nor the day-stars had subsided in the slightest by the time that she reined up outside the stable of the Copper Pot in Hanlis. Nor had the snow diminished. It continued to fall in heavy curtains so thick that Secca could barely make out the half-open stable door and the stable boy who stood there, his mouth open at the figures of horses and men looming out of the snow.

"How many stalls, boy?" asked Wilten.

"A half-score. That's all, ser." The boy's voice trembled.

"Wilten, Melcar . . ." Secca's voice cut out, as if she had strained her cords, and she had to swallow before she continued. "Take care of the rest of the lancers. We have our guards."

"I will offer any aid the sorceresses require." Alcaren eased his mount forward. "My SouthWomen rode ahead, and they secured a barn." He shrugged as he dismounted. "They have their captains. Under such conditions, they would prefer I be here."

"Go ahead, Wilten, Melcar," Secca said. "Look to your men."

"I will leave another four guards so that they may take turns in guarding and resting," Wilten said.

"Thank you." Secca nodded.

"Dyvan! Easlon, Gorkon . . ."

As the guards rode up and listened to Wilten's charge to them, Secca tried to ease herself out of the saddle, but, in dismounting, she staggered. She had to grasp the lower part of the saddle cantle to catch her balance, and just stood for a long moment, hanging on to the saddle.

She slowly straightened and looked up to see Alcaren studying her intently. "Are you all right, Lady Secca?"

"I'm fine," she said.

Alcaren said nothing. While his face—even seen through the daystar flashes that blocked her vision intermittently—showed nothing but a polite smile, she could sense his disbelief.

"Sorcery like that is sometimes hard," she added. "With food and rest, I'll be fine."

"That will help." The Ranuan overcaptain bowed.

Secca didn't mind even that Alcaren walked before her into the foyer of the inn, or that two of the guards carried her saddlebags, lutar, and mirror. She just concentrated on putting one foot in front of the other. Behind her, Richina seemed to be doing the same thing.

The foyer was dark, lit but by a pair of oil lamps on each side of the archway that led into an empty public room to the right. To the left was a short counter desk, no more than a yard wide and less than half that in depth. Behind it stood a graying thin man in a sheepskin vest.

Alcaren stepped toward the man.

"Ah . . . ser?" The thin innkeeper swallowed as he saw the broad-shouldered overcaptain—and then caught sight of the six guards who followed Secca and Richina.

"This is the Lady Secca, Sorceress-Protector of the East, and the Lady Richina. They will have your best room."

"Ah . . . would not the keep at Dolov . . . ?" stammered the innkeeper. "Not that I would not wish . . ."

"It might have been," Alcaren said smoothly, "save for the fact that the sorceresses leveled it and turned all the stones into gravel. Such is the price of rebellion."

"Yes, ser." The innkeeper bowed, once, then twice. "Yes, ser. As you say, ser."

"Not as I say," Alcaren replied. "Either of these two ladies could turn you into dust with a few words, were they so inclined."

"Yes, ser. I mean, yes, ladies. Ah . . . let me make sure all is well. It must be well . . . yes, it must."

"It might be best if you went with him, Achar," Alcaren said, glancing toward Secca.

While still trying to see and appear alert when she felt anything but, Secca offered a nod to the Ranuan.

"And you, Dyvan," said Alcaren. "One of you guard the room, and the other come and fetch us when it is ready."

When Dyvan returned, Alcaren followed the innkeeper, and Secca trailed Alcaren up the dim and narrow stairs, unlit except for an oil lamp set in a bracket in the upper hall.

Once in the upper hall, the innkeeper turned to follow the narrow hallway back toward the front of the building, walking less than ten yards before halting at an open door.

Achar stood by the door. "This is the best for you, ladies. One other is a mite larger, but . . ." His nose wrinkled.

"Thank you, Achar," Secca said, then turned, "and you, innkeeper."

"Thank you," echoed Richina.

The innkeeper bowed, then backed away with a second bow.

The room was not even so large as Secca's bath chamber at Loiseau, and had but two narrow beds, little more than padded cots, and a single window. Although both the inner and outer shutters were closed, the inner shutters vibrated with the gusts of wind buffeting the inn. Secca reflected that the cots probably couldn't harbor too many vermin, and when she felt better, perhaps she could manage a spell to kill them.

Once she had stepped inside the room with Richina, she waited for Easlon to set her gear on the floor. Then she closed the battered door and pulled off the damp and still-frozen oiled leather riding jacket and hung it on one of the two wall pegs. There was no wardrobe or chest in the room, and not even a row of pegs for clothing. The sorceress shivered, looking at the saddlebags before deciding that nothing in them would warm her.

Slowly, she eased herself down onto the edge of the narrow bed. Sitting there, Secca cradled her splitting head in her hands.

In time, she lifted her eyes.

Richina sat on the other cotlike bed.

"Does your head ache?" Secca asked.

"Not so much now. It ached terribly for a time while we were riding in the snow. I couldn't see at times."

Secca closed her eyes, just trying to ignore the rattle of the shutters in the wind and the coldness that seeped from them across the bed to chill her neck and back. She thought about lying down, but was too tired to move and afraid that lying on the bed would be even colder than sitting.

"Lady?"

At Richina's gentle words, Secca jerked herself out of the half-stupor, half-dozing state. Richina stood before her with a large brown mug filled with a steaming liquid.

"Overcaptain Alcaren brought this. He said you should drink it. He said it's a brew that the Matriarch uses after sorcery."

Secca sniffed the substance, catching a bitter odor, then closed her eyes and tried to identify the scent. At the sound of fingers on a lutar, she looked up to see Richina standing there.

"If this be poison or unfit for her to sup
let it turn to dust within its cup."

Secca gaped, then opened her mouth to protest.

By then, the younger sorceress had finished the short verse with a smile—a smile that vanished as she paled, then staggered, barely catching herself on the back of the spindly chair. The lutar thumped the rear leg. Tears poured from the sandy-haired young woman's eyes, and her face was drawn tightly with pain.

Secca looked at the cup, which remained unchanged, then took a sip, then a swallow, before handing it to Richina. "You need this more than I do."

In turn, Richina took a swallow, then a second, before handing the large mug back to Secca. The two sat across from each other, trading the mug until it was empty.

Richina massaged her forehead. "What . . . happened?"

"Darksong," Secca replied. "All food is living—or was. I tried to warn you, but I wasn't thinking very well myself."

"That's what happens . . . ?"

"No. That is what happens in the beginning," Secca

said gently. "If done often or too strongly, it gets worse each time, at least for a sorceress. That is another reason why we send few messages by spellsong."

Richina winced. "I had not thought . . ."

Secca nodded slowly, even as she wondered about the brew Alcaren had offered. While he had to have known that Secca was a sorceress, why would he have brought such a concoction with him? Could the fabled matriarch-leaders of Ranuak use their sorcery to see parts of the future? Or had the Matriarch supplied Alcaren with it, knowing that it might prove useful at some time?

And why? Was the Matriarch looking for the sorceresses of Defalk to support Ranuak? Was Encora where the Sturinnese fleet was headed? And how had the Matriarch known that? Or had she? Or had Alcaren acted on his own? And if so, why?

The questions swirled around in Secca's head.

"We need to eat, lady," Richina said. "They may have something in the public room, might they not?"

"We can but see." Secca rose to her feet, then stepped toward the door, opening it slowly. The narrow hall was warmer, if fractionally, and Easlon, Achar, and Dyvan stood stiffly in the narrow space. "Easlon . . . if you could see if Overcaptain Alcaren would join us. We'll try to get something to eat in the public room below. Achar, if you would escort us . . . ?" Secca managed to smile, hoping it was not a grimace.

"Yes, lady."

Easlon nodded and hurried down the steps ahead of the three. Achar followed the other guard.

The first floor foyer was again deserted, with a chill draft from around the front door. Under the shuttered window beside the door was the faintest dusting of fine white snow. Secca felt as though her breath was steaming, but saw no white.

Richina peered into the public room, seemingly empty, then stepped inside. The small fire in the hearth lifted some, but not all, of the chill from the long and narrow room.

A serving girl, thin like the innkeeper, and not even so old as Richina, scuttled out from the door to the kitchen. "There be not much, ladies . . ." The serving girl glanced from Secca to Richina, then back to the older sorceress.

"What do you have?"

"Just the stew, and bread—the bread be fresh—and ale."

"That will be fine. Four stews, with bread and ale." Secca motioned to Achar, who had followed them. "You can eat first, then go relieve Dyvan."

"Yes, lady." Achar grinned.

"Any table . . . you wish, ladies." The serving girl bowed and scuttled back toward the kitchen.

Secca took the table close to the hearth, pulling up an oak ladder-back chair, stained dark from time and smoke and grease. Achar took the adjoining table.

The serving girl returned and put two of the large bowls on the table, with oversized spoons, then returned with another bowl and a basket containing a single long loaf of bread. Achar got the bowl and Secca and Richina the bread.

"Another may be joining us."

"Yes, lady." The girl bowed nervously.

"And could you put another log on the fire?"

"Yes, lady."

Secca took a mouthful of the stew. While there was a faint odor of beef, what she tasted most was heavily salted pepper, that and soggy roots and squishy potatoes. "It is a hot meal."

The serving girl struggled back into the public room with two largish logs, levering one, then the other, onto the hearth, before slipping back to stand by the kitchen door.

The bread was better than the stew, a rye faintly warm and crusty. As Secca ate, she could feel the last of her headache subside into but a faint throbbing. All too soon, her bowl was empty.

Achar had gulped down his stew, and left, to be replaced by Dyvan, who was sitting and eating at the adjoining table when Alcaren stepped into the near-empty public room, brushing the last remnants of snow and water from his riding jacket. His smooth face was red from the cold, and his brown hair was damp and plastered to his skull.

"I beg your pardon." The Ranuan overcaptain bowed. "I needed to check with my captains."

"How are your SouthWomen?" Secca motioned for him to sit at the table.

"They are warmer than they would be riding, and have managed to start a cookfire in an old hearth off the barn they have taken." Alcaren pulled a chair into place, then smiled. "Better than some of the lancers, I would say, though all are under roof."

Secca immediately felt guilty, but beckoned to the serving girl who stood by the door to the kitchen. "Another stew, please."

With a bob of her head, the girl vanished.

"I'm curious, overcaptain," Secca said slowly. "I was most thankful for the brew you sent, yet that is not exactly something a lancer officer would carry."

"I had forgotten I had it. The guard chiefs of the Matriarch carry two packets of such. Never had I even used one." Alcaren laughed easily. "Did it ease your discomfort?"

"Yes. How did you know?"

"Lady Secca, you have ridden hundreds of deks. You are graceful and poised upon a mount, and then you almost cannot ride and stumble dismounting. That could but be if you were . . . not as you should be."

"I was not, I admit." Secca wondered if Alcaren had an answer—and a good one—for everything.

Was that why she felt so uneasy around him? Or because, while he was an overcaptain, he was probably several years younger than Secca, but seemed far more interested in Secca than the younger and more attractive Richina? Or because she couldn't help but feel attracted, and that worried her?

"You are concerned, Lady Secca?"

"I am. I question where the Sea-Priests take their ships. In the morning, when we are rested, then I will see what we can scry." She shrugged. "Where do you think the ships will go?"

"Encora or Dumar." Alcaren paused, momentarily worrying his upper lip with white teeth. "Encora, I fear."

"Why?" asked Secca.

"There is already a fleet that lays siege to the remnants of Narial, if the white lancers have not already taken it. Were that the Sea-Priests' goal, why would they have sent so many lancers to Ebra? Half that number and no ships and no thunder-drums would have been enough to draw you from Defalk, would it not?"

"It was enough," Secca admitted. "We did not know for sure that the ships were headed to Elahwa or that there were any white lancers in Dolov or with Mynntar's forces. Not when I left Loiseau."

"Loiseau?" Alcaren looked puzzled.

"The keep in Mencha. It was the Lady Anna's, but she left it to me."

"Lady Secca is also the Lady of Flossbend, and a member of the Thirty-three in her own right," Richina pointed out.

For a moment, Alcaren was silent, before asking, "Are all sorceresses from the Thirty-three?"

Secca laughed. "Some are, and some are not. I am, and Richina's mother is Lady of Suhl."

"There are those who are not?" pressed Alcaren.

"Yes, a number of them."

"You do not name them." Alcaren's eyes twinkled.

"One is the sorceress Jolyn," Secca admitted. "The others should name themselves."

The serving girl returned with a bowl of stew for Alcaren and more bread.

"If we could each have another serving," Secca said.

The girl bobbed her head again, and took the two empty bowls.

The thin innkeeper appeared, immediately bowing. "All be to your liking, ladies, ser?"

Secca smiled politely. "It is as it should be."

The man bowed again, and Secca understood. She fumbled in her wallet and brought forth a silver, presenting it to him. "This may help for now."

"Yes, lady . . . thank you, lady." Three more bows followed before he backed out of the room.

"You didn't have to pay him," Alcaren said.

"No, but I could, and it is less costly now than later." Far less costly, she thought.

The serving girl returned with two more bowls filled to the brim.

Secca nodded thanks and began to eat, amazed slightly at her hunger for the overpeppered and mushy stew.

"Are there any . . . ample . . . sorceresses?" asked Alcaren, almost innocently, except for the persistent twinkling of the gray-blue eyes that seldom left Secca.

"There may be," mumbled Secca.

"Not from what I have seen."

"Oh . . . overcaptain, I fear we are the only sorceresses you have seen, save perhaps the Matriarch."

Alcaren flushed slightly. Somehow, Secca felt better about that, although she could not have said quite why.

78

Ashtaar slowly looks from one end of the long dark table to the other, stopping to take in each of the other counselors. The lamps in the sconces on the wall seem to flicker as her eyes pass by each, and the room is hushed.

At last, she speaks. "The Maitre of Sturinn has planned exceedingly well, far better than ever I would have guessed. Dumar lies within his grasp, and before long, the southeast of Liedwahr."

"The Sorceress-Protector has defeated the Sturinnese in Ebra, and the Sea-Priests failed to take even Elahwa," observes a young-faced, but balding, man wearing gold-trimmed brown.

Ashtaar's eyes flash. "Two sorceresses are caught in a winter storm south of Dolov. Another is mired in Esaria trying to support the heir to Neserea against a rebellion fomented by the Maitre, and the last full sorceress and her assistant remain in Falcor, for Lord Robero had not wished to leave his liedburg undefended. The Sturinnese fleet has blockaded both Narial and Encora. The Liedfuhr of Mansuur cannot afford to split his forces, even if he dared send them through the Westfels in winter. He will choose to stand by his sister and her daughter, if he must choose. Only the sorceresses can stand against the thunder-drums and the Sturinnese lancers, and none will reach Dumar this winter."

Again . . . there is silence in the council room.

The Council Leader's dark eyes glitter under the silver hair as she looks to the left. "Marshal Zeltaar? How soon could the first and second fleets reach Dumar?"

"The seas around the Winter Coast have already begun to freeze. We will have to sail westward across the Bitter

Sea. The winds are less than favorable most days." The stocky woman with the iron-gray hair and square face shrugs. "It could be done in three weeks, but it might be six. Do you wish us to prepare? If it is to be done, we should leave within the week."

"Or you may not be able to leave at all?" Covering her mouth with the dark green cloth she carries at all times, Ashtaar coughs, then waits.

"The winter has come hard and early," concedes the marshal.

"Why should we send ships against Sturinn?" questions a figure in a black cloak, her face shadowed by the black hood.

"I am not proposing such," Ashtaar replies. "Yet in these times, I do not wish our fleets to be frozen in unseasonable ice. What would prevent them from sweeping in behind the spring melt to catch us unprepared?" Her eyes sweep the table once more.

The marshal nods slowly.

"Also," Ashtaar continues, "while our ships roam the seas, the Sea-Priests must also take more care in how they deploy their vessels."

"You aid the Defalkans, then?" The voice from the Lady of the Shadows is almost indolent.

"I aid us, without costing us other than provisions." Ashtaar shakes her head. "Lady of the Shadows, if you would consider this. If the Sturinnese must leave some vessels to guard their supply lines and their staging ports, then those vessels cannot support the invasion and conquest of Dumar. That weakens the Sea-Priests. If they are weaker, the Dumarans and the sorceresses, if one can reach Dumar—or Encora—can inflict greater damage upon the Sturinnese. The more they weaken the sea-tigers, the less we will need to face. Would we not be fools not to take steps to weaken our enemies without fighting?" Ashtaar's smile is almost that of a death's head. "And without the use of sorcery?"

"What if they ignore our fleets? Then what?" asks the

Lady of the Shadows. "Will you turn your seers into sorceresses? Or offer the sorceresses of Defalk golds to use their fire-spells to repeat the bitter lessons of the Spell-Fire Wars?"

"Then we attack and sack an undefended staging port in the Ostisles—without sorcery." Ashtaar continues to smile. "Make no mistake. We *will* be the next victim if Dumar and Ranuak fall, for we need the seas to prosper, unlike Defalk and Mansuur, and when the Maitre removes the traders of Ranuak, then he will have even more warships to use against our fleets and traders. Do you wish that? Any of you?"

There are frowns around the table, but none will speak to the Council Leader.

79

Secca glanced around the corner of the public room of the Copper Pot, a room guarded by her lancers and containing only officers, the two chief players, both sorceresses, and Haddev. A low moaning confirmed that the wind still blew, although the snow had stopped falling before it became more than knee-deep. The scrying mirror lay in the center of a square dark oak table.

The red-haired sorceress picked up the lutar, checked the strings, and began the spell.

"Show us now, for all to see
where the Sea-Priests' vessels now may be . . ."

The mirror's surface flashed a blank and dull silver before clearing to reveal a line of ships with a coastline in the background. One of the white-hulled vessels was alongside another dark-hulled and smaller ship.

Secca glanced to Alcaren.

"That is south of the west channel passage," confirmed the Ranuan overcaptain.

With a nod, Secca sang the release spell. She had no desire to hold any image longer than necessary, since she knew she would have to call up at least several more.

The public room remained silent, with everyone looking at her.

"How near are the ships to Encora?" Secca prompted, looking at Alcaren again.

"Southwest of Encora, perhaps twenty deks." Alcaren frowned. "They have set up a blockade of Encora. They would find it difficult to take the city, or to use their storm magic against it."

"Why would they do that?" asked Haddev. "That is, if they cannot take the city?"

"It isolates both Dumar and Ranuak," Secca found herself replying. "The Ostfels and the Sudbergs are impassible in winter. I do not imagine the Westfels are much better. The only way to reach either land is by sea. There are no sorceresses in Dumar now, and all of us are in places where we are blocked by mountains or the ocean." Secca had to wonder if the unseasonably early and heavy snows were the result of some form of thunder-drum weather magic.

"Do we know for certain that the Sturinnese are winning in Dumar?" asked Wilten. "We have had no messages and no news."

Someone snorted. Delvor, Secca thought.

Wilten flushed, but kept his eyes upon Secca.

"I can try to see with the glass," Secca said, lifting the lutar once more.

"Show us now, and in clear sight,
where in Dumar do they fight,
those of Sturinn . . ."

The scene in the mirror showed a single squad of lancers in white in what appeared to be the square of a small town. Although the image was small, Secca could make out at least two figures in red lying on the muddy ground.

"Small forces . . . not good," murmured Wilten.

Secca understood that. If the Sturinnese could send single squads out without hesitation, in at least part of Dumar, the Sturinnese had greater control of the land than did the Dumarans.

After everyone had looked closely, she released the image.

"Can we even return to Mencha now?" asked Richina, slightly too wide-eyed.

Secca managed to swallow a smile, letting her eyes go from Melcar to Wilten, and then to the young Haddev, who had been uncharacteristically quiet ever since Alcaren had joined Secca's force. "I have great doubts, but it might be best to view the Sand Pass, so that all could see."

Wilten nodded.

Secca cleared her throat, then began the simple scrying melody.

"Show me now and with great care
the Sand Pass where we would fare,
the winter's road we'd dare . . ."

The mirror offered a view of the eastern side of the Sand Pass. Everywhere was snow—snow on the evergreens, snow on the birches, and snow so deep that not a stalk of grass nor a low bush protruded from the covering of white, snow so deep that the road could have been anywhere.

Secca let everyone study the image before singing the release couplet.

"I don't think we're about to return to Mencha by the Sand Pass at any time soon," Secca said dryly. Already, her impetuous decision to bring down Dolov in a heap of stones was looking worse and worse. At least, had she merely slaughtered the inhabitants, she and her forces could have had a place to winter over while re-establishing some authority across eastern Ebra—something that Hadrenn had been less than effective in doing, it was becoming all too clear. "And we can do little more in Ebra," Secca said slowly, looking toward Melcar, then continuing. "As we can, we will travel south to Elahwa. There we will see what there is to be done, either to see if we can arrange passage to Dumar or await some message from Lord Robero. We cannot stay here. The town cannot support us for long."

The Ebran overcaptain swallowed.

"I did not mean to suggest that your lancers would accompany us," Secca responded. "You and your lancers have been most helpful, Overcaptain Melcar. Your duties and charges lie within Ebra. You may remain here or return to Synek as and when you see fit."

"We would not wish to be seen in any fashion less than supportive," offered Melcar.

"I understand that, and so will Lord Robero," Secca pointed out. "Doubtless there will be other obligations in the future, and I know that Ebra will respond as it always has." She smiled, hoping it wasn't too false, then turned her gaze to Haddev. "Your support has also been most helpful, Haddev, but your uncle's lancers should not be traveling so far from Silberfels, and not in what looks to be a cold and long winter. While I cannot command, I would suggest that you have them return to Synek as you can and winter over there. Or . . . you could use them here to hold Dolov."

"There is no lord in Dolov," Haddev offered neutrally.

"That is true. Your father has two sons, has he not?" Secca raised her eyebrows.

"Yes, lady."

"I cannot command or even recommend, but were

both keeps to be held by those friendly to Lord Robero, he might well let matters stand. At the least, he would be well disposed toward your and your sire."

"There is that," mused Haddev. "Perhaps I should remain, and ensure that all goes as it should. At least, until he receives my scroll."

Richina glanced to the tall heir, but Haddev avoided her eyes.

"Melcar, Haddev . . . once you discuss matters with your captains, if you would inform me of your plans?" Secca offered another smile. "I will be here, discussing our travel."

Once the two Ebrans had left, Secca glanced to Alcaren. "You have traveled here. What can we expect?"

"The weather will be better in the south along the coast," Alcaren replied. "The snow does not stay so long or so deep when one nears Elahwa."

"Can all the players travel in this weather?" Secca turned to Palian.

"If we have another day or two of rest. Britnay is still fevered and weak, but she is young, and will recover soon. Rowal's lip is healing. He can travel now, but he will have trouble playing." A crooked smile flickered across the face of the chief player. "I fear we will not soon see Loiseau, will we, lady?"

"I have my doubts," Secca admitted. "We—and you—may play for all of Liedwahr." Her eyes went to Delvor.

The chief of second players brushed back lank brown hair and gave a smile even more sardonic than that of Palian. "All my players are tired, but well."

Secca gestured toward the closed shutters. "You will have at least another day of rest. Perhaps two or three."

"Is going to Elahwa wise, lady?" asked Wilten.

"I have my doubts, Wilten," Secca replied, "but we can do little good here, and only create more resentment by remaining. The FreeWomen do have some obligation to us, and should Lord Robero have some charge for us, we need to be where we can carry it out."

Wilten and Alcaren both nodded, the former dubiously, the latter knowingly.

Even though she had known Alcaren for but a few weeks, Secca almost wished he were the one commanding her lancers, but she knew also that such a feeling needed to be resisted until she knew more about the mysterious overcaptain. Much more.

80

Light was beginning to seep through the closed shutters of the small and musty room in the Copper Pot when Secca opened the door and stepped inside. The almost greasy yellow cheese and cold bread that had been her breakfast sat heavily in her stomach, and the cold water, and the spell to clean it, had left her feeling slightly queasy.

Richina had left the public room before Secca, without explaining, but Secca feared she knew where the young sorceress had gone.

Melcar's scouts had returned the evening before, saying that local traffic had packed the roads southward, and the way appeared clear for at least several hamlets. Each day that had passed had left Secca feeling more and more agitated, although the mirror showed only the same scenes in both Encora and Dumar. Something was telling her that she needed to be headed southward, and she recalled all too clearly Anna's observations on feelings—that they were ignored only to the greatest of regrets.

After Secca's announcement at dinner, Melcar had decided that he would begin his return to Synek when Secca departed, accompanying her so far south as to where the river roads diverged. In turn, Haddev declared he would remain in Hanlis to begin preparations for rebuilding the keep at Dolov. In turn, Melcar had agreed to leave one company of lancers with Haddev.

With a deep breath, Secca bent to check the leather wrappings on the traveling scrying mirror once more. She moved from the mirror to repacking the saddlebag that still contained a score of small bottles, bottles she feared would be useful yet.

The door opened. Secca stood quickly and turned as Richina stepped inside, closing the heavy door quickly behind her. The older sorceress waited.

"He didn't even say good-bye. Not really," Richina said slowly. "He just smiled. He wished me well. He said I would be a great sorceress some day. Then he kissed my hand." After a moment she added, "That was all."

"It upsets you."

"It shouldn't. You told me this would happen." Richina sniffed and looked away. "You said it would."

"That doesn't make it any easier. It still hurts," Secca said gently.

"How . . ." Richina shook her head. "I told myself this would happen. I could see it. When he looked at me that day."

"When you used the sabre to save me," Secca said.

"His eyes opened, and he saw . . ." Richina stopped and swallowed. "He saw me, and he didn't like what he saw."

"I know." Secca's voice was low.

"Is that what happened between you . . ." Richina did not finish the sentence.

"No. It never got that far," Secca replied. *It never has. Is that because you have seen too many men back away?*

Another silence, cold as a still winter night, filled the room.

"I'm sorry," Secca said again.

"There's nothing else to say. Nothing." Richina bent over the narrow cot bed and folded her spare riding trou-

sers. She slid them into a saddlebag. Then she reached for
the shirt she had washed in ice cold water two days before
and folded it. She did not look at the older sorceress.

Secca smiled faintly, sadly.

81

Secca looked southward, her breath white in the chill
morning air, squinting against the glare of sun on snow.
The road was already packed in the middle, where the
snow compacted by hoofs and feet followed the contours
of the ruts established far earlier. The only sounds were
those of hoofs and the breathing of mounts, and the occasional jingle or clink of a harness.

After three days on the road, they were still short of the
river junction and the better road toward Elahwa that they
would find there. If the road remained frozen they might
make Rielte by the end of the day, which would provide
some better lodging for the lancers—even if within warehouses.

At some point, they would leave the snow behind, because the mirror showed the roads into Elahwa were only
damp, not even muddy, but without better knowledge and
names, Secca could not use the mirror to find where that
might be, not without exhausting herself.

For the time, Richina rode with Wilten, in front of Secca
and Alcaren. Behind Secca were Delvor and Palian, and
then the remainder of the players. Melcar rode farther
back, with the Ebran lancers.

"If both sun and chill prevail, without wind, we will be
favored by the Harmonies," offered Alcaren.

"At least until we get out of the snow."

"I have been told that there is usually little snow south
of where the rivers join," replied the Ranuan overcaptain.

"You seem to know a great deal about Ebra," Secca said.

"Far more than a overcaptain of lancers from Ranuak should?" A light laugh punctuated his words. "Is that the edge on your blade?"

"Yes." Secca didn't feel like verbal fencing.

"I was not intended to be an overcaptain. As I have told you, my mother wished me to be a trader. Such must learn all about the lands where they trade, and she would tell me all she knew, and then ask me." Alcaren's voice turned dry. "Often I ate but bread and water."

"If you didn't learn?"

"I was stubborn."

Secca smiled. "You learned. That is clear. And you are skilled and intelligent. So why aren't you a sea captain, or an officer learning to be one?"

Alcaren did not reply, and Secca turned in the saddle. "Overcaptain?"

A crooked expression, neither grin nor smile, appeared on Alcaren's face. "The sea and I . . . we did not agree. No matter how many voyages I accompanied my mother . . ." He shook his head. "I did not wish to do what made me most uncomfortable."

Secca suppressed a laugh. Somehow, the thought of the competent overcaptain as a seasick trader was so incongruous. "So . . . your mother let you become a lancer?"

"No. She turned me over to my father, saying that if I were not fit to be a trader then I could at least learn to create beauty."

"He was a sculptor, you said. Did you make any statues?"

"A few. Mostly, I bent chisels and destroyed good blanks of stone. He could scribe a perfect circle with a stick of charcoal, then cut it perfectly. I could not." Alcaren shrugged. "I could make neither happy."

Secca had the feeling, once more, that Alcaren had left much unsaid. Far too much. "So you took up the blade, then?"

"I had some skill there, and that seemed a better thing to do than attempt to be a miserable trader or an untalented artisan."

"I see. What else do you do?" asked Secca.

"Like most good Ranuan men, I can play some on a mandolin, or my lumand, enough to provide pleasant dinner music."

She laughed politely. Again, true as the words themselves sounded to Secca, she still felt as though something were missing. "The more you say, overcaptain, the less I feel I've learned." She paused. "Have you any brothers or sisters?"

"A younger sister only. She will be the trader. Already, she thinks in terms of casks and kegs and barrels, and yards and spans, and golds and silvers, and whether there is drought in Ebra or ice monsoons in Pelara."

"And what do you think about?"

"I wonder now how I find myself talking to a sorceress on a snow-covered road in Ebra."

"I suppose that is strange," Secca admitted, "but the Matriarch is a sorceress, it is said."

"She is, but not in the way that you are." Before Secca could respond, the Ranuan rushed on, as if he had been waiting for an opening. "That sorcery . . . what you used to destroy the keep of Dolov . . . I did not know that two voices could do such."

"The Evult used massed voices, a score of years back," Secca pointed out, certain that Alcaren had been sent as much spy as ally. "There are even old books about sorcery with many voices."

Alcaren, surprisingly, shuddered. "The old sorceries . . . like the evils of the Sturinnese . . . like the Spell-Fire Wars."

"Sorcery doesn't have to be evil," Secca said, thinking about the beauty and grace of Loiseau, wishing she were there, that she could be there. "We don't have to repeat the evils of the past. Can we not avoid such?"

"Can we? There are great temptations to make it so. The

Matriarch has told so many that for so long, as did her mother." Alcaren's words were not quite cynical. "The Sturinnese offer great temptation."

"So you're saying that I'll be tempted into evil in order to stop them? Or that the other sorceresses of Defalk may be?"

"Or someone. I suggest that it is possible. That is because the Sea-Priests did not suffer such as the Spell-Fire Wars and because they also believe what they do is right, as set forth by their great Sea-Father."

"And I suppose the Matriarch believes that we should do nothing, rather than risk some evil to stop a greater evil?" Secca could feel herself getting annoyed.

Alcaren laughed. "No. Hardly that. She would avoid sorcery as she can, for the Ladies of the Shadows are strong in Ranuak, but she sees her choices are most limited. She learned from her mother, and her mother said that she had done much she came to regret, but even later could find no other course."

Secca nodded. She'd heard that enough from Anna.

"Can she not use her sorcery against the Sea-Priests? In some fashion?" asked Secca.

"She is not a sorceress like you." As if sensing Secca's irritation at his repetition, the Ranuan added, "She does not have the ability to meld with the players the way you do, or with drums as the Sea-Priests do. They can use sorcery on the water only with the strength of the thunder-drums."

Secca frowned. Were the massed lutars of the second players something like the thunder-drums? Would they work on or near the water? Could she adapt some spell to reach the Sturinnese ships off Dumar?

"Lady?"

"Oh . . . I was thinking. Is there a reason why the Matriarch cannot use players?"

"She does not. None of the Matriarchs have done so."

"That is a most careful answer, overcaptain."

Alcaren shrugged, almost overdramatically, it seemed to

Secca. "A Matriarch would not talk of such to a lancer, nor about such even around her personal guards."

"It sounds as though the Matriarchs have made a choice not to use sorcery backed by drums or players."

"That . . . I would not be surprised," Alcaren admitted, "but no one has ever said such near me. Nor near any I know."

Those sentences stopped Secca, because the truth rang in every word. But why had Alcaren hedged so many other words and phrases? She rode silently, trying to sort out what she had seen and heard, and getting to no resolution, not one she could have voiced.

"You did not follow Lord Robero's orders, did you?" asked Alcaren, almost absently.

"I had no orders," Secca replied. "Lord Robero requested that I aid Lord Hadrenn and then do what I could to secure Dolov and assist the Free City."

"Doubtless in that order of priority," suggested Alcaren dryly.

His tone brought an inadvertent smile to Secca's lips. "Would you have done otherwise?"

"No . . . but then, I was likely to be one of those thrown against the Sturinnese in desperation had you not put them to flight. So I am most pleased that you acted as you did." Alcaren paused. "I would much prefer to be riding and talking to you than lying in an unmarked grave somewhere."

"I am gratified that my actions please you, overcaptain."

"Not so much as I," responded the Ranuan in a tone that seemed just a shade more than amiable.

Or was that because she wished it so? Rather than reply, Secca studied the narrow fields beyond the road, rather than the woods behind them. Were the grass stalks protruding from the snow an indication that the snowfall was lighter as they rode south, and that they would be in warmer parts before long? She hoped so.

82

Two days after leaving Rielte, and a day after splitting away from Melcar, Secca and her much smaller force rode through a fine mist that was not quite rain. Although they could not see the sun, it was close to midday, and the clouds overhead were almost luminous, as if the sun were trying to break through. The road clay was damp, but not slippery, and the red-haired sorceress could but hope that the cold mist would dissipate as they continued southward.

Strangely, Secca had felt relieved to see the Ebrans go, and that bothered her. Melcar was a far better commander than Wilten. Alcaren, for all that she had tried to get to know him better, and understand him, remained very much unknown. She had less than half the lancers she had commanded a glass before. And she felt relieved?

She shook her head and looked at the road ahead. According to her scrying glass, the maps, and Alcaren, they were about a day and a half from Elahwa. Secca rode beside Palian, while Richina rode with Delvor, before Secca. Alcaren rode at the head of the column, just behind the standard bearers, with Wilten.

Secca glanced at Palian. "What do you think about Overcaptain Alcaren?"

Palian glanced forward, frowned, then lowered her voice. "He has watched the players practice, and once I thought I saw his lips move to the spellsong."

"Do you think he would try sorcery?"

"I know not, save he knows more than he reveals. He would offer himself as an overcaptain of lancers as payment for your rescue of Elahwa. Yet his two companies are SouthWomen, and never have such been led by a man."

"They're not SouthWomen?"

Palian shook her head. "They are indeed SouthWomen. The SouthWomen trussed one overbold bravo like a pig for slaughter and dumped him, gagged into silence, by the cookfires . . . so silent they were that none saw or heard, and he will not yet speak of it."

"Hmmmm . . . Yet they accept Alcaren's orders."

"They accept orders from their captains, who are women. The captains accept orders from him," Palian pointed out.

"He said the same thing," Secca replied. "He did not hide that, yet it remains strange."

"He rides well, like a lancer born, yet there is . . . something."

"A spy from the Matriarch?"

The chief player shrugged. "I think not. The Matriarch would welcome knowledge. That is certain of any ruler. He spars with his captains, and they are better than most of our armsmen. He is better than they. Melcar said that he carried his blade like a lancer, not as a bravo."

"Someone to seduce me?"

"But why, Lady Secca? It would be far easier to seduce Richina, to learn anything from spells to secrets. And, though you are Sorceress-Protector, you are not a regent as was Lady Anna." Palian looks at Secca. "The man listens not as to flatter, but to learn."

"That's why I thought he was a spy," Secca pointed out.

The chief player shook her head again. "I think not. He watches what I do, but makes no gesture to reassure me, nor to flatter these gray hairs. Nor does he court you or Richina. He is not here for our purposes, but what purposes he is here for . . . those are deeper, perhaps deeper even than he knows."

"The Matriarch has a plan for him that he knows not?"

"That would be my guess. He is a man, and he has been offered a freedom to act few men in Ranuak receive. She believes that freedom to act will benefit her and Ranuak."

"But will it benefit us?" questioned Secca.

"Over a score of years, the Matriarch has not acted to harm Defalk or Lady Anna. I do not know her mind, but years of actions speak more clearly than words."

Secca nodded, considering the other side—the Sturinnese, and the Ebrans of Dolov, whose actions had always been against Defalk . . . and women. Perhaps she had not been so wrong to level the keep of Dolov, or not so wrong as she had felt at the time and afterward.

After a time, Secca spoke again. "Yet I worry. There is so much I know not, and so much I have not seen, and I do not seem to be the only one who has not seen it. The Sturinnese have planned what they do for years. That is clear. Have the Matriarchs of Ranuak planned their counter for years as well? And what of the Council of Wei? The Liedfuhr?"

Palian shrugs. "We do not know."

We do not know—what Secca had not known had already caused her to make mistakes, and those mistakes had killed all too many.

"I fear we will need far more sorcery," Secca said. Trite as her words were, they were also true, she knew.

"That I have already told the players." Palian glanced over her shoulder. "I can see a disagreement brewing behind us . . . if you would excuse—"

"Go," said Secca with a laugh.

"Delvor!" called Palian.

The two chief players rode back along the column, and Richina slipped her mount back alongside that of Secca.

"Are you angry with me, lady?" asked Richina.

"Harmonies, no." Secca paused. "Because I have taken time to ride with others?"

"I did not know."

"Palian has much knowledge and experience, and she is one of the few who has been on a campaign such as this before. I wished to hear what she had to say."

"Did you talk of Alcaren?"

"Some," Secca admitted with a smile. "We know little of him, handsome as he is."

"You admit he is handsome?" Richina grinned.

"How could I not? But he is also mysterious and unknown, and that is not all to the good when one must fight alongside such."

"He will fight for us," Richina said.

While Secca felt the same, she did not *know* it, and that worried at her. Did she feel what she felt because it was true, or because she wanted to feel that Alcaren was to be trusted?

83

The Black Kettle—the inn in Sudstrom—was twice the size the Copper Pot in Hanlis had been, and the innkeeper had actually seemed happy to see Secca and her guards.

"We heard of your victory, lady, and most pleased we were," said the beefy, red-faced man.

"I'd wager the girls and I were far happier, Tyras," added the equally hefty woman who stood to his left. "Sturinnese kill women like as look at 'em, and chains are not something any of us would wear with joy." She bowed to Secca a second time. "The big chamber . . . it has a large and a small bed. We would be honored."

"Thank you."

"And a wash stand as well."

"Richina and I could use that." Secca looked at the innkeeper. "We also need lodging for the players and the lancers. We have somewhat less than six companies, and the players."

The innkeeper pulled on his earlobe. "There be ten small rooms, and two other large ones. Be some room in the barn and the stable. Might check with Afgar . . . he's the grain merchant."

In time, Wilten and Alcaren had left the inn proper, with arrangements made for two companies to stay at the inn, while Secca and Richina had headed up the wide stairs to the second floor, and the main guest chamber.

Though probably even older than the inns at Hanlis and Rielte, the Black Kettle had one significant improvement—real glass windows, at least in the chamber where Secca and Richina found themselves. While Secca greatly missed the bath chamber of Loiseau—and even the one in Hadrenn's run-down palace—the basin of warm water, water she reheated with a short spell, and the towels resulted in her feeling far better and less bedraggled.

Once Secca was in cleaner riding clothes, while Richina was washing up, the older sorceress opened the door slightly and called, "Achar?"

"Yes, lady?"

"Could one of you find Overcaptain Wilten and Overcaptain Alcaren—and both the chief players—and tell them we have some matters to discuss at an evening meal with them in the public room here?"

"We can do that." The young guard smiled back.

Secca closed the door, then went to the window and opened the shutters enough to study the muddy main street of Sudstrom. As she watched, she could see Achar hurrying along the board walk in the dim light of dusk toward the chandlery, and the grain merchant's barns beyond. She took a deep breath, not wanting to think too long or too deeply about the comparative luxury of her quarters. While she could tell herself that she could not do sorcery without rest and food, she still fretted and felt guilty.

She closed the shutter and turned. Richina was brushing out her sandy hair.

"Do you feel better?" asked Secca.

"Some. I'm hungry."

"So am I. We should wait a few moments, though, before we go down. I just sent Achar to get Wilten and Alcaren."

"Do you think we will be welcome in Elahwa?" asked

the younger woman, seating herself on the end of the smaller bed.

"We were told we would always be welcome. How welcome . . . I do not know. I worry more about what we must do after we reach Elahwa."

"Because we cannot return home easily?" Richina shifted her weight on the bed, wincing slightly.

"That is part of it." Secca paused before asking, "You're sore?"

"I am raw on the inside of this leg. My riding trousers—they were damp and rubbed."

"I think I have some unguent." Secca opened her saddlebag and, after fumbling through it, came up with a small oiled leather bag. "Here."

By the time Richina had used the ointment, and the two had left the upstairs room, the overcaptains and Palian and Delvor were waiting outside the public room. The only others in the room were an elderly couple at a table in the corner near the fire.

The six seated themselves around the large circular table set directly before a roaring hearth. Almost before they had settled in, a serving girl appeared, doubtless the daughter of the innkeeper, for she had the same round and red face.

"What do you have?" Secca asked.

"We have chicken-chased noodles with a paisino sauce or white fish baked in the husk with potato cakes."

Never having had either, nor having heard of either, Secca looked at the serving woman. "Which is better?"

"I like the noodles, lady, but mayhap that's because we have whitefish so many nights."

"I'll take the noodles. Do you have any wine?" asked Secca.

"Not so as I'd wish to offer it. The amber ale is better."

"The whitefish," Richina said, "and ale."

"Fish and ale," Delvor added.

"Noodles and the wine, no matter how bad," Palian said. "I can't take the thought of ale."

"Noodles and ale," came from Alcaren.

"The same," offered Wilten laconically.

After the server scurried toward the kitchen, Secca turned to Wilten. "Are there quarters enough . . ."

"Not quarters." Wilten laughed. "But we've found spaces dry and warm enough, and provisions. Even the chandler was happy to see us—she was happier to know we'll be leaving in the morning."

A series of *thumps* punctuated the arrival of the ales, followed by Palian's wine, a murky yellowish liquid sloshing in a pewter goblet.

Secca took a sip of the ale. It was weak, almost soapy, but better than making the effort to clean water with a spellsong, and from the glance she'd seen of the wine, to be preferred over what Palian had begun to drink. "We should reach Elahwa late tomorrow, should we not?" She looked at Alcaren.

"That we should, if it does not rain or snow."

"We don't want to just appear in Elahwa," Secca said. "While it is part of Defalk, we should let the city counselors know. I'd be unhappy if an ally showed up unannounced with six companies and two sorceresses."

"I could dispatch a squad with a message," offered Wilten.

"They are men, are they not?" Alcaren's tone of voice indicated that his question was more of a statement.

"All the lancers are men," Wilten pointed out. "Except yours."

"Could you spare a squad to go with Wilten's squad?" Secca asked the Ranuan overcaptain.

"That might be best."

"I'll write a scroll tonight." Secca glanced at Alcaren. "Perhaps you should write one as well, for your lancers to carry."

"I am not so certain that they are exactly mine, but I will write one." Alcaren laughed.

Secca nodded.

"Do you have any thoughts on what you will do once we reach Elahwa?" asked Wilten.

"I'd like to talk to their counselors," Secca temporized. "The glass shows that the Sea-Priests continue to fight in Dumar, and that they still blockade Encora."

"They could not take Encora," Alcaren said.

"Could they starve it into surrender?" asked Richina.

"Over several years, perhaps. Some folk might suffer by this coming summer, but the Matriarch has large granaries, and so does the Exchange. Once winter is over, food can flow from Defalk through the South Pass." Alcaren's lips twisted. "There is enough gold in Encora for that."

"It would seem that the blockade is more to keep anyone from coming to the aid of Dumar, then?" Secca took another cautious sip of the soapy ale.

"Until they have turned the land into a garrison for Sturinn, I would guess," Alcaren suggested. "After that, they will attack Ranuak."

"Why would they go after Ranuak?" asked Richina.

"The best ports in Liedwahr are Wharsus, and Encora, and then Narial," Alcaren explained. "The Sea-Priests already hold Narial, and Mansuur has many, many lancers. They know that the Matriarch cannot use sorcery against them, and few will come to our defense, except the FreeWomen, and they have few lancers."

"Especially now," suggested Wilten.

Alcaren nodded.

"We may just have to wait and rest in Elahwa," Secca pointed out. "We can't return to Mencha until the passes clear, and that will not be until spring." She shrugged. "Then, too, we may be able to find a way to Dumar. I like not dealing with the Sea-Priests, but with each week that passes, they can make it that much harder for us to free Dumar."

"Need we free Dumar?" asked Wilten. "It provides little for Defalk, and we have no orders from Lord Robero."

"You are right about Dumar giving little to Defalk," Secca agreed, pausing for another sip of ale, and to gain a moment to think. "Yet, once the Sea-Priests have gained a firm foothold in any land, such as the Ostisles, none have been able to stop them. As Overcaptain Alcaren has said, once they hold Dumar, then they will take Ranuak. Could we then stop them from taking Ebra and Elahwa? After that . . ."

"That would take many years . . . if it could be done . . ."

Palian snorted. "Three years at the outside, Wilten, if we do nothing. Then we would have to fight, and at a great disadvantage. They could attack through Stromwer from the east or the west, or they could use the South Pass from Ranwa, the Sand Pass from Ebra, the pass from Vult—or they could march north from Envaryl to take the south of Neserea. By then they will have enough lancers and thunder-drums to do all of those at once, and we have but three full sorceresses, and two strong assistants. We may not even have an ally in Neserea, and if we do, that land will be weak."

Wilten looked down at his ale.

Secca could understand the overcaptain's concerns; no matter what they did, the possibility of years of fighting stretched out before them—and she worried greatly that she had heard nothing from Robero. While she did not see that she could do other than she had, and did not wish to spend her energies on trying to discover what the Lord of Defalk intended, she worried. Either Robero did not understand the extent of the danger, or Clayre and Jolyn were so hard-pressed that neither could spare the energy to send a scroll. Neither of those possibilities was reassuring, not with two Sturinnese fleets and scores of lancers attacking all across the south of Liedwahr.

She took another sip of the ale, waiting for the noodles.

....

84

In the bright gray just before sunrise, with the night stars washed out and Clearsong the only light in the sky, Secca stood in the courtyard behind the Black Kettle and strapped her lutar in place on top of the mirror and saddle-bags behind the saddle of the gray mare. The clear air was cold enough that her breath steamed, and the tip of her nose tingled with the chill. Once she finished, she also checked the sabre and scabbard, hoping as always that she would not need the blade, but making sure it would be ready. She adjusted the battered green felt hat once more.

Farther toward the back of the courtyard, some of the players were beginning to mount. One—Britnay—seemed to be having trouble buckling the rear saddle girth. Secca shook her head. If it weren't one thing with Britnay, it was another.

Delvor dismounted to help the young violino player in her struggles with mount and saddle.

Glad that she did not have to deal with Britnay, Secca mounted easily, aware that she was finally feeling less exhausted. As she turned the gray toward the front of the inn, and the street that would lead to the road south, Wilten reined up beside her.

"Good morning, Wilten."

"Good morning, lady." The overcaptain inclined his head. "Just be wanting you to know that the two squads left almost two glasses ago. Overcaptain Alcaren and I saw 'em off."

"Thank you." Secca smiled.

"Be hoping we'll get a warm welcome."

"I'm sure we will."

"The lancers'll be forming up in front. I'll be joining you after I check here."

"I'll wait for you there." Secca eased the gray past the side of the inn and out onto the street where the green company was already formed up and waiting. Behind her rode Rukor and Achar.

No sooner had Secca reined up on the mud-rutted street before the Black Kettle than Richina guided her mount out of the courtyard to join her. Then came Wilten and Palian and the first players, followed by Delvor and the second players, and another company of lancers.

While none of the inhabitants of Sudstrom poured out onto stoops or porches to watch the column of players and lancers leaving the river town, Secca felt as though many eyes studied her from behind window curtains and closed shutters. She felt a very definite relief—if only from scrutiny—when they were out of Sudstrom and traveling the river road beyond the town, a road of gentle curves flanked by a few fields set between larger stands of trees.

The cold of the night before had left a light frost on the exposed upper side of the needles of the pines and the firs, and across the bare branches of those bushes that were not sheltered by taller conifers. Where the rising sun struck the frost, the thin coating puffed into a white mist that drifted upward, and then vanished. As the sun rose above the woods to the east, it played across the frosted trees, and light sparkled everywhere for a time. Secca smiled at the not-quite-sparkling light, but light and smile dimmed as the frost evaporated.

"The sun feels good," Richina offered.

"It's a good thing we're out of the snow," Secca said. "If it's as warm there as it looks to be getting here, the mud will be hock deep there by afternoon."

"With these roads, we'd better hope we don't get rain," Richina said.

"You see why Lady Anna worried about roads?" Secca asked. "We could cross Defalk in the time it takes to go a third as far in Ebra." She wasn't sure if that were the exact comparison, but that was the way it felt.

"It would take years to pave the roads in Ebra."

"It has taken years in Defalk," Secca said dryly. "More than a score."

"How many deks of roads are paved in Defalk?" asked Alcaren, as he rode up beside the two sorceresses, his mount almost on the shoulder of the road.

"I'm not sure anyone has totaled the number," Secca replied. "Mostly the main roads north, south, east, and west from Falcor."

"All the way to the borders?" asked the Ranuan.

"Some places a bit beyond," Secca conceded. "The road from Mencha is paved all the way through the Sand Pass and about fifteen deks beyond."

"That has to be more than a thousand deks," Alcaren said slowly. "And that was done with sorcery?"

"There wasn't any other way. It's taken four sorceresses a score of years," Secca pointed out. "How are the roads in Ranuak?"

"The older roads near Encora are paved, but most to the north and east are not." Alcaren smiled ruefully. "The first Ranuan lancer companies that went to Elahwa could have used such roads to get from Encora to Elahwa. The northern part wasn't too bad. It's always dry as you near the Sand Hills."

"How long did it take?" asked Richina.

"For them, almost two weeks. For us, a week."

"You rode that much faster?" asked Secca.

"Hardly." Alcaren shook his head. "The Matriarch had sent more than ten companies when the Sturinnese first blockaded the Free City. The only way that many lancers could get there was overland, and winter had not yet fallen. For us, the Matriarch wagered against luck and weather. She used coastal schooners to send us to the north side of the Sand Hills. It was but a four-day ride from there."

Secca managed to keep a pleasant smile on her face as she considered the implications of Alcaren's revelations. "She must have felt you would make a difference."

"She could send no more lancers, not without leaving Encora exposed, and she felt that Elahwa might fall before we could ride that way. She risked losing both ships and lancers, had either the weather turned or the captains left the shallows." The overcaptain smiled. "She was right. We did blunt the last attacks, but the city would have fallen in days if you had not come to her aid."

"I am glad we arrived in time," replied Secca. "I was not certain that we would."

"But you did," Alcaren said.

Secca nodded, still mulling over what Alcaren had revealed. The Matriarch had felt she could send no more lancers, and only the SouthWomen, but she had gambled two ships of the type that could evade the deeper-drafted blockade ships to get Alcaren to Elahwa. Or had it been to get the overcaptain to Secca?

Again, the more that the handsome overcaptain said, and the more that he revealed, the further Secca seemed to be from understanding him—and Ranuak. Or was it that she had so much to learn?

85

The sun was low in the western sky, hanging just over the trees on the far side of the unseen river on the west side of Elahwa. Secca shifted her weight in the saddle, trying to present an impression of what a sorceress should be. Under the gray sky, a damp and cold breeze blew from the harbor to the south, carrying the faint scent of seaweed and salt air.

Secca and Richina rode down the gray-brick main boulevard of Elahwa, behind Achar and the banner of the Sorceress-Protector. Behind them rode Wilten and Alcaren, followed by Palian and Delvor, the rest of the players, and then the lancers of Loiseau. The SouthWomen brought up the rear. At the head of the column, before the banner, was an honor guard in the scarlet tunics of the Free City.

Elahwa had no walls or gates. Not that the lack of either was surprising in itself, since the actual towns and cities in Defalk had neither walls nor gates. But from what Secca could see, and from what the mirror had shown earlier, Elahwa also had no walled keeps or fortresses.

Most of the buildings were of the same gray brick as paved the boulevard, and the roofs were of dark split slate. Secca took in the weaver's shop, with its bright blue shutters, and a white sign trimmed in the same blue, a sign showing the outline of a foot-treadle loom. Next to the weaver's shop was a cabinet-maker's, and there the shutters were a light brown. The only touches of color were those doors and shutters—bright green, crimson, sky blue. On each house or structure, shutters and doors matched, but the colors varied from one to the next, often dramatically.

A thin scattering of people stood everywhere—on the porch of the weaver's, under the broad eaves of the cooper's across the boulevard, under the leafless trees at the edge of the green that the column approached. Some smiled, but most just watched as the column rode southward. While a handful of men were among the bystanders, most were women, many gray-haired, but many young, and some only girls. Occasionally, there were murmurs.

"Another of the great sorceresses . . ."

". . . looks so small . . ."

". . . with that small a company . . . has to be powerful . . ."

". . . two of them . . . though . . ."

"Better her than the Maitre . . ."

". . . don't tell that to the shadow ladies . . ."

Secca wanted to shake her head. They talked as though she were the Lord of Defalk or the regent. She was just a sorceress-protector who still was trying to figure out how to do her duty. She couldn't have explained why she was in Elahwa, except that she felt she should be—and there was nowhere else she could take her lancers with the depth of winter yet to come.

On the far side of the green—a parklike expanse of bushes and browned grass surrounded by a stone wall less than a yard high—was the Council building, a structure of a blue-tinged marble. The entire three-level structure was less than forty yards across the front, and perhaps only sixty deep.

As Secca guided the gray mare around the green, she could see that five women waited beneath and before the square stone columns at the top of the stone steps of the Council building. Over tunic and trousers, each wore a long armless scarlet vest that ran from shoulder to knee. A single black braided cord at waist level provided the only cincture.

As requested by the Elahwan captain who now led the honor guard, Secca turned the gray mare when she reached a point in the street opposite the middle of steps to the Council building. Then she rode forward and reined up five yards short of the bottom step.

The woman in the center stepped forward. Secca thought the counselor was the one who had been with Alcaren after the main battle with the Sturinnese north of Elahwa.

"All Elahwa is indebted to you, to you and the great one who came before you." The counselor bowed her head. "Although you have the right to ask for whatever we can offer, beyond that, you are welcome to stay, sorceress and protector."

"I appreciate your welcome." Secca bowed her head in return. "I will ask as little as possible in these troubled times."

A second counselor eased forward and walked down the steps carrying a basket—one gilded and wrapped partly in crimson ribbons. In it, Secca could see a clear glass bottle, a long loaf of bread, and a small cloth pouch.

"For your efforts, we welcome you. May the bread of Harmony sustain you. May the water you drink always be pure, and may you always be the salt of your people."

Secca wasn't sure how to respond, but the ceremony called for something. She bowed her head and spoke. "Thank you for your welcome, and for the bread, water, and salt. For your welcome and your ways, may the Harmonies watch over you and keep you."

Smiles appeared across the faces of the counselors, and murmurs cascaded across the bystanders around the green.

". . . only a sorceress dare to call on the Harmonies . . ."

". . . be why she's a sorceress-protector . . ."

". . . still Sea-Priest ships on the Southern Ocean . . ."

The first counselor raised her voice. "We would like to meet with you in the morning. In the meantime, Overcaptain Alcaren and the honor guard will escort you, your assistant, your players, and your forces to the guest quarters and barracks." The counselor turned toward Alcaren, who had reined up several yards to Secca's right. "Does that meet your satisfaction, overcaptain?"

"I would be pleased, Counselor Veria."

The hint of a frown passed over the woman's face, followed by a rueful smile. "The overcaptain remains under your command, Sorceress-Protector, until you discharge him or until his return is requested by the Matriarch of Ranuak."

Alcaren nodded as if he had expected no less, but Secca had the feeling that Counselor Veria's words were as much a surprise to Alcaren as they had been to Secca, and that they had been deliberately uttered loudly in a public place to ensure all knew. Secca wanted to think about what those reasons might be.

"Until tomorrow, sorceress," offered Veria with yet another bow.

"Until tomorrow, and our thanks for your hospitality after a long journey." Secca inclined her head in return, then eased the gray mare around to follow the honor guard as Alcaren urged his mount up beside Secca's.

"We will turn right at the end of the next block," Alcaren said from behind Secca.

"Thank you." After a pause, Secca leaned back toward the Ranuan and murmured, "You didn't expect that, did you?"

"I was surprised, but I cannot say it was totally unexpected."

"Because it keeps you under the command of a woman?" Secca's tone was light.

"That . . . and . . ." Alcaren shrugged. "Both the Matriarch and her sister are not entirely without humor and wit." His voice expressed a wry humor of its own.

"That's the Veria you mentioned before?"

"The very same." Alcaren gestured. "We turn here."

Once the column had turned right at the corner that held a squarish building without a sign of any sort, Secca and the others rode southward once more. While there were still bystanders who watched them, those grew less and less with each yard that passed.

"Why didn't the older one return to Encora to become Matriarch?" Secca finally asked.

"Veria disobeyed her mother when she came to Elahwa to fight with the FreeWomen. She almost died, and certainly would have been killed had the great sorceress not defeated Bertmynn."

Secca still felt a jarring note when she heard Anna being referred to as the Great Sorceress, even though she knew it to be factually true. With the jarring came the cold emptiness of knowing she would never see, never hear Anna again. Her eyes burned.

"Veria felt her place was here, and soon became a counselor." Alcaren cleared his throat before adding, "That is all that I know. No one speaks of the details. At least, they did not when I was around."

Secca swallowed her grief and asked, "So the two sisters control the adjoining lands?"

"They do not think alike. While they respect each other, they have most different views."

"How are they different?"

"From what I have seen, Veria would use any tool to keep Sturinn at bay. The Matriarch would not."

"She would let the Sturinnese take over Liedwahr?" Secca found her voice rising slightly.

"She might well die attempting to stop them . . ." Alcaren stopped, as if unsure as to whether he could say more . . . or what.

"You know more than that." Secca could see Richina listening intently, and trying to give the impression of paying no attention at all.

"I do not *know*," replied the overcaptain.

"What do you feel, then?"

"All the Matriarchs have done little more with sorcery than scry what happens elsewhere in the world. I have never seen one perform the kind of sorcery that you do. Yet they know all that comprises sorcery, and they understand the Harmonies."

"You seem to be saying that either they do sorcery in secret or that there is some reason that they do not do much sorcery."

"In a land like Ranuak, little can be kept secret for long if it has results." Alcaren's voice again contained that dry humorous tone.

"I see." Secca nodded. Alcaren was definitely telling her something, and she didn't like what she heard because, if he were right, Secca, Richina, Clayre, and Jolyn were all that stood before Sturinn's conquest of Liedwahr.

"So . . ." Alcaren drew out the word, but as an ending, and not an invitation to more questions. Then he gestured ahead and to the left.

There, almost a dek south from the Council building, the honor guard turned to pass though a pair of gate posts set on the left side of the road. A narrow paved lane led to a two-story dwelling that might well have passed for a mansion, with its wide-glassed windows, cream shutters, and double front doors under a covered archway with stone mounting blocks for carriages.

To each side and behind the dwelling were gray brick buildings that stretched back seemingly almost half a dek in a squared-off horseshoe shape. The sides had the frequent doors and windows of a barracks, while the back side of the horseshoe had several wide doors, indicating stables and other working spaces.

"The front building is the guest quarters," Alcaren said. "You will have the master suite on the second floor, with an adjoining smaller suite for Lady Richina."

"What about you?" asked Secca.

"I have a small set of rooms on the lower level. They didn't know where else to put me." Alcaren grinned, and his gray-blue eyes twinkled for a moment. "I was the only man who was an overcaptain in Elahwa." He looked at Wilten. "I expect you will have the suite across from me. The barracks in back will hold ten companies and their officers. The players should get the first set of company quarters, and there are enough rooms in the guest house for your chief players."

"Your lancers worked this out before we came?" asked Secca.

"I suggested it in my scroll. The honor guard confirmed it."

"The lancers and players will appreciate the quarters greatly."

While Secca dismounted and unsaddled her own mount, she did not leave the courtyard until she was certain that all the lancers and players were indeed quartered. Her legs ached by the time she and Richina followed Alcaren through the rear entry to the guest mansion and up the wide staircase. Dyvan and Rukor trailed the three.

"This suite is yours, Lady Richina." Alcaren opened the door and motioned for Richina to enter.

Secca did not enter, just held the lutar, waiting. She could see that the suite was about the size of Richina's rooms at Loiseau, if slightly more starkly appointed.

"I will let you know about the meal shortly," offered the Ranuan as he closed the door. He turned and walked along the corridor, a good three yards wide, toward a set of double doors at the end.

After Alcaren opened the right-hand door, Secca stepped through the shimmering polished oak door frame. Despite the grayness of the day, the large chamber was flooded with light from the wide windows. A working desk faced away from the leftmost of the three windows, so that light would fall over the shoulders of whoever used it. A circular golden oak conference table was set before the right window, with five chairs spaced around it. On the left wall was a tiled hearth with logs already set on a pair of heavy iron andirons. An open door on the right wall revealed a bedchamber, with a bathing chamber beyond that.

The petite sorceress shook her head. Somehow, despite all the words from the counselors, the guest quarters and barracks were more than Secca had expected.

"They owe you and your predecessor greatly," Alcaren said. "They would like to feel that they could repay some of that debt."

Secca wished more rulers felt that way, instead of acting like Bertmynn and his greedy son Mynntar.

"You need but use the bellpull to summon a servant. If you do not mind, I will arrange for the evening meal for those in this building in about a glass."

"And the players and lancers?"

"There is a larger kitchen in the barracks," Alcaren said with a smile. "They will not suffer."

Secca laughed.

Alcaren bowed. "Until later, lady." With his smile still in place, he turned and departed, closing the outer door with an audible *click*.

Secca was still smiling as she walked toward the bath chamber, where two kettles of steaming water stood on the table beside a tub filled with warm water.

86

A distant roaring and groaning filled the dark room, followed by a low grumbling rumble, and then by the sound of metal being wrenched.

Secca bolted upright in the oversized bed in the guest quarters. Ignoring the gumminess in her eyes, she turned her head from one side to the other, trying to determine if the sound had come from the quarters or from somewhere in Elahwa, but all she could hear was . . . nothing. Nothing except her own breathing.

Had she heard metal being bent and wrenched? Or had she dreamed that she had heard it? Or had it been another distant and massive song-spell? The sound had been so much like the sound of tortured Harmonies that had followed the fall of the keep at Dolov. Had it been a dream because she felt she had acted wrongly? Or had it been actual sorcery penetrating her sleep? More Sturinnese thunder-drum sorcery?

She started to lie back, but she could feel her heart pounding. So she swung her bare legs over the side of the bed and sat there for several moments in the darkness, taking deep breaths and trying to relax. After a time, she stood, wincing momentarily as her bare feet touched the polished gray stone tiles of the floor. She eased out of the small bedchamber and into the larger main chamber of the guest suite, listening with each step. The main chamber was dark and silent.

Certain that her chambers were empty of all but her, Secca used a striker to light the candle on the small desk in the main chamber, then eased the travel scrying mirror from its leather case and set it in the small pool of light cast by the candle. Next came the lutar. Her fingers were stiff as she began to tune the instrument, but before long she held the lutar and stood before both candle and glass. What did she need to know?

Finally, she began the spell.

"Show me now and in this light
what great spell has passed this night . . ."

The glass silvered, and then presented an image mostly of grays. With the darkness in the room and the darkness of the scene displayed, Secca found making out details was difficult. As she peered at the glass, she began to recognize a scene showing only shattered rock, much as Dolov had looked, except Dolov was on a bluff overlooking a river, and the structure Secca beheld seemed to be on a low rise of some sort.

She swallowed.

A keep somewhere had been destroyed by sorcery, but where she had no idea. Dumar? Ebra? Ranuak?

With a sigh, Secca lifted the lutar and sang the words to release the first image. Then she tried a variation on the spell.

"Show me now and in this light
Where in Dumar a spell has passed this night . . ."

The mirror remained unchanged, reflecting only the candle above it, and hazy shadows, one of which was Secca's.

Secca thought for a moment, then tried a third spell.

"Show me now and as you must,
the Neserean keep just turned to dust . . ."

The scene was nearly identical to the first, and rather than struggle with keeping the image in the glass, Secca immediately sang the release couplet.

"Belmar?" she murmured.

The fourth spell was an attempt to see if it had indeed been the Neserean sorcerer and plotter.

"Show me now and as you must.
the keep that Belmar just turned to dust . . ."

The third image was near-identical to the first two, and Secca released it quickly.

She swallowed and began the fourth spellsong.

"Show me now and in this light
how stands Clayre in open sight . . ."

The glass showed the dark-haired sorceress, hair disheveled, pacing beside a table holding a scrying glass.

Secca nodded and released the spell. Clayre was safe, but as disturbed as Secca. The red-haired sorceress looked down at her own blank glass and shivered once, then set the lutar on the side of the desk, before turning and walking to the center window, conscious of the chill welling away from the panes, even through the closed shutters. No sounds came from the city beyond the glass.

After a moment, the sorceress unfastened the brass catch, folded back the right shutter, and gazed out on the gray-paved lane, darker and grayer in the night, that led out to the main boulevard.

Belmar? She had felt that it couldn't have been Clayre, not the way that the Harmonies had protested, and the mirror had confirmed that.

And why at night? Not that she had not done spells at night or in the darkness.

Secca leaned forward until her nose almost touched the cold glass, glancing upward . . . Darksong was indeed in the sky, but past its zenith, but Neserea was to the west, where the red moon was higher in the heavens.

So the spell had been sung when Darksong had been high in the night sky in Neserea.

Did that mean that a Clearsong spell for building a bridge would be more effective when the white moon was at its zenith during the day?

She frowned. While there were some mentions of moon positions in the older books, they all referred to Darksong. Yet it followed that they should affect spells under either moon.

Slowly and carefully, she closed the shutter and re-latched it. Then she crossed to the desk, where she re-cased the lutar, but left the mirror on the desk. After another moment, she blew out the candle and made her way back to the bed, where she eased her way back under the comforter.

She took a deep and slow breath, trying to relax, at least enough to get back to sleep.

Belmar? Neserea?

She turned over . . . once, and then again.

87

Secca adjusted the relatively clean tunic, then stepped toward the window of the main chamber of the guest suite. The morning was gray and looked cold outside, but there seemed to be little wind. "It's not snowing or raining."

"Not yet," replied Richina.

Secca walked toward the wall peg on which hung her green leather riding jacket, removing it and slipping into it.

"You don't want me to come?" asked Richina.

"There's no reason for you to," Secca said, trying to avoid pointing out that the invitation was for the Sorceress-

Protector alone. "You could practice or rest. You can practice here, if you like." She sighed. "I wouldn't mind the rest."

"You didn't sleep that well, did you?"

"No," admitted the redhead. "Not after all the work it took to find out what Belmar had done. I still don't know what keep he brought down, except that it's in Neserea, and it's not in Esaria."

"You don't think . . . ? Lady Clayre, I mean?"

"No. She's safe." Secca shook her head, then fastened the oiled leather riding jacket. "I think I would have felt something like that, but I did use the glass last night to make sure. She was as surprised as I was, I think, because she had her glass out." Secca glanced around, then reclaimed the green felt hat, but tucked it into the jacket belt rather than wear it. "I hope I won't be too long, but . . . I just don't know."

"I hope the meeting with the counselor goes well."

"So do I." Secca paused at the door. "Best you study the arrow spell. You may need to use it before we return to Loiseau."

"The arrow spell . . . for thunder-drums?"

Secca nodded before she turned toward the door, then stopped. "Could either of us have stopped them here by ourselves? Do you think that will change when we get to Dumar?"

"We're going to Dumar?"

"If we don't, we'll find the Sturinnese coming to us." The older sorceress smiled. "So practice."

"Ah . . . yes, lady."

Secca slipped out and down the corridor to the stairs.

Wilten and Alcaren were mounted and waiting by the rear entrance when Secca walked out. Behind them, in formation, were four guards—Dyvan, Rukor, Achar, and Easlon—and a squad of lancers from Loiseau.

"Good morning, lady," offered Wilten.

Alcaren smiled and inclined his head. "I trust you slept well."

"As well as could be expected, and certainly in greater comfort, thank you." She returned the smile, before looking back up at Wilten. "Are the lancers comfortable?"

"Most comfortable, lady, and well fed. They are pleased for the respite." The overcaptain smiled.

"And the SouthWomen?" Secca turned to Alcaren.

"They are indeed, lady, and pleased to be back here."

"Good." Secca mounted, conscious again of how she practically had to jump and lever herself into the saddle because of her lack of height, at least when there were no mounting blocks convenient. As she rode forward behind Achar, and the standard he bore, Wilten rode beside her on her right, and Alcaren on the left.

When the short column rode out from the paved lane and turned northward on the gray brick road toward the Council building, the breeze stiffened. Fine misting drops of rain swept into her face, droplets that stung as if they were tiny ice pellets. Secca pulled the green felt hat from her belt and pulled it down on her head, so that the front brim would deflect some of the icy rain.

"Good thing we're here in quarters," observed Wilten.

"Very good," Secca admitted, wondering as she did how long she could impose on the city, and how long she dared. That would depend on the meeting with the Counselor, and on what she could discover in the next day or so through the use of the scrying glass.

"You look worried," ventured Alcaren.

"I am," the sorceress admitted. "We have a respite, but the Sturinnese are still in Dumar." She decided against saying more for the moment.

Alcaren frowned slightly, then shifted his weight in the saddle. "Up there, to the left, you can see the walls for the quarters of the Free City's lancers. Just this side—the building with the pale green shutters—that's the Boiled Pot."

"Boiled pot?" asked Secca.

"It is an odd name for a tavern—it's not really an inn—but it's because the old proprietress said she boiled every pot before cooking anything in it. She claimed that kept food from spoiling."

"Did it . . ." Secca shook her head. Anna had insisted on the same thing for water used in childbirth. "It should work."

Alcaren shrugged. "I wasn't here that long before you arrived, but the local lancers claimed no one ever got the flux from eating there."

"Maybe more innkeepers should boil their pots," interjected Wilten with a laugh.

"Especially in Ebra," added Alcaren wryly.

"I didn't know . . ." Secca grinned at the Ranuan overcaptain.

"I'm fine . . . now. The ride from Hanlis was . . . shall we say I have had more comfortable journeys."

Secca couldn't help a gentle laugh at the wry and self-deprecating tone of Alcaren's response. "I'm glad you're fine now."

As the column turned left at the unmarked squarish building, Wilten pointed to the green across the green. "Don't see anyone there today."

"We wouldn't be out in this if we lived here," Secca replied. "I'd just as soon it didn't turn to snow."

"It seldom does along the coast," Alcaren said.

Anna would have had an explanation for that, Secca reflected, realizing that there was much she could have learned—and hadn't. And now she never would. The redhead reined up the gray mare on the side of the steps leading up to the square columns at the front of the Council building, opposite the bronze hitching rings set into the blue marble wall that comprised the side facing of the steps. She dismounted quickly, and tied the gray to the end ring.

Wilten nodded at the sorceress. "We'll be here till you return, lady."

"I don't know how long it will be."

"We'll be here."

Alcaren dismounted, but did not leave his mount, nodding as Secca turned to walk back to the front of the half-score marble steps. Between the darkness of the clouds overhead and the dampness left by the fine rain on the stone, the pale blue marble steps appeared a darkish gray.

Dyvan and Easlon followed Secca up the steps.

A single woman guard in a crimson short cloak, wearing a brace of shortswords, stepped forward as Secca walked through the square archway and then through the right hand door of the double oak doors.

"Lady Sorceress, Counselor Veria is in the third chamber on the left."

"Thank you." Secca offered a smile.

"My pleasure, lady." The smile presented in return was more than mere politeness.

Secca's boots clicked on the blue marble floor, as she walked toward the doorway indicated by the guard. Her steps echoed loudly enough that the sorceress suspected her heels were worn down and the boot nails were striking the stone. She slipped off the hat, folded it, and slipped it through her belt. She tried to smooth her hair somewhat, knowing that it wouldn't have mattered if she'd used a brush or comb.

The door to the chamber was unguarded, and Secca almost felt foolish as she looked in to see the counselor seated behind a wide table-desk, alone except for a stack of scrolls.

"Lady Sorceress, do come in."

"Thank you." Secca looked to Dyvan and Easlon. "If you would guard the door . . . ?"

"Yes, lady."

Secca eased the polished golden oak door closed and stepped into the chamber, a room roughly four yards wide and three deep, containing a table-desk with a chair behind it, three chairs before it, and a series of footchests lined up against the wall to the left. The table-desk was set before the single tall and narrow window, with two oil lamps upon it—one on each side. Each side of the chamber also had an oil lamp in a sconce. Although all four were lit, the room was still dim.

Veria gestured toward the chairs. "I must apologize, but luxury is yet frowned on in Elahwa."

"The quarters for us are luxury enough in this season and so far from Mencha, and we are most grateful." Secca sat down in the chair to the right.

"We are even more grateful for your presence and your decision to rescue Elahwa before dealing with the keep at Dolov." The counselor studied Secca before speaking again. "Alcaren's message was brief. He only wrote that you had destroyed the keep and left young Haddev there to rebuild and restore the holding. I assume you used sorcery."

"We did. I asked for those within to surrender. They refused. They even tried to kill the lancer delivering the message."

"You decided to destroy the keep, then?"

"The clouds were gathering to the north for another storm. We couldn't stay. We had no siege engines, and not that many lancers." Secca shrugged. "I was tired and angry. Lady Anna pardoned Bertmynn's heirs and gave the keep and lands to them if they were loyal to Hadrenn and Lord Robero. Mynntar rebelled, and his heirs refused to accept Lord Hadrenn's or Lord Robero's rule." The sorceress paused. "I've thought about it since. It might have been better if I had used sorcery to slay all within and left the keep intact."

"I think not," replied Veria. "I say that not because I despise Bertmynn and his heirs. I do despise them, but that is not why."

"Oh?" Secca raised her eyebrows.

"Any who rebuild it will know the effort and golds required. Young Haddev will first call dissonance upon you. In time, he will respect you, for he will learn what it takes to build . . . If you had emptied it and bestowed it upon him . . . then he would have taken it as his due. Even if it goes to the younger brother, the older will not forget."

Veria offered a crooked smile. "They will not like you much, but they also will not cross you."

"I can't say I thought of that," Secca admitted.

"You followed what you felt, and that is oft right more than fine words."

"Others have said that." Secca recalled Anna.

"Remember this. Long after you and I are moldering dust in a fine tomb, for you will have that, men will read of your deeds, and they will call you worse than a rutting bitch because you employed sorcery to slay fine lancers and armsmen. They will praise a masterful battle in which more died and suffered because of the skill at arms of the marshal who won. Yet, in the end, all are dead. Most men, especially lords and holders, wish to be known for their valor and strength."

"And women?" asked Secca. "Are we that different?"

"Some women are like men, and some men think like women, but I would say that most women often care more about what results than how the results were obtained, save they also realize that some means will never achieve the results wished."

Secca nodded, although she was less sure of that than Veria seemed to be.

"If I might ask," Veria asked cautiously, "why did you determine to return to Elahwa?"

Secca smiled, trying to compose a truthful answer that didn't make her seem too simplistic or too calculating. "I suppose because I could see no point in trying to return to Mencha with the Sand Pass drifted deep in snow. The lancers and players need a respite before we try such, and I thought there was the chance that we might be needed to go to Dumar."

"Needed?" Veria shook her head. "Lord Robero should have dispatched one of the other sorceresses the moment he discovered the Sea-Pigs had used the thunder-drums to raise the sea against Narial."

Secca wondered if she should have suggested such, or gone herself—except then Ebra would have fallen.

"You wonder that you should have gone?" asked the counselor. "That would have been no better, for Elahwa would have fallen—and Ebra. Sending a sorceress to Neserea was unwise. A rebellion without Sea-Priests is far less to be feared than ships and lancers in white in Dumar."

"Perhaps not," Secca said slowly. "There is a sorcerer in Neserea. He brought down a walled keep somewhere there last evening. The disruptions were enough to wake me."

Veria leaned forward in the chair behind the table-desk. "You could sense that all these many deks away?"

"Unhappily."

"Can the other sorceress sense such?"

"I don't know about them all," Secca replied. "Some can, and some cannot."

"From that far away?"

Secca offered a laugh. "We've never had this happen before, and I've not been able to talk to them."

"What of the younger sorceress with you?"

"She is still learning," Secca said. "She is the youngest who is beyond an apprentice."

"You were wise to bring her."

Before Veria could pursue more about sorcery, the red-headed sorceress smiled again and asked, "What can you tell me about Alcaren?"

"Possibly less than you already know." Veria smiled in turn. "He was not even yet born when I left Encora. He comes from an old trading family, but not one of the wealthiest. He is trusted by the Matriarch not to harm Ranuak, or she would not have sent him, and he is skilled enough to listen to his captains, but strong enough that they will not overtly disobey him. There is more to him than meets the eye, but he is skilled enough to hide what that may be, but not skilled enough to hide that such exists."

Secca laughed gently. "Much of that—"

"You have already discerned," Veria completed Secca's sentence.

"What is there that is not to be seen?"

Veria smiled. "Besides his interest in you, you mean?"

"Me? He is but interested in me because I am a sorceress."

"I have no doubts that he follows what you do, but he follows more than that."

Secca managed to keep from flushing.

"Do not worry. He will never press, and if he is not to your inclination, then you need not worry."

Secca was not sure what to say.

"That is but a guess on my part, but I have some years more experience in dealing with men." Veria shrugged. "As for the other, he reminds me of my father, although I could not say why in all respects. He was not here long before you came, but he considers matters carefully, and seems to judge wisely."

"Do you know why he was chosen to come to your assistance?" Secca wondered what Veria had seen that she had not.

"There was no one else the Matriarch could have sent. It would have been ill-regarded had the SouthWomen come under their own overcaptain."

"Even when things were so . . ."

"Desperate?" asked Veria. "We would have accepted any aid. That you must know. But the Matriarch must also answer to the men of Ranuak, and they would have been far less pleased. Nor would those in Defalk or Dumar or Mansuur have been pleased with SouthWomen under their own overcaptain. The SouthWomen could not protest, not when they had requested for so long to be sent." The counselor lifted her shoulders expressively.

"Why Alcaren?"

"She trusts him. That is most clear. *Why* she trusts him—that I do not know, although what I have seen and heard would confirm that he is trustworthy."

"He seems so," Secca agreed.

"What do you plan, Lady Sorceress?" Veria's eyes seemed to twinkle as she waited.

"I do not know yet. What I learn in the days ahead will tell me what courses may be open to us."

"Your only course is one that brings you to defeat the Sea-Priests as soon as you can. Each season that you delay brings more lancers and more thunder-drums into Liedwahr." Veria's voice was calm, but almost chill.

"That may be, but even getting to Dumar would seem impossible at this moment," Secca pointed out. "The passes from Ebra to Defalk are blocked. The ports at Encora and Narial are blockaded. We have no ships, and we are not equipped to cross the Sand Hills into Ranuak—even were we to be welcome." Secca paused. "Have you ships that would carry us?"

"None that can easily reach us past the Sturinnese to take you to Dumar," admitted Veria. "We may yet find a way to reach Ranuak, and there the Matriarch could assist you, should you choose to go to Encora."

"How could we be certain that we would not face opposition from the Matriarch?"

"I cannot be most certain," admitted Veria. "I doubt that the Matriarch would make you unwelcome in Ranuak. I do not know that I would be welcome, but most of Ranuak would welcome a sorceress who was devoted to repelling the Sea-Priests from Liedwahr."

"Most?" Secca lifted her eyebrows.

"Most. The Ladies of the Shadows fear sorcery in any form and for any reason, although they will accept that which is but used to watch or gather information."

"There are Ladies of the Shadows everywhere," Secca said.

"But not so many nor so powerful as those in Ranuak," Veria replied. "The Matriarch watches them most closely, and they her."

"They would oppose sorcery to stop the Sturinnese?" asked Secca.

"They fear that Ranuak would again be laid waste, as it was in the Spell-Fire Wars."

"But . . ."

"Exactly. The Wars gave them more freedom than any women in Liedwahr, or indeed in the world, yet they seem to have forgotten such."

"Has the Matriarch?" questioned Secca.

"No. She would use any tool within her power to stop the Maitre. She is young for a Matriarch, and must move with great care. But she would use me—or you."

Secca wasn't quite sure how to respond, or that she should reveal she knew the Matriarch was Veria's sister. After a moment, she said, "You make her sound cold and most manipulative."

"She is not cold, but she is manipulative. Every Matriarch must be so, while seeming to be most caring and direct and honest." Veria raised her eyebrows before asking, "Is that not so with any ruler? For none can be all things to all folk and thus must only appear such."

"I suppose so."

"Is it any different in being the shadow sorceress?"

"The shadow sorceress?" Secca's question was involuntary.

"By remaining in the shadows, you and the one before you let others draw your image as they wished, if with a touch of darkness and mystery."

"We . . . neither of us was or is all things to all folk."

"No, and that is why you chose the shadows, but at noon there are no shadows."

Secca shook her head at the cryptic words. "What do you want?"

"You have already provided what we needed most. We can and will ask no more of you." Veria stood. "You may remain as you wish, all winter if necessary, or until the passes are clear for your return to Defalk."

"You don't think that will happen," Secca replied, standing in turn.

"No. Given you are the daughter in spirit of the great sorceress, given a weak lord in Defalk, and a weaker one in Ebra, and given what the Sturinnese plan . . . I think you will find acting is better than not acting. But that choice must be yours."

"There are many ways to act."

"And as many not to act," Veria replied. "I trust that you will do what is right and necessary, as you have thus far. I doubt that you could do otherwise, however you choose."

"We will see."

"As I said, you are welcome so long as you wish, and I—all of us—sincerely mean that. Without you, we would already be dead or in chains. Nor do I wish to hasten any decision. Whatever you decide, you and your forces need rest first. I will be here when you are ready to decide, and it may be that I can assist you."

"Rest we do need, and we are thankful for your support." Secca inclined her head.

"And *you* will always have it." While the emphasis on *you* was slight, it was definite.

As Secca walked back down the corridor, followed by her guards, Veria's words echoed in her thoughts. *That choice must be yours. That choice must be yours . . .*

Would it be, really?

88

ENCORA, RANUAK

In his small study off the balcony, Aetlen finishes the chord on the mandolin with a flourish, then grins at his daughter. "There!"

"I liked that one," Verlya says. "I haven't heard it before."

"I learned it from your grandfather, Ulgar. He called it a tune to stir the blood. Your mother thinks it's too strident."

Sitting on the stool across from her father, the blonde girl frowns.

"Too loud and noisy," Aetlen explains.

"Sometimes loud feels good. Will you teach it to me?"

"If you promise not to play it often around your mother. She needs quiet these days."

"If you listen," promises Verlya.

"I will." Aetlen looks to his left as the study door opens, and the Matriarch steps into the room.

"Mother!" Verlya leaps from the stool, takes two steps, and wraps her arms around Alya's waist.

The Matriarch returns the hug, the somberness leaving her features as she holds her youngest child. In time, she disengages herself gently and smiles. "Could you go downstairs and tell Cook and Ulya that we would like to eat shortly?"

"You're eating with us?"

"I am," Alya affirms.

"I'll tell them." With a smile, the blonde girl bounces from the study.

Aetlen rises and closes the door. "I heard . . . the shadow sorceress returned to Elahwa," he says slowly. "With Alcaren and the SouthWomen."

"She did not bring Hadrenn's lancers, nor the company from Silberfels." Alya slips into the chair across from her consort. "Your study is warmer."

"It's smaller, and there's but one window and the doors. I was giving Verlya a lesson with the mandolin."

"She may need it," Alya says darkly.

"The shadow sorceress?"

"She may come to our aid. Not with lancers, but with what she knows." Alya's eyes are dark as she looks to her consort. "How can I refuse if she does? If she does not, we must face the old hard choices. We may in any case."

"Do we need her aid? There is no hunger, and no older folk are dying of chill and consumption. We have stores in the granaries—enough for years."

"Do we wait until Dumar falls, and the Sturinnese try

again? Do you think the Maitre will remove the fleets once he holds Dumar?"

"Can we break the blockade?"

"With what? You know what happened the last time. We can protect the channel and keep them from entering, but they can destroy our trade, and in time that will destroy all that is Ranuak."

"Will it come to that? With the shadow sorceress in Elahwa?" asks Aetlen.

"Perhaps not. The shadow sorceress met with Veria," Alya says.

"Your eyes say you are worried—most worried."

"Veria will speak as she sees. She may well persuade the sorceress to aid us. Or she may let the sorceress make that decision."

"You worry that the sorceress *will* come to our assistance?" Aetlen frowns.

"I do indeed, for that will lead us down the trail to the true horrors of a sorcery war. We had almost managed to bury the old knowledge." Alya shakes her head. "Then came the Sturinnese and the great sorceress."

"Is it just the old knowledge?"

"No. The Lady Anna understood beyond the rote spells, beyond the music, and, worse, she has taught at least the shadow sorceress. The spell-poisonings are but the beginning of the horrors." Alya's lips twist. "Yet we cannot bury that knowledge, not to any good end this time."

"If you kill the shadow sorceress . . . ?"

"You want your daughters—all daughters—in chains and under the thunder-drums?"

Aetlen shakes his head.

"Whatever may come, it is but a question of the least of great evils."

"The least of great evils . . ." Aetlen turns toward the single small window, where he looks into the darkness of an early winter evening for a moment before turning back. "Can you see nothing more hopeful?"

"I continue to hope, but I cannot say that I see better."

Alya takes a deep breath, and a smile appears on her face. "Let us go have dinner with the girls."

Aetlen matches her smile with one of his own, then offers her his arm.

89

Still puzzled by her meeting with Counselor Veria, Secca walked slowly up the steps toward her guest quarters. She nodded to Dymen, guarding her door, and stepped inside. Richina looked up from the lutar and the notation, then set aside the instrument and hurried toward Secca.

"How was the meeting with the counselor?" asked the younger sandy-haired sorceress.

"Interesting." Secca paused. "We're welcome to stay here so long as we wish, all winter if necessary." She unfastened the damp riding jacket and hung it on the wall peg, with the green felt hat over it. Her eyes went to the window, where fine ice pellets bounced intermittently against the glass. "It looks like we won't be going west or north anytime soon."

"Lady, might you tell me why you found it interesting?"

"Puzzling, even." Secca turned away from viewing the falling ice mist, certain she didn't want to discuss her puzzlement. "Do you feel up to singing some more scrying spells? You might as well get used to doing more of them." She glanced toward the door. "The players and the overcaptains should be here in a moment."

"You've summoned them all?" asked Richina.

"We need to see what we face, and talk over what everyone knows. That will mean a number of spells. We have to see what's happening in Encora, Narial, and Neserea. You've done scrying spells, and now you've seen enough away from Mencha to be able to visualize things. I can do the first spell, and you look at what the glass shows, and then try the second spell in that area." Secca gestured at the cased scrying glass set on the corner of the desk table. "You'll see."

Thrap.

"Your players and overcaptains, lady," called Dymen, almost immediately following the rap on the door.

"Have them come in."

Palian was the first into the chamber, and she bowed, and then moved farther into the room, almost to the desk. Delvor followed. Then came Wilten and Alcaren.

Once the door closed behind Alcaren, Secca gestured toward the table. "We have some matters we should talk over."

With a look at the five chairs set around the table, Richina slipped into Secca's bedchamber and returned with a stool.

"I can take that, Lady Richina," Alcaren offered.

"I am younger," Richina countered with a smile.

Alcaren returned the smile of the younger sorceress with one of his own. As Richina settled herself in the stool, the Ranuan's eyes shifted to Secca, to whom he offered a rueful and knowing expression.

Secca almost laughed, for Alcaren's face clearly expressed dismay—exaggerated and overdone, but still dismay—at the thought that he was too old to take a stool.

The others seated themselves—Secca with Richina on her left, Palian beside Secca, Delvor flanking Richina, and the overcaptains across the table from the sorceresses.

Secca glanced from one face to the next before speaking. "I have not mentioned to you what I discovered last night, except to Richina," Secca began. "The sorcerer Belmar has begun to use greater powers, even calling upon thunder-drums and possibly Darksong. Last night, he brought down an entire keep in Neserea with sorcery. From what we have already discovered, he intends to bring down Lady Annayal and to become the next Prophet of Music."

"From where did this sorcerer appear?" asked Alcaren.

"He is the holder of Worlan, a coastal town mainly to the west of Esaria. We think that he has been taught sorcery by the Sturinnese," Secca said.

"Can what we do affect aught there?" asked Wilten. "With this weather," he added, gesturing toward the window, "there is little enough we can do."

"Yet everywhere we gaze," Palian said slowly, smoothing back her gray hair unconsciously, "there are the Sea-Priests. They sent lancers and thunder-drummers to support Mynntar. They attacked Elahwa. They ravage Dumar, and now we learn that they are behind the revolt in Neserea." She looked at Wilten, seated beside her. "Do you think such is mere chance, overcaptain?"

"Ah . . . no, chief player. No. I but questioned what we could do in this time of winter." Wilten shifted his weight in the unpadded wooden chair.

"We will not do anything today, or tomorrow, or perhaps longer," Secca said. "The horses are worn and thin. So are the lancers and players. Now is the time to think and plan." She gestured toward the glass in the middle of the table. "To think and plan, you need to see what we can see in the glass."

Secca rose and took the lutar from its case, tuning it slowly. Her eyes flicked to the window. Outside, the fine ice pellets had stopped falling, but the mist seemed to be thickening, cloaking the lane to the avenue with a white fog. She finished tuning and began the first spell-song.

"Show us now and in the glass
what with Belmar comes to pass . . .

As Secca completed the spell-song, the mirror silvered, then revealed the dark-haired holder and sorcerer standing in a library of sorts. Behind a desk sat a heavy-set and older man wearing a rich burgundy tunic. Belmar was smiling as he spoke. The older man frowned.

"The other is not happy," Wilten said.

"We do not know where this is," Delvor murmured.

Secca took the grease pencil and scrawled a line on the rough brown paper before her, then eased it in front of Richina. As Secca seated herself, the younger sorceress stood and cleared her throat, then took Secca's lutar and sang the modified spell.

The mirror showed a low villalike structure set before low hills. Long rows of dark sticklike objects seemed to fill the fields behind the structures that formed three sides of a square around the villa itself.

"Those are vineyards." Palian pointed to the wooden trestle poles. "That has to be in the Ferantha Valley."

Secca frowned, trying to recall the Neserean geography. "That's east of Sperea and south of Elioch, isn't it?"

Alcaren nodded.

With his nod, Secca was most conscious, again, that Alcaren had not watched the glass on the table desk, but had concentrated entirely upon her, and then upon Richina, as each had sung the scrying spell. The Ranuan was all too familiar with far too many things, from geography in lands where he had not traveled—or said he had not traveled—to herbal remedies for overextended sorceresses.

"It is south of Elioch," Palian affirmed.

Secca nodded at Richina, who sang the release couplet.

"So Belmar is raising the south of Neserea against Lady Clayre and Annayal?" asked Wilten.

"Most successfully, it appears," Secca suggested.

"You have dealt with a rebellion and with sorcery," pointed out Delvor. "You are suggesting that matters are different in Neserea?"

"They must be," replied Palian, "or Lady Clayre would not be having such trouble."

"There are large differences," suggested Alcaren slowly.

Those around the table looked to the Ranuan.

"The Evult attacked Defalk, and the Lady Anna destroyed all his forces and buried a goodly section of the northwest under molten rock. Bertmynn rebelled several years later, and the Lady Anna thoroughly destroyed all his forces. Mynntar rebelled, and even with Sturinnese aid, the ladies here have destroyed his forces." Alcaren paused, glanced around the table as if to see that the others were waiting for a conclusion. "The Prophet of Music and his ill-favored son were defeated on Defalkan soil, not in Neserea, and none returned to tell of the disaster, save the few who supported Lord High Counselor Hanfor. Three times has Ebra been crushed. Never has such happened in Neserea. Also, Neserea is far larger than Ebra and far richer. Even were a rebel to conquer Lord Hadrenn, what would he gain? Whereas in Neserea . . ."

The nods went around the table.

"There is little we could do in Neserea, even were the passes clear," Secca observed. "The difficulties there show why we will receive little help from Defalk or the other sorceresses."

"It is but a rebellion," Wilten said.

"That may well be," Secca replied, "but this rebel would make himself Prophet of Music, and both of his predecessors attacked and invaded Defalk. Those attacks are certainly upon the mind of Lord Robero."

"Too much." The murmur was so low that Secca could not determine who said it, save that it could not have been Alcaren, not from the half-smile and nod on his face.

"That may be, but that is as it is," she replied. "Dumar is the problem. It has always been the weakest of the southern lands." Secca stood and took the lutar once more, clearing her throat before singing.

"Show us now and in this glass
where Dumar's battles now come to pass . . ."

The mirror split into six separate images—and in all cases showed the white-coated Sturinnese moving forward, seemingly against no forces whatsoever. Secca watched closely, concentrating on holding the images as she did.

The others half-rose from their seats and also watched.

In the middle image, one of the lancers pitched from the saddle with a long war-arrow through his neck.

After a time, Secca sang the release couplet, set down the lutar, and reseated herself, ignoring the renewed rattling of ice pellets against the window.

"Whoever leads the Dumarans," Alcaren said, "he is trying to avoid large battles. That is all he can do."

"Attack and run before they can bring the thunder-drums into play," Wilten added with a nod. "Use arrows from afar and arch them into the lancers."

"That will but slow them," Alcaren pointed out.

"Perhaps they hope Lord Robero will come to their aid," suggested Palian.

"No one else can," Delvor added.

Alcaren raised his eyebrows, but did not speak.

"Do we know . . . who holds Dumar, or what remains of it?" asked Palian.

Secca shook her head. "The last word we had was that Lord Clehar was mustering his forces, and that was many weeks ago." She took out the grease pencil again and scrawled a few more words on the paper, then slipped it to Richina.

The younger sorceress rose and took the lutar.

*"Show us now and as you must
the one who leads and seeks Dumar's trust . . ."*

The sole image in the glass was that of a younger, dark-haired and sharp-featured man in a crimson tunic astride a dark chestnut. Secca did not recognize the man, although he appeared similar to Lord Clehar. "That's not Clehar."

"It is not surprising," Palian pointed out. "Clehar was gathering his forces when last we heard, and he planned to lead them himself. He had no sorcerers or sorceresses, and his forces were much inferior to those of the Sea-Priests."

Secca nodded to Richina to sing the release couplet.

"They still hold out against the Sturinnese," Delvor said.

"How long?" asked Wilten. "For another season?"

"Not past midsummer, I would guess," offered Alcaren. "Unless they have assistance. Perhaps not that long."

"We cannot reach them from here," Palian stated. "Not unless we cross Ranuak, and, even were we welcome, that would take almost until spring."

"We aren't deciding anything today," Secca said. "I just wanted you all to see what we could bring forth in the glasses. We also need to see what is happening in Encora and where the Sturinnese ships are. If they have left . . . then we could travel by sea."

"They will not have left," said Alcaren firmly.

"You are doubtless correct, overcaptain," Secca replied, standing and lifting the lutar once more, "but we should at least check the glass to see."

At Secca's words, a smile flitted across Richina's face.

Alcaren also smiled, almost ruefully, as Secca began to sing.

"Show us now, for all to see
where near Encora sail and found may be
the ships of Sturinn . . ."

The mirror obligingly displayed the picket lines of ships beyond the channel that Secca had come to recognize all too well. After singing the release song, she moistened her lips and turned to Alcaren. "They seem to be there, yet. Overcaptain, as you know Encora, if you would explain . . ."

"I have told Lady Secca this before," Alcaren said. "The channel from the port harbor is most narrow, and bordered by rocky shoals. Beyond the channel, the water is shallow for many deks seaward, and the Sturinnese sail the deeper waters beyond that. There are ways for coastal ships of shallow draft to avoid the war vessels, but not for the large traders of greater draft. There are large . . . there are many defenses along the channel, and all in Encora, men and women, are trained in the use of blades and bows. Encora could be taken from the sea, it is true, but the costs would be so high as not even the Sea-Priests would wish such."

"So they would prefer to take Dumar first?" asked Wilten.

Alcaren nodded.

"Ranuak can hold out for perhaps years, but it can offer little help to Dumar. Is that how you would say matters stand, overcaptain?" asked Secca.

"From what I have seen, that is so."

"Were we intent . . . *were* we intent on taking the fight to the Sturinnese in Dumar, would the Matriarch allow us passage? Would we be welcome? How would we be received?" asked Secca.

"I cannot speak for the Matriarch, Lady Secca. I am but an overcaptain, and not one of those most favored. I would think we would be well-received, but those are but my feelings."

"With all our lancers except yours men?" questioned Palian.

"There are companies of men in the Ranuan lancers, and their officers are also men," Alcaren pointed out.

"I presume our welcome would be greater the shorter our stay?" Secca studied the Ranuan.

Alcaren laughed. "Not . . ." He paused. "That is most likely so."

"I see." Secca nodded. After a moment, she stood. "There is little else we should discuss at the moment. I would ask that you all consider what we have seen and what has been said. We will meet tomorrow. I will inform you." She smiled. "Thank you all."

As the others stood, Secca nodded toward the Ranuan. "Overcaptain Alcaren . . . if I could have a few moments more of your time?"

Richina glanced at Alcaren, then at Secca.

"If you would practice those spells in your room," Secca said gently, "we'll go over them later."

"Oh, yes . . . lady." Richina bowed and turned.

Secca waited until the door closed behind Delvor, the last to leave, before gesturing for Alcaren to reseat himself. "I need to know more about Ranuak—and about you." She slipped back into her chair.

"What would you like to know?" Alcaren took the chair directly across the table from Secca.

"You have said that the Matriarch could spare but ten companies of lancers, and then two more with yours. Yet you just said that all were trained in arms, and that it would be costly for Sturinn to take Encora."

"Both are true. There are but a few more than twenty companies of lancers maintained by the Matriarch. Their pay comes from the tariffs from the Exchange and from tariffs on goods passing through the port. That is all that the tariffs will support. A good lancer is worth many men and women with blades and bows. But in the streets of a city, where a lancer cannot turn or charge easily and where there are thousands of men and women, a hundred companies of lancers might fail— unless the city were reduced to rubble by sorcery."

"And so long as the channel is defended, the thunderdrums cannot get close enough?"

"Exactly." Alcaren smiled.

Secca wanted to shake her head, even as she found herself being charmed by the Ranuan's wit and knowledge, and by the gray-blue eyes that took in everything, seemingly without judgment. "Why is it, overcaptain, that you have an answer for everything?"

"You have but asked the questions to which I have answers."

"Is your sister like you?"

Alcaren shook his head. "She is like my mother, most able, and most able to calculate sums and tariffs within her head. And she enjoys doing such."

"Do you have any other brothers or sisters?"

"No. I fear that, having raised me, and having seen my sister, my mother did not wish to dare the Harmonies again." The Ranuan gave an embarrassed laugh.

"Most families in Encora are small?"

"Two children . . . no more than three."

Secca nodded. That told her who was indeed in charge of the land. "Why is there still such fear of sorcery? The Spell-Fire Wars took place so long ago . . ."

"You have not seen Ranuak, have you?"

"No."

"There are bogs where the water yet bubbles up stinking of brimstone. There are places where nothing will grow on the land, for morgen upon morgen, save perhaps a stringvine, useful for nothing. There are the Sand Hills, and at times when the winds blow different, another town is uncovered." Alcaren shuddered slightly. "I saw one, once, as a boy. There were bodies, like mummies, clad in what we might wear, or in armor, and they had fallen where they stood, and something had sucked the very juices of life out of them—and out of the land and the soil, and the winds whipped sand over them. There are towns buried there that none have seen in thirty generations or more."

"There are no records of this," Secca said.

"There are many records, and maps, in the archives of the Matriarchs."

"Why have few others heard this?"

Alcaren laughed, without mirth. "Even now, would-be sorcerers sneak into Ranuak each time one hears of

a ruin or town being uncovered, seeking the secrets of
the old sorceries. Would you want the world to look
like the Sand Hills, shimmering grains of lifelessness?
We live in a land where, when the wind blows the
wrong way, we can smell what sorcery has done. Can
you not understand?"

Secca frowned.

"Lady Secca . . . can you not see the dilemma that
faces the Matriarch?"

"I can see that she faces a problem, but not one so
great as we face. If what you say is so, Sturinn will take
us all, save Mansuur, before the Sea-Priests turn on
Ranuak."

"You are correct in that."

Secca stopped. She looked at Alcaren, taking in the
lustrous brown hair, the broad shoulders, and the deep
gray-blue eyes that seemed to hold a veiled sympathy—
or was she seeing what she wished to see?

After a moment, Alcaren added, "If the Sea-Priests
are not stopped, Ranuak will also fall, be it a year or
two later, and all it has stood for will vanish under the
chains of Sturinn."

The red-headed sorceress took a slow and silent
breath.

Alcaren waited, his eyes completely on Secca.

"You are far more than you reveal," she finally said.

"I have told you nothing but the truth, Lady Secca."

"Truth can conceal as much as it reveals," Secca
pointed out softly. "You know geography. You know
about lands where you have not been, unless you have
been misleading me. You know about sorcery. You
know trade, and even Counselor Veria knows of you."

Alcaren grinned, an expression much like that of a
boy with his hand caught in the jar of candied nuts.

"Now why would she know of you, do you think?"
Secca could feel that her smile was somewhere between
amused and almost malicious, perhaps because she felt
as though she wrestled with the wind.

Alcaren spread his hands, helplessly. "Perhaps you should tell me, Lady Secca."

"Encora is far from a small village, yet the counselor knew you. You speak well. You know a great deal, and you have traveled. You have to be from an important family. You might even be a cousin of the Matriarch and her sister."

A quick flicker of the eyes was enough for Secca. "You are a cousin of the Matriarch."

Again, rather than denial, Alcaren offered the boyish and embarrassed smile. "I am. I admit it. I have always been an embarrassment. No matter what I tried, it was never . . . accepted. Except for my being a chief guard, and now an overcaptain." The smile turned self-deprecating. "You can see why I would rather remain as your overcaptain."

"Because you have been successful?"

"I have not been unsuccessful, and what would I do were I to return to Encora?"

"And that is why you decided to help us—or me?"

"That is one of the reasons. Another is even more simple. I fear only sorcery can save Liedwahr—and Ranuak. None in Ranuak can use it." Alcaren shrugged. "You can, and must."

"I must? You're telling me I must?" Secca could feel sudden anger building.

"You are angry. I can only tell you what I see. You will use sorcery because, if you do not, you will die or be chained by the Sturinnese, and then you will die, for you must be free."

Secca opened her mouth, then shut it. Finally, she stood. "We will talk later, overcaptain."

Alcaren rose from the chair, gracefully—and sadly, it seemed to Secca, even despite her anger and her effort not to lash out at the overcaptain.

"As you wish, Lady Secca," he said, bowing.

"When I wish."

"Yes, lady."

Secca watched him slip out the door. Once it closed, she walked slowly to the window.

Had she been angry because he had seen so much of her? Or because he'd seemed to pity her? Or showed her that she was indeed trapped? That she was pushing to get to Dumar, for exactly the same reasons he'd seen? That he *knew* what she faced, and hadn't told her? Except he had, and he had also told her the price sorcery had exacted from Ranuak.

Or because she feared any man knowing her heart and soul?

Swallowing, she looked into the distance, a distance misted by fog and weather.

Outside, the ice pellets rattled against the thick glass of the windowpanes, and the misting fog rose from the gray brick paving stones of the lane below the windows.

90

From where she sat on one side of the conference table in her guest quarters, Secca glanced out the window. Thin streams of cold water oozed down the panes. The rain that had already fallen on the lane and boulevard beyond shimmered silver in the gray midmorning light. Secca had the feeling that rain fell all the time in Elahwa in the winter, and that she would be most tired of the chill, dampness, and gray skies by the time she could depart, if she could determine how best to get her forces safely to Dumar.

Richina followed Secca's glance. "It rains much here. Do you think it does also in Encora?"

"It is on the Southern Ocean, and I would guess so." Secca looked back down at the scrying glass set in the middle of the table. "Were we to go to Ranuak first, what could we do against the Sturinnese?" she asked, musingly. She had some ideas, more than a few, but was interested in what Richina thought.

"Did Overcaptain Alcaren suggest . . . ?"

"He had many suggestions."

Richina flushed and looked down.

"Not those kinds of suggestions." Secca laughed. "Is that all that is on your mind?"

"He watches you, more than he would need, even were he a spy, and he is handsome."

"Striking, rather than handsome. And no, he was most reserved, and anything but forward."

Richina did not look at Secca.

"He is a very private man, Richina. It is most difficult to draw him out, and even more difficult when others are around. I was trying to find out more about Encora and about what the Matriarch is like."

"He speaks well," replied the younger sorceress.

"But seldom about himself or about Ranuak, and Ranuak is the key to what we may be able to do and how we could get to Dumar. The counselor has no ships that will carry us so far as Dumar—only the fleets of Nordwei or the traders' ships of Ranuak could, and we cannot contact or use those of Wei, and those of the Matriarch are bottled inside the harbor of Encora or warded off by the Sturinnese blockade." Secca offered a polite smile. "The Sturinnese ships yet remain off Encora, and from where they patrol, they could intercept any ship that left from here and attempted to land on the coast of Dumar."

"Cannot you discover some sorcery to allow us to travel? You have studied much."

"Those ships are too far from the shore for song-sorcery to carry to them," Secca said. "Yet, unless we can get past those ships, Dumar will fall. Even if we do reach Dumar, until we destroy the ships, they will be back . . . and back."

"The Sea-Priests raised waves through song. Could we not do the same?" asked Richina.

"They had the drums." Secca tilted her head. "Perhaps . . ." She shook her head. "I do not think that waves raised from the shore have the same effect upon the deeper waters. Otherwise, why would sailors head to sea when storms threaten?"

"Storms . . . ? Is there a kind of storm that would threaten a ship? More than any other kind?"

"I would have to ask," mused Secca.

"The overcaptain would know." Richina grinned.

"I am most certain he would."

"He must have made you most angry, lady."

"Angry?" Secca shook her head, all too conscious of her attempted deception—and self-deception. "I think not."

"You act . . ."

Secca smiled. "As you felt with Haddev?" She raised her eyebrows, wishing not to dwell too much on Alcaren. "He was handsome as well."

"He did not care enough."

"He may have cared more than you think," Secca said. "He saw you, and he did not hurt you, and he did not lead you on. He was bright enough to realize that, beautiful as you are, you would be unhappy in Synek, and, in time, so would he. He will make a better lord than his sire, I think."

"I would suppose so."

"Richina . . . would you have been happy in that shabby hold? In a land where a woman must still request all through her consort?"

"I . . ." The sandy-haired sorceress shook her head. "Why does it have to be so?"

Secca did not have an answer, either for herself or for Richina. Did Alcaren watch her merely for his own ends? Or for the Matriarch? Did he seek to understand her better to manipulate her for some unknown end? Yet . . . so far . . . he had refrained almost scrupulously from suggesting anything. Was that because her actions accorded with what he wanted? Or because he did care for her? Or because he actually did not wish to push her? Or some of both? Or neither?

Finally, Secca stood and walked to the window. She

would not speak of Alcaren, not to Richina, not after his declaration of what she must do.

And yet . . . did she have any choice?

She took a deep breath. Perhaps tomorrow she would talk to Alcaren again. Perhaps tomorrow.

91

The sky to the south was clear for the first time in weeks, but displayed the cold blue of a winter day. From the center window of the main chamber of the guest quarters, Secca could see the topmost branches of the trees across the boulevard bending in the wind.

Her eyes went to the mirror on the table, the mirror that had shown skirmishes continuing in Dumar and snow piled even deeper across the Sand Pass, and that Sturinnese ships yet patrolled the coast of Liedwahr south of the Shoals of Discord. Lord Robero sat in his gilt chair and frowned, and the sorcerer Belmar was riding somewhere with his players and lancers, a force that had grown in size to resemble the armsmen of Sturinn. And Secca was sitting in Elahwa, doing nothing and going nowhere—and she had done nothing in three weeks but sit and watch.

She had to do *something*.

With a snort, she pulled the riding jacket off the peg on the wall and stuffed herself into it, then walked out of the doors, with a brusque nod to Easlon and Gorkon as she passed. One of them followed, but she didn't look back to see which as she marched down the wide stairs and then back along the corridor to the doors opening out onto the rear courtyard.

Once at the entrance, Secca fastened the riding jacket more tightly before she stepped out into a cold and stiff breeze that swept across the rear courtyard behind the guest quarters. She glanced across the expanse of gray brick paving toward the barracks, then began to walk swiftly toward the red-painted door that was supposedly an armory of sorts.

Each step clicked on the brick paving, reminding her again that she needed new heels on her boots. She probably should have considered that before she left Loiseau, but she had to admit to herself, if not to anyone else, that she'd had no idea what she had been riding into or how long everything would take.

A group of lancers from Loiseau stood a good fifty yards beyond the armory door. All of the lancer rankers straightened as they saw her, but Secca merely smiled. She turned and opened the red-painted door, trimmed in black, and stepped inside.

A broad-shouldered woman with short-cut white hair and muscular forearms looked up from a pedal-driven grindstone as Secca closed the door behind her. "Yes, lady?" The gray eyes twinkled.

"You are the armorer?" Secca ventured.

"Such as there is," admitted the older woman.

"I was hoping," Secca continued, "that you might have some blunt practice blades."

"For your lancers?" The armorer shook her head. "All I'd be having are rattan ones, and most lancers be not happy with such. Rather they would break bones and claim pride than learn."

"You have a pair?" asked Secca.

"More than that." The armorer slipped toward a rack in the left rear corner of the room. "Let me see . . . Four pair and one."

Secca smiled. "Might I see them?"

"Of course, lady." The armorer brought forward a pair and set them on the smooth and clean, but battered, bench to the left of the door through which Secca had entered.

As Secca began to try each of the practice weapons, the armorer brought the others to the bench as well. Secca hefted each. The smallest was still longer than the saber at her belt, but about the same weight, if of different balance.

"Could I borrow this pair?" asked the sorceress.

"You may have them so long as you like for all that you have done." The armorer smiled. "You may also change either for another set, if they be not to the liking of your lancers."

"One is for me." Secca picked up the pair, then turned toward the door. "The other may be exchanged." She smiled. "Thank you very much."

"I hope they will suffice."

"I'm sure they will." *One way or another.* Secca opened the door and stepped back out into the chill winter day.

Before taking three steps along the barracks row, Secca caught sight of a captain in the green of Loiseau. "Captain Drysel!"

Drysel—an angular young man a good head and a half taller than Secca—turned quickly, then inclined his head. "Yes, Lady Secca?"

"I have found some practice weapons—they're not blunted iron, but rattan. I would appreciate it if you would spar with me."

Drysel bowed his head more deeply and nodded, looking down at Secca. "As you wish, lady."

"Captain . . . I am in a foul temper. Please do not humor me more."

"Ah . . . yes, Lady Secca."

Drysel was one of the newer captains, a younger son of a cousin of Lord Robero's consort Alyssa, and the last officer to come to Loiseau. He'd been picked by Anna, but Secca hadn't seen him or sparred with him before, nor had he seen her work with a blade. She wondered if she were making a mistake, but decided that if she were, she would pay for it, and if she weren't and Drysel were as arrogant as his attitude indicated, he would. "These are not iron, and I would prefer we avoid head cuts. Other than that, if you can strike, do your best." Secca extended the longer weapon. "You may exchange this for another from the armorer if you wish." She inclined her head toward the black-trimmed red door.

Drysel took the rattan weapon, hefted it, then nodded. "This will be fine." His smile as he looked down at Secca was almost patronizing.

Secca set the rattan weapon down, then slipped out of the riding jacket. While it wasn't too restrictive, and she'd certainly worn it in battle, she didn't want to be hampered at all. Then she unfastened her own real sabre and scabbard. She didn't want that banging her legs and getting in the way. Across from her, the young captain also took off his jacket, folding it carefully, almost as if it were a gesture to her. He left his sabre and scabbard on his belt.

The group of lancers who had been standing farther away began to edge toward Secca and Drysel, and Secca could hear a few of the words they exchanged.

"Captain . . . never crossed blades with her . . ."

". . . only those wooden things . . ."

"He's good . . . she'll be lucky that way."

Secca could feel anger rising in her, and she wondered why she was so touchy. Wrong time of her season? Or something akin to what Anna had felt—where people condescended to her because she was small, but simultaneously deferred to her because she was a sorceress? Secca pushed the thought away, taking a deep breath and positioning her feet on the smooth bricks. The snow and rain had washed away any grit, so that she wasn't likely to slip.

Across from her, Drysel squared his shoulders, then tested his footing by scuffing his boots on the bricks.

The two moved forward, Drysel watching Secca's rattan blade far more than her eyes, Secca aware of all of the younger man's movements.

Almost casually, Secca feinted toward Drysel's left shoulder, then pulled back. Drysel's weapon did not move. She tried another feint, this time toward his left thigh.

He eased to his left, blade still in guard position.

Secca feinted left, then ducked and swept under and

inside his weapon and tapped Drysel on the right shoulder, almost before the taller captain blinked.

"Quick . . . she was . . ."

"No force in it . . ."

Secca pushed that back. It wouldn't have been right to use full force on a captain who was just trying to avoid either being struck or striking his commander. She wanted to shake her head. She wouldn't have had the problem if she had been a man. She'd seen enough lancers try to strike Jecks, Rickel, Himar, and others.

Drysel feinted, and Secca offered a half-parry, as if she didn't know his move were a feint, then came over the top of his weapon and forced it down into the bricks before dancing back.

Still, the young captain avoided striking directly at Secca. If she struck him, under those conditions, she would be unfair, and she might even hurt him.

So she concentrated on his weapon, deciding to see what she could do to make him look silly, since he was clearly wrapped in his own superiority.

With his next half-thrust, she ducked and came up under his weapon, putting her full weight, if momentarily, behind her weapon, and taking her hilt against the rattan with enough force to drive the weapon out of his fingers. With a smile she stepped back and beckoned for him to retrieve it.

Drysel frowned momentarily, flexing his fingers as he retrieved the practice weapon.

Secca could sense his grip on the rattan blade was firmer, but he was obviously determined merely to defend.

After another series of engagements, blade against blade, Secca hammered his weapon into the bricks with enough force that, in order to hold the weapon, Drysel went almost to his knees.

As the captain straightened and stepped back, Secca caught some of the murmurs from the onlooking lancers.

". . . he won't strike . . . see . . . she knows it . . ."

". . . she won't either . . . won't take advantage . . ."

". . . trying to disarm him . . . done it once already . . ."

In the next set of exchanges, Secca managed to force Drysel's blade higher and more to the side, then slammed her blade into the side of his weapon just above the hilt. As Drysel's practice weapon seemed to bend in his hand and then drop to the bricks, Secca tried to break the momentum of her follow-through, but even so, her rattan slammed into his upper arm.

She stepped back. "I'm sorry, captain. I was only trying for your weapon, not for you." As she watched, she could see blood oozing through the fabric of Drysel's sleeve.

Drysel concealed a wince. "I know, lady. That was obvious."

"I am most sorry," Secca apologized again.

"That is all right." Drysel started to bend to retrieve the rattan weapon, then paused, with a less-well-concealed wince.

"I didn't . . ." Secca stood back, taking a deep breath, wondering what she could say. She shouldn't have let her temper, even focused into the weapon, get the better of her. Just because she wasn't big . . . everyone seemed to think she was fragile.

"So . . . you are beating up on your officers, lady?"

Secca turned to see Alcaren standing there. "I was trying to get some exercise. I'm not used to the rattan, and I didn't realize . . ." She broke off as she saw the amused expression in his gray-blue eyes. "Perhaps you would like to take Captain Drysel's place, overcaptain?"

"And if I injured our sorceress, then where would I be?" Alcaren shrugged.

"The same place you are now—waiting in Elahwa." Secca's words were as chill as the wind she scarcely felt.

"I can see you will not accept my deferral."

"Not at the moment," Secca replied.

"Then, if you will allow me, captain . . ." Alcaren stepped toward Drysel and scooped up the blade off the gray bricks.

"Captain Drysel?" Secca said.

"Yes, lady?"

"I am most sorry for being overzealous. I would appreciate it if you would have Chief Player Palian look at your shoulder. She is a fair healer."

"If you would allow me to watch for a moment before I do?"

"Of course . . . but not too long." Secca turned toward Alcaren, who had not bothered to remove his riding jacket.

"Limitations, lady?" asked Alcaren.

"No head thrusts. I might still have to sing, and you might need to give orders."

"Most fair."

Alcaren was even more cautious than Drysel, parrying Secca's exploratory cuts, but not attempting to slip by her weapon or begin an attack.

The Ranuan followed the same pattern as Drysel had, except Alcaren was willing to attack Secca's weapon, and she was the one who almost lost her rattan blade. After the first set of exchanges, her fingers tingled, and she circled, flexing them as she did, trying to get more feeling back into them.

Abruptly, Alcaren stepped back. "A moment, Lady Secca, while I remove the riding jacket."

Secca nodded, stepping back and taking a deep breath. She noticed that there were more onlookers, mostly SouthWomen, easing forward from the northern wing of the barracks.

Alcaren finished folding the jacket and stepped forward with a nod, then began a tightly focused series of attacks, always at Secca's weapon.

She slipped aside, then managed to strike his weapon with fair force before falling back.

They circled again.

Secca could feel the dampness all over her body, despite the chill wind, and she could see the sweat beading on Alcaren's forehead.

She feinted, then struck upward under his weapon, but he recovered and came slashing down. She pulled his rattan blade to the side, and almost drove it into the bricks, but, again, he recovered, and was on the attack again, and Secca had to circle back.

For a moment, they were almost hilt to hilt, but Secca managed to disengage before his superior strength literally lifted her off her feet.

Even so, he pressed the attack so fiercely that Secca had no choice but to slide his blade. The rattan did not slide as smoothly as did steel, and the effort sent a jolt down her arm. She danced back, barely avoiding a slashing thrust that, while possibly not intended, swept toward her right thigh, then stepped inside and used the comparative roughness of the rattan to help his weapon along.

While Alcaren staggered for an instant, he was back on balance almost before Secca was.

They circled again, and Secca began the attack, but had to back off.

Alcaren returned the favor.

How many times this continued Secca did not know, only that she wondered how long she could continue. Yet she'd started it, in a way, and she hated to be the one who called the match—if that was what it was.

Abruptly, Alcaren eased back. "You . . . are more . . . dangerous than you look . . ." he said between gasps.

"So . . . are . . . you." Secca wished she weren't breathing so hard, but keeping up with the bigger and stronger over-captain had taken everything she had.

"I . . . am sorry," Alcaren continued quietly. "I did . . . not . . . understand." He grinned. "I will be . . . very sore in many places . . . because . . . I did not." He paused. "You have made . . . your point, lady—pardon . . . my pun, and I . . . would humbly . . . suggest . . . that . . . we cease before . . . you render . . . me . . . unfit for . . . duty." The grin was strained.

Secca straightened, still breathing heavily. "I accept . . . gratefully . . . your advice . . ."

After a moment, she slowly bent to recover the riding jacket, although she was sweating all over, and dared not don it until she cooled off. Then she refastened the sabre and scabbard to her belt.

Alcaren slowly followed her in reclaiming his own jacket. Then he bowed.

Secca bowed in return.

"Like cats ... they were ..."

"So alike ... because ..."

Secca couldn't hear the last words, because Wilten moved in front of the SouthWoman who was talking and stepped toward Secca.

"Lady Secca?"

"Yes, Wilten?" Secca smiled politely.

"It has been some time since I have seen you work with a blade. You use it like the best of lancers now. Even the men saw it."

"Yes ... the overcaptain and I did put on quite an exhibition. I trust our form was good enough to inspire the lancers?"

"It was most inspiring." Wilten's smile was warm. "It was also most impressive to the SouthWomen and their captains." The Defalkan overcaptain laughed. "It matters not to them how impressive we men are, but how impressive you are."

Secca nodded. "I do hope they were impressed." She paused. "If you will excuse me ... ?"

Wilten bowed.

The redheaded sorceress turned and walked across the courtyard toward the main guest quarters building, still carrying the rattan exercise weapon. She was going to be sore in more places than she wanted to count, but no one was going to see that, especially not Alcaren.

92

Secca eased into the chair at the conference table that would let her look out the windows to the southwest. She had too many stiff muscles, more than she would have thought after the weeks of riding, but riding and sorcery were not bladework against bigger and stronger men. Her left shoulder hurt especially. At times, she detested being small.

She glanced toward the window, not that there was much to see, since the clear skies of the previous day had been replaced with gray clouds and a drizzling rain.

"I wish I could have seen you sparring with Captain Drysel and Overcaptain Alcaren," Richina said. "Drysel's whole arm is black, and there's a slash that will take weeks to heal."

Secca winced. "That was an accident, and bad blade work. I never meant to strike him. He was being kind and refusing to engage anything but my blade. So I was trying to disarm him."

"He said that."

"How do you know? You said you weren't watching."

"I was working with Palian and the players when he came in to have her look at his arm. He was most uneasy. Palian told him not to worry, that you were far better with a blade than most lancers, and that your size meant nothing."

"It does, though. I have to work harder with a blade, and I can't do as much sorcery as Anna could before I get tired." Secca shook her head. "Size has its advantages. If you learn to sing as well as I do, then you will have the strength to do more sorcery. Lady Anna thought she was small, but she was not." Anna hadn't understood what small was, Secca thought.

"How could she think that?" asked Richina. "Only a handful of women are taller than she was."

"I asked her that once. She said that in the Mist Worlds, she was a small woman, and that many women were near two yards in height, if not taller."

"They must be giants there."

"She was strong . . ." Secca mused. "Her warhorses . . . all of them raider beasts. None but her or a few favored ostlers could handle the first." As she recalled Anna, she could feel again that gaping emptiness, and she swallowed.

"Despite your size, lady, you are strong," Richina said quietly.

With her sore muscles, Secca felt anything but strong as she gazed out into what seemed endless rain.

Suddenly, there was a dull *clunk*, and the odor of hot metal filled the main chamber.

Secca glanced around. On the working desk, not two yards from the conference table, rested a bronze cylinder that had not been there moments before.

Richina was the one to use her riding gloves to lift the bronze cylinder before it scorched the table desk.

"Careful . . ." The appearance of the message cylinder had Secca even more worried.

Slowly, Richina extracted the contents of the cylinder— three parchment scrolls. Two were unsealed, the third was beribboned in blue and set inside the second.

Secca began with the first scroll, one from Jolyn, she confirmed by a quick look at the signature at the bottom.

Dear Secca—

 I have been watching your progress through the glass and relaying what I have seen to Lord Robero. He was pleased with your defeat of the Sturinnese, but concerned about the retreat of their ships to the south. I was also surprised that he was so pleased about your destruction of the keep at Dolov . . .

Secca nodded. She could see why Robero would be pleased.

Clayre is having great difficulty with Belmar. The Neserean sorcerer travels quickly, and from place to place. He knows what a glass will show, and what it will not, and often remains separated from his lancers and his players. He has a group of players, and uses four thunder-drums as well. He has taken the keep at Sperea through some kind of treachery, and most recently, just two days past, he destroyed the hold of one Jysmar, near Netzla . . . Why he did so is unclear, unless Jysmar opposed Belmar's efforts to claim the seat of the Prophet of Music. Lord Svenmar has declared his support for Lord Belmar, as have several other holders in the south of Neserea.

Lady Annayal has refused to consider a consorting until Belmar is removed as a threat, and the Liedfuhr of Mansuur has moved more than fifty companies of lancers to the western border of Neserea. He has sent a scroll, which took more than four weeks to reach Lord Robero, asserting that he had no intention of attempting to conquer Neserea, but that he would not see his sister's daughter lose her birthright for lack of armed support.

Lord Clehar was killed in the early battles in Dumar against the Sturinnese, and his brother Fehern has taken on his title and duties. He did not tell Lord Robero, and I fear that Clehar had died before I had dispatched the last scroll to you through sorcery. I discovered this only within the past week, when Lord Robero received a dispatch from the Council Leader of

Wei. Leader Ashtaar wrote that Nordwei has sent all its fleets out of the Northern Ocean for fear that they might be trapped there over the winter.

The roads to Stromwer are blocked with deep and early snow, and there is no way through the Sudbergs or even through southern Neserea and across the lower Mittfels.

Be most careful in whatever you decide.

Secca moistened her lips, then set Jolyn's scroll aside and picked up the second one, the one with the blue seal of Defalk with the scrawled signature of Robero at the bottom. Secca smoothed it out slowly, fearing the worst as she began to read the words set upon the parchment.

Sorceress-Protector of the East,

Know you that the snows have left us prisoned within walls of winter, and there is no manner in which the Assistant Sorceress of Defalk can reach Dumar. Either treachery or the Sea-Priests have killed Lord Clehar. His brother Fehern has taken over his duties, although we have received no word of such, perchance because of the weather, but, given that his death was before the worst of the storms, the failure of the one who now acts as Lord High Counselor of Dumar to inform us is more likely to reflect more than the death in battle of Lord Clehar. . . .

The Sturinnese now hold Narial and Dumaria. The sole major city holding out is Envaryl, and it is unlikely to withstand the Sea-Priests into summer unless Dumar receives aid.

While we have grave concerns about the current Lord High Counselor of Dumar, we have even greater concerns about the growing power of Sturinn in Dumar. For this reason, we would

request that you consider most carefully and seriously how you might undertake an effort to
assist Dumar. With the rebellion and destruction
in Neserea, the Lady Clayre cannot now leave
that land. Even if she desired, she would have
to gather forces and travel southward for nigh
on two weeks or more through the rebellious
south of Neserea and then through the high
snows of the southern Mittfels.

We trust in your enterprise and judgment. In
the event that you will need such, I have also
requested that Lady Jolyn enclose a scroll for
the Matriarch of Ranuak. The scroll suggests
that all Liedwahr is at risk, and requests her assistance in aiding you as she sees fit. You may
use this or not, as you see fit.

Our hopes and best wishes are with you.

Secca shook her head. That Robero would even consider a scroll to the Matriarch was the strongest sign of
all that all was less than well and getting worse.

"What is it?" asked Richina.

"Best you read them both. I would rather not repeat
their words," Secca replied. "Don't open the third one.
That's from Lord Robero to the Matriarch, should we
need such." She passed the two opened scrolls to the
younger sorceress. "I'll need to meet with the overcaptains and chief players, and then with Counselor
Veria."

"Is it bad, that bad?" asked Richina.

"It might be worse." Secca glanced out into the gray
and rainy day, considering how fate and the Harmonies—or Discord—often left one with few choices indeed.

93

Outside, the midafternoon clouds were darkening, as if the misting rain were about to turn into a colder and heavier downpour. Inside the guest quarters at Elahwa, seated at the table with her back to the windows, Secca shifted her weight in the chair, ignoring the twinge in her left shoulder, and glanced across the faces seated around the conference table—two overcaptains, two chief players, and one sorceress besides herself. The logs set in the hearth previously had died into a wall of red-banked coals that provided a gentle and welcome heat to the room.

"I called you all together because we have just received some scrolls from Defalk. By sorcery." Secca gestured toward the now-cool and empty message tube in the middle of the conference table.

"From your countenance, Lady Secca," began Palian, "it would appear that the news is not the most welcome."

"Perhaps it would be best if I passed the scrolls around, and each of you can read them," Secca suggested. "When you are done, then we will discuss what we may do." Secca handed both scrolls to Palian, who sat to Secca's left.

Secca could have read the scrolls aloud, but felt they had more impact if each person read them, and she was fortunate that Anna had insisted all chief players and officers had to be able to read. Also, Secca could watch each person as he or she read the scrolls. Palian nodded slowly several times, then passed the missives to Delvor with a faint smile. Delvor absently brushed back the lock of lank brown hair that had been falling across his forehead for as long as Secca could remember, but his face remained impassive as he in turn passed the scrolls to Wilten.

Wilten glanced to the bottom of each scroll before he began reading, as if to assure himself of who was writing each one. Unlike the two chief players, the Defalkan over-captain frowned more deeply with each line he perused. As he passed the scrolls to Alcaren, Wilten cleared his throat and, looking at Secca, shook his head.

Secca returned the headshake with a faint smile, and waited for Alcaren to finish reading.

Alcaren read through both scrolls quickly, his eyebrows lifting slightly, then passed them to Richina, seated to Secca's right. Richina looked at both briefly and then re-turned them to Secca.

Secca took another study of the faces before looking across the table directly at Wilten. "Overcaptain . . . you looked concerned. I would be most interested in your thoughts."

"I am most concerned," Wilten began, "most con-cerned." He gestured toward the grayness beyond the win-dow that he faced. "Snow has made all the mountains impassable. Here the rain has turned the ground into swamps and bogs, and two mighty fleets patrol the south-ern coast of Liedwahr. We have six companies of lancers, not even a full six companies, yet we are being asked to find our way to Dumar in some fashion, and there take on perchance fifty or more companies of Sturinnese lancers with thunder-drums to back them. For all we know, there may be even more lancers than that."

"It does appear difficult," Secca observed. "The glass shows that the Sturinnese have not yet taken Dumar. While they continue to fight and to push back the Dumarans, the Sea-Priests' efforts are costing them lancers. If we wait for the weather to allow us to travel through the mountains to Dumar, they will doubtless have taken all of Dumar, and will have forces and thunder-drums awaiting us."

"We could have more lancers and more sorceresses, could we not?" asked Wilten.

"Lord Robero can muster at most forty companies of lancers," Secca pointed out. "And he cannot call up the levies unless Defalk is invaded. He would not hazard all those lancers in Dumar. So we might gain little in additional lancers, but much in greater numbers of enemies were we to wait until late spring or early summer."

"Any number would be most helpful," Wilten offered. "Most helpful."

"That is true, but we cannot count on such."

"Against the Sturinnese?" The older overcaptain raised his eyebrows.

"Will Lord Robero send lancers southward against the Sturinnese if this Belmar becomes the Prophet of Music in Neserea and if the Liedfuhr sends fifty companies into Neserea?" asked Secca.

Wilten did not answer.

"Will Lord Robero wish to send us another sorceress if such should happen?" Secca pressed.

"These are most perilous times," murmured Wilten.

"Indeed they are," Secca agreed, as she turned her gaze on Alcaren. "What do you think, overcaptain?"

"I cannot speak fairly of what is best for Defalk. I will not try." Alcaren shrugged. "I can only say that, from what history shows, waiting has benefited none in opposing Sturinn. Your great sorceress is the sole leader in Liedwahr who did not wait to face the Sea-Priests. In fact, she is the only one in the world who did not wait, and she is the sole leader to have bested them."

Palian nodded, and Secca turned to the chief player.

"What the overcaptain says is so," began Palian. "I was there. Some told her to wait, and she did, but only briefly, until she knew what spells she would perform and how she would use them and where. She attacked the Sturinnese in the rain and storms when others would have waited, and she prevailed."

Delvor offered a brief smile.

"Chief Player Delvor?" asked Secca.

"I can add little, except that I would rather see battles waged with sorcery fought in lands other than mine."

Alcaren nodded to that comment.

· Secca glanced around the table once more. "Lord Robero would wish we find a way to Dumar, and soon. While Overcaptain Wilten is most correct in noting that having more lancers is better than having less, there is no certainty that we will have more if we wait, and great certainty that we will face more enemies. The problem is not one of will, but of manner. We need a way to travel to Dumar that will not exhaust our lancers and players and that will not take forever."

Alcaren cleared his throat.

Secca gestured for him to speak.

"We traveled here partly by riding, but part of the way on fast coastal schooners of shallow draft. It may be that the counselors know of some such. While those vessels will not suffice for travel to Dumar, they might aid in reaching Encora. They could carry us to the south of the Sand Hills. From there the riding to Encora is swift and mostly upon dry roads."

"That would not get us to Dumar," Wilten pointed out.

"No," Secca admitted, "but it would get us closer, and should the Sturinnese vessels move, or should we find a sorcerous way to·remove them, we could travel swiftly. Even if we could not, we could travel across Ranuak well before spring and take the passes through Stromwer. At the very least, we would be in better position to strike earlier, even were we required to wait for spring."

"That is true." Wilten's words were heavy, almost as if grudged.

"I will see if I can meet with Counselor Veria tomorrow. Perhaps there is some way we can get to Encora." As she stood, Secca did not mention that she had already requested a meeting with the counselor. "I would like a few moments with the chief players next . . . and you, Richina, after you take a message. We must discuss spellsongs."

As Wilten and Alcaren rose, Secca beckoned to Richina. Bending forward, she said in a low voice, "Would you ask Overcaptain Alcaren, most discreetly, if he would meet with me after the players depart?" She added quickly. "I want his opinions without Wilten around, and I don't want to announce that."

Richina smiled. "Yes, lady." She turned and followed the overcaptains out into the corridor.

Secca waited until the door closed before reseating herself. She looked at Palian. "Is there any other choice?"

"None that I can discern, lady. The Sturinnese have planned this for many years, perhaps waiting until Lady Anna passed, and they will pour more and more lancers into Dumar if once they hold the land."

Secca inclined her head to Delvor.

The brown-haired man smiled. "I am not a sorcerer, nor a lancer, but those who wait give more venues to their attackers."

All three looked up as Richina slipped back into the chamber. The younger sorceress nodded to Secca, then seated herself.

"Could all your players perform upon a vessel?" Secca looked once more to Palian.

"If it did not pitch too wildly, I would guess, lady," offered Palian. "That is but a guess, for none of us have attempted such."

"I would say it would be easier for the second players," suggested Delvor. "Strumming and fingering the strings is easier than bowing under difficult conditions."

"The falk-horn and woodwinds would not be so affected either," mused Palian. "You ask because we may need to defend ourselves at sea?"

"That is possible," replied Secca. "I did not wish to request vessels unless we have a sorcerous defense."

"We would need to play where there is no water or spray," Palian said.

"And high enough on the vessel that our tones—and yours—would carry," added Delvor.

"We would also need a vessel with enough space for all to play," Secca continued.

There was silence around the table. The red-haired sorceress looked to Richina. "Do you have any thoughts on this?"

"What about the wind? If it were behind us . . ."

"Then it would carry the spells further." Secca's lips curled as she wondered how many more things they did not know. "Is there anything else?"

Palian shook her head.

"No, lady," murmured Delvor, as did, a moment later, Richina.

"You may go, but if you do think of other considerations," Secca said, rising, "I would hear them."

Once the three had left, Secca walked to the window, where she stared into the gray and the rain that now fell in heavy leaden drops that occasionally *splatted* against the glass. The gray and the rain and the gloom weighed on her, and she realized that she missed the sunlight, the light, and the grace of Loiseau. Would she ever even see her hold again? At times, she had to wonder.

At the *thrap* on the door, she turned. "Yes?"

"Overcaptain Alcaren," announced one of the guards, Easlon, Secca thought, from his voice.

"If you would have him enter." Secca stepped toward the table and waited.

Alcaren stepped inside and bowed. "You requested my presence, lady?"

"I did. You are very perceptive, and most gallant, overcaptain," Secca said.

For the first time since she had met the Ranuan, Alcaren looked almost puzzled, as if pondering how to respond. After a moment, he offered the boyish, embarrassed grin. "I fear you have me at a loss, Lady Secca."

Secca thought for a moment, but could see no answer that would not lead to greater difficulty and misunderstanding—no answer except the truth, much as it grated on her to have to speak it. "Our blade *skills* are close, although you are somewhat better. You are far stronger than I, and larger. You allowed me to retain more respect than I deserved. I appreciate it."

Alcaren bowed again. "I learn much of you as time passes, lady, and it is a pleasure. Would that all ladies of power had your determination and grace."

Secca could hear that the words were more than formality, and carried a touch of warmth unusual for the always polite and discreet overcaptain.

"For your grace . . . and kindness, I thank you." Her words sounded too formal, but anything less formal might have been misunderstood. So she added quickly, "That was not all I had in mind, but I did want you to know that." Why she did, Secca wasn't totally sure, except that Alcaren's grace had made her feel small in spirit, and she hated feeling petty—even if she had been. "Would you sit down?"

Alcaren took the same chair he had used earlier.

Secca seated herself as he did, then spoke. "I wanted your thoughts on other matters. We have discussed storm spells, overcaptain. You have been a trader. Are there any types of storms that are more deadly to a vessel than others, or any more deadly to a warship?"

"All storms can damage a ship, but few are strong enough to sink a good vessel outright."

"A strong thunderstorm?"

"Such might rip away sails if the master were caught unaware, and break a mast, perchance, but the ship would remain sound."

"What of typhoons?"

"A strong typhoon can drive a ship upon the coast or rocks or shoals." Alcaren frowned. "A good master can keep a good ship far enough at sea to avoid such—unless the storm is most sudden and far larger than likely to be created by sorcery."

"Sometimes, in the spring, there are whirlwinds—they can tear apart a cot," Secca offered.

"Waterspouts can do such to a ship as well." Alcaren smiled. "But they are infrequent and most capricious, and they seldom last long."

"I wonder if we could create such," mused the sorceress.

"If you could, and *if* you could direct such, you might destroy many ships."

"We will have to think." Secca nodded. "For we cannot be sure to reach Dumar before late spring, except by ship."

"Spring—that will be too late."

"Not for Wilten," said Secca with a laugh.

"I do not understand why you have as overcaptain such a soul as Wilten," Alcaren said slowly. "At a time when you must act, or risk losing all, he sees not that."

"That is true," Secca replied. "And that I brought him, that also is my failing. He is the most experienced of my officers. Before you joined us, I relied more heavily on Stepan. He was the arms commander for Lord Hadrenn."

"The one whose body you sent home with an honor guard?"

"He gave good advice, and understood much. He held off the last attack of the Sturinnese before they broke, and saved the victory."

"Ah . . . that explains much." Alcaren nodded. "Still . . . you inherited Wilten as your most senior officer from the great sorceress, and she was no stranger to battle . . ." The Ranuan fingered his chin.

Secca paused to think. Why had Anna retained and promoted Wilten? Then she smiled. Of course!

"Why do you smile?"

"In her later years, Lady Anna wished to avoid pitched battles. She was able to deal with most matters with subtle sorcery. Would a senior officer who was more aggressive have been suited to such a post?"

Alcaren smiled knowingly. "And the lady died just shortly before you were required to leave on your expedition, and you trusted in her choices."

"I had not worked that closely . . ." Secca shook her head. "Before this winter, it was years since any sorceress in Defalk had been in a pitched battle."

"That is, alas, true of most of us," Alcaren pointed out. "In that, those of Sturinn have us at a great disadvantage." He smiled. "You have fought more battles than all those lancers in Encora who did not come to Elahwa."

"What of the others?" Secca asked.

"The Matriarch sent ten companies in addition to the SouthWomen. Perhaps six companies worth remained when you routed the Sea-Priests. Those who could ride began the long coastal ride back to Encora within days."

"How many companies could the Matriarch raise?"

"There are twenty. There would be twenty still, but with the strength of sixteen, or perhaps more, if new recruits have been found."

The two looked at each other, and Secca knew they understood the same truth—not enough lancers existed in all Liedwahr to stop the Sturinnese by force of arms.

Finally, she eased back the chair. "Thank you, over-captain. I will meet with the counselor in the morning, if she will see me. Then we will know what we may do." Secca stood, forcing herself to move smoothly, and not to show the stiffness she felt.

Alcaren also rose, speaking as he did. "She will see you. Elahwa will not remain the Free City unless Defalk remains strong and with power in the hands and spells of the sorceresses."

Power in the hands of the sorceresses? Secca could feel an unseen and cold mantle of . . . something . . . dropping onto her shoulders.

Alcaren smiled, half sadly, then bowed, before turning and departing.

Secca watched him go, almost with regret. What else could she have said?

Outside, the heavy rain splatted against the glass of the windowpanes, as the late afternoon darkened into a gloomier dusk.

94

Secca pulled off the dripping green felt hat after she hurried up the steps and under the outside columns of the Council building. She squeezed the water from the hat, folded it into her belt, smoothed her hair, and then stepped toward the single guard.

"Counselor Veria is expecting you, Lady Sorceress," the tall woman in the crimson guard's uniform told her.

Again, Secca felt somewhat overguarded as Dymen and Achar followed her inside and down the corridor to the counselor's chamber. Both guards remained outside when Secca entered and closed the door.

The sorceress bowed. Veria did not rise from behind the table-desk, but inclined her head to the chairs. Secca took the chair on the right side.

"You requested this meeting, Lady Sorceress," Veria said.

"I did. Yesterday afternoon, I received several scrolls from Falcor." Secca extended the two to the counselor.

"You received scrolls? In this weather?" Veria looked at the two rolled sections of parchment, but did not begin to read them.

"By sorcery," Secca explained. "Those scrolls were written yesterday. We can send scrolls in a bronze tube. It is exhausting, perhaps the only sorcery a sorceress can do for a day—or longer—and a sorceress can send less than a handful in a year. It is seldom used because there is usually so much of greater import."

"A scrying glass takes less effort?"

"Much less," Secca admitted.

"Scrolls sent hundreds of deks in moments." Veria

shook her head. "I almost understand the wailings of the Ladies of the Shadows."

Secca offered a polite smile.

After a moment, the counselor began to read the scrolls.

Secca took in the chamber. The outside wall was the same polished blue marble, while the inner walls were the golden oak—but none of the walls bore any decorations, except for the simple baseboards and crown moldings. Even the bronze brackets and wall lamps were simple and smooth metal, and the glass mantels of the lamps curved gently.

Veria set down the scrolls, then belatedly extended them to Secca, who rerolled them and slipped them inside her jacket.

"You wish our assistance in getting to Dumar, I take it?" asked the counselor.

"That might be difficult. You might help us reach Encora, I was led to believe."

"No doubt by Alcaren?"

"We did discuss it," Secca admitted.

"The Matriarch would be pleased to see you, for she—as do I—knows that without sorcery, Liedwahr cannot resist the Sturinnese." Veria paused, and her eyes met Secca's. "Not all in Encora will be pleased to see a sorceress, and even less would they be pleased were they to know the extent of the sorceries you have accomplished. I have seen you raise the wind, and dispel the fog. I have seen you call forth fire and lightning, and direct arrows through sorcery." The counselor's smile was faint and chill. "I doubt that I have seen near all that you can or may do."

"I have ideas," Secca offered, "but whether any will work . . . that remains to be seen."

She paused for but a moment. "Is Alcaren right that you might be able to assist us? You had suggested that you might when I met you first."

"Alcaren is correct, and I did suggest such. We have no means that would aid you in reaching Dumar, but it is possible that we could find enough coastal vessels to land you along the southern side of the Sand Hills or perhaps farther south. It might be dangerous. The Sturinnese do have shallow draft patrol schooners, but they have but few, for they are ill-suited to deep ocean crossings. We have not seen any in a season or more. The larger war vessels dare not venture into the shallows."

"How long?" asked Secca warily.

"A week to make ready, two or three days for the crossing. You would still face a hard ride of three or four days."

"If it can be done . . . we would be most grateful," Secca replied.

"It will not be without cost." Veria held up a hand. "Traders, even those of Elahwa, do nothing without recompense, but the Council will provide such."

"You expect something in return?"

Veria laughed mirthlessly. "We will obtain much in return. Either you will defeat the Sea-Pigs, or you will occupy them for another few seasons or years. If you defeat the Sturinnese, we obtain freedom from their domination for many years. If you occupy them, while that occurs, we can recover our strength."

"I would hope we would do more than occupy them for a time." Secca did not voice the thought that all that depended upon their reaching Encora at the very least.

"So do I, but I must be prepared to justify the golds even under the worst of happenings."

Secca nodded, even as she wondered about a system where a leader had to justify every action in terms of its costs. Could one really put a price in golds on women not wearing chains? Or being able to reject an ill-chosen consort?

"When will we know what is possible, and the timing?" asked the sorceress.

"Late tomorrow, or early the day after. As soon as I know, so will you—or almost, although we have no magical ways to send scrolls." Veria smiled and stood. "If we are to have you on your way soon, I must be finding those who can make this happen."

Secca stood and bowed. "We thank you."

"Thank me best by surviving and defeating the Sea-Pigs."

Behind the cool words, Secca sensed an old and cold anger. She recalled what Alcaren had told her. Had the counselor been tortured? Secca was not about to ask. "We will do our best."

"I am certain you will, and for that, I am most grateful." Veria offered a last smile before Secca turned and slipped back out the door.

With each echoing click of her boots on the polished blue marble floor as she walked back toward the front entrance, Secca felt more alone—even with two guards following her.

95

From the window of the guest chamber, Secca looked out into the midday drizzle. Her left shoulder still twinged, and she hadn't even realized that she had pulled the muscles there when she had been sparring with Alcaren, not until a day later. The wet weather did little to help the soreness that had come from that sparring.

It had been almost two days, and she had heard nothing from Veria. The rain of the previous days had stopped, but the clouds remained—featureless, dull gray. She shook her head. She missed the bright and clear skies of Loiseau. Finally, she turned and looked down at the table-desk, her eyes taking in the spells she had scrawled on brown paper.

She stepped back and uncased the lutar, then tuned it. As she stood over the desk, looking down at the modified flame spell, she strummed the lutar and mentally tried to match the note values against the words on the page. After running through the spell melody twice, she set the lutar aside. The last line still bothered her.

Before she could sit down with the paper and grease pencil, there was a *thrap* on the door. "Yes?"

"A messenger for you, lady," called Easlon from beyond the door. "From Counselor Veria."

"Have . . . them come in." Secca wasn't sure whether the messenger would be man or woman, not in Elahwa. She turned and waited.

The young woman who stepped through the door was a taller and more slender version of the counselor, with short-cut dark hair, wearing the crimson tunic of a lancer of Elahwa. She bowed. "Lady Sorceress."

"Welcome." Secca smiled. "Are you . . . related to Counselor Veria?"

"Her daughter." The lancer smiled. "I'm Averra."

"I'm sorry. You must be asked that often."

"Not so much any longer. She says that's because her hair is so gray." The lancer's smile was warm and open, and Secca wondered if Veria had once smiled so.

"I am sorry," Secca apologized again. "You bring a message . . . perhaps about our travel?"

"Yes, lady. She sent me to tell you that the Council has managed to arrange for enough vessels for four companies. We can attempt two trips, or we can send you and three of your companies and one of the SouthWomen . . . and then we would be pleased to escort the other two companies along the longer coastal route."

"Only four companies?" Secca frowned.

"It is not the lancers, lady," Averra said. "It is the mounts. For such a short trip we could take twice the number of lancers, but mounts are heavy and take more space. Also, we needed vessels with a crane and hoist."

Secca nodded. She just hadn't thought about the size and weight of mounts. "Do you know why three of my companies?"

"The counselor said that you would like most of your

forces with you, but, should you leave Ranuak quickly, the Matriarch will need all the forces that can be mustered."

Secca's lips quirked. She doubted that was the only reason. "When will the ships be ready?"

"You will need to start loading no later than midmorning the day after tomorrow." Averra bowed. "What shall I tell the counselor?"

"We need the ships, but I need to talk to my overcaptains and players before I can say which arrangement we prefer."

"She thought you might."

"I can send a messenger later this afternoon," Secca said. "To the Council building?"

"She will await word, lady." Averra bowed.

"Thank you, and give her our thanks for all her efforts."

"That I will, lady."

Once Averra had left, Secca sent Dymen to collect the overcaptains, the chief players, and Richina. Then she took out the scrying mirror and set it in the middle of the conference table. She glanced out the window, but nothing had changed. The sky was still gray, but no rain fell.

Secca picked up the spell she had been working on and studied the last line, but still had no better words when Palian—the first to arrive—stepped inside the chamber.

"Delvor will be here shortly. He was repairing a lutar, and was setting the joins." The gray-haired player smiled, then asked, "Have we word on ships?"

"We do, and that is what we need to talk about."

The door opened, and Wilten, Alcaren, and Richina entered. Secca gestured to the table. "Please be seated. Our other chief player may be a few moments longer." She took the chair with its back to the window. With the seemingly constant grayness of Elahwa, she didn't mind not looking out.

"How is Captain Drysel?" Secca asked Wilten.

"Much bruised, lady, but recovering. He appreciated your note."

"I was sorry. It was an accident, but I'm sure it was painful."

"It cannot hurt him to learn that size is far from everything." Wilten's voice held a dry humor that Secca had not heard before.

Alcaren kept his mouth from smiling, but not his blue-gray eyes.

The door opened a last time, and Delvor slipped in.

"I am most sorry, lady . . ."

"Palian told me," Secca said. "I would not have you hasten a repair to a lutar. We will need every lutar in the weeks and seasons ahead." She waited for him to take a seat before she continued.

"I have talked to Counselor Veria, as you know, and they have gathered enough ships to take us to a point on the south side of the Sand Hills. We can ride from there to Encora in several days. There is one problem." Secca paused. "There are not enough vessels to carry all of us and our mounts at the same time. The most they can take is the players and perhaps four companies." She paused. "The counselor also made it clear that they would prefer that one of the four companies be one of those commanded by Overcaptain Alcaren."

"Lady Secca . . ." Alcaren said, "that was not my doing."

"I was led to believe that the Matriarch wants at least one, if not both, of the companies of SouthWomen back in Ranuak to be ready in case the Sturinnese attack there."

"And we are considering going there?" asked Wilten.

"Does it matter?" riposted Secca gently. "We will have to fight them in one place or another. If we go to Ranuak, and the Sturinnese attack, we do not fight alone, and then, at the very least, that may slow the conquest of Dumar. Here, we do not even pose a threat to the Sea-Priests."

Palian nodded slowly.

Delvor brushed back a lock of his lank hair.

Alcaren shifted his weight in his chair, but did not speak.

"What if we take the three companies and one of the Southwomen first," asked Richina, "and then wait to determine if the ships can make a second trip? We can use the glass to see. If they can, we wait. If not, we start for Encora and wait there."

Secca looked at Wilten. "What do you think?"

Wilten shook his head. "Against the Sea-Priests, four companies or six . . . it makes little difference. If your sorcery does not hold, then two companies will not change matters. I would favor Lady Richina's suggestion, though, for if the ships can travel the inner gulf again, it will be far easier on the riders and mounts."

Secca hoped so, but sea travel was out of her experience.

"Do you know where the Sturinnese ships are?" asked Alcaren.

"I thought I would try to call their images in the glass, so all could see." Secca eased from her chair and reclaimed the lutar, checking the tuning before beginning the scrying spellsong.

"Show us now and upon the sea
those ships near where we may be . . ."

Even after the end of the spellsong, the mirror remained blank. Was that because the spell was faulty, or because there were no ships on the inner gulf between Elahwa and the southern end of the Sand Hills? Secca didn't know. She tried a second version.

"Show us now and in the light of day
any ships that may oppose us on our way . . ."

This time the mirror split into more than a dozen fragmentary images, each fragment showing a different ship, and all but two were white-hulled. Even before the others could really look at the images, Secca sang the release couplet.

"What—" began Alcaren.

"It showed every ship that could sail to the inner gulf," Secca said. "The spell wasn't right." She lifted the lutar and tried a variation on the spell.

"Show us now and upon the sea,
vessels in the inner gulf that be . . ."

Again the mirror came up blank.

The fourth spell—the one that asked for vessels south of the inner gulf, showed five large Sturinnese warships and three smaller vessels, rigged as schooners.

After letting everyone see the images, Secca sang the release couplet.

"There are no Sturinnese ships in the inner gulf now . . . is that what the glass shows, lady?" asked Wilten.

"It is."

Wilten turned to Alcaren. "How long will it take them to sail northward?"

"Into the inner gulf? Several days." The Ranuan paused momentarily before adding, "But the last part of the voyage will take us out of the shallows of the inner gulf."

"I would say that we take as many as we can on the first voyage, lady," Wilten suggested. "Even have they scrying glasses, they will have to see us depart in such and then find us."

There were nods around the table.

Secca was forced to agree that his suggestion made the most sense—and it agreed with the suggestion of Counselor Veria. "Then, that is what we will tell the counselor."

She still wondered about the South Women—they seemed better disciplined than most lancers, and supposedly they fought well, but no one seemed to want them around, and that bothered her.

96

Secca glanced from the piers out into the harbor, empty except for the vessels tied at the heavy wooden piers. The morning was chill, made more so by the wind blowing off the dark gray water. There were five vessels of varying lengths at the piers—but the largest was perhaps sixty yards in length, the smallest little more than thirty. A line of mounts stretched along the pier. Secca watched as one was led up a gangway and onto the deck of the *Foamsprite*, the nearest vessel.

"We'll do what we can, Lady Sorceress," offered Weyla, captain of the largest schooner, the *Alycet*. The captain was a wiry woman almost as tall as Drysel, and a good fifteen years older, but Secca would have wagered her golds on Weyla in any contest between the two. "Luck and Harmonies with us, and we'll get well south of the Sand Hills. If not . . ." She shrugged. "We land you where we can." Her eyebrows lifted. "Unless your sorcery can help."

"It's possible. I'll certainly try if we need it, but I've never tried it on a ship."

"Like you," the captain continued, "I'd be wishing we could carry all on one crossing. The problem was not the lancers, but the mounts. Easy for a company or two, but six be a problem. Safer to make one crossing with five vessels than five with one."

"That's what Counselor Veria told us," Secca replied.

"Take the morning to load, and then we'll sail. Usually get a southwesterly by afternoon. Sweeps inland to the Sand Hills, especially this time of year. Small pier at Ilygot. We can't get that far, and you'll have to swim them ashore . . . won't be bad . . . we don't draft that deep . . .

and the water here's not that cold, not like up near Os-twye."

"Why couldn't we get that far? The Sturinnese?"

The weathered captain nodded. "We can go shallow along the Sand Hills. Know the waters and the shoals. South of that, the shallows narrow, and they can get to us unless we hole up in one of the shallow bights. There we'd have to hoist the mounts clear, and you'd swim 'em in. Probably not more than a hundred yards—fifty in some places."

"Let's hope we can get to a place with a pier," Secca said. "Maybe sorcery can help."

"We'd prefer such, lady," replied the captain. "Faster for us, and it will let us make a second run without the Sea-Priests havin' time to bring in one of those patrol schooners that can go where we do. 'Course, better here than in their lands. They got slave galleys there, and with thunder-drums and oars, and shallow draft . . . best you not be anywhere close."

"They don't have anything like that here, do they?" asked the sorceress.

"Only the smaller schooners, but they take Dumar, and it won't be long before Dumuran captives'll be rowing galleys." Weyla inclined her head. "Be seeing you on board."

Secca bowed. "I'll be there shortly." She watched as the weathered captain walked down the pier toward the sea-ward end where the *Alycet* was moored.

As she watched, Alcaren and Wilten appeared from behind a group of sailors in pale blue trousers and jackets and walked up the pier from where they had been over-seeing the loading of the SouthWomen's mounts on the *Foamsprite*.

"How is everything going?"

"It's not the loading I'm worried about, lady . . ." Wilten coughed, then fingered his chin. "The captain there . . . she said . . . we might have to swim the mounts to shore."

"So did the captain of the *Alycet*," Secca replied. "I

don't know that many of our lancers can swim." Secca wasn't that sure she'd do well in the water, either.

"That be true, lady," admitted Wilten.

"All they have to do is hang on to the mounts," Alcaren offered. "The water isn't that deep except in the center channel."

That was easy enough for Alcaren to say, Secca reflected. "Can you both travel on the *Alycet* with me and the players? We need to have some time to talk over things."

"My captains would not object, I do not think," said Alcaren.

"Nor mine." Wilten shrugged. "They cannot go off somewhere on their own."

Secca nodded. "I'll tell Captain Weyla." She looked toward the *Alycet*, hoping again that she wouldn't have to swim her mount from the ship to a strange shore.

97

With the sea spray misting around her, whipped by the brisk wind, Secca walked forward, along the right side of the *Alycet*, her hand not all that far from the heavy wooden railing, trying to adjust to moving on a surface that slowly pitched with the long rolling and following swells.

To her right, to the west, she could just make out a long and low dark smudge that one of the crew had said was land—swampy wetlands that were still a part of Elahwa. South of the swamps were higher and far drier bluffs, and south of the bluffs—well out of sight—were the Sand Hills.

Stiff as the wind was, with the full late afternoon sun falling on the schooner, Secca felt warmer than she had at the piers in Elahwa that morning. She eased up to the railing where Alcaren leaned on the polished but worn wood, looking to the southwest.

The Ranuan did not turn as Secca joined him. "We might just get to see a hint of the Sand Hills before sunset."

The wood on which Alcaren's hands, overlarge for his frame, rested was battered, but buffed smooth and varnished. The Ranuan followed Secca's probing eyes. "You have to keep the wood sealed. It splinters and rots, otherwise. Doesn't matter so much on the rails here, except for you and me, but anywhere the sails could touch, you don't want splinters or sharp edges—put a rip in the canvas, and then where would you be?"

"In some sort of trouble. Why did you say the rails didn't matter except to you and me?" Secca frowned.

"Real sailors scarcely ever touch the rails."

As if to make that point, the *Alycet* pitched forward more steeply. Secca had to grab the railing. The ship then rode the following swell, still maintaining a southwest heading, or so it seemed from the position of the sun.

"Do you always stay up here on the front?" asked Secca, loosening her grip on the varnished but salt-sticky railing.

"The bow?" Alcaren grimaced. "I do indeed. Here, the air is cool and fresh."

Secca glanced southward. "This seems wide enough for a larger vessel."

"Here . . . it is, but before long, the deep part of the channel will narrow, and it would take less than a glass for the captain to have us in water where you could walk to shore. That's why we pitch so much with so little wind."

"Because the water is shallow?" asked Secca. She thought any water over her head was too deep.

Alcaren nodded. "Where you see the waves break . . ." He pointed to the west, his arm almost in front of Secca's nose. "That is where there are shallows and shoals."

Secca followed his gesture, seeing white spray less than a dek away. "It doesn't look shallow."

"One of those big Sturinnese war brigs would get hung

up there and break her back, just like that." Alcaren smiled. "But they know that. We won't see them until the channel widens."

"How long will that be?"

"Late the day after tomorrow at the earliest."

Secca glanced upward. As the mast seemed to move, she could see Clearsong, almost at its zenith. It would be high in the sky well into evening. She hoped that was a good sign.

98

A few scattered high white clouds scudded across the late morning sky, moving to the south with the wind that carried the *Alycet* southward. Somewhere to the west— just beyond the horizon, according to Alcaren—were the last traces of the Sand Hills. Secca stood on the raised rear deck of the *Alycet*, close to the railing around the wheel platform. To her left was Weyla, although the captain's eyes were never still, and never turned toward the sorceress. Alcaren stood almost at the starboard rail, facing into the wind. Richina leaned on the railing as well, less than two yards from Alcaren, but farther forward.

Perhaps a half-dek astern and to the north of the *Alycet* followed the *Foamsprite*. For a moment, Secca watched the smaller vessel, her bow cutting into the long swells, with spray and foam seemingly almost touching the base of the bowsprit. Then the sorceress looked forward again.

On the lower mid-deck, Palian was rehearsing the first players, and the sound of strings and horns drifted aft to Secca. The second players stood on the raised forward deck, as if waiting for the first players to finish rehearsing.

"A good half-day out of the channel . . . another few

glasses, and we can run for Ilygot," said the tall and wiry captain.

"How far are we from there?"

"Half a day, if the wind holds."

"Sail to the east!" came a call from the lookout above.

The captain turned away from Secca, peering to her left and back toward the east. "Can't see yet, but can't be other than the dissonant Sea-Pigs." She glanced eastward, then looked toward the helmsman. "Bring her ten starboard."

"Ten starboard, aye. Coming starboard."

As the *Alycet* swung to the west, with the wind coming into the sails more directly, Richina climbed up the ladder from the lower deck. "We're turning . . ."

Secca gestured toward the east. "There are ships there."

Behind Richina, Wilten appeared, his face slightly pale. "Sorceress?"

"The Sea-Priests may have found us."

Weyla glanced upward, toward the lookout. "How many?"

"Four, mayhap five!" came back the call.

Five vessels had to be Sturinnese, Secca reflected. She stepped forward until she looked down on the mid-deck. "Players, stand by. The lookout has sighted the Sturinnese."

"Stand by," called Palian.

"Second players to position," ordered Delvor.

The second players began to climb down the ladders to the main deck.

Secca walked back toward the captain, who pointed eastward. "Just out there."

Secca could see but specks of white above the dark blue water.

"They're running with the wind, and they carry far more sail than do we."

"Can we make it to Ilygot?" asked the sorceress.

"I'd wager against it." Weyla looked westward, then walked toward the raised platform that held the helm, where she studied the map fastened on an inclined plot.

Secca eased behind the captain, leaving Richina, Wilten, and Alcaren by the railing, all three now peering out to the east.

"We are here . . . most exposed." Weyla pointed to the map, at a series of dotted lines in the green space that seemed to represent water. "The shallows to the west of us are narrow. Don't offer much protection. Another five deks south, there is a reef, and we could almost reach Ilygot behind it."

"That's where we're headed?"

The captain nodded. "For now. Need to watch, see how fast they're closing."

Secca frowned, catching the concern in the older woman's voice. "You think they're faster than we are?"

"The wind favors them, and there was but a short time between when the lookout sighted them and when we could see sail from the deck."

For a time, all watched the dark blue waters to the east, and the specks of white on the horizon that quickly grew into sails above white hulls. Secca began a vocalise, trying to warm up slowly, sensing she would need sorcery, and wondering how singing on the sea would affect the results of the spell.

"Five vessels—two brigs and three of the shallow-draft schooners—all full-rigged," Weyla pointed out.

Secca frowned. "I thought there were only three of those schooners. That's what the glass showed."

"They had to be using their own glasses," suggested Alcaren from behind Secca. His face was pale.

"They use scrying glasses often," Secca said, "and they were following us all the time in Ebra." She paused. "I worry about the drums on the water."

"You think the thunder-drums work better at sea?" questioned Richina.

"Why else would they have developed them?"

The captain inclined her head, and Secca slipped away from the railing toward Weyla.

"Sorceress," Weyla said slowly, her voice pitched low,

"never have I seen a ship that size move with that quickness. On this course we cannot reach the reef before they reach us." She gestured again. "The three small war schooners can follow us into the shallows."

Secca glanced at the oncoming vessels, white sails billowing in the midday sun. The Sturinnese were not within normal spell range, but . . . could she speed the five Elahwan ships with a wind spell? "I will see what I can do." She stepped forward, looking down on the main deck, and called to Palian, "Players! The fourth building song!"

"Form up! The fourth building song!"

Secca's command was echoed by both Delvor and Palian, and both sets of players formed up on the mid-deck, the second players forming an arc around the first, both facing eastward. As the scrambling for position died away, and renewed tuning echoed upward, Palian glanced to Secca.

"When you're ready," called Secca.

"The fourth building song. On my mark . . . Mark!"

The gentle pitching of the deck had little effect on the players as the first bars poured forth from the strings and horns—and from the lutars of the second players. Secca faced forward and sang.

> *"Turn the wind from them to our sails,*
> *and let us fly before the gales . . ."*

The sails billowed and the *Alycet* seemed to lurch forward, spray cascading in sheets almost to the forward rails, with a salty mist drifting aft toward Secca. Several players lurched sideways with the ship's motion.

Secca took a deep breath, then looked at the wiry captain. Weyla glanced from Secca to the helmsman, and then to the pursuing Sturinnese.

The sorceress followed the captain's eyes. While the five Elahwan vessels clearly were increasing speed, the sails of the Sturinnese remained billowed and taut, and the distance between the Sturinnese and the *Alycet* continued to decrease, if more slowly.

Were the Sturinnese using wind sorcery backed by drums, as Richina had suggested and Secca feared?

Whatever the Sturinnese were using, it was allowing the pursuing vessels to close on the Elahwan ships, despite the increased speed afforded by Secca's sorcery-boosted winds.

"We need to run for shore, sorceress."

"Do what you think best, captain." Secca eased to the rail, putting a hand out to steady herself. From there, she studied the oncoming vessels, trying to think of what spell she could use, and how.

"Starboard thirty!" Weyla ordered the helm. "Bring her round easy!"

"Aye. Starboard thirty. Easy as she goes."

Richina eased up beside Secca. "They must be using sorcery, too."

"I fear so." Secca looked to the north, where the other Elahwan vessels stretched almost in a line abreast, except for the northernmost, which had begun to fall behind the four others.

The two sorceresses continued to watch as the white-hulled vessels drew nearer to the *Alycet* and the other four ships carrying Secca's force.

Secca ran through another vocalise, trying to fix the spell in her mind—a spell she wasn't sure would even work. Yet she *knew* the Sturinnese had to be closer before any spell would carry to them.

The five Sturinnese vessels were less than a dek to the east, when Weyla barked an order. "Fire parties on the deck! Fire parties on the deck!" She looked toward Alcaren, Wilten, and the two sorceresses. "Best you move forward of the helm. Put the mast 'tween you and the Sea-Pigs."

As Secca slipped to the starboard side of the *Alycet*, following the captain's directions, from somewhere below appeared nearly a half-score sailors, six men and four women, each carrying two buckets. Of each pair, one bucket held sand, the second was empty but was attached to a long coiled line.

The *Alycet* and the *Foamsprite*, and the two vessels immediately abreast of them, were pulling away from the other Elahwan vessel.

Weyla shook her head. "Told Ilspeth that rig wasn't right."

"The rig?" asked Secca.

"*Wavesinger*'s rigged for a northern run. Tighter, but you don't get as much sail in a following wind."

"So she can't use the wind as fully?"

Weyla nodded. "Afore long, they'll be using the big crossbows to send fireshafts into us. Could be before we cross the shallows."

Secca could see whitecaps ahead, but they seemed distant, more than deks away, and the land beyond was but a thick line on the horizon. Her eyes darted back to the white-hulled pursuers, the closest—one of the smaller schooners—less than five hundred yards aft.

"Can you offer another spell?" asked the captain. "The flame shafts will be striking soon."

Secca tried to gauge the distance. How would she know? Too early and the spell would be wasted. "Perhaps . . ."

Hisssssssss . . . thunk!

Secca's head jerked up at the sound, her mouth opening as a flaming shaft slammed into the deck. Before she could utter a word, one of the women sailors had stepped forward, struck the shaft with an iron hammer to knock it loose and flat on the wooden deck, then covered the flames with damp sand from the bucket she carried.

Hissss. . . .

Secca ducked, but the second flaming shaft had already passed a good yard over her head at an angle and plunged into the dark blue waters of the Southern Ocean. A flicker of orange caught her eye. She swallowed as she saw flames begin to climb up the canvas of the aft mast of the trailing *Wavesinger*. She looked at her companions. Alcaren and Richina looked greenish. Wilten's countenance was drawn. Even Weyla looked worried.

Secca stepped forward and looked down at the players. On the deck below, Palian's face bore a greenish cast, as did Rowal's. "The third building song!"

Secca's command was echoed by both Delvor and Palian, and both sets of players began to re-form, now facing southeast, not quite toward the pursuing Sturinnese.

"The third building song . . . on my mark!" Palian's words were forced.

"Now!" ordered Secca. On the third bar, the one that began the spell proper, she launched into the words.

> *"Come wind and rain, too fierce to fight,*
> *strike with power, and all storm's might,*
> *lightning bolts to cleave day into night . . ."*

As she finished the spell, Secca could only hope her visualizations of the stormwinds were accurate enough, and that her voice and the tones of the players were strong enough. Yet, even before the echoes of the spellsong died away, the once-clear sky began to darken, and a lightning bolt flashed from above, striking the second Sturinnese vessel.

Winds whipped through the canvas above her, cracking the sails like the whip of a teamster. The *Alycet* pitched forward in swells that had become waves five yards or more from crest to trough.

A line of dark rain—almost like a black curtain—formed to the south of the ten ships, and began to move northward . . . but too slowly. The leading Sturinnese brig surged before the storm, less than a hundred yards from the *Alycet*, plunging directly toward the *Alycet*'s stern quarter.

"Richina—get me a lutar! Any lutar!" Secca yelled.

"A lutar! A lutar!" Richina's voice rose over the storm, penetrating the whistle of the wind, and the crashing of the bow into heavier and heavier swells. "A lutar for Lady Secca!" The younger sorceress was half-way down the ladder to the mid-deck, swinging one-armed.

A player staggered and slid toward the blonde sorceress, thrusting a lutar at her. Richina grasped it, and then struggled up the ladder one-handed.

Secca tried to move forward to meet Richina, but found her feet sliding, carrying her aft. An arm—Alcaren's arm—reached out and lifted her toward the railing, which she grasped with both hands to steady herself. Then she made her way forward, hand over hand.

Richina thrust the dark-bodied instrument at Secca.

Taking the heavy lutar in her left hand, Secca half-walked, half-lurched along the side of the taffrail until she stood just to the starboard of the back of the helm platform. The Sturinnese ship was so close that she could see the letters of the name stenciled beneath the bowsprit. She braced herself with one leg against the taffrail, ran her fingers over the strings quickly, hoping the instrument was close to being in tune, cleared her throat, and began the spell.

"Turn to fire, turn to flame,
all those who stand against our name.
Turn to ashes, turn to dust . . ."

More lightnings flared out of the blackened sky, some so close to Secca that she felt the heat across her face. Screams echoed from the doomed Sturinnese vessel. The smell of charred flesh swept across the *Alycet* in waves . . . between spray and wind.

Secca clasped the borrowed lutar with one hand, the railing with the other as the *Alycet* pitched away from the burning mass that had been, moments before, a proud and dangerous white-hulled warship.

The black storm curtain swept over the three trailing Sturinnese vessels, and they vanished from Secca's vision.

Despite the torrents of rain and wind, the sole remaining white-hulled ship—one of the smaller war schooners—plowed toward the *Wavesinger*, striking the Elahwan vessel midships, even as the storm curtain swept over both ships.

Secca watched, trying to breathe as the wind sucked air from her very lungs, but she could not make out either vessel.

Then . . . suddenly, the air began to clear, the swells to diminish.

Still hanging on to the railing, Secca glanced out at the circles of debris that appeared and disappeared in the swells. Not a single white-hulled vessel remained.

"Hard port!" snapped Weyla. "Make for the *Wavesinger!*"

The *Alycet*'s bow swung to port, seemingly away from the other Elahwan vessels, before settling on a heading almost due north. The ship seemed more sluggish, and a crackling and cracking overhead drew Secca's eyes. The mainsail was almost in two pieces, and four sailors aloft struggled to furl the whipping canvas.

As the *Alycet* neared the wreckage that had been the *Wavesinger*—and the Sturinnese schooner—Secca could see shattered timbers, shredded canvas, several barrels . . . and more than a few heads bobbing in the water, some attached to immobile bodies. Most of those in the water waved as the Elahwan vessel neared, but there were far fewer heads than had been lancers and crew upon the *Wavesinger*.

At the sound of a particularly loud *crack*, Secca glanced up at the tattered mainsail, and the sailors struggling to finish furling it, and then back at the wreckage of the *Wavesinger*.

Weyla issued another set of commands, and the *Alycet* slowed, turning somehow into the wind so that the sails went limp. "Get that mainsail furled!"

As Secca watched, Alcaren wrapped a line over his shoulders, then tied the bitter end to the railing. After making sure there was loose line hanging, he dived into the water. He surfaced and swam strongly toward a limp figure, then swam back toward the *Alycet*, towing the lancer. One of the sailors lowered a line with a loop in it, and Alcaren slipped the figure into it before swimming after yet another struggling lancer.

One figure dropped below the water as Secca watched, as if dragged down, and did not reappear.

A smallboat appeared in the water, lowered from the davits on the port side of the *Alycet*, and the crew rowed toward a group of figures clinging to a wooden hatch cover.

Richina slipped up beside Secca. "It happened so fast. One moment, they seemed deks away, and then . . . suddenly, they were just . . . right there."

"All battles are like that, I fear," offered Wilten. The overcaptain's eyes remained on the figures in the water. "Some of those are lancers. I think the one swimming there is Drysel."

Secca tightened her lips. Drysel . . . her lancers . . . those who drowned had died because she had wanted to get to Ranuak, and because she had not really been prepared to handle sorcery upon the sea. Why did she have to learn so many things the hard way—and so late?

She wished she could swim like Alcaren—or do something—but the dayflashes before her eyes told her she could do no more sorcery, even had she known any sorcery that would suffice. So she watched in silence as the other Elahwan ships and their smallboats joined the search.

The sun hung low above the western horizon before the smallboat returned to the *Alycet* for the last time, the third officer shaking her head when she positioned the craft under the davits. "None left, captain."

As the crew turned the winches that lifted the boat, Weyla walked toward Secca.

The sorceress turned. "I'm sorry, captain."

The older woman gave a slight, but firm headshake. "Risk we all understood, sorceress. Wasn't all your doing. I told Ilspeth she needed to re-rig for the Gulf and southern waters. Didn't believe me."

"Is she . . . ?"

Weyla shook her head. "Second said she was dragging lancers topside, then got caught in something. Went down with the *Wavesinger*."

"I'm sorry."

"No one made us take you, sorceress. We all wanted the risk golds. Besides, first time in a year that any caught by the Sea-Pigs have come clear."

"I cost you a ship." Secca glanced up at the main mast, where the tattered mainsail had been furled. "And more."

"This is war, Lady Secca. You lost half a company, and all their mounts." Weyla smiled grimly. "I would trade a sail for my life and my ship any day, and one ship for five Sturinnese." Weyla smiled grimly. "None will reach us afore we make port at Ilygot. Maybe not even for weeks."

Secca hoped not. She wondered if trading one ship for five would be enough, given the vast Sturinnese fleets she had seen in her glass. Again . . . her lack of experience had cost everyone dearly, no matter what the Elahwan captain said.

" 'Sides, this way, with those Sea-Pigs gone, and them having no other shallow water vessels, we can slip back along the coast and pick up your other lancers, neat as you please. Also be a while afore they try the Gulf." The captain gestured toward the helm. "Best we

get on with it. Be a bit tricky coming in after dark."
With a brisk nod, Weyla turned and moved toward the
helmsman.

Secca returned the nod. She felt numb, far number
even than after the land battles that had killed many
more lancers on both sides.

Alcaren reappeared, wearing a dry set of blues,
doubtless his only other uniform. His face was almost
as pale as Secca felt hers was. He looked at her with
eyes that seemed to look within her. "Few could do
what you did."

"I did not know." She shook her head. "I acted too
late."

"It is difficult to cast spells on a moving deck, and
more so to do it in a storm, as you did with the last
spell."

"You're kind," she replied, "but I almost failed, and
many died because I was slow and did not understand."

"Most of us live because of you." His voice was firm.

She shook her head a second time, turning away from
him and looking aft, back toward the wreckage that still
marked her failure, and the watery grave of half a company of lancers, good mounts, and too many sailors.

Alcaren stepped to the taffrail, standing beside her,
not speaking.

Secca was grateful for his presence, and for his acceptance of her need for silence.

They stood there, without speaking, as the *Alycet*
swung southwest once more, leading the way toward
Ilygot . . . and Ranuak.

99

A s dawn seeped past the closed shutters into the small
inn room, Secca turned over, to avoid facing the light.
Even with her eyes closed, her head ached, and dayflashes
seared through her skull. The light strengthened.

Finally, the sorceress sat up and swung her feet over the
side of the bed. The floorboards were cold . . . and gritty.
Sitting in the gray light that seemed far brighter than she
knew it was, she used her left hand to massage her forehead and then her neck. Her head still ached, and her eyes
burned, whether she opened them or closed them. But
headache or not, Secca was a person who woke early, and
once awake, seldom if ever could return to slumber.

She could smell the harbor of Ilygot, the dampness of
a winter mist, the odor of fish decaying somewhere.
Slowly, she stood and tottered toward the basin and pitcher
on the side table. She began to wash, reflecting on the day
before, and upon her slowness in reacting to the Sturinnese. Had it been thunder-drums upon the other vessels,
drums she had not heard, or had it simply been because
she had been attempting sorcery under most unfamiliar
conditions?

Weyla and the three other Elahwan captains had managed to rescue slightly more than half the lancers aboard
the *Wavesinger*, and most of the crew, simply because they
had been topside. The losses had not been nearly so great
as in some battles, but they still bothered her because she
knew they could have been avoided by a more experienced
sorceress.

She snorted quietly to herself. The only problem was
that there weren't any sorceresses or sorcerers who were
more experienced in warfare—except among the Sturin-

nese, who never seemed to stop fighting somewhere.

After she pulled on her riding clothes, Secca pulled back one shutter and looked downhill at the empty piers. The *Alycet* and the other Elahwan ships were gone. Although Weyla had told Secca that she would sail before dawn, to catch the land breezes, Secca somehow felt regretful and alone.

From the adjoining narrow bed came a groan as Richina turned over. "How . . . lady . . . it is most early . . ."

Secca did not reply for a moment, finally closing the shutter and turning. "I was too uncomfortable to sleep longer. You can sleep for a bit. I'm going down to get something to eat."

She sat on the edge of the narrow bed and pulled on her boots, then stood and reclaimed her riding jacket. All her clothes felt clammy and chill, and her head still throbbed.

After opening the door, she stepped into the narrow hall where Rukor and Dymen stood. "Lady Richina may be a while yet."

Rukor smiled. "I will accompany you, lady."

Secca descended the staircase, a passage so small that her shoulders almost brushed both walls, and stepped out into the foyer off the public room. The odor of bread and grease wafted toward her, and she swallowed.

With Rukor standing guard behind her, Secca debated entering the small public room, empty as it was save for Wilten, her own officers, and Alcaren. The two over-captains had been sitting at a corner table, and, upon seeing Secca, Alcaren rose and bowed in her direction.

Secca stepped forward.

"Good morning, lady." Alcaren's voice was cheerful.

Secca nodded, but did not speak immediately as she seated herself.

Wilten gestured toward the single serving woman. "Something hot for the lady."

"Cider be all we got."

"Fine." Secca's voice cracked on the single word. "And some bread and cheese, please."

"You be wanting any mutton, lady?"

"No . . . I think not. Thank you." Even the thought of mutton sent cramps through her stomach. She waited until the serving woman turned. "How is everyone this morning?"

"All the lancers that got saved are fine, lady," Wilten replied. "Good thing as the ocean is warmer here, though. Some were pretty chill, and a lot of bruises, but only two were hurt beyond that—one got a broken arm and another a slash across the shoulder. We used the elixir on both and set the arm."

With a *thunk*, the serving woman set a tall mug of steaming cider on the plank table. "Here ye be. Two coppers."

Secca fumbled for her wallet, and Alcaren slipped a pair of coppers onto the table, coppers that vanished into the large hand of the woman.

"Thank you," Secca said.

"Best you not be opening that wallet here," murmured the Ranuan.

The Sorceress nodded and then sipped the hot cider slowly. After several small swallows, she broke off a chunk of the warm and moist dark bread. As she ate, she could feel some of her headache recede. She still was seeing occasional dayflashes.

"Captain Weyla said it could be six to eight days before she'd be able to return with the last two companies," Alcaren volunteered after a time of silence. "Especially to bring more mounts."

Secca ignored the fact that Weyla had told her the same thing the night before, and looked at Wilten.

"I can wait here for the other two companies, Lady Secca," offered the older overcaptain.

"You wouldn't mind that?"

"Lady Secca, I'd just as soon be here as in Encora. I'm not a town lancer, not in a large town, anyway."

And not in a city run by women, either, Secca suspected. "You'll need to keep one company."

"The one without mounts is fine. Won't have to worry much about feed," he replied. "You should leave as soon as you can."

"Why do you think so?" Secca repressed a frown. Wilten had been the one who had been most opposed to traveling to Ranuak. "It's likely to take several glasses to straighten matters out."

"The Sturinnese are after you, Lady Secca. They might well send vessels here if you linger. If they believe you to be heading to Encora, then the last two companies will find sailing less . . . disputed . . . and we will have more lancers when we need them, whether that be in returning to Defalk or in going on to Dumar."

Secca took another swallow of the cider. While it had a deeper clove taste than she would have preferred, the hot liquid was definitely easing the tightness in her throat.

"And, begging your pardon, lady, you are not looking up to great sorceries in the next days," Wilten added.

Her overcaptain was definitely right about that. She turned to Alcaren. "Should we not send messengers ahead to request the Matriarch's permission to come to call upon her?"

He nodded. "Only four initially, I would suggest."

"Two SouthWomen, and two lancers?"

"That would be best."

"They can depart when we do." Secca frowned. She'd have to give them golds for lodging, and she was beginning to doubt that the hoard of coins she had brought, extravagant as the amount had seemed when she had left Loiseau, would see her through the coming weeks, let alone an expedition into Dumar.

She took another mouthful of bread and cheese, wondering what she could really do in Encora. Would she just have to wait until spring to travel overland to Dumar? Or would Dumar be completely in the hands of the Sturinnese by then?

She lifted the mug.

100

The winter mist collects on the window beyond the Matriarch's study, gathering, and then oozing down the ancient glass in slow rivulets. Inside, in the glow of the oil lamps set in white bronze sconces on the white walls, Aetlen sets down the mandolin and looks to the woman who sits behind the flat table desk. "You look like you are listening, but your mind is elsewhere."

Alya says slowly, "The glass tells me that the shadow sorceress fought a sea battle with the Sturinnese south of the Gulf. She destroyed four ships with storms and the fifth with fire."

"Upon the open ocean?" asks Aetlen.

"Upon the open ocean. She is riding south from Ilygot with two companies of her lancers and one of South-Women. She will arrive here in three days."

"Is Alcaren with her?"

"He is. I cannot say what transpires between them, save he is acting as overcaptain for both her lancers and his."

"It could be worse." He leans forward and sets the mandolin on the polished wood of the table-desk, then leans back, his eyes still on the Matriarch. "Using Alcaren so . . . you risk much."

"Not so much as not using him. At worse, he guards our ally. At best, he will learn enough to help her . . . and us."

"That is a frail reed," Aetlen points out.

"As my mother said, it is the only reed we have, except trust in the Harmonies."

"You both have had this habit of assisting the Harmonies."

Alya shrugs and smiles. "Where I can . . ."

"Do the Ladies of the Shadows know the Sorceress approaches?" asks the sandy-haired consort.

"I would think not yet, but within glasses they will." Alya sighs. "Best we make ready the guest quarters and barracks, and put on extra guards."

"You expect them to act that soon?"

Alya laughs. "I would be most surprised if they did not. A true great sorceress within Encora? One who has no scruples about using her powers?"

"I would say she must have some."

"She uses them. To the Ladies of the Shadows, that means she has none."

Aetlen winces. "They would die rather than be chained, as are women in Sturinn, yet they would kill one of the few hopes of holding off the Sea-Priests."

"The Sea-Priests have already lost fleets and more than a hundred score lancers to the sorceresses of Defalk, and Defalk has no interest in exerting power beyond Liedwahr. Yet the Sea-Priests persist. Who is more foolish?"

Aetlen laughs, his tone bitter. "And we are caught between those who will not use sorcery to save us and those who will use it to enslave us."

"Ever it has been, dearest. Those who are blind slaves to principled belief would claim virtue while murdering for their beliefs. Yet they claim that they are exalted above those who profess no such principles at all, even as the bodies pile up."

"It is indeed a pity that you cannot say such openly."

"That . . . I cannot do. Not while the dismal swamps yet dot Ranuak, or the Sand Hills shift across the north, covering towns and uncovering others to reveal mummies of mothers still holding babes in arms."

"I know." Aetlen's voice is soft. "I know. So, again, we must put our trust in the Harmonies, and in others."

"And post guards," Alya says dryly. "And train sorcerers whom we cannot avow."

Both laugh, half in irony, half in bitterness.

Dark gray clouds loomed over the valley to the west of the road, clouds so dark that the early afternoon felt more like twilight. The road, while not paved, was of a firm clay and just wide enough for two wagons to pass side by side. The valley itself was split by a narrow river. To the east of the river, below the road, was an ancient-looking conifer forest, although the trees displayed a coloration that held as much black and purple as green.

Beyond the river to the west were small ponds fringed with yellowish reeds and linked by patches of sickly greens and orangish-browns. From amid the browns protruded leafless polelike trees. Secca could see not a single dwelling in the entire valley, which stretched a good fifteen deks from northeast to southwest, and more than ten in breadth.

A light mist drifted across the riders heading along the ridge road to the southwest. Secca and Alcaren rode near the front of the column, behind a small vanguard of four lancers, and in front of Richina and Palian. With the mist came a sickly bitter odor from the valley, not quite like burned meat, nor like swamps, nor like rotten fruit, but reminding Secca of all three.

"Not a pleasant place," she said quietly.

"No," Alcaren admitted. "These are the Great Dismal Swamps of the north. They say that once the entire valley was like the western side."

"What caused them?" Richina's voice drifted up from behind Secca and Alcaren.

"The Spell-Fire Wars," Alcaren replied. "There are many valleys like this throughout Ranuak."

"From sorcery?" Richina's voice carried a tone of disbelief.

"From sorcery," Alcaren affirmed. "You have seen a battlefield blasted black by Lady Secca, have you not? Do you think she or the Lady Anna were the first to harness such power?" He glanced at Secca.

"We have blackened the land in a few places," Secca admitted. "But nothing I have done would turn a valley into something like this—even after scores of generations. Nor did Lady Anna create any destruction such as this."

"I would hope not, lady." Alcaren's voice was calm. "Yet this was the price for the freedom of both Wei and Ranuak from the Mynyan lords. These valleys once held hamlets and towns, and the sorcery of the Mynyans turned them into spell-blasted holes that filled with water and became poisoned bogs and swamps. The Sand Hills are where the ancient Matriarchs turned the once-fertile borderlands of Mynya into desert heaped with sand. When the spring storms shift the dunes, folk still find hamlets where lie the bodies of those poor folk buried under the sand in those long-ago days."

"Are you sure that the dunes date back that far?" asked Richina. "I thought the Evult used sorcery to move the Sand Hills to block the Sand Pass."

"He moved the Sand Hills." Alcaren turned in his saddle. "He did not create them. The first Matriarchs did that through their sorcery."

Had sorcery done all that? Secca glanced to the dark and misshapen trees, and then to the sickly greens of the bogs and swamps. After a moment, she considered the contents of the notebooks locked behind iron at Loiseau . . . and shivered.

Alcaren did not remark upon her reaction, but continued to ride beside her. Secca looked ahead, where the road followed the ridge line toward the southwest . . . and Encora.

$\mathbf{S}$ecca shifted her weight in the saddle, glad for the morn-ing's sunshine, hazy as it was. She rode between Palian and Delvor, and behind Alcaren and Richina. The road followed the northern bank of a small river that wound through low rolling hills generally covered with scattered grasses and scrub bushes. At times, Secca had seen small flocks of sheep in the distance, but the size of the flocks suggested that the grazing was indeed poor.

"Is there a better way to set up the players if we must offer spells from a ship again?" she asked, looking first to Palian, and then to the lank-haired chief of second players.

"The sound of the instruments might carry farther from the rear deck," offered Delvor. "They would from the front deck, but there is much spray, and damp strings lose their tuning in moments."

"Do you think we will need to use ships against the Sea-Priests?" Palian frowned.

"I cannot see them bringing their fleet into a harbor so that I can sing a spell over it," Secca replied.

"Did not the Lady Anna . . . ?"

"She destroyed one of their fleets by building the giant dam on the Falche, and letting it gather water for seasons. When she tilted the dam with sorcery, the flood destroyed the fleet because it was anchored in the harbor at Narial. That was because the Sturinnese held the city," replied Secca. "They don't hold Encora."

"I doubt there's a river that big flowing through En-cora." Palian nodded to the narrow stream flanking the road.

"Or that the Sturinnese will anchor somewhere like that

without watching the river through their glasses," added Delvor.

"We won't have that much time, either," Secca pointed out.

Silence fell over the three for a moment.

"What is that?" Richina's voice contained such curiosity that Secca looked forward and followed the gesture of the younger sorceress. The hilltop a good five deks to the north of the road glistened black in the hazy morning sunlight.

"It is called The Last Encampment," Alcaren said. "It is said to mark the farthest advance of the Mynyan lords into Ranuak. There the first Matriarch cast the first true Darksong spell and turned all of the Mynyan forces there into stone, but the spell was so violent that even the stone figures melted like wax." Alcaren pointed farther west. "That smaller hill there, do you see it?"

"It's black, too," Richina observed, "but smaller."

"That was where the Matriarch stood. The spell recoiled upon her and those around her."

Secca winced at that thought. She cocked her head, thinking exactly about his words, about the spell recoiling upon the first Matriarch, and about the feeling behind those words.

"Lady?" asked Palian.

"I'm fine. Just thinking."

"Have you ever been there?" Richina pressed.

"Only to the lower part of the hill," Alcaren replied. "Nothing lives where it is black, and often animals still die if they spend much time among the shining black stones."

"Have you seen that?"

Alcaren nodded. "The hair falls from their fur in clumps, and they bleed from all over their skin. If they live for more than a few days, all their hair vanishes and their teeth fall out. Any animal that eats the flesh of one of them also dies."

"After all these years?" asked Delvor, his voice skeptical.

"None will stop you if you wish to test what I have said," replied Alcaren. "But none will touch your body or aid you, either."

Delvor shuddered.

Palian nodded, sadly and reflectively.

Somehow, reflected Secca, the concerns of the Ladies of the Shadows did not seem quite so strange, not if a fraction of what Alcaren had said happened to be true . . . and she had yet to hear a word from him that she knew to be untrue.

103

As the gray mare carried Secca to the crest of the road that passed between two hills almost tall enough to be very small mountains, the sorceress could see a broad plain spreading before her, filled with winter-turned fields edged with stone walls and interspersed with infrequent woodlots, also marked by stone walls. Every morgen of land seemed to be in use, either for homes or fields or barnyards—and the trees in every woodlot or orchard ran in neat rows.

To the south, perhaps ten deks from the road, lay the dark blue-gray expanse of the Southern Ocean, empty of either sails or whitecaps that could be seen from that distance. A dark smudge appeared on the horizon to the southwest—the island that sheltered the port.

A good fifteen deks to the west was a second set of low ridges, topped with lines of white stone walls that shimmered in the midday winter sun.

"There! Those are the northern and eastern walls of Encora." Alcaren gestured toward the ridge hills.

"Walls?" While Secca had seen more than a few walled

keeps in Defalk and in Ebra, she had never seen walls around an entire city—or even parts of it.

"They are older than the city. They have never been used for defense, but they were built in the generations after the Spell-Fire Wars."

"I suppose there are seawalls as well?" asked Secca.

"Of course." Alcaren nodded. He did not smile. "Even all the fleets of the Sea-Priests would have difficulty in taking Encora from the sea."

"There don't seem to be any ships out there," ventured Richina, from where she rode behind Secca.

"The Sturinnese would have to be either to the southeast or much farther to the southwest. Except for a few narrow channels, those waters are too shallow for most of their war vessels." Alcaren smiled. "We have never marked the channels, and they change often."

"They cannot scry the channels?" asked Richina.

Secca winced.

"Lady . . ." Alcaren's voice was patient.

"Oh . . ."

Secca could sense the flush and embarrassment of the younger sorceress. At times, it was hard to remember that Richina was still several years shy of a full score—until she asked a thoughtless question that betrayed a lack of experience at variance with her very womanly appearance.

"Is that why the Elahwan vessels cannot travel farther south than Ilygot?" Richina asked quickly.

Before they had left the small town of Zedal that morning, Secca had used the scrying glass to seek out the lancers of Loiseau that followed her to Encora. The glass had shown that the two remaining companies were sailing southward on three of the Elahwan vessels and that there were no Sturinnese forces near the ships. Secca only hoped she had phrased the spell correctly enough that there would be none near by the time the three vessels neared Ilygot.

"Yes," replied Alcaren. "The secrets to the channels are held most closely. Also, it would be difficult to maneuver more than a ship or two in the shoals and the shallows, and even the most experienced Ranuan captains will not traverse the East Sound in rough waters or in storms."

"Encora is well-protected," offered Palian easily.

"With our past, could we afford otherwise?" countered Alcaren.

"After more than a thousand years?" questioned Secca.

"Whose fleets blockade our ports?"

At the dryness of Alcaren's tone of voice, Secca laughed, even as she considered the memories of a war so violent that scars remained everywhere throughout the land after scores of generations. "You make a good point, over-captain."

The light breeze was chilly, but not unbearably cold, as the column began the descent into the valley that lay between them and the white walls of Encora.

"We should dispatch the messengers now, should we not?" asked Secca.

"It would be best," answered Alcaren.

While they had already sent one set of messengers from Ilygot, and while it was almost certain that the Matriarch already had known of their journey and approach to Encora even before those messengers had arrived, the courtesy of a more formal and immediate notification was certainly due. Secca and Alcaren had earlier decided on sending eight more lancers, four from the SouthWomen and four from Secca's diminished forces.

"Messengers to the fore!" called Alcaren.

The eight riders rode forward along the shoulders of the road, passing the players, and then Richina, Delvor, and Palian.

"You have your scrolls?" asked Secca.

"We do, lady," answered the squad leader—a South-Woman in a crimson-trimmed blue riding jacket.

"Convey our regards to the Matriarch and to all others as well," Secca continued.

"Yes, lady . . . overcaptain."

Secca and Alcaren watched as the lancers trotted ahead and down the road that angled northward on its initial descent toward the flatter land of the valley below.

"You are certain we will be welcome?" Secca asked in a low voice.

"Who else can use sorcery against the Sturinnese?" replied the Ranuan.

"With what I have seen in the last few days, I would question whether the use of sorcery is that welcome." After a moment, she added, "Unless the sorcery is performed beyond Ranuak."

Alcaren shook his head ruefully. "I am most certain the Matriarch would have few difficulties with that and would support any such efforts."

Secca still wondered as she shifted her weight in the saddle, her eyes going again to the distant white stone walls of Encora.

104

By late afternoon, heavy gray clouds had drawn across the sky, and a fine mist sifted down, carried by a light wind out of the south. Each fine droplet felt like a tiny point of ice on exposed skin. Secca had refastened her jacket and pulled the green felt hat from her saddlebags. Alcaren rode bareheaded, but Secca could see the redness from the damp and chill on the tips of his ears and on his cheeks.

The road itself was similar to the main highways in Defalk—stone-paved and straight, raised a half-yard above the plain through which it passed, and very slightly crowned so that rain would run off the broad and graveled shoulders. The thoroughfare was far, far older than any of the stone highways in Defalk, as the fine cracks and more than occasional replacement stones indicated. Those darker replacement stones were also much smaller than the massive slabs that represented the original paving.

Each of the scattered dwellings that flanked the highway was also of stone, with a slate roof. Stubble in the fields had long since been turned under, leaving neat rows. Although the dwellings varied in size, all were scrupulously kept, as were the outbuildings. Perhaps because of the cold, Secca saw few souls out, and those she did see paid little attention to the column of riders plodding westward toward Encora.

The column was less than two deks from the base of the ridge holding the city walls when Secca could make out through the mist both a crossroads coming directly from the north, and more than a score of riders reined up in two lines just beyond the crossroads.

Alcaren gestured toward the riders waiting at the crossroads ahead. "We have an honor escort waiting."

"Let us hope they are just an honor guard," replied Secca.

"Were they not, the gates would be closed, and there would be no guard at all," suggested the Ranuan.

Secca debated taking out the lutar, then decided against it, since the rain would do it little good, and displaying it would only offer offense. She did begin a gentle vocalise.

Alcaren looked at her, eyebrows raised.

"I prefer not to ride into a strange city with no defenses at all, overcaptain."

"You have a certain ability with a blade, lady."

"It is not sufficient to make a would-be enemy hesitate, as you well know." She paused, then said with a smile, "Your blade might, but not mine."

"I would not wish to cross blades with you again, my lady." As Secca turned, he added, returning her smile with one of his own, "Not if you were angry."

Secca laughed gently, enjoying the moment of banter, but she continued to warm up until she had ridden to within a hundred yards of the riders beyond the crossroads.

The twelve lancers that Secca and Alcaren had sent as messengers waited, mounted, on the flat of the road below the inclined and paved road that wound upward through four switchbacks to the gates above. Behind the twelve were two companies of Ranuan lancers wearing pale blue riding jackets identical to the one worn by Alcaren—one company on each side of the road.

The overcaptain of the Ranuan lancers rode forward and halted her mount. "Lady Sorceress! The Matriarch welcomes you and your company to Encora."

Secca reined up the gray and inclined her head. "Thank you. As you know, we come in friendship, and in hopes of finding a way to defeat the Sturinnese."

Behind her, Richina and the other riders slowed to a halt.

"The Matriarch knows such and welcomes you as friend and ally. All Encora is open to you."

"Thank you, and the Matriarch."

"We are here to escort you to the guest quarters and barracks."

"We appreciate your courtesy and grace." Secca nodded again.

One company of the Matriarch's lancers swung onto the road to lead the way up the road to the gates above, while the second waited and then brought up the rear.

Alcaren's SouthWoman squad leader eased her mount up beside the Ranuan overcaptain. With her was Delcetta, the SouthWoman company captain.

"Overcaptain, ser?" offered Captain Delcetta.

"Yes?" replied Alcaren.

"The Matriarch has requested that we remain under your command until the problem with Sturinn is resolved. The South Council has concurred."

"I appreciate the support of the Council," Alcaren said.

So did Secca, especially after riding through Ranuak. The SouthWomen seemed more likely to support sorcery than many throughout the land.

With a nod, the captain and the squad leader turned their mounts.

While she rode up the inclined road toward the gates,

Secca studied both the road and the walls as best she could through the mist. The road narrowed slightly, and indented stone rain gutters appeared on both the uphill and downhill sides, gutters that drained into stone channels at each of the four switchbacks. Once Secca neared the top of the ridge, the scale of the walls became even more apparent, ramparts of gray-white granite that towered a good fifteen yards above the rocky ground out of which they rose.

Secca held herself ready to use sorcery, even without the lutar, should it be needed, but those massive walls held no guards, nor were any evident near the gates. The single gate opening was but four yards wide, and framed with massive stone pillars, two on each side. Each pillar had been cut as a single unit. Between the pillars were the edges of the gates, each nearly a span in thickness. Each gate was designed to slide out from between the pillars, and the city walls behind them, along stone channels more than two spans deep and across the gate opening, one before the other, so that when the gates were closed there were two thicknesses of timber, each tightly anchored in stone on three sides. Where the channels crossed the roadway, they were covered with thin oak planks to ensure neither horses nor people broke legs in them.

Secca studied the stone of the walls as the gray mare carried her past the unguarded gates. She nodded.

"Lady?" asked Alcaren.

"The stone work was accomplished with sorcery."

"You recognize the method?"

"I have some familiarity with it. I don't think those gate pillars could have been put there any other way. Not that I know of, anyway."

"That may be, but it might be best if you did not voice that too widely."

Secca snorted. "Use the fruits of sorcery, but do not mention it?"

"You have seen what sorcery has done to this land."

"Like any tool, it can be used for good or evil. One should not blame the tool."

"Blaming the tool is far easier, especially when the user may have had little choice."

Secca did not reply. She understood Alcaren's point, but also felt that those who restricted what tools could be used often deserved the results that befell them.

Once through the gates, the Ranuan lancers turned slightly right and began to follow a gray stone boulevard that, within fifty yards of the wall and gate, arced downhill through a grassy park toward the dwellings and structures of the city below. For the first time, in the park, Secca saw hardwoods and fruit trees, rather than the endless conifers that had seemed to populate the land of Ranuak all the way from Ilygot.

"Are there many such parks in Encora?" she asked.

"One cannot go a dek in any direction without finding a large park, and less than that for small greens," replied the overcaptain.

To the southwest, Secca thought she could make out long stone piers at the edge of the dark circle of water that formed the harbor, and seawalls to the east of the piers. At least two vessels were tied up at the longer pier, and there might have been others, but the taller structures near the center of the city blocked a full view of the wharfs and piers.

Below the park, the boulevard straightened, pointing like a quarrel toward the harbor, and settled into a gradual decline toward the water. Raised stone sidewalks flanked the boulevard, and the dwellings on each side were generally of two or three stories, built of stone, with covered balconies looking out in front, and over rear garden courtyards.

Less than four blocks from the base of the park and toward the harbor, Secca glanced up at the topmost balcony of a three-story dwelling on the left side of the boulevard. There stood a figure in a dark hooded cloak, the face lost in the hood and the gloom of the growing twilight. A Lady of the Shadows?

Why?

To warn Secca against sorcery?

For the first time since they had begun to ride through Ranuak, Secca noticed people who actually looked at her, and at the others, although indirectly. No one seemed to stare or study the column intently, but they were not traversing the city without notice.

The guest quarters and barracks lay just on the northwest side of the boulevard less than half a dek from the harbor. They were so similar to those in Elahwa that they might have been designed by the same person, save that the walls of the structures were of the whitish-gray granite, and that a wall a good five yards in height surrounded the entire compound. The blue-painted iron gates were swung back and locked open. When the Ranuan honor guard swung through the gates, the stone walls threw the echo of their hoofs on the stones of the drive back at Secca.

The drive was flanked on both sides by a low boxwood hedge that did nothing to mute the echo of hoofs, and before the guest house itself was a circular rose garden, one whose roses had long since been cut back to ready them for the spring still many weeks away.

Standing on the steps at the rear of the guest quarters was a tall and squarish woman in the pale blue of the Ranuan lancers, but with a single red rosette embroidered upon each shoulder of her riding jacket.

Alcaren reined up and bowed. "Commander."

"Overcaptain." The commander smiled at Secca. "On behalf of the Matriarch, Lady Sorceress, I bid you and all those with you welcome to Encora. The Matriarch offers her hospitality and support, and assures you that you will lack for nothing as you prepare to deal with the Sturinnese invaders."

"We are pleased to be here and greatly appreciate your support and that of the Matriarch," replied Secca.

"We are even more pleased to welcome you." The commander bowed deeply. "Once you have rested, the Matriarch looks forward to meeting you."

"As I do her," Secca replied, wondering how long before the meeting would actually take place.

105

Secca stood over the small round conference table in the main chamber of the Matriarch's guest quarters, holding her lutar and looking down at the scrying glass laid in the center of the table. She studied the image in the silvered glass. The Sturinnese vessels appeared where they had been for weeks—south of the harbor of Encora.

After singing the simple release couplet, Secca laid the lutar on the table and walked toward the middle window of the quarters' main chamber, halting well back so that she would not be that visible from the open gates or from the boulevard itself. The air was so still that the dismal gray mist and fog of the previous days continued to hold Encora prisoner. She could only see the vague outlines of the warehouses that fronted the stone piers less than half a dek away.

After a time, she spoke to Richina, who remained beside the table. "If we are not summoned in the next day or so, I will see if Alcaren can arrange for us to travel the western bluffs overlooking the channels south of the harbor."

"Why has she not met with you?" asked Richina. "The Matriarch, I mean."

The older sorceress turned. "She cannot be that hasty."

"You have traveled across half of Liedwahr, and now . . ." Richina shook her head.

"I am a sorceress, and they fear sorcery," Secca pointed out. "Have you not seen the scars of sorcery upon this land?"

"I have seen things which the Ranuans claim are scars of sorcery."

"Do you know of any other way to build roads with such large stones? Or the walls of this city?"

Richina glanced down at the floor.

"I cannot but worry about those who fear sorcery," Secca said slowly. "If the Matriarch waits to see me, so that none will claim she rushes to greet a sorceress, then their power may be great." She glanced at Richina. "Perhaps you should spend some time with your glass and try to see what you can discover about the Ladies of the Shadows here in Encora."

"I will try, Lady Secca."

"Good." Secca paused. "Will you send word that I would see Overcaptain Alcaren and Captain Delcetta?"

Richina's eyebrows lifted.

"I doubt the SouthWomen—or the good overcaptain—have any love for those in the shadows." Secca concealed a wince at the way her words had come out. More than once, she had been accused of being in the shadows.

"Yes, lady."

When the door closed behind Richina, Secca replaced the lutar in its case, and then seated herself behind the working desk. That morning, the scrying glass had shown her that the remaining two companies—and the mounts for the understrength company—had landed in Ilygot and were riding southward. Lord Fehern still held the lands around Envaryl, and it seemed as though the Sturinnese were no longer attacking. That disturbed Secca, although she could not say why, unless the Sea-Priests had decided to wait for better weather in the spring.

She took out the sheets of brown paper with the spells she had used to create the storms that had destroyed the Sturinnese vessels, looking across the lines. She shook her head. Two spells on mostly calm waters, and the weather had made it impossible for the players to continue, and the third had been all she could manage. Three spells for five vessels? And the Sturinnese had almost three score warships left in the Southern Ocean?

"Overcaptain Alcaren and Captain Delcetta," called out Easlon from the corridor outside.

"Have them come in." Secca set aside the spells.

Once the two Ranuan officers entered, Secca gestured to the small round conference table, seating herself and waiting for them to do so as well.

"Tell me about the Ladies of the Shadows, if you would." Secca glanced at Captain Delcetta.

"They do not believe in sorcery, save for gathering information and sending messages." The words of the captain with the short-cut strawberry blonde hair were clipped.

"They would seem to be especially powerful here in Ranuak," ventured Secca.

Neither officer spoke.

Secca looked at Alcaren. "How much does the Matriarch fear them?"

"She fears them not at all, not for herself certainly." Alcaren offered an amused smile.

"Yet she fears meeting with me upon my arrival, and would that not mean that I should be concerned?"

"There are double guards outside the wall, and they do not care who leaves," said Delcetta.

"Does anyone know the names—"

"No. They know sorcery's limits."

"Perhaps not mine." Secca stood, then bent and uncased the lutar. Her fingers skipped over the keys as she began the spell.

> *"Show me now and in this light*
> *the Ranuan shadow lady of greatest might.*
> *Show her face as it may be*
> *clear for all to see . . ."*

The mirror silvered without hesitation, revealing a round-featured and gray-haired woman with a surprisingly sharp jawline attired in pale blue. Secca's eyes darted from the image to the two Ranuan officers. Delcetta looked at the image, frowning. Alcaren's eyes widened ever so slightly.

"You know her, overcaptain." Secca's words were not a question.

"Only by sight and position, Lady Secca. That is San-thya, the Assistant Exchange Mistress."

One-handed, Secca pushed an empty sheet of paper toward the overcaptain. "If you would write down her name."

Alcaren glanced from Delcetta to Secca, then at the paper. He reached for the quill beside the inkstand. Secca nodded. Alcaren wrote a single name.

Secca began the spell again.

*"Show me now and in this light
the shadow lady of next to greatest might . . ."*

The image in the mirror was that of a narrow-faced woman with hennaed hair, and deep-set gray eyes. Secca looked at Alcaren again.

"Felcya of the Artisan's Guild . . ."

The sorceress managed eight more versions of the spell before she had to stop with the onset of dayflashes. Alcaren had known four others, and Delcetta had named two Alcaren had not known.

Secca set aside the lutar, and began to eat the biscuits in the tin on the sideboard. Her head was throbbing, if not so badly as with battle sorcery. After several biscuits, interspersed with cold water, she looked up from the conference table at the two silent Ranuans.

"What will you do with these names, lady?" asked Alcaren.

"For now . . . nothing. Should I?"

He shook his head.

"You aren't saying something," Secca suggested.

"I would be most careful, that is all, Lady Secca. Some of the shadow ladies have had rivals vanish—or be killed within locked rooms."

That was all Secca needed—another type of attack to worry about. She avoided sighing and took another swallow of water from the goblet, emptying it. "You didn't mention that."

"Ah . . . I did say that the Ladies of the Shadows did not like sorceresses, lady." Alcaren looked almost embarrassed.

Secca was supposed to have guessed that the group included professional assassins? She did sigh. Then, Alcaren had warned her, if slightly belatedly.

"That is very seldom," suggested Delcetta quickly. "They would prefer that those who profess sorcery leave Ranuak."

"I would like to," Secca replied. "The Sturinnese and the winter snows make that difficult. I hope the Ladies of the Shadows would consider such."

"I would not know." Alcaren shrugged. It was a most unconvincing shrug, and one clearly designed to suggest that Alcaren did know, and that the Ladies of the Shadows had little interest in Secca's concerns. "They have not had a great sorceress within Encora before. I could not say what they might do."

If that did not happen to be a warning . . . Secca hadn't heard one.

She rose. "Thank you both. I appreciate all you have told me." She smiled, an expression obviously as false as the overcaptain's shrug.

The falsity of the shrug and his few words about the Ladies of the Shadows troubled her. Not their falsity, but what that falsity conveyed. Alcaren did not lie well, and that meant he had not lied to her in the past. He had evaded answering some questions, but he had not lied, not the way he just had, and that troubled her more than if he had.

Finally, Secca ate another pair of biscuits, and then took out the brown paper and the grease marker. She needed another set of spells, and before the evening.

106

MANSUUS, MANSUUR

The Liedfuhr holds his aching head in his overbroad hands for a moment, then massages his temples before looking up at Bassil, who stands, patiently, before the study desk. "The shadow sorceress is in Encora?"

"That is what your seers show. The Sea-Priests did not fare well in Ebra and retreated to their vessels. She destroyed five in the short passage across the Gulf to Ranuak."

"That is well, but hardly enough. Now the sorceress will remain blocked in Encora unless she can break one of their fleets," Kestrin points out. "The sea has always been the strength of Sturinn. Until then and unless she does, what can she do?" He frowns, leaning back in the padded desk chair. His eyes flick to the windows at the howling of the late afternoon wind that promises yet more snow, then back to the overcaptain. "She will not divert the Sturinnese for a moment. Nor will it help Aerlya."

"For the moment, your niece holds Neserea," Bassil states.

"For the moment, and only because the Sorceress of Defalk has removed two of this Belmar's allies, and destroyed bridges and who knows what else, but it is not enough. Each week that passes tempts more to back the usurper."

"The sorceress is hampered by having to defend Aerlya and Annayal, as well as fighting Belmar and his Sturinnese sorcerer."

"Yet Lord Robero will send no other sorceress to her aid. So I must send aid."

"You will risk his wrath?"

"What wrath? I will send the lancers in Unduval through

the Mittpass, along with another fifty companies, including the thirty in Deleator. They will answer to Aerlya, Annayal, and the Sorceress of Defalk—in that order—and I will send a message to Lord Robero to affirm that, although he may not receive it until all is moot. Still, he wants Belmar as the new Prophet of Music even less than do I."

"I foresee even greater conflict," Bassil says quietly.

"So now you think I err?" Kestrin looks at the overcaptain.

"No, sire. I fear I may have advised you too cautiously. I would have your lancers proceed against any of Belmar's allies who stand without his sorcerous aid. Leave Belmar to the sorceresses. I would also place what companies you can northwest of Envaryl."

"To give the Sturinnese in Dumar pause?"

"If anything will," admits Bassil.

"And should I prepare to send another set of lancers through Aleatur once the snows melt?"

"If you can."

Kestrin stands and looks to the northmost window, studying the dark clouds that loom in the late afternoon. "To think that all Liedwahr is at war or stands on the brink, when all was calm and peaceful not a half-year ago."

"Much has happened since then, sire."

"What? Two people died . . . just two people."

"They were not just two people," Bassil points out. "They were the two who created that peace and who ensured that all Liedwahr was united against Sturinn. Now you must do the same."

"Me? And who else?"

Bassil does not answer.

In time, the Liedfuhr's eyes turn toward the window and the clouds massing to the north.

107

In the dim light of the single lamp still lit in the main room of the guest quarters, Secca lifted the brown paper and read. After studying the words yet again, Secca slowly picked up the lutar and began the spell.

> *"Bell to ring and crystal sing*
> *should any step within the door,*
> *louder still, the air to fill*
> *should they weapons bring . . ."*

After completing the spellsong, she set the lutar in its case on the side table on the west wall of the main chamber, leaving the case open. After wicking down and out the last lit lamp in the main chamber, she stepped into the smaller bedchamber, sliding the thin iron bolt shut. She examined the bolt, shaking her head. She wasn't sure that she couldn't undo the bolt from outside with a thin knife. Then, that was another reason for the spell, although the lingering nature of the spell would drain some small part of her strength, but not that much, since it was a warning songspell, and not one requiring great energy.

But it was clear she needed such a warning. Although Richina had also had little luck in uncovering anything about the Ladies of the Shadows, the younger sorceress had reported to Secca that she had called up many faces, but had found none engaged in anything other than normal activities. Secca shook her head. That was always the problem with scrying—all too often the glass showed nothing useful . . . although the number of faces Secca and Richina had seen in their glasses was dis-

turbing enough, and another reason for the warning
spell.

Once in the bedchamber, Secca slipped from her riding clothes into a simple shift. Before going into the
small bath and robing chamber, she removed the sabre
from its scabbard and set it on the bedside table away
from the door. Her eyes dropped to the iron bolt she
mistrusted, and she found herself shaking her head.

With an upper room, two locked doors, guards outside her door, and a warning spell . . . she should have
felt safe. But then, she knew nothing of the Ladies of
the Shadows, save some were either assassins or could
call on such, and assassins often found ways around
guards and locks. She also knew, cryptic as Alcaren had
been, that he had wanted to warn her, yet not obviously.
Why?

She still had no answer for that, unless he feared ears
were everywhere, and that an obvious warning might
make matters even worse. Secca liked that idea even
less.

Finally, she climbed up into the high bed and snuffed
out the candle.

For a long time, she lay in the darkness, thoughts
whirling through her mind. Eventually her eyes closed.

Clannnnnnnnnnnggg . . .

The clanging of the bell and the ear-splitting ring of
the crystal jolted Secca full alert, and she flung herself
sideways from the bed, her hand closing around the
sabre on the table, even before her bare feet touched
the cold wooden floor.

Secca blinked away sleep, or tried to, as she stood
there, sabre in a near-instinctive guard position, peering
back toward the door.

After what seemed long moments, Secca could make
out the shadowy form sliding toward her. The sorceress
lifted her blade and eased along the side of the bed and
then around the foot of the bed to get away from the
wall.

The intruder—more than a good head taller than Secca—moved forward with grace toward the foot of the bed, trying to back Secca into the corner. The intruder's longer blade flicked in the dimness at Secca, and Secca barely managed to parry it, as much by feel as sight. She gave ground as she did, trying to ignore the ringing and the clanging that continued unremittingly.

"Lady Secca! Lady Secca!" came the calls of the guards outside the room, calls barely audible over the bell and ringing crystal as the two guards pounded on the door to the main chamber.

Secca kept her own blade high, trying to gather her thoughts, and the spell she thought she had prepared. What were the words?

Another thrust slash from the intruder, and Secca circled away from the corner of the room where she'd almost been skewered by the very skilled and silent attacker.

After another cut-slash from the silent intruder, Secca circled back, still mentally fumbling for words, coughing and trying to clear her throat.

Finally, she had the words, the all-too-simple words and melody.

"Flay . . . flay . . ."

Another attack, and a dry throat, and Secca had lost both melody and timing, and had to scramble aside.

As she circled back, she bent and half-slid, half-shoved the stool toward the dark and taller figure, who stepped aside gracefully.

Secca used the moment to begin the spell again.

"Flay with fire, flay with flame,
this one who'd defy my name
kill this one with fire's thrust,
as fire can and fire must!"

Secca again skipped aside, barely parrying two more thrusts before the miniature flame lances appeared from nowhere. The intruder continued to try to bring the longer blade against Secca, even as the taller woman shuddered noiselessly under the impact of the fires.

The ringing of the crystal ended with a *snap*, and crystal shards tinkled onto the floor. The clanging of the bell stopped as abruptly.

Secca just stood, blade up, scanning the room, hoping there were no others nearby.

"Lady Secca! Lady Secca!"

Still with blade in hand, Secca fumbled the striker left-handedly and managed to light the candle on the table beside the bed. The yellow-orange light was enough that she could tell no one else was in the bedchamber, and the door to the main chamber, slightly ajar, suggested how the intruder had gained access.

The sorceress cleared her throat and edged toward the door, using a quick flick of the sabre to open it all the way. The main chamber was empty, but the draft from the open end window gave a good indication of how the attacker had reached Secca's chamber.

Secca edged toward the door of the main chamber. "I'm all right."

"Are you sure, lady?"

She recognized Easlon's voice. "Who is on guard with you, Easlon?"

"Rukor, lady."

"I am, lady."

The two responses were near simultaneous.

She slipped the iron bolt, ready to close it—or spell-sing—as necessary, but the only ones in the hallway were the two guards. "Come in. Lock it behind you."

She eased toward the lutar she had left on the side table, checking the strings in the dim light before slipping toward the open window. Almost without pause, she began the second spell.

> *"Flay with fire, flay with flame,*
> *all those who with this one came*
> *Kill them all with fire's thrust,*
> *as fire can and fire must!"*

Three firebolts flared from the dark gray clouds, striking once behind the boxwood hedge by the drive, and twice beyond the walls. This time, there were screams.

Secca took a deep breath, then used the striker in the main chamber to light the desk lamp. After that, she walked slowly to the window. The would-be murderer had edged her way along a ledge barely a span wide from the corner where a step-chimney had offered access to the second level. She looked down, closely. A pry bar had been set carefully next to the wall, obviously to be retrieved on the way out.

Followed by Easlon and Rukor, Secca returned to the bedchamber where she looked down at the dead figure, whose face was crossed with blackened lines. The intruder had been a tall woman, well-muscled, with dark brown hair. Before the sorcery, she had been handsome. She had also been one of those whose visage had appeared in the glass, but whose name neither Alcaren nor Delcetta had known.

"Find a blanket or something to wrap her in," Secca said tiredly. "We'll need to deliver her to the Matriarch. Roust out some of the lancers and do the same with the others."

"Others?" stammered Easlon.

"Those firebolts outside? Each struck someone, and they were with this woman."

The two exchanged glances.

"Yes, lady."

"As you wish, Lady Secca."

Secca closed her eyes for a moment as she stood there. She really could use more sleep, but wondered if she would ever sleep that well again in Encora.

108

Secca rode on the north-south boulevard, away from the harbor and the guest quarters and toward the dwelling set amid a parklike garden and behind granite walls that appeared pale blue. The more she thought about the assassin of the night before, the angrier she felt. Even though Alcaren had warned her, even though she had seen the scars of sorcery throughout Ranuak, Secca still smoldered. She had always disliked the pettiness and the maneuvering for power, the use of politics she had seen among the Thirty-three and in Falcor, and the Matriarch was clearly using Secca for her own political ends.

Perhaps that had been another of the reasons why Anna had insisted on taking Secca to Loiseau. A fiery temper did not mix well over time with the intrigues in the corridors of the liedburg of Falcor—nor in other corridors of power.

A few words drifted in her direction as she rode past what appeared to be a shop dealing in all manner of baskets.

"The Lady Sorceress of Defalk . . . has to be . . ."

"Her hair . . . like flame . . ."

". . . looks stern . . ."

". . . in great anger . . ."

". . . is said that some already attempted to remove her . . ."

Secca could not catch the rest of the words of those few who turned to watch as she was escorted along the wide stone-paved boulevard by the two companies of lancers, one in the green of Loiseau and the second in the crimson and blue of the SouthWomen. Yet the fact that those in the street knew of the assassination attempt told her again that every wall in Encora might well have ears—or worse.

"You are still angry," offered Alcaren, riding beside her. "Perhaps I should have been more direct . . ."

"No. I understand that. You thought that if you said something very direct and obvious that word might get out that I'd been warned, and I would find it even harder to protect myself."

"I am most sorry . . ." Alcaren's voice was soft, but strained.

Even in her anger, Secca could sense both the truth of his words and something more than mere professional concern. She turned, wanting to ask, then stopped what she was going to say. Finally, she spoke. "I can see that. It was not your fault, and I do not blame you. You have always spoken truth to me."

"I have tried."

"Unlike others." Secca snorted. "But your truth also says that Encora is a pit of vipers with spies everywhere."

"That it is," Alcaren admitted. "Why do you think Delcetta and I prefer to serve you?"

"That just makes me more angry. If Sturinn weren't such a problem . . ." She shook her head. "Still, the Matriarch has much to answer for. Last night was totally unnecessary. It was an easy way of dealing with a problem that should have been handled generations ago."

"How?" asked Alcaren. "By using sorcery? So that even more women would flock to the shadows? By imprisoning mothers and giving their daughters another reason to hate the Matriarch?"

"I don't know." Secca shifted her weight in the saddle. "All I do know is that allowing assassins to attack me is not exactly hospitable . . ."

"The Matriarch had guards everywhere, lady. Yet they did not, or could not, stop your attacker. Does that not tell you something?"

"Yes. It tells me that too many women in Ranuak are stupid and fearful. And possibly men as well."

Alcaren winced. After a moment, he added, "Say what

you will to the Matriarch, but essay to say it without the fire of anger that consumes you."

Secca forced herself to take a deep breath. Alcaren was right about that, and he was daring to offer good advice to a very angry sorceress, which offered another message. That message could wait—would have to wait—until after she dealt with the Matriarch. In dealing with the Matriarch, Secca needed to be cooler, the way Anna had been. It had never done Secca any good to lash out—and the Matriarch was not unintelligent. She could not be, and rule.

Secca took a slow deep breath, then nodded to Alcaren. "Thank you."

They rode silently toward the opening in the bluish-white granite walls that surrounded the Matriarch's grounds. There were no gates, not even decorative ones, only the opening leading through a single high stone arch. Above the keystone of the arch was a single white-bronze fire lily. The stone drive inside the walls curved to the side of the three-story dwelling in the middle of the parklike setting. There, under a low portico barely high enough to allow a rider on a tall mount to pass without ducking, was a long carriage mounting block. Toward the dwelling from the mounting block were three wide stone steps leading to another archway.

The SouthWomen lancers had already passed under the portico and re-formed, facing Secca as she dismounted and handed the gray's reins to her guard, Dyvan. Alcaren dismounted as well.

"Grace and strength, lady," offered Captain Delcetta, her voice strong but not booming, carrying over the light mid-morning breeze.

Secca turned and inclined her head before taking the first step toward the archway. "My thanks to you all."

Beyond the archway was a square foyer—and a single staircase. There were no doors beside the one through which she and Alcaren had entered. At the foot of the staircase was a single guard in a pale blue uniform absolutely without insignia. "You are expected, lady and over-captain."

The staircase leading to the second floor landing was not overly broad—less than three yards from one plain stone wall to the other. A single guard stood at the top of the landing, looking down at Alcaren and Secca.

Alcaren walked up the stone steps beside Secca, close enough to offer his arm, though he did not do so. As they crossed the landing and approached the single door of golden wood set in the wall at the far side of the landing, the guard spoke.

"The Matriarch will see the Lady Sorceress alone, over-captain."

Alcaren nodded. "I will wait here."

The guard turned and eased the door ajar. "The Sorceress-Protector of Defalk, Matriarch."

"Have her enter."

Secca stepped into the formal receiving room. Despite her resolve to be calm and not to lash out in anger, she could feel the fire in her amber eyes as she looked toward the dais and the woman seated on the blue crystalline chair that was not quite a throne. The hazy light that fell through the floor-to-ceiling windows onto the shimmering blue stone floor offered little cheer and less warmth.

"Welcome, Lady Secca." The silver and blonde-haired Matriarch inclined her head in greeting. "It has been long since a sorceress has visited Ranuak as friend and ally."

"After last night, it may be a great while before another does." Secca managed to keep her voice even, but she could sense the edge it carried. She stopped several yards short of the crystalline chair, sensing that the chair was far more than ceremonial.

"That might be best," replied the Matriarch. "Sorcery is not favored by many in Ranuak."

"Yet you use it, and you would have me use it to assist Ranuak."

"I do not believe Ranuak has even asked such of you."

Again, there was the hint of a twinkle in the eyes of the Matriarch.

"I would not be here were it otherwise," Secca pointed out. "And I am not much interested in further employing words as blades."

"What am I to do with you, Lady Secca?" Although the Matriarch's voice was calm and firm, there was an even greater hint of a smile in her eyes, very much at odds with the tone of her voice.

"Perhaps you could begin by apologizing for the behavior of those who tried to kill me. You have their bodies, and you would know better than I what occurred," Secca suggested. "You could then advise me of what you intend to do to redress the grievance. And then, perhaps, we could discuss how we can work together to remove the Sturinnese from Liedwahr."

Alya laughed, gently, humorously. "You are as direct as the blade you bear."

Secca drew the two scrolls from within her riding jacket and extended the first. "This I bring from Lord Robero."

"Thank you." The Matriarch took the scroll but made no effort to open it.

"And this is from me." Secca handed the unsealed short scroll. "I thought you might find this helpful in dealing with those who have in their hearts less than the best interests of Ranuak and Liedwahr."

Alya took the list, her eyebrows raised. "This is . . . ?"

"A list of some of the more powerful within the Ladies of the Shadow in Ranuak."

Alya laughed. "It will indeed be most helpful, perhaps even in ways neither of us might envision."

"It is very possible I would not envision those ways," Secca said carefully, "but I cannot imagine that you have not considered all of them."

The Matriarch shook her head slowly. "Although I never met the Lady Anna, you are as she once might have been."

Secca cut off her immediate response and considered the Matriarch's words before replying. "I would not know, but

I have always thought most highly of her. More highly than any other I have ever met."

"And she of you, most clearly, and with great reason." The Matriarch pursed her lips. "I am truly sorry about the events of the past evening. I had hoped that my guards, and those of the SouthWomen, would have deterred the Ladies of the Shadows. I had hoped . . . but I still feared."

"Yet . . . ?" Secca waited.

Alya frowned. "You have seen my dwelling. You have seen how few guards I have. I can muster fewer lancers than can Lord Robero."

"Ranuak is richer than Defalk."

"Ranuak is as rich as it can be. It cannot be much more than it is. Defalk can be far greater and more prosperous than Ranuak."

Secca's face expressed skepticism.

"It is simple. You rode from the east. You saw the swamps and the bogs, the trees that grow less than well. All the land that bears good harvests, all that is used. We have turned to the sea, because we have little good land, for most of Ranuak is poisoned or poor, or both."

"Poisoned? After all these years?"

"Not just from the Spell-Fire Wars, lady. Once the sorcerers and sorceresses of the east, and not just the Mynyans, employed sorcery for creating all manner of devices and materials. When they wrenched metals from the earth, the rain seeped into the pits, and leached forth noxious substances. When they pulled iron from the soil, trees and plants withered and died. There must be a balance within the soils and within the lands, and there is none in much of Ranuak, and it will be many hundreds of generations before the Harmonies restore such."

Secca tilted her head. The Matriarch seemed truthful, and what Secca had seen bore out her words. So did— now—some of Anna's words, words she had scarce heeded in years past.

"You have heard this before?" asked Alya.

"Lady Anna . . . she offered some words. She always said that the least sorcery was the best."

"She was right." Alya paused, then asked, "How can Ranuak help you defeat the Sturinnese? Is that not why you came to Encora?"

"I had thought to come here to reach Dumar," Secca said. "So that I could keep the Sea-Priests from subjugating that land and using it to conquer all of Liedwahr."

"You cannot reach Dumar by sea from here any more easily than from Elahwa. Not while the white-hulled ships hold the Southern Ocean," pointed out the Matriarch. "And we of Ranuak have few ships left from the attacks of the Sea-Priests. Even were their fleets to vanish, hard years would face us. Would that we could take some of their ships in recompense for the suffering that they have caused. Have you spells that would destroy them, but not their vessels?"

"That *might* be possible . . . but only for a few vessels," Secca admitted. "It took all my efforts, and those of my players, to destroy a mere five vessels. Sturinn has fourscore warships in the Southern Ocean."

"Mere?" Alya arched her eyebrows. "One sorceress, a score of players, and five mighty ships are gone."

"Compared to the task at hand . . . mere," Secca replied. "What I can do with sorcery is limited, and more so upon the ocean, it would seem. I can scarcely sing spell after spell on a ship pursuing the Sturinnese." She paused. "With their thunder-drums, after my first sorcery, they would use the drums to speed from us."

"What if they were gathered together?" asked the Matriarch. "Could you not come up with one spell that would leave at least a few ships untouched, and then a mighty enough spell to destroy the others?"

"Perhaps. I might be able to sing a spell that would affect them all. I'll need to try out some things on the shore, though." Secca frowned. "Spells dealing with the oceans or objects upon them are harder."

"So it is said."

"How would one gather all the Sturinnese ships together?"

"That . . . that we might well manage." Alya offered a wry smile. "The Sturinnese fear and respect you, lady. If all our trading vessels were armed, and gathered as if to carry you to Dumar, what would the Sea-Priests do? Especially after they found five ships less than able to halt you?"

Secca nodded slowly.

"It will take a week, maybe two, for they must see in their glasses what we do . . ."

As the Matriarch explained, Secca listened, forcing herself to concentrate on the problem of the Sturinnese and to put aside her anger at the Ladies of the Shadows and the Matriarch's inability to deal with them. The problems of the Ladies of the Shadows would have to remain those of the Matriarch.

Not so a few other problems, Secca feared, but she forced herself to listen carefully.

109

ENCORA, RANUAK

The Matriarch sits upon the blue crystal chair on the dais in the formal receiving room.

"The Assistant Exchange Mistress, Matriarch."

"Send her in." Alya's voice is even more chill than the gray clouds that she can see through the long windows, clouds that have returned to cloak the skies over Encora in the late afternoon.

A gray-haired and round-faced woman steps through the door that is quickly closed behind her with a dull *thunk*. The Matriarch watches as the woman steps toward her, then stops and bows, if almost indifferently. The Matriarch waits.

"Why am I here, Matriarch?" asks the gray-haired woman after a time. "Have I done aught to displease you? What, I can scarce imagine."

"I believe you can, Santhya. I do believe you can." The Matriarch studies the Assistant Exchange Mistress. "Last night, there was an attack on the Sorceress-Protector of Defalk. I thought you might know something about it." The Matriarch's voice is mild.

"I am less than pleased to have a sorceress of power in Encora, but that is true of many, as you must know." Santhya bows her head slightly and waits.

"The assassin was one of your number, Santhya. The sorceress killed her face-to-face. You and the others of the Ladies of the Shadows underestimate the sorceress—in that fashion, and in others." The Matriarch lifts a roll of parchment. "She provided me with a list of all those in authority within the Ladies of the Shadows."

"That is a lengthy list, Matriarch. Their absences would be noted."

Alya laughs, if mirthlessly. "That they would. Fear not, Santhya. I see no point in executing you all—not at the moment. You will all merely be my guests in the White Tower until the Sorceress-Protector leaves Encora." A cold smile crosses her lips. "So long as no other attempts are made on her or upon any in her party . . . why, nothing will happen."

"I cannot speak for the others."

"Oh, I understand that. Indeed, I do. That is why you will join all of those on the sorceress's list—and a few other names I have come across—as my guests. I am also keeping your daughters—as my honored guests, of course—in the Blue Tower. As we speak, they are being gathered."

Santhya nods. "I cannot say I would expect any less."

"Those keeping watch over your daughters will be the third and fourth companies of the SouthWomen."

"You cannot—"

"Do not tell me what I can and cannot do."

Santhya's ruddy color pales.

"I might add that there are two others who know sorcery with the sorceress. It is most unlikely that all three could be killed at once. The others would have my leave to turn their sorceries upon every name in this list. From the White Tower it would take but a single spell." Alya's eyes fix on Santhya. "I do hope you understand."

The older woman's eyes are as cold as those of Alya. "I understand, Matriarch. You will revisit all the horrors of the Spell-Fire Wars upon us."

"Better that than chains for generations to come. You may go. Your escort awaits you."

The Matriarch's eyes appear as gray as the clouds as she watches while Santhya turns and walks slowly toward the door at the back of the formal receiving room.

110

In the light cast by the lamps set in the middle of the conference table, Secca looked down at the lines scrawled on the single sheet of heavy brown paper, then at the stacks of brown paper piled around her.

"Dissonance . . . frigging dissonance . . ." Tiredly, she took the grease marker and lined through the words she had just written, as she had lined through others earlier. "Note values . . . not right. Again!"

She rubbed her forehead and then took a sip from the water goblet. She turned the sheet of heavy paper over and lifted the grease marker.

"Lady . . . why do you not write another spell melody?" asked Richina, as she refilled the goblet.

Secca pursed her lips tightly together. She could tell she was ready to lash out at Richina, and Richina didn't deserve it—not too much. She looked up at the younger sorceress for a long moment.

"I am most sorry . . ." As Richina backed away from Secca and the piles of brown paper, her hip struck the table. Water slopped from the pitcher.

"Richina," Secca said slowly, "I will be asking the players to perform upon the deck of a ship that may be pitching. Fire arrows may be falling around them. Some may feel their stomachs lurching within them. Is that not so?"

"Ah . . . yes, Lady."

"How well are they likely to play a spellsong they have practiced but for a few days?"

Richina's mouth opened, then closed.

"That is why I struggle with words and note values. That is why I call on dissonance. That is why . . ." Secca let the words die in her mouth.

"Yes, lady," Richina said, as if she knew not what else to say.

"I must also worry about whether the Matriarch's plans will work, whether the spellsong I have yet to write will do what it must, and whether someone else in this dissonance-forsaken land will try yet again to kill me." *And whether sorcery will lead to yet another spell-fire war where whole lands are again devastated.*

"Did not the Matriarch sequester all those Ladies of the Shadows?"

"Did we not have double guards the other night? Did Alcaren not have SouthWomen patrolling the grounds and the walls?" Secca took another swallow from the goblet.

"Yes, lady."

"It is not your fault, Richina. It is not . . ." Secca set down the marker. "Perhaps I will think better in the morning." She stood. "I must hope so . . . I must." She bent down and blew out one of the lamps, wondering as she did whether the mixture of great and shadow sorcery she was attempting would be sufficient.

Yet . . . what other choices did she have? Her lips twisted in a bitter smile.

How many others had thought those same words over the generations? Had the ancient Matriarchs felt so . . . before they turned hilltops into shimmering black rocks and inundated villages with hot sands?

111

ENCORA, RANUAK

Cold droplets of water collect on the windows of the third floor of the Matriarch's residence, droplets not quite chill enough to freeze in the late winter night of Encora. Across the table where they share a late supper, long after their daughters have been tucked under their covers, Aetlen looks at his consort.

"How went matters with the sorceress?"

"She is strangely old and strangely young, as are all who would use the Harmonies." Alya fingers the empty wine goblet.

"As are you."

The Matriarch shakes her head. "It is not the same. A sorceress—or a sorcerer—cannot help but feel the sorrow and pain that accompanies sorcery. Yet, to do what she must, she cannot dwell too greatly on the consequences of each spell. Not as a young woman. Not if her mind is to remain whole."

"Will she do what you feel necessary?"

"I do not know. I suggested she consider a spell to empty some ships of their crews and officers, but that sorcery verges on Darksong and will not carry far upon the waters."

"Do we need the ships that badly?" asks Aetlen.

"We have lost close to a score since last summer. Need I tell you what that loss has done to us, to the Exchange?"

"No." Aetlen's voice is dull. "Yet sorcery for survival is one matter, and sorcery for gain . . ."

"Trade is survival for Ranuak, dear one." Alya's voice is almost as flat as that of her consort. "Do you think I would suggest such were not matters nearing desperation?"

He nods slowly, then clears his throat before speaking. "There is one other matter. About the Ladies . . . the sorceress could not have known all those names, not even with Alcaren's assistance."

Alya offers a twisted smile. "Of course not, but she handed me a list with eight out of the highest half-score, and the two most important, including Santhya."

"You waited for the Ladies of the Shadows to act . . . just so that you could claim that you were not being hasty, and that you were protecting them?" He shakes his head. "What if they had not acted, but waited for you?"

"They did not. They could not wait, not after so many years. You must admit, dearest, that it was effective." Alya takes a sip of the amber wine that is more bitter than she would prefer.

"Effective, but most risky," he suggests. "What if the sorceress had not been able to kill Jesreya?"

"That was a risk, but it is unlikely that a sorceress unable to think facing an intruder would also be able to deal with the Sturinnese."

"Dear one . . . she could have been a sound sleeper, and very alert when awake. Or unable to hold off Jesreya with a blade for long enough to cast a spell. You . . . we . . . were most fortunate that she is the kind who wakes quickly."

"I know." Alya sighs. "I was wrong there."

"You were most fortunate. I would not risk such again. We need the sorceress if we are to avoid worse."

"I will not. My few seers are watching all the time. So are the SouthWomen, and not just those under arms."

Aetlen winces. "You will have a revolt here, just as is happening in Neserea, if you do not tread with great care."

"I know that, also. Yet . . . what else can I do, matters

being as they are? If aught else befalls the sorceress, we are lost."

Two pair of eyes meet. Both are bleak and dark with worry.

112

The wind blew out of the south, gentle but chill. As Secca rode southward behind the squad of South-Women that served as a vanguard, she tightened the fastenings on her riding jacket, and pulled down the green felt hat more tightly. Already they had ridden more than a solid five deks southwest of the harbor along the west side of the channel, and Secca had seen no sign of the sheltered cove Alcaren had promised.

She watched the road and the gentle indentations of the coast, and tried not to shiver in the raw and wet wind under a hazy gray winter sky. While the day was colder than she would have preferred, she had little enough time before the Matriarch's orders for readying the handful of ships were conveyed to their captains and owners.

Every so often, she glanced sideways at Alcaren, but his eyes darted between the road ahead and the dark waters below. The road followed the curve of the time-worn low bluffs that formed the shoreline of the channel south of the harbor of Encora. The short space to her left between the road and the channel was mostly filled with water-smoothed boulders. To the right of the road was a line of low hills, sloping gently upward to rises which were no more than twenty yards above the water.

She felt foolish in some ways, accompanied as she was by two full companies of lancers and a full squad of the SouthWomen, but she could understand Alcaren's concerns, even with most of the leaders of the Ladies of the Shadows supposedly under guard in the White Tower—and their children in the Blue Tower. She twisted slightly in the saddle, looking briefly at Alcaren and wondering if she would ever have children when most men looked either to bed her and leave her or consort her for her power and lands.

"You look fretful, lady," offered Alcaren.

"I was thinking of the daughters and children in the Blue Tower." Secca wasn't about to say exactly what she had been thinking, especially not to Alcaren. While he intrigued her and seemed to be more than politely interested, too much was hidden behind the pleasant demeanor and the polite manners.

"That is most necessary. Did Jesreya offer a word when she attacked you? Did she cry out when your sorcery killed her?"

"You *knew* who she was?"

Easing his mount slightly closer to the sorceress, Alcaren shook his head emphatically. "I never met her. She was once a lancer officer. I had heard her name in years past, and once, when I was guarding the Matriarch, a Lady of the Shadows called upon the Matriarch. The woman had the same long hair, and was of similar height, but I did not see her face clearly. It might have been Jesreya."

Secca studied Alcaren's face, but the penetrating gray-blue eyes seemed to hide nothing. She wanted to shake her head. The Ranuan had been attentive, interesting, and appealing in a reserved fashion, yet . . . there was something more, and she was less than certain she wanted to know what it might be. Was that because she would have to trust him? She tried to push aside that question. "Do you think it might have been her?"

"I would judge so, but it would be but a guess." He laughed. "The guards of the Matriarch do not question."

"You are an overcaptain, but you have questioned me."

"Suggested, my lady . . . never questioned." Alcaren looked away abruptly for an instant, peering at the road ahead, before turning back. "We are almost there."

Somehow . . . in his words themselves, or in the way they had been delivered, or in looking away, Alcaren had offered something, and Secca could sense it, but not name it, as if he had almost said more than he wished, and was uneasy about it.

Her lips tightening, Secca leaned forward in the saddle, her hand going back to brush the lutar case strapped behind her saddle, her eyes on the dark gray-blue water of the channel.

The road curved back southward. As the gray mare carried Secca around the curve, before her appeared a circular sheltered cove or small harborlike expanse of water, perhaps two deks across, and almost cut off from the channel by two ancient rock jetties, whose ends were less than a hundred yards apart. Rising out of the channel waters a half-dek eastward of the antiquated seawall was a long sand bar. Roughly ten yards below the road, gentle sandy beaches circled most of the cove, except where yet another jetty, barely visible because of the sand drifted up and around it, protruded from the westernmost edge of the shallow water.

Alcaren again eased his mount toward Secca's gray. "Will this do for what you essay?"

Secca continued riding, studying the waters and the shoreline, before she replied to the Ranuan, "Was this another result of the Spell-Fire Wars? It looks like it was once a harbor."

"It was a harbor, although so far back that nothing remains save the seawalls and the jetty." He smiled at her, warmly. "Several generations back, my mother said, traders from the Ostisles asked permission to dig a channel from here out to the main channel." He shook his head. "It sanded up almost as fast as they could dig. I do not know if sorcery created it or changed it, only that it is a pleasant place to swim in the summer."

"You have swum here?" She could not but help wonder with whom he had swum—if anyone.

"At times. It is a favored bathing place—in summer."
He laughed. "The water is too cold except then."

"This should do." Secca pushed away the thought of
swimming.

"Good. It is the closest place to Encora that would come
close to what you requested." He gestured. "The road will
carry us within fifty yards of the inner jetty."

Once the column had reined up on the section of the
road closest to the jetty and after Alcaren had sent out
squads along the road a half-dek in each direction, the
Ranuan looked to the sorceress. "Whenever you are ready,
Lady Secca."

Secca dismounted and handed the gray's reins to Easlon,
still mounted beside Mureyn. The two guards glanced at
the road that led back to Encora.

"I would doubt we will be here more than a glass or
so," Secca said as she began to unstrap the lutar case.

"Yes, lady." Easlon nodded.

Deciding to leave her hat on, and carrying the uncased
lutar, Secca slowly walked halfway out the sand-covered
rocks of jetty. Even after all the years of wind and water,
the regularity and smooth finish of the dark stones suggested that the walls and jetty had been created by sorcery.
After a single shudder as she thought about yet another
evidence of ancient sorcery, she stopped walking and
glanced toward the darker waters of the main channel to
the east, before surveying the shallower gray and more
placid waters of the ancient harbor.

Alcaren stood on the jetty a good ten yards closer to the
road, his head moving slowly as he surveyed the channel
beyond the ancient seawalls, the road that arced around the
sanded-in harbor, and the lancer guards stationed there. His
eyes brushed across Secca, lingering for a moment before
resuming their searching pattern.

Secca squared her shoulders, then took a deep breath
and began to tune the lutar. Finally, she lifted the lutar and
began to play, running through the melody without the
words, but concentrating on them in her mind. On the flat

gray water, a cone of mist swirled for a moment, then vanished as Secca frowned, losing her concentration for a moment.

She forced her mind back to the spell and began to play the spell melody again from the beginning, ignoring the second mist funnel.

When she finished, she looked around, noting that Alcaren's eyes darted away from where the ephemeral mist funnel had appeared.

Finally, after taking a series of deep breaths, she looked to the channel and, holding the lutar but not playing it, began to sing the spell, softly and without any projection.

> *"Water boil and water bubble*
> *like a caldron of sorcerers' trouble . . .*
> *build a storm with winds swirling through*
> *in spouts that break all ships in two . . ."*

The light, hazy gray mist of the sky darkened into almost blackness, so dark that the day became dusk. From nowhere came a howling wind that ripped at Secca's riding jacket, at her hat, and at the lutar in her hands. Sand lifted from the jetty and the beaches blasted her clothing, and the back of her unprotected neck, each grain feeling like the bite of some insect.

Under the pressure of the winds she took several steps eastward, before she dug her boots in and caught her balance.

In the center of the sanded-in harbor, less than half a dek from Secca, rose a gray-black funnel. The water-spout towered nearly forty yards up, and the water level in the ancient harbor had dropped over a yard as the swirling mass of gray water swayed away from Secca and toward the seawalls and the main channel beyond.

Secca swallowed, and sang, if not quite raggedly, the special release couplet.

> *"Stop! Stop, the water in its spout;*
> *let it fall in rain and rout!"*

Sheets of rain cascaded around her for several moments, before she found herself buffeted by a last violent gust of cold wind. She looked down at the lutar, then pulled a strip of cloth from her belt—usually used for blotting her own forehead—and began to wipe off the lutar and blot away the water. She hoped she could get it dry enough before the water affected the strings too much. The half-soaked sorceress finally looked up to see Alcaren watching her intently, his face somber.

Then he grinned, shaking his head. His grin faded. "We need to get you back to Encora where you can dry out and get warm."

Secca couldn't help returning his grin with a smile. "It does work . . . with just the song and no accompaniment." Her own smile faded. "But we still have to get close enough so that it will strike enough of their ships."

"That is the Matriarch's task, is it not?"

Secca nodded, repressing a shiver. The wind had not subsided to the gentle breeze it had been before the sorcery, and she could feel the chill as it gusted past the damp legs of her trousers.

113

NETZLA, NESEREA

The golden sheen of the wood panels set between the ancient built-in bookcases, also of golden oak, glistens in the light from the half-score manteled lamps set in bronze free-standing sconces, well away from wood and books.

The door to the study opens, and two men step inside. The taller closes the door. He is dark-haired, and his blue eyes are as cold as the snow that covers the fields and hills beyond the walls of the keep. The shorter wears gray. Both nod but slightly to the blonde-bearded man who remains seated behind the writing table, but who gestures to the pair of unpadded and straight-backed oak chairs across the table from him.

"Now that spring is but a few weeks away, at least in the south, I thought we might discuss how we will be proceeding." Belmar bows to the blonde-bearded man before seating himself.

The man in gray bows and sits without speaking.

"I see, most honored Belmar," begins the bearded man, "or should I begin to call you honored Lord Prophet Belmar . . ."

"I think such is premature, perhaps by years, honored Ayselin." Belmar laughs good-humoredly, but his eyes do not laugh with his voice and face.

"Chyalar has begun to refer to you as such," Ayselin replies.

"I was not aware that he thought so highly of the office of Prophet."

"He does not. Nor do most in Neserea. That is why he ties your name to such with every opportunity. But then, that is why you sent assassins after him. It is a pity that their success did not match their fees."

"Golds are but a tool." Belmar laughs again.

"Indeed they are, and that is why I have supplied such to you, but they are not endless, and I would suggest that they be spent with greater return."

"While they did not succeed, Chyalar may proceed with greater caution," suggests the younger holder.

"Yes . . . he may suggest to Lady Aerlya that his suit to be consort to Lady Annayal might be well preferred to a forced suit by you."

"He is already consorted."

"For now."

Belmar laughs, delightedly. "What a most wonderful idea! Have her murdered in a way that casts great doubt about the most noble Chyalar and his motivations."

"I thought that would appeal to you." Ayselin nods, then touches his beard for a moment. "You still have not been able to bring the Sorceress of Defalk to bay, for all your sorceries and lancers, and when spring comes, what is there to prevent Lord Robero from sending more lancers or another sorceress or both to the aid of Lady Aerlya? Already, there is word that the Liedfuhr may send fifty companies of Mansuuran lancers to support his niece. With all your sorceries, and a mere forty companies of lancers beholden to you, you cannot fight both Defalk and Mansuur."

"*We* will not have to do such. Lord Robero will do nothing beyond what he has done," suggests Belmar. "He hoards his lancers, and he spends but two sorceresses—one here and one in the east."

"There are two in the east," jerGlien says mildly.

"Two . . . and what have they done in almost two seasons? Propped up a puppet in Ebra, and barely managed to struggle to Ranuak. There they must deal with an indecisive Matriarch and murder attempts by the misguided Ladies of the Shadows."

"It is not that insignificant an effort for two women with but a handful of lancers," suggests Ayselin.

Belmar shakes his head with a broad and condescending smile. "No. It is not. But does that weakling in Defalk use their actions to his advantage? Does he request lancers from High Lord Counselor Hadrenn? Or even golds?"

"Lord Robero is overly cautious, but he could well agree to allow his sorceresses to work with the Liedfuhr's lancers to restore all of Neserea to Lady Annayal. And he would do such in a moment rather than send his own lancers, as well we all know."

Belmar fingers his chin, frowning. "There is much to that, and we must ensure that such does not occur." He glances toward the man in gray. "Is this an area where your masters might provide some suitable mischief, master jerGlien?"

"They would not wish such an alliance, that is true. Perhaps a fleet sent from the Ostisles to patrol off Defuhr Bay?" He raises his eyebrows in inquiry.

"You suggest that so readily that it is apparent such has already been planned," offers Ayselin.

The Sturinnese shrugs. "It would not be opportune to invade Mansuur at this time, but such a maneuver will keep the Liedfuhr from sending more lancers eastward, for they cannot be recalled quickly."

"And it will bring more ships closer to Dumar—and Ranuak," suggests Ayselin. "Doubtless filled with lancers."

"I would not guess what the Maitre plans," jerGlien replies. "One does that with great risk."

"That still will not offer us much assistance," Ayselin points out.

"You have been insistent that no lancers or ships from Sturinn enter Neserea. Do you wish that to change?" asks the Sturinnese.

"No," Belmar says, "but perhaps a chest of golds for us to raise and arm more lancers. That would be far cheaper for the Maitre."

A second shrug follows. "I can but ask."

"That is true," Belmar says politely. "But . . . if we are better armed, then neither Defalk nor Mansuur will be nearly so interested in what may occur in Dumar—or Ranuak."

"That is true, and I will convey those thoughts," says jerGlien.

"As for other plans," Belmar says, "I had thought perhaps a little sorcery in the vineyards to the east of Itzel might prove useful."

Ayselin waits.

"Well . . . those who hold those lands, they still support Lady Aerlya and her ill-gotten daughter, and many of their coins come from their vintages . . ."

The other two in the library nod as Belmar continues to talk.

114

Secca stood on the rear steps of the guest quarters in Encora as Wilten and the two additional companies of lancers rode up the drive between the boxwood hedges toward the guest quarters and barracks. Leading the column was a squad of Ranuan lancers in blue, not the SouthWomen, although the last company in the column wore the crimson and blue riding jackets of the South-Women.

In the late afternoon, a chill winter sun tried to break through the white and hazy clouds that covered most of the sky like a thin layer of gauze. Secca could see Clear-song for a moment, before a heavier and grayer cloud obscured the larger moon.

As the first squad of Ranuan lancers turned aside, Wilten rode to the steps, where he reined up and half-bowed from the saddle. "Lady Secca."

"I am most glad to see you, Wilten."

The overcaptain bowed again. "And I you, Lady Secca."

"How was the journey?"

"Longer than one would like, but the weather was mild. The air to the north is warming, and spring may come early." The overcaptain smiled politely.

Secca returned his smile with one equally pleasant. "We need to discuss some matters—once you have the companies settled. If you and Overcaptain Alcaren would join me, we have much to do, and little enough time in which to accomplish it."

Behind Secca's left shoulder, Richina nodded.

"A half a glass, lady?" asked Wilten.

"I will await you. My chambers are located as they were in Elahwa."

With a bow, Wilten turned his mount toward the barracks.

"He is worried and tired, lady," offered Richina as the two sorceresses reentered the building.

"Are not we all?" asked Secca, dryly. "The rebellion worsens in Neserea. The Sea-Priests will hold all of Dumar in a season if we do not act. We must use great sorcery in a land that has already once been prostrated by it, and that land is our sole ally willing to offer more than mere words of concern." She glanced at Richina. "I would like a moment to myself. If you would escort the overcaptains . . . ?"

"I would be happy to do so." Richina inclined her head.

Secca turned and walked back through the arched door and along the corridor to the stairs, then up to her guest quarters, nodding to Dymen as she entered. Once inside, she walked to the working desk, reaching down and lifting the goblet. The water was warmish, but cleared her throat.

For a time, she stood alone in the main chamber of the guest quarters, looking toward the harbor where sailors swarmed over the mast of one of the vessels there while they worked on the rigging. Several more ships had appeared from their previously hidden anchorages or ports to tie up in the main harbor, and on all sailors toiled, making ready for the voyage ahead.

Secca wondered if the sailors did not feel a greater surety in the future than did she, with all the unknowns that surrounded and faced her.

"Overcaptain Wilten, Lady," called Dymen. "And Lady Richina and Overcaptain Alcaren."

"Have them enter."

Wilten stepped into the guest chamber, his tired eyes avoiding the stack of brown paper on one side of the small round conference table. He took three steps forward and bowed. Behind him followed Alcaren and Richina, who offered bows in turn.

"I will not keep any of you overlong. Especially you, Wilten. You have had a long journey, and the one most recent." Secca did not seat herself.

"As you must, lady." Wilten frowned, and his eyes did not quite meet Secca's.

Alcaren's eyes betrayed no surprise, and Richina merely watched Secca.

"You must know that we are going to try to use sorcery against the Sturinnese. I met with the Matriarch, and we have come up with a plan. A sorcerous plan." Secca looked directly at Wilten.

"I can see no other way, lady. That troubles me."

"We must strike against their fleet. That was the only way in which Lady Anna drove them from Liedwahr, and it will be the only way in which we can do the same."

Alcaren nodded.

"You know, Lady Secca," Wilten said carefully, "that their ships do not come near the shore, and this will be even more so now that you have destroyed those few of shallow draft that challenged you in the Gulf."

"I know. The Matriarch is providing us with ships."

"As she should," said Alcaren.

"Could she not just provide the ships to carry us to Dumar?"

"She does not have enough ships to protect us from the warships of Sturinn. Also, that would not destroy the Sturinnese fleet," Secca pointed out.

"I see that." The older overcaptain's voice was cautious.

"I intend to take but one company on board the ships—and without mounts. They will be there to protect me and the players and Richina."

Wilten's eyes flicked to Alcaren, then focused on Secca. His brow crinkled.

"To ensure that all works as it should, we will be preparing to load all lancers the day after tomorrow with their mounts."

"All lancers?" asked Alcaren.

"You will take but one company, but we will prepare to load them all?" followed Wilten.

"Yes." Secca nodded. "The Sturinnese have scrying

glasses. They will doubtless be watching us closely now that you have arrived. The weather is fair, and the winds would favor us. So they will expect us to act quickly, and that we will."

"But they will watch you, and if you do not board a vessel . . ."

"We all will be boarding vessels—very carefully. The Sturinnese will doubtless use sorcery to create much disruption in the channel and upon the sea. Their great sorceries are much like mine, and cannot be repeated quickly, and that is when we will strike—with sorcery."

"Perhaps I am overly tired, but if you would explain . . ." said Wilten.

"We will begin to load the vessels. It is likely the Sturinnese will send a great wave down the channel and into the harbor to destroy ships and delay our departure. The channel is too shallow for a great wave to travel far, and it will break far away from the harbor. There will be flooding, perhaps water several spans deep in the streets, even a yard deep. That sorcery is like great battle sorcery and will tire greatly both the drummers and the Sturinnese sorcerers. When the water from that great wave retreats, I will board the largest of the Ranuan ships, and we will take sorcery to their fleet. They will believe, we hope, that I am traveling to Dumar to stop their conquest. That is why Richina and Alcaren will be with me, and why you will prepare the remaining lancers as if for an overland ride." Secca shrugged. "That is the plan."

"And you will take but one company with you?"

"That way, it will look as though I am trying to reach Dumar in desperation. Also, there is little point in hazarding the lives of brave lancers to no end," Secca pointed out. "If I am successful, we will return and embark all within a few days. If I am not, you will return all the lancers to Loiseau when the weather permits and await Lord Robero's commands." Secca offered a broad smile. "I do not expect the latter, but I would be a poor sorceress-protector if I did not have orders for all possibilities."

Wilten bowed. "As you command, though I would that you take greater protection with you. Another squad, at the very least."

"I will consider that, and we can talk tomorrow, when you all have had a chance to consider these plans." Secca smiled again.

When the door closed behind the three, the warm and enthusiastic smile faded from the lips of the sorceress as she turned back toward the conference table, and the spell that lay there, underneath a plain sheet of heavy brown paper.

Secca disliked the expansion of the shadow sorcery, but the songspells involving poisons, such as the one she had used against Mynntar and his captains, required more of the crystals than she had carried with her. Likewise, using a variant of the flame spells would prove too exhausting.

She bent over the table and uncovered the words of the spell Anna had written years earlier, reading the opening lines slowly. "Infuse with heat, and turn to steam, the water . . ."

Shaking her head, Secca paused. When Anna had explained how the spell worked, Secca had been horrified—but, horrified or not, she could see no other alternative for what needed to be done. Secca needed the Matriarch's support, and the Matriarch needed the ships, and both knew the Sturinnese needed to be stopped, and that could not be done without great sorcery—and more ships for Ranuak.

Secca straightened and looked, bleakly, toward a setting sun that was turning the hazy clouds into a bloody pink froth.

The predawn gray seeped into the main chamber where Secca checked the sheaf of spells she had readied. She doubted she would have the time to check them again, or even use any except the first two, but she slipped them into the saddlebag anyway.

Moments earlier, as she had finished dressing, she had heard the first companies of lançers riding toward the harbor, and that had meant she needed to head down to the lower level and to play her part.

Abruptly, the very air began to shiver around Secca, or so it seemed, and then an anguished chord rattled through her. She glanced toward the windows, but they were not shaking. A wry smile crossed her lips. The wrenching of the Harmonies was an indication that the Sea-Priests had indeed called up their great wave. The smile vanished as she wondered if Alcaren and the Matriarch had been right—that the wave would not greatly damage Encora.

She forced herself to the window to watch.

For a long time, nothing happened. Another company of lancers rode out of the guest quarters, and then a third.

Secca squinted. A silver-gray was filling the lower part of the drive—water! Rushing water. From the guest quarters windows she watched as grayish water flooded up the drive from the harbor, then seemed to stop. The water was only a bit more than hock deep on the trailing mounts of the next lancer company to leave the guest barracks.

To the south, she could see masts swaying . . . but only swaying. She hoped that the Matriarch's judgment about what a great sorcerous wave could do to Encora had been correct. She watched for several moments longer, but the water across the drive got no deeper, and, in fact, seemed to be slowly receding.

With a nod to herself, she picked up her saddlebags and lutar, and then the traveling scrying glass. She opened the door and stepped out into the hallway. There Gorkon took the mirror and saddlebags and followed her down the wide stairs. Richina, who had been watching from her doorway, scurried to catch up.

Secca had barely stepped through the archway above the rear steps to the guest quarters when Alcaren rode up the paved lane, his mount spraying water from the puddles remaining. The Ranuan overcaptain had a grim smile on his face.

"The wave wasn't that deep, was it?" Secca asked.

"No. It was just what you and the Matriarch had hoped for. The Sturinnese raised the ocean, but the shallows spread it thin."

Secca gestured toward the south and the damp streets and puddles between her and the harbor. "This was scarcely like what happened to Narial." She still couldn't quite believe the difference.

"Of course not. Great waves can break over the land only when there are deep waters and narrow shallows. Here the shallows stretch for tens of deks, and widen as they near Encora, so the great waves break far from the harbor, and the harbor level rises but little. The Matriarch warned those in the coastal towns to move to higher ground. While there was doubtless much damage in Nerula and Gherste, we can hope few lives were lost." Alcaren paused. "As you and the Matriarch discussed, such sorcery is most difficult, and now that the waters are receding, we should hasten to the piers before the Sturinnese can refresh themselves."

"I am ready now."

"So am I," added Richina.

"If you would summon the players, Richina," Secca requested.

"Yes, lady." Richina turned and hurried across the damp

stones, her boots occasionally splashing water.

Secca turned full to Alcaren. "Is it likely that they could raise yet another wave while we are in the channel, or just leaving it?"

"It is possible. Anything is, but they have never done so two times on the same day."

"Let us hope they do not today," Secca said as she stepped toward the gray mare that Rukor was leading from the stable.

At the end of the long courtyard that separated the wings of the barracks, the players were gathering and mounting, strapping instruments in place. Secca watched for a moment before she saw Palian's gray-haired figure, and Delvor chivvying the second players into order. Richina began to hurry back across the courtyard, this time mounted and riding around the players, and the last company of lancers—and the squad of Alcaren's SouthWomen that would also accompany Secca.

After fastening the saddlebags with spells and her cased lutar in place, Secca half-climbed, half-vaulted into the saddle, then turned to wait for Palian and the players.

Palian was already riding from the barracks courtyard toward Secca, raising her hand. "We stand ready, lady."

"Then let us go." As Secca replied and turned the gray back toward the harbor, the sky was turning a brighter gray—not orange, for the heavens held the same hazy formless clouds that seemed to be almost constant through the winter in Encora.

Riding down the damp stones of the lane, past the boxwood hedge toward the boulevard, Secca tried to check everything. So did Alcaren, riding slightly forward and to the sorceress's right.

Two full companies of SouthWomen blocked the boulevard heading north, and as the gray mare carried Secca through the gates, Captain Delcetta rode forward. "If you don't mind, sorceress, we would like to ride as shield."

"Thank you." Secca offered a smile, understanding all too well that if any of the supporters of the Ladies of the

Shadows wished to act, now would be their last opportunity before Secca tried to deal with the Sea-Priests.

Richina rode to Secca's left, and Alcaren to her right, both behind the SouthWomen and their shields. Behind Secca came the players, also shielded by the second company of SouthWomen. Secca felt as though she were almost in a moving box, with lancers all around her. Those nearest her bore silvered shields, held so high that she could barely see the buildings on each side of the boulevard.

The city area near the harbor held the odors of fish and salt, and all the walls of the buildings—from the chandlery to the weavers—showed an almost even water line at about half a yard above the paved and raised sidewalks. Those flooded streets were empty, except for the lancers, and the players. While it was still just before dawn, Secca wondered if the Matriarch had ordered the streets cleared.

Looking past riders and shields, Secca's eyes searched every side street, but all she saw were lancers—regular Ranuan lancers in blue. She could also see that the water was quickly receding, as fast as it had risen, if not faster.

"The Matriarch had this whole part of the city cleared, didn't she?" Secca said in a low voice to Alcaren.

"She did not tell me such, but it appears so." The overcaptain flashed a brief smile. "It would certainly ensure that the Sea-Priests would know we are trying something."

"So that they will attack us instantly?"

"Not instantly, but once we clear the channel and the shallows."

At the open stone-paved plaza between where the boulevard ended and the loading area for the piers began, Wilten was waiting, mounted, looking north. As he saw the SouthWomen, and then Secca, a momentary smile of relief crossed his face. He rode forward toward the sorceress and her escorts.

"How did it go?" asked Secca.

"Everyone was prepared. Some mounts got skittish when the water rose around them, and we had to pull a couple out of the harbor. Drysel thinks he lost one lancer, unless he's hanging onto a pier post or a rock somewhere."

"Now it's our turn," Secca said. "Make sure everyone gets dry. It's still winter, even if it's late in the season and warmer than Loiseau."

"That we will, lady. You be most careful." Although Wilten's words were addressed to Secca, his eyes rested on Alcaren.

"We will look after her most closely," Alcaren said.

"I am most certain you will," Wilten said firmly. "And you, Lady Richina, take great care as well."

"Thank you, Wilten." Richina inclined her head.

With a last nod and smile at Wilten, Secca urged the gray forward once more.

"The *Silberwelle* is at the second pier at the end," Alcaren said.

"I can see the ship." Secca reined up at the base of the second long stone pier, now merely covered with a film of water. After dismounting and handing the gray's reins to Rukor, she unfastened the lutar and saddlebags. Easlon and Dymen scrambled to dismount—as did Richina and several of the SouthWomen.

Still surrounded by guards and lancers, Secca walked seaward along the pier until she neared the gangway to the *Silberwelle*.

"Lady Sorceress!" called a voice. Although the voice was deep and strong, the woman who stepped forward to the railing beside the gangway was less than a span taller than Secca and not all that much broader. Her face was tanned and weathered, and a broad smile showed even white teeth. "Denyst, captain of the *Silberwelle*."

"I'm Secca, and this is Richina. She's also a sorceress." As Secca stepped on board, she nodded to Alcaren. "You know Alcaren?"

"Since he was mayhap knee-high." Denyst smiled. "Glad to see he's been put to good use."

As he half-bowed to the captain, Alcaren's smile was somewhere between amusement and relief, Secca judged.

"He was one of those to persuade me to help you, sorceress," continued Denyst. "I can't say any of us much like sailing out to a war fleet."

"Nor do I," Secca replied. "But we have to do something."

"We do. We'll not sail anywhere if we do not," Denyst nodded. "Being as this is a short voyage, you sorceresses can have my cabin, and the players can use the mess."

Secca glanced to Alcaren.

"I'll show Palian and Delvor," the overcaptain affirmed.

"They'll need somewhere to keep their instruments dry until it's time to play."

"The mess will do for that."

Secca turned as she caught sight of Palian leading the players toward the gangway. "Here are the players." She waited until the two chief players were on the deck.

"Palian is my chief of players, and Delvor is the chief of the second players." Secca gestured toward the two.

"Welcome to the *Silberwelle*." Denyst inclined her head to the two. "We'd like to be setting sail in less than a glass. Take us three glasses to clear the channel." Denyst turned to Alcaren. "The overcaptain will be showing you where you'll be hanging your cloaks." She turned to Secca. "If you'd not mind . . ."

"Go ahead, captain," Secca said. "Alcaren can get us settled."

"Once we're under way, I'll find you. There are a few things we need to talk over while we're headed down the channel." For a moment, Denyst turned to watch the SouthWomen and lancers walking up the gangway. She looked back at Alcaren. "They'll have to be quartered in the fo'c'sle bay."

"That will be tight."

"Put some in the port crew room if you have to."

"Yes, ser." Alcaren nodded.

Denyst turned aft and climbed the ladder to the poop deck.

As the Ranuan captain stepped away, Palian looked to

Secca. "In what fashion would you like us to proceed?"

"The Sturinnese may call storms or something upon us. You and the players will wait in the mess room until just before you are to play. That way we may avoid wet strings and soaked players. Richina will summon—"

"It might be best if I summoned them on your signal," Alcaren suggested from where he stood to the right, near the railing. "You might need the Lady Richina's skills."

Alcaren's suggestion made sense, but Secca wondered if she were coming to rely too much on Alcaren. "You'll summon the players on my signal." She addressed Palian. "You know the two spellsongs we plan to use, but we still may have to use the long or short flame song."

"We understand."

Alcaren gestured toward the lancers who were forming up behind Secca and her group on the main deck and then at the players milling by the starboard railing.

"Alcaren . . . perhaps you'd best get everyone settled," Secca suggested. "Then the five of us should meet again. Richina and I will wait here."

"With your guards and some lancers." Alcaren smiled. "I'll have Dymen take the lutar and mirror and saddlebags to the captain's quarters so that you don't have to keep carrying them. If that meets with your satisfaction?"

Secca nodded.

Alcaren gestured, and Easlon and Dymen stepped forward, along with a half-score of the SouthWomen.

Boxed in as she felt, Secca repressed a sigh, but handed the lutar to Dymen, and then the saddlebags.

As she waited for Alcaren to return and for the *Silberwelle* to move from the pier, Secca studied the vessel itself. The main deck was higher above the water, and the ship had greater freeboard than the *Alycet*. The *Silberwelle* was also a good thirty yards longer and ten wider, clearly a deep-ocean vessel built for long voyages while heavy-laden. The three masts were all square-rigged.

As had been the case with the *Alycet*, every surface was

smoothed and varnished or oiled, and the brasswork gleamed.

"It is a beautiful vessel," murmured Richina.

"Single up!" came the command from the poop deck. "Harbor rig!"

"Aye! Harbor rig!"

Secca watched as the crew, men and women, swarmed up masts and let out canvas, and then cast off.

Under the light northeast wind, the *Silberwelle* glided away from the pier and toward the southwest, but long before nearing the shore, eased onto a more southerly heading, in the middle of a channel that seemed deks wide. But even Secca could see the lighter shades of the shallower waters, not all that far to either side of the ship.

"If you'd join me, Lady Secca," called Denyst.

"Why don't you wait here for Alcaren, Richina?" Secca said.

"As you wish, lady."

Secca turned and climbed the ladder. Denyst stood several yards to the left of the helm platform, itself raised above the upper deck.

"Most have not talked of this, but the Sea-Pigs could raise another wave as we clear the channel," suggested Denyst.

"Alcaren said they couldn't create as large a wave here."

Denyst laughed. "Not so large as elsewhere, but it might be a good ten yards from crest to trough just beyond the channel. Hit us sideways, and we'd go over."

"Oh . . ."

"In the open sea, wouldn't be near as big, and a good ship'd hardly notice it, just a big even swell." Denyst laughed. "Well . . . we'd notice it, because the sea flattens, but any good ship mistress could handle it. They do it offshore, and it'd break at the end of the channel, and that's where it's dangerous. Once beyond the shoaling, the break would lift everything maybe two yards in foam and water."

"What would you suggest?" asked Secca.

"I've told the others to hang back. *Silberwelle* will be battened down. If the wind holds, two-three deks shy of the channel end, we'll pile on full canvas and race for the open water. There's but a one-or-two-dek space where a great wave could break."

"That's why everyone should be below?"

Denyst nodded.

"Including us?"

"You won't be doing us much good, lady, if you're washed overboard before we get to the Sea-Pigs." The captain offered a humorous smile, as she continued, "And I wouldn't stand well with the Matriarch if I allowed that to happen." She turned to watch as Alcaren climbed up the last few steps of the ladder and crossed the poop to the two women.

"Captain." Alcaren bowed. "All the lancers and players are settled." He turned to Secca. "Your chief players have begun the tuning and practicing."

"Thank you," Secca said.

"Before long, in the next glass or so, best you settle yourselves in my quarters," suggested Denyst.

"We will," Secca promised. "Could we stay up here for a bit, though?" She thought Alcaren would appreciate the fresh air as well.

Denyst nodded.

Secca eased to the starboard railing and gazed out to the west. The vessel had already passed the ancient harbor where she had practiced her sorcery. She pointed back to the northwest. "Is the old harbor about there?"

"I think so," he replied. "It's hard to see from the channel."

A jetty and a breakwater—all that remained of a harbor once created and maintained by mighty sorcery. She shook her head and studied the coast and the dark rocks, rocks that began to lighten as the orange ball that was the sun rose out of the Eastern Sound.

The wind seemed to strengthen as the *Silberwelle* sailed

farther from Encora itself, and spray began to mist over the bow.

The sun stood well over the isle that formed the eastern side of the channel when Alcaren looked toward Denyst, then touched Secca's arm.

"I know. It's time," she said.

Richina waited on the main deck as Secca and then Alcaren climbed down the ladder.

"We're headed below," Alcaren said. "It could get very rough when we start to leave the channel." He gestured for Richina and Secca to enter the doorlike hatch he held open. "The captain's quarters are the farthest aft." After Richina eased past him, he smiled and looked at Secca. "You're fortunate that Denyst likes you. Not every ship mistress would offer her quarters."

Secca smiled. "I think I am fortunate that she likes you."

Alcaren flushed. "Ah . . ."

"Oh . . . you knew her before?" Secca wondered if Denyst had been a former lover, knowing that it was none of her affair, yet . . . She pushed the thought away.

"No . . . not as a friend or acquaintance . . . She is one of my mother's closest friends." The Ranuan shook his head. "I had not thought to presume . . . but she offered the *Silberwelle*, and it is one of the largest and most seaworthy, and she is noted for surviving storms that have sunk other vessels."

"We are both fortunate." Secca hoped the captain's abilities and fortune would continue. With a smile, she turned and eased toward the hatch door, suddenly aware of how close the broad-shouldered overcaptain was, but she slipped past him without flushing and made her way along the narrow passageway. While she did not have to duck, anyone much taller would need to be most careful.

The captain's quarters were spacious—for a vessel— nearly five yards in width and almost as deep, with a recessed double-width bunk against the forward bulkhead, a series of built-in chest cabinets against the rear, and a round table in the middle of the room. Secca noted that all the chairs around the circular table were fastened to the wooden deck, as was the table itself. Alcaren, or Dymen, had placed the lutar in a net-covered open wooden bin fastened to the bulkhead with brass-studded heavy leather straps.

"Why did the captain want us in here?" asked Richina.

"She thinks that the Sturinnese may try to bring another great wave against us as we leave the channel before we can get to the safety of the open seas," replied Alcaren.

"Safety of the open seas?" Richina looked puzzled.

"The safest place for a ship in a storm is well away from the coast and from the shallower waters right off the coast," Alcaren explained. "A truly safe harbor, such as Encora, is best. After that, the open seas are to be preferred."

Secca and Richina exchanged glances.

Alcaren shook his head. "The shallows will break a ship."

After several moments, Secca turned her head to Richina again. "We need to start some vocalises. I don't know how long it will be after we leave the channel before we find the Sturinnese." Or before they find us.

Alcaren nodded slightly.

The two sorceresses had completed a series of two long, drawn-out, and gentle warm-ups, when the pitching motion of the *Silberwelle* began to increase.

"I think we're out of the channel," offered Alcaren, straightening in the chair he had taken closest to the hatch door. He swallowed.

A half-smile flitted across Secca's face as she recalled Alcaren's discomfort with sea travel.

A deep bass rumbling filtered through the hull of the ship, a rumbling that seemed to go on and on. At the sound or sensation, Secca cocked her head. Across from her, Alcaren frowned, also tilting his head slightly.

Secca glanced at Richina. "Did you . . . ?"

Richina nodded, her face showing apprehension.

Secca's eyes went to Alcaren again.

He shook his head.

Then, not all that later, the pitching of the ship stopped, almost abruptly, as if the *Silberwelle* had entered an area of calm water. Alcaren frowned again, then lurched from his chair to the forward porthole where he looked out through the green-tinted thick glass.

"What . . . ?" began Secca.

"Hold on to the chair. Hold tight!" Alcaren wrapped his arms around one of the circular posts framing the captain's bunk.

"Why—" Richina tightened her hands over the carved arms of her chair.

"Another wave! Hang on!"

Secca gaped as she felt the deck tilting, the forward bulkhead of the cabin seeming to rise a good two yards above the rear one, and she could feel her feet dangling away from the deck for a long moment.

Then abruptly, the bow dropped with a lurch, and Secca's stomach dropped with it, and her boots slammed down on the deck. The light from the portholes vanished momentarily as dark water appeared outside, and then was replaced with foam, and then the gray of day. Despite the closed hatches and the raised coaming of the hatch to the captain's quarters, a thin sheet of gray-blue water poured across the wooden deck of the captain's cabin.

The *Silberwelle* continued to ride through a series of maneuvers, combining a slight tendency to corkscrew with irregular pitching of decreasing intensity.

Secca wasn't sure which had shocked her more, the fact that the Sea-Priests had been able to use sorcery for another great wave or the fact that Alcaren had sensed the disruption of the Harmonies, as though he were a sorcerer. Alcaren . . . a sorcerer?

Secca wanted to shake her head even while the ship continued to ride out the aftermath of the wave. A sorcerer! That made sense, and yet, the fact that he had used no sorcery somehow reassured her, but she couldn't say why. Nor was she ready to struggle with all that implied—not right before a sorcerous sea battle, and not when Alcaren had been trustworthy in all that he had said and done.

Richina looked pale and Alcaren positively green by the time the hatch door opened to reveal a figure in blue.

"Selya, first officer. Captain would like you topside." Selya did not wait for their response, but disappeared as quickly as she had appeared.

Secca took the saddlebags and the cased lutar and headed along the passage to the open main deck. Outside, in the chill sea air, she glanced around. The *Silberwelle* looked little different, save that all surfaces were wet and water sloshed along the decks.

Turning, she climbed the ladder to the poop deck, and crossed to the railing around the helm platform where Denyst stood.

"Quite a ride there, if I do say so," said the captain. "Nothing we couldn't handle, though. Been through worse in the fall storms in the Bitter Sea. Lookout has sighted sails to the southeast. They're faster, but the wind's with us. I thought we should let them catch us. Otherwise, they might get suspicious." She looked at Secca.

"How long will it take?"

"A glass, I'd wager."

"That would be good. Can you let us know about a quarter-glass before they get in range for their fireshafts?"

"You want all of them close?"

"At least a handful," Secca said. "We can't do spell after spell."

"The Matriarch said we might be able to pick up a few ships . . ."

"That's possible—*if* the spells go right."

Denyst nodded. "Spare crews are on the *Schaumenflucht*."

Secca glanced forward, noting that the swells remained constant, and still almost two yards from crest to trough. About every third swell, a thin spray rose over the bow, but only a little water struck the fo'c'sle, and only within a yard or so of the base of the bowsprit.

"More sails to the southwest, captain! Looks like a half-score!" came the call from the lookout above.

"Starboard ten," ordered Denyst.

"Aye. Coming starboard ten."

"Alcaren . . ." Secca began, then shook her head.

"You want the players on deck?" Alcaren swallowed as he finished the question.

"They don't have to run, but better now than later."

"I'll tell Palian." The Ranuan overcaptain turned and climbed down the ladder to the main deck, crossing the deck beside the mainmast.

Secca looked down at the lutar and saddlebags.

Richina took both with a smile.

Secca began another vocalise. "Holly-lolly-pop . . ." For some reason, she had to stop and cough up mucus, but after the second run-through, her cords felt clear.

"They're running under full sail, captain, even the ones coming into the teeth of the wind," reported the lookout.

"Sorcery?" asked Denyst.

"Wind sorcery," Secca confirmed. She frowned as she realized the implications. The Sturinnese had raised two mighty waves, and each took a sorcerous effort that was similar to fighting an entire battle, at least from the way the Harmonies protested, and yet there were some Sturinnese strong enough to call up winds to speed their vessels. Just how much sorcery could they do?

Shortly, Alcaren returned. He glanced at Richina, carrying Secca's lutar. "It might be better if I held this."

Secca nodded.

"Thank you," said Richina as Alcaren took the lutar.

Secca glanced out upon the fleet bearing down upon her three vessels. She could not even count how many, so numerous the sails appeared, but she saw no point in using sorcery just to discover numbers.

"A third of a glass or less before the lead frigate closes, sorceresses."

Secca walked to the railing at the edge of the poop deck that overlooked the main deck and called down, "Players!

First spellsong will be the third building spell. The third building spell. Less than a quarter-glass."

"Run through on the third building spell!" ordered Palian. "At my mark . . . Mark."

Although she managed to keep smiling, within herself Secca winced at the first few bars. The pitching of the *Silberwelle* had definitely affected their playing. But by the fourth or fifth bar, the raggedness smoothed out, and she let out a breath she hadn't even realized she was holding.

She looked up and out off the port side of the ship. Three of the white-hulled Sturinnese frigates were less than a dek away. Another three were closing on the *Schaumenflucht*.

She glanced toward Alcaren. His face was composed, but pale and greenish. Richina's eyes were still fixed on the nearing Sturinnese vessels.

Secca closed her eyes for a moment, concentrating on the first spell she would use, trying not to think too deeply about it. According to Anna's notes, it wasn't Darksong because it referred only to water as a substance, and not to any living aspect, but Secca wondered how close she would be coming to Darksong with it. Still . . . she had promised the Matriarch she would try.

She stepped back to the railing overlooking the main deck, where the players faced southward, to the port side of the *Silberwelle*. "Chief players!"

"We stand ready."

"Third building song. Now," ordered Secca.

"At my mark!" called Palian. "Mark!"

The opening bars were far smoother than with the run-through, and Secca concentrated on a smooth and free production, not worrying about actual projection, as she launched into the spellsong.

"Infuse with heat, and turn to steam,
the water within the veins and bloodstream
of each Sea-Priest and all whom they command;
Boil within their blood right where they stand . . ."

An off-key note chimed through the gray skies, followed by the sound of crystal shattering. Secca blinked, staggered, then went to her knees on the hardwood of the deck, one hand thrust out to keep from falling totally on her face.

Alcaren had an arm around Secca, and was helping her to her feet almost immediately. Waves of light and dark washed across her vision, and it took all her effort to stand, even with Alcaren's support. For a time, she just stood on the deck, unseeing.

Alcaren and Richina exchanged words. Secca had no idea what the two had said, but Richina moved away and then disappeared.

Secca tried to make out what was happening around her. Her head was throbbing, and double images flashed before her eyes. Alcaren seemed to be two separate men, one looking at her with kindness and concern, the second leering and sneering simultaneously. She closed her eyes.

"Lady Secca! Drink this. You must."

Even Richina spoke in two voices, and Secca had to struggle to make out the words. She swallowed whatever Richina tendered, feeling the liquid splash across her cheeks and chin.

Some of the headache began to subside, and the double images of those around her seemed to fade slightly, so that each person carried a silvered shadow, rather than a double of their entire self. She blinked again, her eyes watering in light that seemed far too bright, even though the sky was filled with high gray clouds.

"You need to drink more, my lady," said Alcaren gently.

His breath and words seemed close enough to caress her neck, and she wanted to lean back into his arms. Instead, she forced herself to take a longer swallow from the mug Richina held.

"Dissonance! Lead frigate swept starboard right into the other one!" The words came from the lookout above, sounding very far away. "Looks like none at the helm, captain."

Secca shook her head. At least the first spell had worked on one of the Sturinnese vessels.

"Two of 'em, like as in irons," reported the lookout after several moments.

After taking a biscuit from Alcaren, who was still pale and greenish, Secca slowly ate it, interspersing the biscuit with sips of water to get it down her suddenly dry throat. She looked up as a shadow fell across her, squinting to make out the figure of the captain.

"Whatever you did, Lady Secca, there are five, maybe seven, of their vessels unhelmed," said Denyst. "The others are regrouping and starting to close on us once more."

"How long?"

"Another half-glass."

"I'll be ready." Secca began to eat the second biscuit offered by Alcaren.

"Lady, you cannot do more sorcery. I can use the flame spell against them," Richina offered. "I can."

"Not yet." Stepping slightly away from Alcaren, Secca took another swallow of water, reaching for another biscuit. "I can do one more spell. If that is not enough, then you will have to use the flame spell. Tell Palian to be ready with the first building spell. The first building spell."

"As you wish, lady." Richina did not turn toward the players, but remained looking at Secca.

"Let her do the flame spell, my lady," Alcaren whispered. "She must try herself, and whatever she does will leave less for you."

Secca opened her mouth, then closed it. Finally, she spoke. "Richina . . . perhaps you should try the flame spell on the nearer vessels."

"Yes, lady." A trace of a smile flitted across Richina's face, then vanished.

A glance passed between Richina and Alcaren, but

Secca ignored it. She would still have to handle the storm spell . . . somehow. The flame spell wouldn't reach far enough. Nor would the wind spell she had used against the Sturinnese before. And Richina had not the feel for the storm spell.

The Sturinnese recovered quickly. Before long, unless Richina could destroy the Sturinnese ships, both she and Secca would have to fight off the effects of the thunder-drums, as the Sea-Priests neared the *Silberwelle*.

"Chief players!" called Richina. "The short flame spell."

"Standing ready with the short flame spell."

Richina watched as the white hulls of the Sturinnese closed. "On your mark, chief player!"

"The short flame spell. Mark!" called Palian.

When the second bar of the accompaniment began, so did Richina's spell.

"Turn to fire, turn to flame
All ships here with Sturinn's name . . .
Turn to ashes, on this sea . . ."

As the younger sorceress's words finished, a curtain of flame flared southward, wrapping itself around the nearest two vessels, and the bow of a third. In moments, the three were blackened hulks.

Secca's eyes went from Richina, now holding the rail for support, to the remainder of the seemingly endless white-hulled vessels, watching as those untouched by the first two sets of spells, once more turned toward the *Silberwelle*.

Secca nodded to Alcaren, squinting to make the two images she saw of him into one. "Tell Palian I will need the first building spell."

"Can you do this?" whispered Alcaren, leaning toward Secca.

"I must . . . All is lost if I cannot."

Alcaren looked directly at Secca. Even through the silvered, half-double images that were those of but one man, she could see the concern on both his faces. Then he turned and called out loudly, "The Lady Secca will be using the first building spell. The first building spell."

"We stand ready with the first building spell," came back Palian's reply.

A flaming quarrel flew toward the *Silberwelle*, falling short, and plunging into the blue-gray waters fifty yards off the ship's quarter. A heavy vibration filled the air, and then died away.

The dissonant drums! In moments, they would begin to support the Sea-Priests. She had so little time.

"Be but a few moments before they're in range, sorceresses!" called Denyst.

Secca took a deep breath and stepped up to the railing above the main deck. "The first building song. Now!"

"The first building song," repeated Palian. "At my mark. Mark!"

Secca pushed the headache, the wavering vision, the double images, even that of Alcaren holding the lutar case and watching her, all out of her mind and concentrated on the spell, on the words, on meshing with the melody that rose from the players below.

She began to sing, and she was the spell that rose from the Silberwelle.

> *"Water boil and water bubble,*
> *like a caldron of sorcerers' trouble . . .*
> *build a storm with winds swirling through*
> *in spouts that break all ships in two . . ."*

Secca managed another breath between the stanzas, knowing that she needed at least two complete stanzas to build the spell fully.

> *"Ocean boil and ocean bubble,*
> *crush to broken sticks of floating rubble*

ships crewed by those in Sea-Priest white
and let none escape the water's might . . ."

As the last notes died away, a silence seemed to creep across the afternoon. The swells around the *Silberwelle* flattened, and the gray light filtering through the hazy clouds dimmed even more, until the sky was almost black—and silent.

From somewhere in the distance came a low and growling rumble, followed by a high-pitched whistling whine, before the two sounds merged into a rushing and roaring torrent.

Secca tottered, her hands on the railing, trying to hold herself erect as a series of black columns reared out of the suddenly flat waters of the Southern Ocean. Each waterspout column split into two, one silver and one black, just as each player on the deck seemed to have doubled, and each sail and white hull.

The spouts moved slowly, inexorably, toward the white hulls, touching one, then another, and as each dark spout touched a Sturinnese vessel, that ship disintegrated into splinters flying in all directions. With each disintegration, the screams unheard by few others— that Secca understood—reverberated inside her skull, until she wanted to lift her hands to her ears to block out the sounds of death and destruction.

Richina's hands went to her ears, and Alcaren staggered as if struck, but straightened.

Scattered drumming rose—and then vanished.

Both the roaring and the screams continued to rise, until their combined din was all that Secca could hear, a roaring shriek that began to drive her to her knees, a roaring so powerful that she could not even lift her hands to block the sounds that prostrated her. Her fingers, trying to hold to the railing, failed, and she could feel her body crumpling, sliding down beside the railing, until she was sprawled on the deck of the *Silberwelle*.

Lying on the deck, her life being wrung out from within and without . . . she shuddered as the darkness fell across her, sensing that her chest was frozen, that she could neither speak nor breathe.

"No!" screamed Richina. "No!"

Someone was singing, but she could not hear the words.

A voice from far away—far, far away—announced gravely, "The sorceress has left the shadows."

No! she wanted to scream. I'll always be in the shadows now. I'll never live, never love. For she could feel the cold darkness, and the blackness, and the dissonance, all gathered above her, descending. . . .

116

SOUTHERN OCEAN, SOUTH OF RANUAK

The *Silberwelle*'s sails flap once and then hang from their yards, limp, in the sudden stillness that surrounds the Ranuan trading vessel, a stillness at variance with the roaring and rushing sounds that rumble toward those standing on the deck.

Alcaren's eyes dart from the massive water spouts that have begun to shred the Sturinnese fleet to the slender, almost-fragile redheaded figure who grasps the railing overlooking the main deck of the *Silberwelle*. He swallows as he watches her fingers spasm and her body shudder, as if pummeled by forces no one else can see or hear.

As she grasps the railing to steady herself, Richina's eyes are fixed on the white-hulled ships being shattered by the dark spouts, as are those of the ship-mistress of the *Silberwelle*.

Only the gray-blue eyes of the Ranuan overcaptain see Secca crumple, see her slide down beside the railing, her fingers limp, her eyes closed. Lutar case in hand, Alcaren takes two steps, then rushes toward the forward railing and the fallen sorceress.

At the sight of Secca collapsing, Palian turns from the players and the destruction on the sea to the south and begins to scramble up the ladder.

Richina turns, slowly, her mouth opening into a soundless cry.

The redheaded sorceress lying on the deck on her back opens her eyes, then her mouth, as if to speak, then shudders, her eyes wide, seemingly sightless.

Alcaren fumbles open the lutar case, snatches Secca's lutar from within, and stands over her. He clears his throat and begins to sing, his voice true, but carrying an edge that threatens to overwhelm training and past discipline.

> *"With my voice and with my song,*
> *Keep her safe and make her strong.*
> *Still within her that darker spell,*
> *so all within her is mended fair and well.*
> *With my voice and with my song . . ."*

Palian stops at the top of the ladder and shudders, her eyes flicking back and forth between the sorcerer and the dying sorceress.

Richina moves step-wise toward the pair by the railing, as if uncertain as to what she could or should do even as Alcaren's voice completes the spell.

A single long note—somehow half-harmonic, half-Clearsong, and half-dissonant, half-Darksong—vibrates through the air, and the entire ship shivers. Crystalline shard notes slash at those who can hear the Harmonies. Richina and Palian shiver again, as if slashed by unseen knives.

The strings on Secca's lutar snap, and the metal ends flay Alcaren's hands and jaw, leaving long red lines. His legs fold under him. He topples forward, like a tree cut with a single swing of an axe, and the lutar drops from his limp fingers and strikes the deck with a single half-melodic *thunk* that echoes far more loudly than it should.

Richina and Palian stare for a long moment before rushing toward the fallen couple.

"Darksong," murmurs the chief of players. "Twice."

Tears stream down Richina's cheeks as she looks helplessly down at both figures on the deck before her.

Palian drops to her knees, her fingers searching for signs of life.

117

In the time just before midmorning, sunlight flowed through the windows of the main chamber of the Matriarch's guest quarters, the first sunlight Secca had seen in days, if not in weeks. A warm and light breeze flowed through the partly open end window, bringing in the smells of an early spring.

Secca looked down at the scroll before her on the conference table, her eyes skipping over the lines she had struggled to write, struggled because with each word, she fought another battle, one having little to do with the words before her.

> . . . were most successful in destroying all but a handful of the Sturinnese ships in the Southern Ocean. According to the scrying glass, there are less than a half-score such vessels remaining, and four have turned their sails toward the Ostisles . . .
>
> . . . were able to remove the crews from six vessels and make the ships available to the Matriarch in recompense for the losses suffered by Ranuak, both in supporting us and otherwise . . .

She shook her head. "Writing this is hard."

"Writing anything might be a little harder than usual," pointed out Richina. "After all, you did so much sorcery you almost died, and that was less than a week ago."

Although Secca knew better—she had died, or had come so close as to make little difference—she did not correct the sandy-haired young woman.

At the *thrap* on the door to the guest quarters, Secca sat up straighter in the armchair pulled up before the conference table. She laid aside the quill with which she had been writing to Lord Robero.

"Overcaptain Alcaren, ladies," called Rukor. "If the Lady Secca can receive callers."

Secca swallowed, her eyes going to the door.

Richina looked to Secca.

"I'll . . . I'll see him," Secca finally said.

"Have him enter," Richina said quickly, standing and striding toward the door, as if to make sure that Secca did not change her mind.

Secca turned her head at the sound of hoofs on the long drive outside the windows of the guest quarters, although she could not see the drive from where she sat at the table. As the door opened, she looked back toward the broad-shouldered figure who stepped inside.

"Come in," said Richina belatedly, holding the door wide. "She is much better."

Secca felt as though a bolt of Clearsong had shivered through her heart and thoughts, freezing her where she sat for a long moment.

Richina closed the door, her eyes on Secca.

Secca felt all eyes were on her, from everywhere, even though there were but three of them in the chamber.

Alcaren stepped toward the armchair, and Secca could see that the red welts on his cheeks had begun to fade. The overcaptain swallowed, his eyes full on Secca. "I did not want to intrude until you were well enough

. . . I brought this for you . . . something to take with you," he offered, stopping just short of where Secca sat and extending a rose, the perfect white bronze rose with an iron stem, so delicate-appearing it seemed the slightest breeze would rip off the petals.

"It is beautiful." Secca hesitated, glancing down at the uncompleted scroll, then turning her eyes back to Alcaren.

"Like you, it is far stronger than it appears," said the sorcerer/overcaptain gently.

Secca did not speak for a moment, a moment she knew was as fragile as appeared the rose Alcaren held. What words could she offer? How could she say what she felt?

"Though it is not so beautiful," Alcaren murmured, his voice so low she could barely hear the words.

Secca wanted to reach out, to draw him to her. Instead, she looked into Alcaren's gray-blue eyes. "Thank you . . . for the rose . . . for my life . . . for everything." But thanks were not enough. Could she say more? How could she not? And yet . . . what? How?

Alcaren looked down for a moment, then raised his eyes to Secca's amber ones. The faintest of smiles showed at the corners of his lips.

The silence drew out, as eyes met eyes.

"You . . . no one . . ." Secca felt as though each word tripped over the one previous. "I wish I had . . . seen . . . sooner."

"I saw you had," he answered slowly. "I was unsure if I should come . . . after that. I was not well . . . either . . . at first, and then . . ."

Secca ignored Richina's puzzlement, concentrating on Alcaren, trying to find the words, trying to step from behind the years of walls so carefully built. "I'm . . . glad . . . you did. I do not know . . . if I would have had your courage."

"My lady . . . I could do no other."

Secca laughed, softly, warmly. "I did not mean your

saving me . . . although that was a sacrifice no one could expect . . . and most courageous." Her eyes dropped to the rose for a moment before meeting his gray-blue eyes again. "I meant coming here."

"That . . . was harder. I thought of coming yesterday."

"I thought of seeking you," Secca said slowly. "I was not brave enough."

"You nearly died," he offered with the smile that warmed her. "Few would question that bravery."

"You couldn't say . . . could you?"

"I feared you saw," he replied. "I thought you might guess every time I looked at you."

"I did guess," Secca admitted. "I was afraid to believe it." She looked up at Alcaren.

"As was I," he replied.

At the click of the door opening, both turned their heads, as did Richina.

Another figure stepped into the room, just ahead of the announcement by Rukor. "The Matriarch of Ranuak."

Alcaren turned. "Matriarch?"

Alya laughed, gently, as she approached the pair by the table. "I had not thought to find you together, but that is as it should be."

Secca could not help but smile at the slightly puzzled expression and knit brows displayed by Richina.

"The sorceress understands, Alcaren, and so does your heart, if not your mind," said the Matriarch.

"It never ends, does it?" said Secca, fighting for a way to say what she needed to without the Matriarch saying it for her. "No matter how mighty the battle and how great the victory?"

Alcaren's eyes flicked to Secca, then back to the Matriarch.

"No." Alya shook her head. "The rebellion burns hotter yet in Neserea, and the Sturinnese still hold Dumar, and they will send more fleets. And if you destroy those, as did your predecessor, you will still have to fight battles in sunshine and shadow."

"More battles? The lady . . ." Alcaren began.

"The lady needs you," Secca managed to blurt out, her mouth dry, before anyone, anything, could stop her, before someone else spoke for her.

Alcaren turned to Secca, the gray-blue eyes wide, his lips parted slightly.

"You're the first in years to give without asking, without expecting," Secca said. "And no one has ever risked so much for me."

"I had not . . ." Alcaren turned to the Matriarch. "If the lady will let me serve her, I would ask your leave to be released from your service."

Alya laughed. "Separating you two would be worse than your mixing Clearsong and Darksong. Far worse, and there is no way you can remain in Ranuak, not now that the world knows you are indeed a sorcerer. Though I will keep the Ladies of the Shadows in the towers until you are both departed."

"But . . . you said I could never be a sorcerer," Alcaren replied.

"Not in Ranuak," Secca said gently. As Alcaren turned to her, she felt the moment freeze, everything becoming as still as it had upon the *Silberwelle* just before the waterspouts had destroyed every Sturinnese ship, before the recoil had killed her, and before Alcaren had offered his spellsong and life to save hers. She had to make it clear to everyone, but especially to herself. "Liedwahr and Defalk need you." She swallowed and repeated, "So do I." She felt even more defenseless than she had on the *Silberwelle* as dissonance had swooped down on her. But she waited, hoping. Hoping she had not waited too long already.

"I had hoped . . ." he began, bending toward her, his eyes bright.

Secca lifted a hand, reaching out and touching his

cheek. "I had not even dared to hope . . . not for so long."

"Nor I." Alcaren's right hand took her left, his fingers entwining with hers, as he set the perfect rose on the table and lifted her from the chair into his arms.

Her arms went around him, as the sunlight fell across them, and, outside, the first sounds of spring murmured in the midmorning air.

Look for

SHADOWSINGER

From Tor Books

Now available at
your local bookstore!

The late-morning sunlight poured over the two-story structure that held the Matriarch's guest quarters, but the wide second-story windows that faced west were still in shadow. The air in the main chamber was hot and still, foreshadowing summer in Encora, although by the turn of the seasons, spring had even yet to arrive.

Rather than using the small working desk that faced away from the leftmost of the three windows, Secca had seated herself at the circular golden oak conference table, her back to the windows. Alcaren sat on the opposite side of the table, leaving four chairs vacant. The tiled hearth on the south wall held several logs set on a pair of heavy iron andirons, but it had been weeks since Secca had needed a fire.

The petite and redheaded sorceress looked at the rose that lay on top of the papers before her on the conference table—a perfect white rose, appearing so delicate that the slightest breeze would rip off the petals. But like so much in Liedwahr, the rose was not what it seemed, for the petals were of white bronze and the stem of a greenish iron— and it had been Alcaren's love gift to her, one she had never expected.

Her amber eyes went from the rose to Alcaren—narrow-waisted and broad-shouldered, almost too short for his breadth to be handsome, yet not stocky, with short-cut brown hair and gray-blue eyes. He wore the pale blue Ranuan uniform and the collar insignia of an overcaptain. As he felt Secca's eyes upon him, he looked up from the map he had been studying and smiled warmly.

In spite of herself, Secca flushed.

"I do the same thing," he said with a slight laugh, adding, "when you look at me."

She shook her head. "It is hard to get used to."

"I know. No one ever looked at me that way."

Secca wondered about that, and yet, she didn't. Alcaren was barely a head taller than she was, and he was striking, but not necessarily handsome. He was a largely untrained sorcerer in a land that feared sorcery, and a strong man in a land ruled by women. "We still need a consorting ceremony," she said slowly.

"You sound dubious, my lady. Am I that much of a burden to bear?"

At the mock-woeful tone of his voice and the twinkle in his eyes, Secca laughed. "You are no burden. Far from that! Still, it is strange."

Alcaren waited, his smile encouraging her to speak.

"It is strange, and it is not. After these years, I had not thought to find love."

"Though I have not traveled as you have, my lady," he replied gently, "neither had I."

"I had thought, were I ever to be consorted, it would be in Falcor, or Flossbend, or even Loiseau . . . not in a strange land."

"We could wait," he suggested. "I would not wish to rush you into such."

Secca shook her head. "Lady Anna waited even to acknowledge her love for Lord Jecks, and I fear she lost years of happiness because she delayed." A sad smile crossed Secca's lips as she thought of the woman who had been more than a mentor, more than a teacher—a mother as well, in fact, if not in name. Secca doubted that she would ever recall Anna without love, emptiness, and a sense of regret that she had not told Anna how much the older woman had meant to her.

After a silence, Secca added, "I need you, both for myself and for what we do. I would not have it said that our alliance was disharmonious or merely of bodily needs."

Alcaren raised his eyebrows.

Secca found herself flushing again, wondering how she had been able to ignore the sheer magnetism of her consort-to-be for as long as she had. "I did not say . . ." She laughed once more, shaking her head as she did.

Alcaren laughed as well.

As the moment of shared joy passed, Secca cleared her throat gently, repeating, "We must have a consorting ceremony before we leave Encora."

"Because you're a Lady of Defalk."

"And so that the Ladies of the Shadows know that I'm going to carry you off away from Ranuak." Secca smiled mischievously for a moment. "Does the Matriarch perform such ceremonies?"

"Seldom . . . but she can."

"Surely, she would do that for a beloved cousin."

"She would more likely do so to make sure her beloved cousin was leaving Encora forever," replied Alcaren dryly as he rose from the chair and stepped back, stretching, before looking past Secca toward the windows and the harbor beyond.

"I think she would like to see you happy," Secca said.

"Oh . . . that she would. Happy with a lovely woman and a beautiful sorceress . . . and happily gone from Encora and on our way to save Liedwahr from the scourge of the Sea-Priests. With song-sorceries used to great effect elsewhere."

Secca nodded agreement, even as she sensed the underlying bitterness. "But she would perform the consorting ceremony."

"I am most certain she would."

"I will send her a request by messenger," replied the petite redhead, "after we meet with the others."

"Will you also send a message to Lord Robero?"

"Yes, but not by sorcery, and not soon. Perhaps I will wait to tell him personally." Secca grinned. "He did say that I needed to consider the matter of heirs."

Alcaren's mouth opened.

Secca laughed once more. "Not now, but with you able

to do sorcery, I could have children without fearing all
would be after me while I was weakened."

"I am not . . ." he replied slowly.

"You can certainly sing a scrying spell already," Secca
pointed out. "That is not forbidden, even by the Ladies of
the Shadows."

"The idea of greater sorcery—it feels strange," Alcaren
replied.

"Best you get used to it if we are to contend with the
Sea-Priests." Secca eased to the working desk, bent over,
and lifted the lutar from the case beside the left end of the
desk. She began to check the tuning.

"You want me to try a scrying spell now?" he asked.

"Why not? We need to check on the Sturinnese ships
before we meet with the others. I'll do the first one, and
then I'll write the words for the second."

"You have high visions of my ability."

Secca shook her head. "I know what you can do." She
pulled on the copper-tipped leather gloves, then stepped to
the conference table and looked down at the scrying glass
in the middle before clearing her throat. She'd already run
through a series of vocalises before Alcaren had arrived,
and they should have been enough for scrying spells.

Chording the lutar, she sang.

"Mirror, mirror, show me clear and as before,
any ships of Sturinn near Liedwahr's shore . . ."

Even after Secca had finished the spell and lowered
the lutar, the mirror remained blank silver, showing only
the white plaster of the ceiling.

Secca frowned, then handed the lutar to Alcaren. As
he strummed it and hummed the spell-melody, Secca
dipped the quill in the inkwell and then jotted down the
words she held in her mind. Careful not to tilt the paper
or brush the wet ink, she set the sheet on the table
between Alcaren and the scrying glass.

He studied the words and ran his own chords, not

quite like hers, mouthing the words silently. Finally, he
sang the spell in his true and light baritone voice.

"Show me now, most clear and as must be,
ships of Sturinn near our southern sea . . ."

The glass remained blank.

Secca jotted a third spell—one asking to see Sturinnese ships in the Western Sea near Mansuur. Even after
Alcaren sang it in his true baritone, the glass came up
equally blank.

"My singing?" he asked.

"I think not. Try this one." She slipped a fourth spell
before him.

"If this doesn't work, you get to try it again," he said.

"It will work."

He raised his eyebrows for a moment, then concentrated on the spell.

"Show us clear and show us bright
ships of Sturinn that share Ostisles' light . . ."

The glass displayed a bird's eye view of a wide harbor filled with vessels.

Secca swallowed. Never had she seen so many ships
in one place—even through a scrying glass. "You see.
You can do it as well as I."

"I can do it, but not so well," he countered.

After trying to count the vessels in the glass, she
lifted her eyes. "Can you do a release spell?"

"It will fade without it," he pointed out.

"But it takes energy from you. The release spell ends
the drain immediately."

He frowned, then sang, chording the lutar.

"Release this vision of what we see,
and let the glass a plain mirror be."

Secca laughed. "I haven't heard that one."

"I couldn't remember yours," Alcaren confessed. "So I made that one up."

"That just shows you are a sorcerer, no matter what you say."

"Don't tell the Ladies of the Shadows, thank you."

"I won't." Secca frowned. "I lost count at threescore ships."

"The spells showed that all those ships are still being readied in the Ostisles," Alcaren pointed out.

"Right now."

A solid *thrap* on the door interrupted their conversation.

"The lady Richina is here, Lady Secca," called Easlon, the lancer stationed outside her door.

"Have her enter."

The tall blonde sorceress—the youngest of all of the full sorceresses of Defalk and not even a year beyond being more than an apprentice—stepped into the main room of the guest chamber, inclining her head to Secca, and then to Alcaren. Her green eyes smiled with her mouth. "Wilten and the chief players will be here shortly."

"Has your glass . . . ?" Secca shook her head. "You can tell us all at once when they arrive."

Richina, more than fifteen years younger than Secca and nearly a head taller, moved toward the conference table with the kind of tall grace that the all-too-petite Secca had often envied in others. "It's most pleasant outside, if with a chill breeze."

"It looks to be," Secca admitted.

"You should get out more often, lady," suggested the younger sorceress.

"The chief players," announced Easlon.

Spared the need for a response, Secca replied, "Have them enter."

The gray-haired Palian stepped through the door, her light gray eyes offering a smile as they passed over

Secca and Alcaren. Delvor followed, his lank brown hair flopping over his forehead. Both inclined their heads to Secca, and to Alcaren and Richina, if slightly less deferentially. Two steps behind came Wilten, the overcaptain of Secca's undermanned four companies of lancers. The overcaptain nodded reverently, if stiffly, to Secca.

Secca waited for Richina and the other three to seat themselves before she began, slowly. "The Matriarch has gathered crews for some of the Sturinnese ships." As she spoke, she found herself thinking again how dearly the spell that had destroyed the Sturinnese sailors and armsmen had cost her. Yet, had Alcaren not offered his own life with Darksong to save hers, she never would have known the depth of his love. Still . . . remembering how she had felt sprawled on the ship's deck dying, she almost shivered, and she had to swallow before continuing. "And there are also another half-score of Ranuan ships that will accompany us when we leave for Dumar."

"Are there other Sturinnese warships near?" asked Wilten.

Secca nodded to Alcaren.

"There are none near Liedwahr," explained the Ranuan overcaptain. "The glass shows that the Maitre gathers ships in the main harbor of the Ostisles. That is a voyage of two weeks with the most favorable of winds."

"The seas are clear," pointed out Wilten, "but the Sea-Priests hold Narial and the coast all the way east to the Ancient Cliffs, do they not?"

Secca nodded. "We will have to use the glass to find a landing where we will not have to fight our way ashore. There are few Sturinnese lancers on the lowland coasts west of Narial. It's a longer voyage, but there are roads north to Envaryl."

"They could take Envaryl any day, could they not?" pressed the overcaptain.

"Not with the lancers they have within fifty deks of

that city," replied Alcaren. "They have sent companies of lancers throughout Dumar to root out those who oppose them. Even if they tried to regroup the very day we set sail for Dumar, they could not gather more than twenty companies and send them to the coast by the time we land."

"This you are sure of?"

"It might be fifteen; it might be twenty-five," Alcaren conceded.

"That is why we need to sail as soon as we can," Secca said. "We cannot count on the Sturinnese to keep their forces spread, and we do not wish to wait until another fleet is gathered and filled with armsmen and lancers." *And drummers and sorcerers,* she added to herself.

"How long will that be?" asked Palian.

"I hope not long," Secca replied. "I meet with the Matriarch tomorrow, and we will see." She turned her eyes back to Wilten. "Can all be ready within the week?"

"We can be ready," the Defalkan overcaptain responded.

Secca looked to Alcaren. "And the SouthWomen?"

"They have been ready for several days. A few more days will help in training the new recruits."

"Recruits?" asked Wilten.

"Among the younger SouthWomen there has been no dearth of volunteers to go fight the Sturinnese. Captain Delcetta and Captain Peraghn have been able to be most selective in those they accepted."

Wilten nodded slowly, almost stolidly. To his left, Palian offered a knowing smile, while Delvor bobbed his head, and then pushed back the lock of brown hair that always fell across his forehead, and always had in the score of years Secca had known him.

Secca stood. "We'll meet after I've talked to the Matriarch. Then we should be able to finish planning how we can retake Dumar."

As the chief players, Wilten, and Richina stood, and then slipped out, Secca kept a smile on her face, despite the near absurdity of what she had so blithely proposed. With perhaps a half-score of ships, six companies of lancers, two groups of players, and three sorcerers, she was talking about reconquering a land held by more than a hundred companies of Sturinnese lancers, supported by dozens of Darksong drum sorcerers. While she might expect two companies of SouthWomen, her own four companies of lancers were already well understrength, and she could expect few if any reinforcements, while her enemy gathered a fleet of between two- and fourscore warships and transports and scores more companies of armsmen and lancers. To the north of Dumar in Neserea, a rebellion raged, and if that turned out badly, she might find another sorcerer arrayed against her—one who had powers similar to her own, and interests far closer to those of the Maitre of Sturinn.

The smile remained, and she said nothing until the door closed. Then she sighed as she turned to the window and looked toward the harbor, although she could see only the masts of the ships tied at the piers.

"Everyone thinks we can do this," she said slowly.

"If we cannot, the Liedwahr we know is doomed," Alcaren said, stepping up behind her and slipping his arms around her waist, if loosely.

"If we can, it is also doomed," she replied softly.

"I know."

For a long moment, they stood together, enjoying the moment, before Secca turned in Alcaren's arms, hugged him, and kissed his cheek. Then she slipped from his loose grasp and stepped back toward the conference table, looking down at the papers and scrolls. "With the new recruits, the SouthWomen will be nearly as strong as my lancers."

Alcaren shook his head. "You still have nearly three companies' worth."

"And a very cautious overcaptain."

"Wilten does not care that much for me," Alcaren observed.

"We have talked about that before. He does not dislike you. He dislikes anything that is unknown or offers a risk. You are both." Secca tilted her head, thinking, realizing that, even after all the years of seeing Wilten, she would be hard-pressed to describe the overcaptain, except in a general way. He affected neither beard nor mustache, and he was neither tall nor short, neither ample nor excessively slender. His eyes seemed to take on whatever color surrounded him, and his face was not oval or square or round or thin.

"He is like too many in Encora these days, then." Alcaren snorted. "They would have someone else bear the risk, essay the song-sorcery, and then complain that the way in which their liberty was preserved was not to their liking."

"That is true in all lands, perhaps in all worlds." Secca pulled out a sheet of parchment, then shook her head and took one of the crude sheets of brown paper. "We still need to send a request to the Matriarch."

"We?"

"It takes a man and a woman to be consorted. We both should sign the request."

Alcaren laughed. "That way, neither those in Defalk nor those in Ranuak will be pleased."

"Are they ever?" Secca raised her eyebrows.

They both laughed.